PRAISE FOR CAROLYN MILLER

"I am emerging out of my book hangover after reading *Checked Impressions* by Carolyn Miller....The romance, humor and themes of identity are so enjoyable and make for a great read!" - *BECKY'S BOOKSHELVES*

"A fun sports-themed contemporary romance, this makes for a great, quick read...perfect for those days that you want a story about trust and love and navigating the ups and downs of being with that special someone." ~ *GOODREADS review*

"Carolyn Miller's ability to pull you into a story is outstanding! ...*Love on Ice* is a brilliant story of romance, exhilarating sporting excitement and devastating disappointment of hurdles to be overcome... I never thought I would give 5 stars to a book about ice hockey and speed skating!" ~ *KAYE'S REVIEWS & NEWS*

"Adrenaline, chemistry, romance, and lots of wooing!...You do not have to be a fan of sports or even knowledgeable in hockey and short track to appreciate *Love on Ice*." ~ *GOODREADS review*

"Carolyn Miller scores another win with *Love on Ice*, the second book in her Original Six Hockey series. I absolutely loved the faith thread in this story. It's message that success does not lie on what we do, but who we are is powerful." ~ *GOODREADS review*

"*The Breakup Project* is a fun, charming, and faith-filled contemporary romance with adorable characters set in the competitive North American ice hockey world. Highly recommended." ~ *NARELLE ATKINS, Author of Solo Tu & Her Tycoon Hero*

"Displaying a flair for comedy and witty dialog, Miller is clearly an author to watch...with clever, snappy repartee, creating an exciting and fast-paced read." ~ *LIBRARY JOURNAL*

CHECKED IMPRESSIONS

CAROLYN MILLER

CHAPTER 1

Chicago
August

"And now, may I draw your attention to what I consider the room's finest work if you, like me, are someone who appreciates that first impressions need not last forever."

Allison Davis smiled at her silly pun and moved to the opposite wall, the museum's visitors shifting their stance to follow like sunflowers following the light. Sure, some might prefer Monet and his haystacks or waterlilies or Renoir and his ballerinas, but Georges Seurat's *A Sunday Afternoon on the Island of La Grande Jatte* was one of her very favorite pieces in all of the Institute's hundreds of thousands of artworks. Something about the light and optical effects called to her, inspiring her with her own work.

"At first glance it may seem easy to dismiss this painting as simply a collection of tiny dots. But this is one of the most iconic paintings of the Post-Impressionism period and demonstrates pointillism at its best. Here we see many figures that represent different walks of life as they gather on the banks of the Seine river on a Sunday afternoon. The use of color makes the artwork seem very alive, yet there is a stillness, with everyone bar a handful of figures facing the Seine on the left. There are things to ponder here: Why is the boater seated on the left so much larger compared to the couple sitting next to him? Why is the girl in white facing the viewer? And why did Seurat paint this?"

She watched as the museum's visitors paused, their faces melding into expressions of what she hoped was interest and not simply a desire to know how many more minutes remained of her tour on this sticky, stifling late-August day.

"Pointillism is a technique of painting in tiny dots, often in complementary colors. Avant-garde artists in the late nineteenth century would consider complementary colors of the color wheel and how to use them to create effect. Complementary colors include yellow and purple, blue and orange, and red and green. When placed next to each other, they have a flickering quality, the pigments almost having a shimmer to them. Pointillism was a completely different approach to painting."

She talked more about the significance of the shadows, Seurat's process, and related works by Seurat, including how this piece perfectly complemented his previous painting, *Bathers at Asnières*, which hung in the National Gallery of London. "Because of Seurat's technique and subject matter, this is one of those paintings that we can return to again and again and not grow tired, because there is always something else to find that is unusual, that makes you think differently about what you thought you knew. To my mind, this is the sign of a great painting, and it's one of the reasons I love the Impressionist movement so much."

She turned to the small group of art enthusiasts signed up for this free tour. "And that concludes our tour of the highlights of the Art Institute. I trust you have enjoyed our time today and will take the opportunity to visit the other galleries, filled with many other treasures. I'm happy to answer any questions you may have, but once again, thank you for your visit, and we hope you will enjoy your time in the Windy City."

No questions—save for directions to the nearest restrooms —and after a couple of murmured thanks, she was released to slowly wander back to the staffroom. Some days she still pinched herself to think she got to work here. She truly had one of the best jobs in the world.

She paused to look at Renoir's dancers, taking a moment to let the colors and shapes infuse her senses, then, conscious that Dave, the security guard, was looking at her with his usual tilted-head expression of concern, she smiled and moved on. How people could not stop and linger at every painting amazed her, and while most people who worked here were art enthusiasts, some, she knew, viewed this as merely a way to make a living.

Wryness tweaked her lips. Few artists made much of a living from their work, as she well knew. Oh, to be successful…

She pushed open the staffroom door and was greeted by the scent of stale coffee and perspiration.

Selina Wemble looked up and waved her hands in a fanning motion. "It's so hot today."

Allie nodded, swiping a curling strand of damp dark-blonde hair behind her ears. Selina had always made her tongue-tied, ever since that first encounter years ago when the polished, pretty art student had met her as they waited for a job interview, casting a look over Allie's Target ensemble with a raised brow and curled lip. Of course, Allie's lack of chattiness hadn't helped matters either and had possibly been construed as unfriendly. In reality, it stemmed more from a case of literally not having the words to say. Allie's lips curved to one side. It seemed some first impressions could last.

She moved to the fridge to collect her now-chilled eco-bottle of water, briefly resting it against her forehead. These late-summer days in Chicago often reached a point of heated heaviness that even the building's stone walls did little to alleviate. Thank goodness her two shifts of tour guiding were done for the day and she could now relax into the administrivia of her role as part of the Public Relations and Learning team. She pitied whoever had to run the kids' tour this afternoon with the intern. Given this late stage of school vacation, that was bound to be lots of fun.

"How was the highlights tour?" Selina asked.

"G-good."

Selina glanced at her and shrugged. Surely she was used to Allie's lack of detailed replies by now. "Did you see the roster changes?"

"No."

Trepidation slowed Allie's progress to the whiteboard, where a glance at the new roster evoked an inward groan. Kids' talk. Again. On hot days like today, the air-conditioned Art Institute was a favorite place to take kids who were *really* ready to finish vacation and go back to school. She loved kids, and as the favorite aunt to two nephews, kids seemed to like her in return, but seriously. Again? A protest formed in her brain, then faltered. Was there any point in complaint? She released a sigh instead.

"Hey, it'll be better than last time, I'm sure."

Allie hitched an eyebrow. If Selina was so sure, then why hadn't she volunteered?

"Don't look at me like that. I would've done it, but I'm working on the wording for the new promotion, and—"

Allie's chest grew tight, thumping sense from the rest of the words. That was supposed to be hers! Myra Fordley had as good as *promised* that promotion to her. "Since when?" she said carefully.

"Oh." Selina's face instantly melded into contrition. "Myra just wanted someone who could articulate things very quickly, and, well, we all know that's not exactly your forte, so I volunteered."

Volunteered? Or snatched it from her? She didn't buy Selina's innocent act for a second.

She glanced at Myra's office door. Shut. Which meant she was either busy or not in.

"Myra's out, if that's what you're wondering."

As per Myra's usual policy on sticky summer days, when she managed to either be elsewhere or what she liked to call "developing strategic partnerships with other museums," which Allie strongly suspected was code for visiting the nearby Holborne Museum—more specifically, its director of programming, Neil Blanchard.

Tension gnarled knots in her stomach. Her scruples protested Myra's frequent visits to a very married man and made her vacillate between wanting to tell Neil's wife and praying that God would reveal it another way. As he wasn't on staff here, it wasn't something that broke protocol as far as the museum's policies, but the morality of it had sunk her opinion of Myra very low. And the knowledge that Myra *knew* that Allie knew, due to an unintended and most unfortunate glimpse of their encounter in a supplies closet, and that Myra was so far unwilling to say anything, had led to a strange standoff between them in which Allie was reluctant to make the first move. This news was just the latest in a series of events that showed the power games some people liked to play. Selina had learned from the best.

"Look, I'm sorry, Allie. I did try to tell her you were the best for the job—"

Sure she had.

"—but I'm afraid it can't be changed now. And those kids will be here soon, and Taylah really needs someone to keep her in line so she doesn't spend the whole time on her phone."

Anger rose in Allie's chest. Taylah, the summer intern who

had impressed Myra so much in the interview, then done virtually nothing since. Allie couldn't help but be glad that Taylah's time with them was nearing its close and she wouldn't have to work with her again.

"And it makes sense that the person with the most patience is the one who deals with the kids now," Selina continued.

And the one least likely to complain.

"I'm sorry, Allie." Selina shrugged. "I wish I could help."

Swap then, Allie longed to say. But the words stayed stubbornly locked inside, refusing to spill from her mouth.

The phone rang, and Selina snatched it up. "Hello, Public Relations and Learning, this is Selina speaking."

The door opened, and Taylah entered in her usual sliding manner that denoted the level of enthusiasm she seemed to hold for her role, the bouncy gait of those first few days most definitely gone. No point trying to impress Myra now.

Taylah glanced at the whiteboard and made a face. "Kids? Again?"

Looked like Allie would have to dredge up enthusiasm for the two of them. She forced a smile. "I'm sure it will go really well."

There. Why could she talk so smoothly in moments when it didn't matter, but other times she might as well have her piano on her chest?

"At least it's with you," Taylah muttered, casting a glance at Selina, who was still talking animatedly on the phone, waving a hand and flashing a grin like she was a celebrity filmed for a TV telethon event. "I think Selina thinks I'm an idiot."

Selina likely thought the same about Allie. Shaking off the thought, she motioned to the cupboard where the kids' activities were stored. "We'd better go and get things set up."

"It's still half an hour until we're due to start."

"By now you know what some parents are like—that they like to get there early."

"Yeah. They're happy for some free babysitting."

Which Allie didn't mind—not if it meant their children were being encouraged to explore their God-given creativity and dream larger than their immediate worlds. Unless, of course, their kids were bratty. Then it was a problem when the parents weren't there.

She moved to the cupboard and began withdrawing the papers she'd printed off last week along with the stencils and pencils in their respective baskets. Best not to think about the injustices but on the positives. She was blessed with this job. Blessed to work so close to home. Blessed with family, friends, and a great church nearby.

Allie pushed her hair behind her ears, slid her glasses up her nose, and internally braced for the next hour. This would go well. God was still on the throne, even if it felt like He'd dropped the ball on a few things lately. He'd straighten her paths. Eventually. She could do this, just like she'd done it a hundred times before.

Beckoning for Taylah to follow, she moved to the creative learning space and began setting up. Sure enough, families soon started gathering, waiting for the magic moment when the rope enclosing the creative learning space would drop and the children were welcomed in.

Twenty minutes later, given the space was heaving with kids already, Allie signaled for Taylah to place the *Sorry, we're at full capacity* placard on the easel nearby and judged it best to begin. She drew in a deep breath.

"Good afternoon, boys and girls, moms, dads, and caregivers. We're so glad you've decided to join us today for the Summer Art Spaces series here at the Institute. My name is Allie"—so much easier for the kids to say than Allison—"and this is my colleague, Taylah"—Taylah grinned and gave a wave —"and we hope you'll enjoy yourself this afternoon as we learn about the wonderful French artist Claude Monet."

She glanced around at the faces lifted expectantly to her—apart from one man, glasses and baseball cap on, looking at his phone already. Indignation rose in her chest. "I would like to take this opportunity to encourage parents and caregivers to explore the world of art with their children, to be in *this* moment right now."

Did that sound too sharp? Taylah's raised brow suggested yes. Allie softened her tone. The man still hadn't looked up. Oh well.

She went on to explain the usual procedures, then began the brief slideshow of some of the Institute's more famous treasures, some of which she'd also covered in the painting tour this morning. But kids liked the treasure hunting aspect, and after this, they would be released to go and explore with their families using the special kid-friendly "treasure maps" of the Institute, a concept she'd designed and implemented two years ago, for which Myra had taken the credit.

Speaking of being in the moment, she needed to forget the injustices of the past and focus on right now. She completed her spiel and outlined instructions for the activity, unable to ignore the baseball cap man who *still* hadn't looked up.

"Are there any questions?" She glanced around, saw a small boy put up his hand. "Yes?"

"Yeah, I want to know something."

From the edge of her vision, she noticed the man finally lift his gaze to pay attention. "Yes, what is it?"

"Why do you talk so weird?"

She blinked, all thought of further talk draining away in a special two-for-one deal of frustration and mortification. For that man looked exactly like none other than her favorite hockey player of all time, the one whom she'd had a crush on since she'd first learned of his existence: the left wing for Chicago's top line, the fastest man on ice.

Jai Mullins.

~

GUILT SHOVED Jai's phone into his back pocket as a titter raced around the room. He became aware that the woman who'd been speaking—a classy looking, glasses-wearing blonde with a mesmerizing, musical voice—had stopped and was staring at him.

Then he heard that other voice again. "You talk funny."

Air pushed past his gritted teeth. Kyle. Why on earth had he agreed to help Kat out today by looking after her son? "I'm sorry," he muttered, pushing forward. He sure hoped nobody here recognized him. He squatted until he could eye his nephew. "You are being rude. You need to apologize to the nice lady."

"Don't want to."

And this was why he'd agreed to help Kat out. Imagine having to put up with this disrespect every day. "Now, or we're leaving."

Kyle crossed his arms, his bottom lip projecting.

Jai sighed, glanced up with an apologetic smile for the museum employee. "Sorry."

She shook her head, her gaze not meeting his, her cheeks bright pink. The knife in his gut twisted harder. He placed a firm hand on Kyle's shoulder and gently squeezed.

"Sorry," Kyle muttered.

Jai wasn't sure if the museum employee had heard, but he'd take it as apology enough. It might be the first time Kyle had apologized this week. Or was it this month?

A glance up showed the woman had retreated to the farthest corner, as if determined to get away from both Mullins men, and her college-aged associate was now leading things.

Man. Now he *really* needed to apologize. He glanced at Kyle, who had started coloring a picture Jai thought might have been a haystack. Maybe the kid could manage a minute of scribbling unsupervised while Jai made up for Kyle's rudeness.

A glance around the room revealed that nobody here had recognized him—he'd put that down to the cap and glasses—so he shifted through the groups of chatting parents to where the art guide talked with a round-cheeked, redheaded woman. He listened and was once again caught by the musical cadences of the art guide's voice. Then she pivoted and caught his gaze, and her mouth fell open as her words stumbled to a halt.

"Hey, I'm sorry for interrupting. Please continue." He made a small gesture to reinforce his words.

"Oh, it's nothing," the plump redhead said before giving him a quick scan and a smile that rippled uncertainty within. She moved on, leaving him standing awkwardly with the lady his nephew had embarrassed. His glance drifted down past her tiny cross necklace to her name badge: Allie.

She cleared her throat, and his gaze snapped up to her now-narrowed eyes as he suddenly realized how his gaze might be construed. No. No, no. "Allie, uh, I mean, Miss, I wasn't, um, checking you out—"

Her jaw dropped.

Kill me now. Could he insult her any further? "I mean, not that you're not pretty, because you are, and I, well, it's obvious that"—he shared his nephew's gift for rudeness. He took a breath and tried again. "I'm really—"

"E-excuse me," she murmured, then hurried away.

Whoa. He'd really outdone himself there.

"Uncle Jai?"

He spun to hurry to his nephew. It'd be better for all concerned if the people here didn't know his identity. It wouldn't help the team PR if they knew their left wing was prone to random spurts of obnoxiousness. "Hey, buddy. What have you got there?"

"It's a farm."

"Uh huh." Looked more like a squiggled mess, but okay. Good to have the clarification.

He snuck another glance at Allie, whose gaze instantly shifted away before she removed her glasses and wiped them. That was hardly surprising, seeing it was so hot in here, the collection of smaller and larger bodies contributing to a heat that probably rivaled outside, as if the building's air-conditioning had given up.

The noise level seemed to ramp up, echoing off the hard interior surfaces, and another sneaked peek revealed a wash of what looked like fatigue on Allie's face as her smile dimmed and dropped and her fingers clutched the back of a chair.

He gestured to the other girl—her name tag read Taylah—and murmured, "Is your boss okay?"

"She's not my boss, but"—her gaze flicked to Allie—"she doesn't look great, does she?"

No. Allie was wiping her forehead. "Is there something you can do to help?" he suggested, eyebrows raised.

"Oh. Maybe. I dunno."

He figured Allie wouldn't necessarily appreciate any more of his verbal vomitings, so any further approach from him might need to be avoided. "How much longer is the session supposed to go for?"

"Um, I dunno. Maybe ten minutes?"

"We started early, so we're probably close to being finished anyway. Maybe you could start cleaning up. That might help people get the idea that it's time to go."

"Oh. Yeah. Okay." Her eyes lit. "Then we all could go, right?"

Good to see that her desire to finish didn't stem from self-interest at all. "Right."

"It's so hot, isn't it?" she said, waving a hand to fan herself.

He nodded. "Should I help you start clearing up?"

"Aren't you nice?"

Or maybe still feeling a little guilty. He shrugged. "Maybe you should make an announcement that you're ending soon."

"Oh, yeah. Good idea." She batted her eyelashes.

He stepped back, turned to help Kyle clean up. Please. As if he needed to encourage some clueless college girl to start flirting with him. "Kyle, it's time to go. Let's clean up now."

"But Uncle Jai—"

"Now."

Kyle's bottom lip protruded, but Jai was made of stronger stuff than his sister and ignored it. He grew aware of Allie moving closer, asking Taylah what she was doing.

"Oh, it's so hot we thought it might be best to finish up."

A beat, then, "I beg your pardon?"

Jai glanced at her. Smiled. "This has been great!" He clapped Kyle on the shoulder. "You've enjoyed yourself, haven't you, buddy?"

"Yeah."

Okay, so that disconsolate tone wasn't exactly selling enthusiasm. Judging from the twitch of her lips, Allie might even agree. He needed to try harder. "I'm sure the other parents here would agree. You do a great job of helping kids learn more about art."

Her lips pressed together, and she nodded, her eyes still not meeting his. What had he said now?

She murmured something to Taylah, then shifted to the middle of the room and clapped her hands. "Thank you, everyone," she said in that slow and gracious way she had. "We trust you enjoyed yourselves today. If you can assist us by helping to put the pencils and crayons back in their baskets, that would be most appreciated. And if you would like to explore more of the treasures of the Art Institute, then you may wish to obtain a special treasure map from Taylah near the exit."

"Treasure?" Kyle exclaimed at the top of his lungs. "I want some treasure."

"They don't mean real treasure, buddy," Jai said in a voice he thought was for his nephew's ears only. Apparently, it was heard by Allie, even above the sounds of rushing and exiting by people who seemed to have ignored her request for help to clean up in their haste to leave.

"This *is* real t-treasure," she said, her brown-eyed gaze finally meeting his before dropping to his nephew. "But I'm afraid it's only for looking at, not for keeping. Unless, of course, you want to buy a postcard at the gift shop."

"Aww," Kyle complained in that high-pitched whiney sound that always got Jai's goat.

"Perhaps it's t-time for you to take your son home," she said, thrusting a paper at him, then hurrying away with a murmured, "He seems very t-tired."

His son?

Kyle glanced up at him, then back at Allie. "Hey, lady, Uncle Jai is my *uncle*, not my dad. Are you stupid or something?"

God, help me. Jai hoisted Kyle to his feet and hurried after the woman, whose look of shock mirrored the sensation stealing across his chest. Yeah, he couldn't believe Kyle's rudeness either. "I'm so sorry. He's not, well, he's just—"

How to explain his nephew had neither the smarts nor the filtering wherewithal to understand let alone practice good manners. Or that his sister seemed to have long given up her understanding of what parenting actually was.

Allie shook her head, and he thought he glimpsed tears before she turned away and began stacking chairs.

Man. What a fail this had been. He blew out a breath, crouched to Kyle's eye level, and muttered, "You have been very rude to this poor lady. You need to say sorry."

"Why?"

He had a feeling that reasoning with an eight-year-old was not going to succeed. He'd never been one for giving up though. "Because you've hurt her feelings and made her cry."

"Are you crying?" Kyle said in his too-loud voice.

She paused in her chair-stacking endeavor, facing away from him as the noise that had dropped at Kyle's comment picked up into whispers again.

As much as Jai wanted to help with stacking chairs, and knew a weird desire to help her any way he could, he figured the best way he could help her was probably to leave with big-mouth Kyle as quickly as he could. And ensure that neither of them ever visited this art museum again.

~

HAWKS & SQUAWKS ONLINE CHAT

TubularBells: Saw Alex Petrovsky in Chi-town today. Looking fine!
PucktheMagicDragon: OMG!!
PipeDreams27: Heard in the group that Tesci is retiring.
CoolplayismyJam: So who will be new alternate captain?
PucktheMagicDragon: Drago?
TubularBells: LOL!
ArtHeart101: Guess who came into work today.
PipeDreams27: Benny?
CoolplayismyJam: Lasertaser?
ArtHeart101: JM17
PucktheMagicDragon: OMG!!!!

CHAPTER 2

Okay. So yesterday may have proved one of her worst in history, even surpassing that oral report in her senior English class that had led to new depths of classmates' bullying and no prom. After all, Allie had expected kids at school to be cruel and hadn't had a crush on them for ten years. Heavens to Murgatroyd. Would she *ever* forget the unfortunate incident at the kids' talk and how she'd created the worst first impression in all the world? Could she have embarrassed herself any further?

But today was a new day. And as this morning's Bible reading reminded her, she could do this. God would give her strength. Allie internally braced and pushed open the staffroom door.

"Oh, look who's here," her boss said, glancing significantly at the clock.

"G-good morning, M-Myra." Allie glanced at Selina and Taylah and summoned a small smile.

"Are you feeling better today?" Selina asked sympathetically.

Huh? Oh. Yesterday, after the kids' talk fail, she'd pleaded a headache—her migraine hadn't been feigned—and gone home

15

early. Allie nodded, then deposited her bag on her desk and took her seat. Funny how everyone had decided to come early for once, on the one day all year when her arrival might be construed as being late, even though the hand had barely scraped past the nine on the clock.

"I heard the kids' talk yesterday was a bit of a disaster," Myra continued.

What? Allie glanced at Taylah, who looked away.

"Something about a little boy who made you cry?"

Indignation heated her chest. "I didn't—"

"Perhaps we really should reconsider your role here if such things prove too difficult."

"It…it wasn't t-too difficult," she stammered. "It was just that it was my third t-t-talk of the day, and I…I—"

"Others manage it," Myra said, brow raised.

"Who?" Allie burst out before drawing back in surprise. Never had she spoken back to her boss, something Myra clearly recognized too, if her affronted expression was any indication.

"I beg your pardon?"

"Who else h-has done three t-talks in a day?" Oh, *why* couldn't she speak smoothly? She really needed to calm down, practice the breathing that helped her smooth her speech into that singsong tone that allowed for greater fluency, even though she sounded like she was on Valium. She drew in a deep breath and noticed Taylah straighten, a smile twitching as she glanced between Allie, Myra, and Selina like she was watching a Broadway show.

"Are you sure you're feeling well enough to be here today?" Myra continued. "You're behaving most peculiarly."

"Perhaps you should go home," Selina added in her ever-helpful, sycophantic way.

And be intimidated into taking a sick day to suit the agendas of these women? "I'm fine." Allie turned to her computer and focused on the email awaiting attention, pressing her fingertips on the keyboard to stop them shaking.

Lord, give me peace. Help me be calm. Be my vindication.

Hissed murmurs filled the room as she continued to pray and work through her to-do list. Her first talk was scheduled for just before her lunch break, and she planned to take her sandwich outdoors, regardless of the humidity. As much as she loved this building and adored the many treasures old and new it housed, sometimes it was necessary to escape the staleness inside.

A knock was immediately followed by the door opening and the sound of Billy's voice as he spoke to Myra, drawing Allie's attention. The custodian was one of her more favorite people who worked here.

"Miss Davis?" Allie straightened as Billy held out a mid-sized bouquet. "These came for you."

"What?" Who would send her flowers? She could count on one hand the times she'd received flowers, and it had been from a family member every time. But this time there was no birthday of significance or special promotion. Who—?

"Really, Allison, you should know by now that work time is not to be used for personal matters."

The irony of Myra, of all people, saying this made Allie level her gaze at her as words burned to escape: *Try telling that to Neil's wife.*

"Who's it from?" Taylah asked. "You never told us you had a boyfriend."

That's because she'd never had one.

"She never tells us anything," Selina said in a volume Allie was sure she was supposed to hear.

Curiosity drew Allie to open the envelope, to stare at the words, heart rippling with emotion.

Dear Allie.

Thank you for a most informative and entertaining kids' art talk yesterday. Please accept these flowers as an apology for the way certain attendees *made things even more difficult on an already challenging day.*
Sincerely,
Jai (and Kyle)

Breath lodged in her chest. Was she now actually living last night's fantasy?

After the tumultuous events of yesterday and a semi-coherent explanation to her parents and sister late last night, Allie had managed to finally get to sleep only to be plagued by images and questions and half-remembered words as she tossed and turned. Had Jai Mullins really been at her work? And she'd spoken to him? What had she said? Well, not actually *said*, more like word-spat at him. In between all the other awkwardness, had he really said she was pretty?

It was like her best dream ever—the one she hated waking up from to face reality—albeit shaded with a degree of despair. For the fantasy of being dressed to kill, then descending a staircase before uttering witty and wise words and heading off to dance with Jai in her perfect *Bachelor*-like golden moment would forever be elusive.

And yet she had now finally met him, bad though that meeting had been. Not that she'd admitted it to anyone. *Especially* her family, whose rabid enthusiasm for the Hawks had earned them the title of superfans and whose ability to keep a secret clocked in at zero. No way would she ever admit to having encountered him, to having spoken to him. Or that he'd spoken with her. And while it hadn't exactly been the conversation of her dreams—try more like nightmares—it still counted, right?

She'd been prepared to dismiss yesterday's encounter as a

one-off—her chance to meet the man of her (literal) dreams, even if she'd blown it. She would've been content with that.

But now this. Flowers. From him. From *Jai*.

Emotion stabbed her eyes.

"Allison? What is it?" Taylah asked. "Are you okay?"

"Oh. Did somebody die?" Myra asked.

What? Allie glanced up at the trio of faces. "No. It's a…th-thank you."

"Oh." All traces of sympathy fled from Myra's tone. "As I said, you really shouldn't be engaging in personal matters—"

"For my t-talk yesterday," Allie persisted stubbornly.

"What?"

Myra and Selina rushed to read over her shoulder, but Allie refused to hand the card over despite their snatching at it. It wasn't like Jai had actually written this—a florist had, for sure—but she couldn't let anyone touch his words. Even letting the others read his words felt like they were trespassing on something sacred.

"Jai? Who's Jai?" Selina asked.

"He was the guy with the bratty kid, wasn't he?" Taylah asked.

Allie nodded. His nephew he'd said, inducing one of the greatest rushes of relief in all of history. When she first realized Kyle belonged to him, she'd heard a sound like a Ming vase crashing off a pedestal into a million tiny pieces, shattering all she'd thought she'd known about Jai. Call her narrow-minded, but she'd never thought the never-married vocal Christian had a secret child. When she heard Kyle utter the magic word *uncle*, she could have keeled over in a faint. The rush of blood to and fro had likely caused the migraine.

"Yeah, it's probably fair enough to get flowers," Taylah continued. "Yesterday was so hot, and that kid was pretty rude, right? I would've liked to have sent him out, but his uncle seemed…rather nice." She flapped her hand as if warm.

Wait. Had Taylah not recognized him? Granted, nobody here suspected Allie of holding the biggest NHL-player crush, but how could Jai's utter amazingness slide past with a mere "seemed rather nice"?

"Oohh. Sounds like there's more to tell," Selina said, ruffling the edge of a rose before slinking back to her seat.

Breathe in. Allie breathed out with, "No more."

The tension knotting her insides said differently.

"Hmm. Well, you'd better put them in water so we can finally get focused on what needs to be done today," Myra said, her words punctuated as her office phone rang. "Hello?"

Allie clutched the flowers and moved to the tiny adjoining kitchenette, taking a moment to inhale the aroma. It was stupid to get caught up in what this might mean. Stupid. But the fact she'd registered at all in his awareness—let alone that he'd taken the time to craft such a kind note—was enough to tangle her heart and whisper hope to her dearest dream. Well, one of them, anyway. And if she never became a famous artist, then attention from a famous hockey player would just have to do.

Water in vase, flowers artfully arranged, gift wrap disposed of—but not the card, *never* his card—Allie moved back to her desk and placed the bouquet on the corner where she could admire it.

Her next talk was in an hour, and she had a mountain of emails to deal with, especially those relating to several school visits scheduled for the next few months. She dealt with these, then moved to prepare for the next talk—one on her special field of Impressionism and Post-Impressionism. With a nod to the others and a last look at her flowers, she headed to the Impressionism Gallery, mentally gearing up for her talk. As she walked, she took a moment to admire the paintings—Monet, Manet, Pissarro—then took her place in the large square room designated for talks.

Celeste, the Pacific Islander guard, lifted a hand. "Hey, Miss Allie."

"How are you, Celeste?"

"Can't complain."

"No one listens," Allie responded.

"You know it."

Allie grinned. See? This kind of small talk she could do, especially with someone like Celeste, all relaxed and easy. Even doing her talks was okay, as there had only been a handful of times when so-called experts in the group had questioned her facts and proved to be embarrassingly problematic. It was only the big talks—the public address types or the kind where she felt a degree of intimidation, like with Myra or Selina—that made her fumble her words into foolishness.

"How's your son?"

Celeste shared about her son and his challenges with ADHD, some of which sounded eerily similar to what she'd seen with young Kyle yesterday. Not that she should be surprised. She'd undergone training for working with various kinds of child behaviors before. But theory could be awfully different to practice.

Allie glanced at the room, which was slowly filling, and murmuring an apology to Celeste, moved to the gold-etched inlaid wood at the center of the floor, nodding as various people enquired whether this was the right place for the talk.

A glance at her notes. A deep breath and smile. "Good morning, ladies and gentlemen. Welcome to our talk today on Impressionism and Post-Impressionism. My name is Allie, and I look forward to sharing with you for the next little while about my favorite period of art." She kept her smile on as she made herself glance around the room, only for her gaze to alight on a man near the corner. Tall, broad-shouldered, wearing shorts and T-shirt, baseball cap and glasses on, hands in his pockets. Her words stuttered to a halt.

Jai Mullins was here.

Again.

~

JAI NODDED, gave a half shrug as Allie's spiel wound to a halt, her glorious voice fading as she stared at him like she recognized him or something. Not what he'd been aiming for. He didn't mind people knowing that not all hockey players were only into sports, beer, and girls, but it wasn't like he was here because he was any great art fan. Although, if she started talking again, maybe he could be. The stuff she'd said yesterday had been pretty interesting, and he'd bet today's talk would be too, given the fact her face had been aglow when she mentioned this type of art was her favorite. Mind you, her face held a very different kind of glow now…

"Miss?" an older gentleman asked.

Heads swiveled from her to Jai and back, as if they expected some kind of confrontation. Yeah, he wasn't the one in his family who did conflict—save on the ice, of course. He didn't want to be recognized, so he hunched deeper and pulled out his phone, studying the screen as he prayed for her.

Allie cleared her throat and started again. "T-today we are going t-to look at—"

Was she nervous he was about to start acting like an idiot again? He'd hoped the apology flowers would've arrived by now, but if they hadn't, it wasn't any wonder she was worried about him being here. Maybe her talk would go better if he left. He moved away, near an enormous painting of a whole bunch of people dressed in fancy old-fashioned clothes standing in the shadows under trees while staring at the water. Huh. Weird. Why was the little girl the only one facing him? He peered closer, eyebrows rising. It was dots. The whole thing was done with paint dots. How cool was that?

"Excuse me, sir." A large woman of Islander heritage moved closer. "You need to stay behind the specially marked ropes."

"Okay. Sorry."

Great. So much for staying under the radar. He shifted back, glanced at the woman, and caught her nod. Another glance over his shoulder and he saw Allie's gaze instantly avert. Maybe she was worried about him being too near her precious paintings also. And he bet they *were* precious. He'd seen a few art heist movies. Some of these would likely fetch a couple of million.

As if aware of his thoughts, Allie said, "This Monet of haystacks here forms part of the Institute's *Meules* series, the collection of six the largest in the world, with each painting worth over ten million dollars."

A whistle split the air. Wow.

Jai listened a little longer, glancing around the room as Allie continued her talk, shifting to focus on the large waterlilies painting, which had a whole wall to itself. What she shared was fascinating, maybe more so because he could hear this was her passion in the same way people could no doubt hear his passion when he spoke about hockey. She clearly knew her stuff, and he found his gaze returning to her, her composure very different to yesterday's debacle. Of course, it likely helped that a storm last night meant today's temperatures were far more moderate, and it probably helped to not have obnoxious small boys—and their uncles—displaying their ignorance of good manners.

What had happened to those flowers? Mom had promised they'd arrive this morning when he scrawled that note. Maybe traffic had held things up.

He took the time to study Allie. The springy dark-blonde hair wound in a low bun, the glasses, the slim figure her professional white shirt and dark-green knee-length skirt hinted at— she was all class. Something he definitely was not. His gut gave a disconcerting twist.

"Monet is a great favorite of many art aficionados, but some prefer the more muted works of Pissarro. Camille Pissarro was one of Monet's contemporaries, and as we examine the paintings here, we can see a number of similarities in technique and the like."

Jai drew closer, her words weaving a spell of intrigue, and positioned himself behind a large man wearing a Disneyland T-shirt. He didn't want to distract her, but neither did he want to miss a drop of what she said.

Pissarro moved to Renoir, then it was something called Post-Impressionism and the painting he'd admired before. "This technique is called pointillism, and as you can see if you come a fraction closer, Seurat has painted this in a form most unlike the others, with thousands upon thousands of little dots of paint. The pigments here use complementary colors, which serves to highlight both the color and forms and gives a sense of shimmering light. Isn't it beautiful?"

Jai nodded, joining in the chorus of appreciation.

"I don't mind confessing it's one of my favorites," she confided.

A few minutes more, then she opened the time for questions, including some from a British-sounding art professor, which she handled with a grace and calm equivalent to every other part of today's talk. It was enough to make him wonder if his—and Kyle's—efforts yesterday had thrown her off her game. Maybe she just didn't do noisy kids. Heaven knew he barely did. After dropping off Kyle, he'd had a whole new appreciation for his sister's patience—and a boatload of incentive to keep the relationship/family thing on the back burner for a whole lot longer. God knew Jai had no intention of screwing up a kid the way he and Kat had been.

"Well, thank you once again for coming today. I hope you've enjoyed your time."

Jai clapped, the sound echoing through the muted building,

causing more than one startled look in his direction. Oh. They weren't supposed to do that here?

He waited until she was clear of the quiet questioners who hadn't been bold enough to ask in front of others, then cleared his throat. "Hi."

She glanced up, her cheeks pinking, her gaze darting down. "H-hello."

Man. She was still nervous of him? Maybe he shouldn't have been so hard on Kyle. Except Kyle had been more than a little bratty and painful.

"My name is Jai. I was here yesterday for the kids talk."

A beat. Then her brown eyes met him again. "I remember."

"I don't know if that's a good thing or not," he confessed with a sudden burst of honesty that he couldn't quite understand. "I mean, between us, my nephew Kyle and I seemed to do our best to make things difficult. And I really wanted to apologize, because the last thing I ever want to do is insult a woman."

Her mouth opened, then closed, and he wondered suddenly —and completely inappropriately—what it would be like to kiss her. Which was stupid. He barely knew a thing about her. She probably had a boyfriend or—he discreetly checked for a ring, but her left hand was tucked under some index cards—a husband. But he knew a tug to keep on talking.

"Anyway, I sent some flowers, but you probably didn't get them yet. But when you do, I hope you know that it's a genuine apology for making life difficult yesterday."

"Th-thank you."

He nodded and moved to turn away, then pivoted back. "You know, I really think you're good at this."

"I beg your pardon?"

"This." He waved a hand at the paintings. "I can't pretend to know much about art, but I really learned a lot from your talk today—and your talk yesterday, but there were other challenges then." He smiled.

Her lips half curved into what might be wry amusement.

"So I hope you know you're doing a good job. You had everyone here fascinated, even the art professor dude, so yeah. Be encouraged."

She bit her lip, and again he got the impression she might cry. Man. He had a gift. What had he said now? He was only trying to be nice.

"Yeah, anyway, thanks. And sorry. And…" Man, he needed to get out of there.

"Th-thank you for your flowers."

"I hope you enjoy them. My mom is a florist, and I think she does as nice work as anyone here in the city, so I hope you like them when they finally arrive."

Her gaze connected with his again, and he blinked. Man, she had pretty eyes. What would they look like without glasses in the way?

"Does…th-that mean you wrote the card?"

Huh? He took a moment to refocus. "Yeah." Wait. How'd she know there was a card?

Her half-smile curved into full bloom. "Please tell your mom that the flowers were beautiful, and the card, well, thank you. That meant a lot too."

"Wait, you got them?"

She gave a small nod. "They arrived this morning. The others in my office were really impressed."

"Well, I hope nobody will be offended or anything. It's not like I go giving flowers to random women all the time—not that you're random, but it's not like we really know each other or anything—"

Who needed a Kyle when Jai was in charge of his own mouth? "Hey, I'm sorry. I've always been bad at talking with pretty women." Maybe that was a better approach, seeing as the confused look from a moment ago had transformed into some-thing sweet. "Um, anyway, I just meant before that I hope there's no boyfriend or husband who's gonna get upset because I sent you flowers. That's all."

She made a sound like a husky burble. "There isn't. You're safe."

"Oh, good. I mean, not that I'm glad you're not married, but —oh man, I should just shut up, shouldn't I?"

Another smile escaped. "It's okay. I know what you meant."

"Good. Anyway, I should probably go. You've probably got another talk to do or something."

She shook her head, her gaze shy. "I'm actually going for my lunch break."

Was that a hint? As if. He was so bad at this. "Um, okay then. Well, I'll see you around." He stepped back, caught a flash of something that he might almost call disappointment cross her face. Please. As if a classy, intelligent, art-loving woman like her would ever be interested in a dumb jock like him. Better save the rejection and leave her in peace—the kind of peace that could be found *away* from Mullins men who always seemed to wreck things.

"Th-thank you," she said.

"No problem. And hey, thank you for being so gracious." He smiled, paced back, then added in another burst of honesty, "You know, you really have one of the nicest voices I've ever heard."

She blinked, mouth dropping open, and he spun on his heel. Looked like now would be the perfect time to go for his run. And run fast away.

CHAPTER 3

The thick canopy of leaves above rustled in the light breeze, a welcome escape from the sun and the muggy heat that still lingered after yesterday. This section of lawn was different to Allie's usual location, nearer the paths used by cyclists and joggers, yet it still contained a modicum of privacy and peace. Allie sat with her sunglasses on, eyes closed, listening as the sounds and scents of the park washed over her senses and the tension inside gradually faded away.

Never had she been so glad for the timing of her lunch break. It had allowed her to collect her sandwich and water bottle and slip outside to this space she prayed would bring some sanity to the tumult of her heart.

Jai Mullins had been there again? They'd talked—or at least word spurted at each other—again? But oh, her conversations with him in her dreams had definitely never sounded like that. Between them, she and Jai had more than a gift of awkwardness. They navigated their interactions with all the success of the Titanic, every blunder or faux pas another iceberg sending conversation and ease to a watery grave. Ugh.

It was hard to believe her idol had feet of clay, but there it was. She might stutter, but he seemed to have the gift of foot-in-mouth, with his awkward apologies and bursts of impromptu confessions.

Her heart rippled. Had he meant his last line about liking her voice? She couldn't quite believe it—had been sure he was teasing her until she realized that was hardly in keeping with the rest of his kind words. Nobody had *ever* complimented her about her voice before. But she supposed some people might think it had a soothing quality, given its resemblance to a kindergarten teacher's singsong tone—something that demanded much mental strain. Oh, to be so relaxed with him that she could speak like she could with her family or colleagues like Celeste.

But at least this conversation had proved a mite easier than yesterday's. Of course, his kindness had helped. Had he really called her pretty? For the second time? That was almost enough to make her think he meant it.

This had definitely been a day of firsts. First flowers from a man—even if they were apology flowers. First time feeling a sense of appreciation from a man. She hadn't imagined that; he'd said as much, hadn't he? Even the first time of feeling like she'd halfway impressed her colleagues, between the flowers and the positive reports from Mr. Weinberger, the deputy director, who had apparently heard her talk as he showed some potential donors around. Thank *goodness* she hadn't seen him, otherwise her already tongue-tied performance would've been three million times worse!

But Mr. Weinberger's praise—his encouragement not unlike Jai's, actually—had lifted her spirits and lips, especially as he'd shared it just as Myra and Selina passed, prompting him to congratulate Myra on her choice of Allie as her second-in-command.

"Oh! Well, Allie does her best, I'm sure."

"She certainly impressed me—and Mr. and Mrs. Donohue, who are potential donors. I wonder…" He glanced at Allie, then back at Myra. "I'll be in touch soon. But this one…" He nodded to Allie. "We need to keep this one."

With Myra apparently struck dumb, Allie had managed to murmur her thanks and slip back to the office before Myra and Selina could wonder aloud in that ever-draining way of theirs. "Thank you, God, for vindication," Allie said aloud now.

Maybe God was paying attention, and these twisted ropes of disappointment and frustration could one day be straightened and woven into something lovely after all.

Maybe the fact that Allie's younger sister was getting married before Allie had ever had a boyfriend was okay. Maybe the fact that Allie had never felt Myra would support her career ambitions could be sorted too. It was funny how she could sing about God's goodness but then seem to forget it so very quickly. She exhaled and opened her eyes, wryness tugging at her lips. She must be about the most human of humans she knew.

She collected her eco-friendly water bottle and moved back along the shaded path. This was a nice part of Chicago, all prettified near the lake. She peered up at the tall residential towers, wondering about those lucky enough to live nearby. Her family's house was in a modest suburb populated mostly by families like hers—middle-class, employed. She liked it, but it was all she knew. Rents here were sure to be abysmally expensive, but living in the city was like moving to the west coast. She could add it to her list of impossible dreams.

Joggers moved along the path, committed to fitness in a way she'd never own, especially as they ran in the heat of the day. Admittedly, today wasn't as hot as yesterday, but still, she couldn't help but admire the effort. She stepped out of the way of an oncoming female jogger when—

"Allie?"

She turned, breath hitching as her heart had a conniption.

"Jai? Remember?"

Allie nodded. How could she forget?

She swallowed. And looking at him now—T-shirt taut over a muscled chest, sweat glistening off tanned skin—she would likely never forget this, either. Get the girl a fan already. Or an ice bath. Or a camera.

"Just had your lunch, huh?"

Another nod. Oh, how this man tangled her tongue in knots!

"What'd you have?"

"A s-sandwich. Salmon, from a can." Because she certainly hadn't been counting on talking to Mr. Hot Hockey Player when she'd made her sandwich last night!

Could he smell her breath? *Dear heavens, please let him not smell my breath.* She paced back. Faked a cough and covered her mouth with her hand and sniffed. Was that *eau de salmon?* This must be why her sisters always screwed up their noses whenever she made such a sandwich.

"Do I smell?" he said, sniffing at one underarm. "Sorry. I'm trying to keep up with the training, and for some reason, my trainer seems to think it's good to run in the heat."

Embarrassment that she'd embarrassed him faded at his later words. *That's weird*, she wanted to say but couldn't. *Weird when you work on ice.*

"Which is strange," he continued.

"Why?"

He shrugged. "Because I play hockey on ice."

Yes. Yes, he did. She bit her lip. Should she admit she knew this about him? She didn't want to come across all stalker-like, but neither would things end well if she professed total ignorance. "For the Blackhawks."

"You know hockey?" A grin lit up his face.

Her insides tensed as she wavered between admiration of his perfect teeth and an admission she could never speak. "A bit."

"Wow. Classy, pretty, and she knows hockey. I don't suppose you're a Christian?"

She stiffened. "Why don't you suppose that?"

"Huh." He drew off his cap, ran a hand through his curly brown hair. "Does that mean you are?"

Her breath suspended as he drew closer. No way did she want him to smell her salmon breath. But no way could she move away from the glistening, sweaty hotness of him. Not when she felt herself standing on the precipice of something extraordinarily wonderful.

"Yes."

He smiled, and again she felt that answering kick low in her stomach. "What church do you go to?"

The same as you. She told him, enjoying the widened hazel eyes.

"No way. How come I've never seen you there before?"

"My family and I go to the early morning service. You must go later."

"Yeah. Wow. Well, okay. I guess this makes it official."

Her heart spun and danced in a crazy mix of foxtrot, salsa, and rhumba. *Stop it, stupid heart. Come on, Allie, talk!* "M-makes what official?"

"I'm officially an idiot. I can't believe you've been there all this time and I've never noticed you."

Ouch.

"Wait—I didn't mean that to sound like that. I just meant—"

"It's okay. I know what you meant."

His smile sent her heart's dance moves to pirouettes. She grasped the water bottle more firmly. Obviously she was losing grip on reality.

"So, Allie—"

He knew her name? *Oh my gosh, oh my gosh—*

"Do you have lunch here often?"

She took a breath, willing herself to talk slowly even as her blood rushed at great speed. "Most days. When the weather's nice enough. And I have time." Speaking of time, she should probably check how much more she had before her break was—

"I'll keep an eye out then."

Now her pulse seemed to have caught her mouth's propensity for stuttering fun. But no. He didn't mean it. He couldn't. *Come on, Allie, speak!* "Do you run here often?"

"Most days." His grin flickered. "When the weather is nice enough. And I have time."

Amusement pushed out in a chuckle. She'd definitely be keeping an eye out then.

His grin hitched higher. "Okay then."

"Okay."

"Well, I guess I'll see you around, Miss Allie."

"I guess you will, Mr. Mullins."

"You know my last name?"

She froze. She didn't want him to know she was likely his biggest superfan. That she moderated—okay, had started and basically ran—an online fan club devoted to Jai Mullins. "I follow the Hawks," she allowed, "so I might've heard of you a time or two."

His forehead furrowed. "Did you recognize me yesterday?"

She swallowed. *Admit it now.* Let him know her room had a poster or three of him, like she was some sad chick from the 1990s with her room covered in boy band posters.

"Sorry." His brow cleared. "That makes me sound so arrogant, doesn't it? Forget I asked. Hey, good to see you."

Her tongue unclenched enough to offer a lame "you too," and he grinned, saluted, and jogged away. She exhaled, watching his long stride, his steady gait, wondering at the fitness of the man and whether he'd score the title of fastest man on the Hawks' roster this year for the third year in a row. Then also wondered whether he'd turn and catch her looking. She forced her feet to move, but her disobedient head refused to follow, watching him until the last moment.

He didn't look. Her heart felt a stupid pang of disappointment.

This was *ridiculous*.

But also awesome.

This was *stupid* for her emotions to be getting so far ahead of reality.

But also exciting. Judging from the last couple of encounters—three encounters in two days, no less—she was almost prepared to think the man might sort of like her.

Which was a miracle of the big God variety. A miracle of an answered-dreams variety.

As she moved back to the artwork of the past, her heart sang the "Hallelujah Chorus." *Dear God. Thank You. Thank You. Thank You!*

"ALLIE? HELLO? ARE YOU PAYING ATTENTION?"

Allie blinked, stuffing her stupid imagination back into its box, and refocused on Chrissy, the song leader at tonight's music rehearsal for Sunday's service. "Y-yes."

"Are you sure? Because you're going to have to introduce the song, and we all know that's not always worked out well in the past."

No. It hadn't. But at least most people in this church were far more patient and gracious than some members of the worship team at music practice.

"If you can't pay attention, then maybe someone else should do the solo," Chrissy said. "Remember, we're simply trying to minister to the Lord here."

Allie ducked her head.

"Now, let's go again from the top."

Allie closed her eyes, listening as Chrissy counted the musicians in, and let herself sink into the music written by Sarah Maguire of Heartsong Collective, the Australian worship group whose songs were sung in churches around the globe. There were only a few times when Allie felt completely like herself, and worshipping in church was one of them. For some reason, her voice always seemed to do what it was supposed to do, articulating sounds in a way that never came as easily in mere conversation. She didn't have to try. She could just be. She could relax and feel almost normal for once.

"Lover of my soul, You are always with me," she sang.

The words of awe-filled surrender, of hope and trust, rippled from her soul, reminding her once again of God's faithfulness and mercy. Reminding her that He was always with her, that He'd been there in the depths of her embarrassment yesterday when she'd failed to restrain tears after her flop of a kids' talk time. That He'd been there, even when Selina had basically stolen her work. That He'd been there today, when she'd returned from her hallelujah of a lunchtime to discover that Myra had suddenly scheduled her to do the Tots and Paint Pots activity that afternoon. She'd nearly earned another migraine from the ear-piercing shrieks and chaos that such afternoons always induced, while the second-guessing that seemed to be the soundtrack to her life whispered that she'd misread things and misunderstood, because why would *Jai Mullins* of all people think she was remotely interesting?

Now such embarrassment didn't matter. God reminded her it didn't matter. And here, worshipping Him, she had no reason to feel ashamed or overwhelmed. She could simply be herself with the One who already knew all her flaws and imperfections, and she could do and be what she'd always felt she was created to be: a worshipper of the ultimate Creator.

"And I need not fear, because I know that You're my God."

She kept her eyes closed as the music washed around her.

God. Her God. Regardless of what others said or did or how she felt about herself. God still deserved worship. This Sarah who'd written this song really knew her stuff.

The music faded, the auditorium emptying of sound as if pausing to take breath.

"That was really good," Chrissy said, her voice holding a note of surprise.

"Really anointed," a deeper voice said.

Allie opened her eyes and smiled. Josiah Abrahams, the pastor of the church Allie and her family had attended for years, had a real gift of encouragement. He also had a love for hockey, and she knew Jai was part of a special online Bible study he ran, along with several other players like Mike Vaughan and Brent Karlsson, both of whom had recently married. Not that she kept tabs on the relationship status of Christian hockey players or anything.

"When will the church be blessed by this song?"

"This Sunday, sir," Chrissy offered.

"Hmm. Both morning services?"

Chrissy raised an eyebrow at Allie. Allie's family usually only attended the earlier service, but she nodded anyway.

"Wonderful."

She hoped it would be, anyway. She didn't know many who attended the ten-thirty service, most of them belonging to the hip-and-happening crowd. Her experience showed that their tolerance for those who were a little different tended to be on the lower end of the spectrum.

"So, we're all set then? Allie will do the solo, and we've got the rest of the songs sorted. You'll sing both services, yes?"

Allie nodded.

"And don't forget you'll need to introduce the item."

Another nod.

"That means talking, Allie."

Her sense of humor bit, and she nodded again.

Chrissy—fortunately—saw the joke and laughed, which tugged another smile from Allie. Okay, so maybe tonight's practice hadn't turned out to be so bad after all. Now if only she could forget that someone like Jai Mullins existed, she might be able to find her emotional equilibrium once more.

IT'D BEEN a long time since Jai had felt the need to get to church for the 8:30 a.m. service. Games that finished late on Saturday night didn't exactly encourage waking early on Sundays. Especially when he'd always preferred to stay up and sleep in. All the more so when church required a twenty minute drive to get there. But today, traffic seemed much lighter, and the thought of why he was going earlier compelled him.

He'd explained to his mom that the reason he couldn't stay for breakfast with her was because he hoped to take the girl he'd met properly the other day—who just so happened to love his mom's flowers—out for brunch after the service. "You could come too," he'd offered, hoping she might finally say yes.

"And cramp your style? No, thank you. I don't mind you missing time with me if it means you finally get a chance to take a girl out. What's it been? Six months? A year?"

He shrugged.

"Whatever it is, it's been too long. And I'm getting older and would like to see you married, like Kat."

Yeah, maybe not like Kat. Her marriage hadn't exactly been a recipe for happiness. He refrained from saying the obvious and went for caution instead. "There are no guarantees, Mom. Anyway, she seems a bit too good for me."

"Too good for you? Honey, who's the person with the multi-million-dollar contract?"

"I don't think money is that important to her."

"Uh huh. Sweetie, I can't help but think you're a tad naïve to think money ain't important to a girl."

"She's not like that," he protested.

"And you know this how?" She hooked a tattooed eyebrow.

"I kinda meant she's really smart."

"Hmm. Smart enough to know how to pick up a hockey player, I'll give her that."

"Mom! There's no picking up. If anything, it's me chasing her." When was the last time he'd done that? "Oh, and let's not forget where we're meeting. At *church*."

"Maybe I should go. I might meet a nice man myself."

He'd saved his sigh for the car and chased it with a bunch of prayers, even as his heart wondered if maybe he really had finally found someone nice himself.

It had been a long time since he'd dated or had a girlfriend. His friends in the hockey Bible study group weren't much better. He knew Dan didn't date. Beau hadn't for months, or was it years? Mike had waited for Bree to finally pay him attention, and Brent had taken time out from the dating scene to rebuild a reputation soured by the so-called perks of too-quick success. A Cup by the age of twenty-four? A gold medal from the recent Vancouver games? Where did you go from there? Mind you, he seemed to have found someone good in his Aussie short track skating pocket rocket. Jai had met Holly a few times before Brent's wedding two months ago, and he liked her forthright nature and sass. She was good for Brent and would no doubt prove a steadying, calming force in the volatile world of pro hockey.

It was funny how, in this sport, the measure of success seemed to be found in contracts, money, and wins, but he knew —only too well—how promises weren't always kept, money could disappear, and the magic of a win could fade as quickly as the sound of a car pulling away. Yeah. Success could turn a man's head, that was for sure.

Which was why he needed to stay grounded in truth and hang with people who were honest and could keep him accountable. Jai had dated fans before, as had some of his teammates, and experience showed that honesty wasn't always their preferred policy. Which was why he'd made it his policy to never date fans. He wasn't about to invest his time with liars.

He pulled into the church parking lot, found a spot, and killed the engine. Here went nothing. Was it too bold a move to come to this service? He barely knew what was considered okay and wouldn't be misconstrued by women these days. Maybe he should've waited. But hey, he still needed to go to church, and if today gave him a bit more insight into who Allie was, well, he'd take it.

Two minutes later he was in the foyer, looking through the glass doors leading into the auditorium and wondering where he should sit. He was used to his little corner near the back of this large church, where he could pretty much come late and leave early as he needed, thus avoiding hockey-related conversations other than those his friends or Pastor Josiah Abrahams instigated. This service time he figured might be different.

"If it's not my Jai-man, here early for a change."

Jai completed the hand-slap-handshake thing his pastor insisted on every time they met. "Hey, Jo."

"What brings you here today?"

Aim for cool. He shrugged, stuck his hands in his pockets. "Just thought I'd check things out. No game means I don't have to sleep in."

"Hmm. Never stopped you before, but all right." Jo eyed him with a tweak to his mouth that suggested he knew Jai was not being completely forthcoming. "Any more word on tickets for training camp?"

"Nope. You'll be the first to know though."

"Counting on it. See you inside."

Jai nodded and shifted his weight to his other foot. Would it be weird for Allie if he met her out here? She'd said her family attended this service, and he wasn't so green that he didn't know things with Allie were *way* too new to think about meeting her family yet. Maybe this was a mistake. Maybe he should leave. Maybe he—

"Jai Mullins?"

He turned and met the gaze of a woman with dark eyes and blonde hair.

"Oh my word, it *is* you. I couldn't believe it when she told us, and yet here you are."

"Here I am," he agreed. Huh. He hadn't figured Allie as the kind to spill her secrets. "And you are?"

"Marcie. Marcie Campbell." She gestured to a wide man with a pink, cherubic face. "That's my husband, Steve. We're big fans."

"Oh." He smiled, further words trucking away like they were powered by a semi. What was he supposed to say? *Thank you? I'm glad?* He'd never been too good at this small talk stuff.

"We haven't seen you at this service before. Are you church shopping? If so, we can definitely recommend this place. They have the most wonderful music. These musicians have a real heart for the Lord, and the people are real friendly too."

"I can see that," he said politely.

"Aren't you sweet? I thought you might be, but—hey, Steve!" she called. "Come over here and meet Jai."

"Oh, ma'am," Jai protested, "I was just about to go in and find a seat—"

"Well, you sure can't sit by yourself on your first day! That would be right unneighborly, now. No, you'll just have to sit with me and Steve, y'hear?"

Jai gritted his teeth, pasting on politeness as Steve ambled closer, his broad grin hitching wider as Marcie introduced them.

"That's really kind of you, Marcie, but I'm afraid I have plans already."

"Oh! You know someone here? Well, apart from Gloria?"

"Who?"

"Gloria Abrahams. The pastor's wife?" She waggled fingers at a woman who grinned and drew near. "She's the one who mentioned you before."

His chest knew a ping of relief. So it hadn't been Allie who'd mentioned him to Marcie.

"I've heard about you," Gloria said with a wink.

Okay, no way was he about to admit he'd spent many an evening discussing hockey with Jo while Gloria waited patiently in the kitchen. "How are you, Mrs. A?"

"Just fine, thanks, Jai." She spoke to his super-friendly hostess, then gestured him inside, adding in a lower voice, "Nice to see you here today. What brings you to this early service?"

Did he need to have a sign over his head admitting to the truth? How could he ever stay under the radar with all this attention?

He shrugged. "Felt like a change."

"Well." She patted his arm. "I hope you'll enjoy. Now, don't worry about Marcie. She and her entire family are hockey-mad, so don't get too concerned. Oh, look, here come the musicians. I best let you get your seat. See you tomorrow night?"

He nodded. Every second Monday was the usual Bible study catch up via Zoom. Of course, living in Chi-town meant he and Jo were often able to be in the same room.

Jai took his seat—as far as possible from the overly-enthusiastic Marcie—and checked out the printed program, all the while wondering where Allie was. Was she sick? Had his hints at coming today scared her off? Maybe his bouts of word vomit had proved too much to handle. Not that he'd blame her.

He glanced up, his mouth falling open. The person moving to the center of the stage holding a microphone in her hand was none other than the mysterious art-loving Allie.

Should he wave to catch her attention or slink down in his

seat to avoid it? Every time he'd seen her in a setting like this—out the front, eyes on her—she seemed to get distracted and lose her place. And it was one thing to lose focus on a talk about paintings, quite another to deliberately steal her attention when she was about to lead worship.

"Good morning, everyone," she began in that smooth voice he was quickly coming to love. "I'd like to invite you to stay seated and listen as we sing a special song unto the Lord."

There. Decision made. He'd stay slumped in his seat and out of her line of sight.

The keyboards began, and soon did her song, the notes, clear and true, wrapping around his heart, squeezing air from his lungs. Wow. He'd visited some of Chicago's famous jazz clubs, and he'd bet Allie could give them a run for their money. And she spent her day telling others about art?

"You are the Lover of my soul, You are always with me…"

Oh. Yeah. He closed his eyes, leaning forward to prop his elbows on knees and place his face in his hands as he refocused on why he was here. Seeing Allie was only a bonus, not the main purpose of his time in church. Now had to be about reconnecting his heart with God. Realigning his focus and steps and submitting to God's ways.

Lord, forgive me. Guide me, lead me, show me what You want me to do.

The music continued to sweep around his heart, as if reminding him of his prayer and encouraging his commitment to sink deeper, and in the words, he heard an echo of his musings on the trip here.

Fame meant nothing. Money didn't last. A win could be savored for only a certain amount of time before one had to stop living in the past and think about the future. These measures of success were transitory at best, an illusion through which the world so often viewed this prism of life.

He wanted God. He *needed* God. God had saved his life from

a path of destruction, and Jai knew that a life spent in service for others was healthier than one spent serving himself.

And, he thought as the song concluded and he straightened and finally smiled and waved at Allie, he wanted someone who wanted those things too.

CHAPTER 4

*A*llie's chest grew tight. He'd come? She'd thought he'd been joking, flirting, just saying what she wanted to hear. But Jai had come. Was waving at her, grinning. Oh. Her pulse sped to double time. He was giving her a thumbs-up. So her solo had been okay?

The music for the first of the regular songs played quietly in the background until Josiah opened the service in prayer.

She couldn't look at Jai. Or her family who, after Marcie had rushed in and spoken urgently to Mom and Dad, had all looked back en masse at Jai as he studied his church bulletin. Dear heavens. She hoped nobody had embarrassed him. Or told him about the posters in her room. As soon as she got home today, she was tearing them down! Or at least, carefully removing them and storing them for a rainy day. Like when Jai moved on, at which point she'd no doubt cry and need a little reminder of the time when he'd actually seemed to like her.

Stop it! Focus. She had to focus. *God, help me focus.*

And she did, singing her part through the songs, experiencing a touch of heaven in her own heart that she hoped the congregation felt too.

"

"That was great," Chrissy murmured as they took their seats on the side near the stage.

Allie exhaled, refusing to look across the rows of seats to where Jai sat. He was allowed to come to church. Even this particular service at this particular church. It was no biggie. What *could* prove a biggie would be if her family ever found out about her accidental meetings with him and started making a mountain out of something rather less than a molehill. That would not be pretty.

Her eyes didn't seem to want to play fair with her brain and stole across to where Jai sat. As if he felt the weight of her gaze, he glanced across, smiled, and lifted a hand.

She could hardly ignore him, could she? So she lifted her fingers in what surely had to be the most non-committal wave of the century—literally, a flap up and down of four fingers—and immediately returned her attention to Pastor Jo at the front.

Ridiculous. Her foot started to jiggle. These stupid hormones racing around her body like they were on spring break were simply being ridiculous. Stupid. Juvenile.

"You okay?" Chrissy asked.

Allie nodded, picked up the program, and started waving it, like she had to cool down. Of course, she *did* have to cool down, because Mr. Hot Hockey Player was over there at a service he didn't normally attend, and her crazy hormones whispered it just might be because she'd said she did, and her brain was so befuddled she didn't quite know what to do with that.

"Let's pray."

Oh dear. How had her brain managed to filter awareness of everything about the service and the sermon except where Jai was sitting? *Sorry, God.*

Chrissy beckoned for Allie to follow, and they moved back to the stage, waiting for Josiah to finish. But now she couldn't pretend to not pay attention, and her smile felt a little wavery and unsure as she faced the congregation.

She drew in a breath and hitched her lips higher, her gaze flicking from her parents to her sisters with their respective husband and fiancé, then across to where Jai had straightened, a smile on his lips, his gaze bolted to hers until she dragged hers away. She couldn't look at him—he drained sense from her brain and strength from her knees—so she fixed her attention on the back of Josiah's head until he finished speaking and turned expectantly to them.

This was it. Chrissy wanted her to speak, to introduce the song. Allie opened her mouth—

But words refused utterance, clamping in her throat, her tongue refusing to move around the rock-sized panic in her mouth. She pushed air out, but no sound came, and she felt her chest constrict, sweat trickle down her back. No. No, no. She couldn't fail. She couldn't fail right now. In front of *him*.

A desperate glance at Chrissy saw her bend to the microphone and speak—speak blessed words so smoothly fluent that Allie's entire body seemed to prickle with envy. Oh, to be normal. To be able to *speak*. To not have this terrifying panic shut down her life.

Somehow, her vocal cords managed to work enough for her to join the song halfway through the chorus—a moment which might have appeared planned, but she knew better. Chrissy knew better. The musicians, her family, Pastor Jo—they all knew better.

Allie might have moments of fluency where she could articulate artistic theory and endeavor as well as the next person, but today just proved why she should never, could never, aspire to be more than what she was. Because this condition had defined her whole life, and despite Jai's attention causing her heart to leap treacherously into hope-filled waters, she knew the truth.

She'd never be more than a stutterer. And she'd never be equal to him.

~

SHE'D FROZEN. Again. Jai knew a disconcerting twist low in his gut. He sure wasn't used to being the cause of such embarrassment. Most fans seemed super eager to talk to him. Would spy him in a store and bustle up to chat, which he didn't really mind, depending on what he was trying to do. Some of his teammates just wanted to be left alone and would get a little touchy when their privacy was invaded. Others drank in the adulation, especially with the girls. Jai had encountered plenty of girls who liked to chat—not as many as flirted with the bigger name guys like Brent Karlsson, but enough to recognize signs of interest and availability for more. With Allie, he'd seen little of that, her aloofness something that had piqued his interest as much as her obvious class, intelligence, and good looks.

But this...this obvious dismay at his presence? Yeah. Well. He shouldn't have come. *Sure misread this one, Mullins.*

The service concluded, and the musicians and singers left the stage, Allie escaping without once looking at him. Man. He knew a kind of crawling inner loathing for having embarrassed her. Maybe he should escape too—

"Jai?"

He glanced up. Oh. "Hey."

Marcie smiled. "Did you enjoy the service?"

"Yeah."

"Did you like the music?"

"Yep."

"You don't talk much, do you?"

"I do when I have something to say."

"Oh. Right. Okay."

He knew a moment's regret that his bluntness seemed to have left her so nonplussed.

"Well, we like to pride ourselves here on being welcoming to strangers and wanted to know if you'd care to join us for a special morning tea for visitors after the service."

"Thank you, but I'm not exactly a visitor."

"What? I've never seen you here before."

"I usually attend the later service," he confessed.

"Oh." Her eyes widened. "So what brings you to the earlier one today?"

Hadn't he answered this enough already today? "Felt like a change."

"Oh. Okay. Well, it's good you could come. Do you know some people here, or would you like me to introduce you?"

"I should be okay," he said, adding, as he noted her chagrined look, "but thanks for thinking of me."

"Of course."

He smiled, waited until she'd left, then exhaled. Yeah. This had been a bad idea. He was totally getting out of—

"You're Jai Mullins, right?"

He closed his eyes, pasted on pleasantness, and turned.

"I'm Peter," an upper-middle-aged man said, holding out a hand for Jai to shake, which he did obediently.

"Jai."

"I knew it! You were just talking to my daughter, weren't you?"

Jai coughed. "Marcie?" The man nodded. "She's very friendly."

"Yeah, sometimes a little too much so, but hey, you never heard me say that." Peter grinned. "You've played for Chicago for the past five years, right?"

"Yeah," Jai said.

As the man shared about his long love for the Hawks, ever since they won the Cup way back in 1961, Jai resigned himself to another long chat. Yep, they felt the pressure of being one of the Windy City's premier sports teams without a recent championship, and plenty of people in this town had plenty of opinions on just why that might be.

He snuck a peek past the man's J.Crew-clad shoulder to see if Allie was around. Still no. Maybe he should simply resign himself to this being a bad idea and letting go of the hope of anything more.

"Hey, I'm sorry. I'm chewing off your ear, aren't I? And I bet you hear from rabid fans like me all the time."

"It's fine," Jai said politely.

"You sure?"

Jai smiled. "I'm part of a Bible study headed by Pastor Jo."

"Enough said then."

Indeed.

"Hey, I have a super crazy question—don't freak out on me or anything, okay?"

Uh oh.

"Seeing as we're family—"

"Excuse me?"

"You know, church family, part of God's family and all, I was wondering if maybe you'd like to come to lunch today."

Jai blinked.

"Or maybe come for lunch another time. We keep it casual, whoever is available. My wife always cooks enough to feed an army, but it's always pretty relaxed and fun."

"Uh huh."

"I bet someone like you probably already has plans for today, and I know it's a little last minute and all, but hey, any time after church on Sunday." Peter chuckled. "Or maybe you'll have plans from now on because you're worried about the random man with his random invitations and all."

Yeah. That. Jai's smile grew tight. Definitely true.

"Well, I can understand you might not be able to come today. Maybe one day though?"

"Maybe." Keep it non-committal. No obligations, no expectations…

Movement beyond Peter's shoulder distracted him. Finally. Allie. He lifted a hand. Noticed her glance at him, the way her cheeks pinked as she hesitated.

Peter must've tracked his distraction, because he turned around. "Wait. Do you know Allie?"

Barely. But… "Yeah."

"Allie, get on over here," Peter said, gesturing her near before wrapping an arm around her shoulders in an overly familiar way. People sure were friendly at this service. "Why on earth didn't you say anything?"

Allie's dark gaze met Jai's, then dropped away as she shrugged.

He knew a twist of disappointment followed by a sudden urge to know why she hadn't said anything, an urge that chased rational thought from his brain and propelled tease to his mouth. "Yeah, Allie. Why not?"

Something that looked like amusement—or maybe it was annoyance—flashed in her eyes. "I, um, didn't want…"

"Didn't want what, Allie?" Peter asked—demanded, really.

Protectiveness surged. Who did this guy think he was, talking to Allie that way? "It's okay," Jai assured her. "We can talk later."

She shook her head fractionally as the man looked between them. "What? Talk later? What's going on?"

Jai had to change the subject. Fast. "Hey, you did such a great job with that song."

A brief smile, a briefer glance, then she looked at the floor as her cheeks grew pinker still.

He tried again. "I didn't know you could sing like that."

"Keeps her light under a bushel, this one."

"Peter?" A new female voice chimed in. "Oh, here you are." The woman, who seemed to be Peter's wife judging from the way she cozied up to his other side, looked between them all. "So, is someone going to introduce me?"

Peter clapped Jai on the shoulder, like he thought they were best buds or something. "Sweetie, this is Jai Mullins."

"Hello. Oh! Not the Chicago player? Oh my." She fanned herself. "Oh, it's an honor. I didn't know you came to this church."

"I usually attend the second service," he admitted, sneaking a peek at Allie. She still studied her toes.

"So you're a Christian?"

"Yes, ma'am."

"Oh, how wonderful! To think we've been Hawks fans since before we could walk, and to now meet you! Oh my stars!" The hand fluttering picked up in pace. "Oh, this is wonderful!"

It was wonderful, but Jai still didn't know who she was. "Excuse me, but who are you?"

"Oh!" Peter sparked to animation again. "This is my wife, Merrilee."

"Nice to meet you, ma'am." And a little overwhelming, to be honest. He should probably see about leaving soon—

"Oh, Peter. Have you asked him?"

"Asked him what?"

"Asked him to join us for lunch."

Oh. No.

"Oh, Jai—you don't mind if I call you Jai, do you?"

What could he say? *No, I prefer Mr. Mullins.* "Uh, no."

"I'm so glad. I feel like we're family already. Oh, I should ask —do you have family here?" She looked around.

"Nope. Just me."

"Oh, does your family worship elsewhere?"

Yeah, at the golden temple of retail and consumption.

Before he could answer, Peter said, "Now, Merrilee, we don't want to badger the man. In answer to your previous question, I've already asked the man to lunch, and he's said he's busy." He slid a look at Allie. "Unless you've had a change of mind." He raised an eyebrow, as if in question.

No way was Jai ever gonna get involved with superfans. He appreciated Allie's calmness—her knowledge of hockey seemed general, not too specific. He wouldn't be tumbling off any pedestal there, at least.

Allie inched away. "I need to go."

"Oh. You're not joining us for lunch?"

She glanced at Jai, then away. "I'm doing music for the second service."

"Oh, I forgot," Merrilee said, and Allie's lips flattened.

"Are you singing again?" Jai blurted, then wished he hadn't, as Peter and Merrilee glanced at each other, then Allie, then him, eyes wide as pucks.

Way to welcome the new guy and make him feel comfortable, like every word and action was being measured and judged.

Allie's wide eyes held a streak of deer-in-headlights panic as she nodded and shifted farther away.

He didn't blame her. He had to get out of here, too, and shut down the intense speculation he could read in the dynamics here. "'Kay. Well, nice to see you," he said as nonchalantly as he could. "Nice to meet you, Peter, Merrilee."

"Oh, but are you sure you can't join us today?" the latter pleaded.

"Sorry. I've got plans."

Was that disappointment creasing Allie's face? Likely not. What kind of idiot would think that when she hadn't given him a drop of encouragement all day? Come to think of it, maybe he'd just gotten everything confused and she had no desire to have anything more to do with him in any context anyway.

That thought sharpened his goodbye to something a little

terser than he'd aimed for, and he spun on his heel to avoid Allie's lack of interest and the sounds of regret from the way-too-interested Peter and Merrilee so he wouldn't be waylaid any longer. He lifted a hand of farewell to Josiah, hurrying outside to escape the heat from within. Climbed into his truck. Turned on the ignition for the air-con to cool.

Okay. He'd come. He'd seen. And he'd definitely not conquered this stubborn attraction to this girl. Allie. She who'd given him not the slightest sense of encouragement. And judging from the fact this service seemed filled with superfans, he sure wasn't going to come hurrying back at this time any time soon.

What to do now? He'd as good as told his mom he wouldn't be back for lunch. Going back early to her place meant a sure date with an empty house, as she would be—as she always was—at the mall, searching for the insta-joy retail therapy seemed to bring her. If by some miracle she was home, it would only prove a lesson in patience as she worked to worm out more information about the girl and why things hadn't worked out, and he'd be forced to weave and dodge around complaint and comparison. He sure wasn't a saint, but honestly, nobody needed that much patience.

He tapped the steering wheel, watching as various individuals, couples, and families exited. There were Marcie and Steve. There were Peter and Merrilee, chatting to a bunch of others. Man, they were friendly. A little too friendly, actually. For a second, Jai imagined what lunch at their place might be like: filled with questions and conversation about the team and what the upcoming season's roster might look like and what he thought their chances might be like at the Cup this year. But he also got the impression theirs would be a place of relaxed chatter and laughter and a help-yourself kind of meal that wouldn't involve grand showiness or pretense. Their talk of family seemed warm and genuine, something that by turns intrigued and scared him. Something he'd not grown up with, but perhaps better than going home to a sandwich and a too-quiet apartment.

Should he accept their offer?

No. He didn't need the chaos. Didn't need the noise. He did okay by himself. He wasn't lonely.

Except…if Allie was going, then he'd be an auto-yes.

"She doesn't even like you," he said aloud, his car's interior filling with his discouragement.

Except…had she just been shy? From his admittedly limited interactions with her, she wasn't especially forthcoming. The most he'd ever heard her speak was during her talks at the Art Institute. Maybe she was like him and found the whole interacting-with-the-opposite-sex thing kind of hard and exhausting, wondering what was safe to talk about in the minefield of conversation. Maybe he should hang around for the second service and see if he could get a chance to talk to her properly.

Man. He didn't even know her last name. Or her phone number. How could he be so fast on the ice and yet so slow to figure this stuff out?

He watched as the over-friendly crew from this morning hugged and waved and got in their cars. Knew another tug of envy. It'd be kinda nice to feel accepted and part of a warm family-type group like that, more so than the fractured family of his origin. Sometimes he felt that sense with his team, especially in playoffs, when months of playing together tended to bond them close like brothers. Even so, there was always this awareness that a team only lasted as long as a contract did and the guys who had played together could get traded away. Mike Vaughan had seen that two years ago, traded away from Boston, another of the Original Six teams, to Calgary. Teammates couldn't be relied on, although he could count on his Bible study crew.

But it would be nice to have local people who he could feel

as comfortable with as he imagined some people felt with their families. Would the risk of rabid fans entering his world prove exhausting? Probably.

He'd simply wait until they left, then return inside and hopefully talk to Allie instead.

CHAPTER 5

He was here. Again.

Allie's skin prickled as she glanced out into the congregation already waiting for the second service to begin. Yep. Her eyes hadn't been playing tricks. That was definitely Jai Mullins up in the back corner, surrounded by a group of similarly cool congregation members. Yet he didn't seem to be paying attention to them. Rather, his focus was on her, if that smile and wave thing was any indication.

Her stomach tugged with anticipation. So maybe her impression of a mute hadn't scared him off after all. Or the crazy obviousness of her folks. Honestly. Could her parents have been any more painful? The fact Jai had hung around interacting for as long as he had proved him a man of immense courage.

Or...maybe he was just here because he wanted more of God. Oh, who was she kidding? Of *course* Jai was here because he wanted more of God. Which was good. Which was as it should be. She wanted a guy who was focused on growing in his relationship with God, just as she was trying to do. So that was great. Really.

The service began, and she knew she had to tune Jai out so she could tune God in.

Deep breath. Focused heart. Focused thoughts. *Be still. Know that God is here. Know that He is in control.* He was big. Powerful. All powerful. Could raise people from the grave. Nothing was impossible for Him.

The words reminded her soul to relax, her shoulders to release tension, as a cavalcade of God's faithfulness and goodness—non Jai-related—rolled through her mind.

Her family. Her job. Her art. Creativity. Friends. This city. Freedom. Forgiveness. Peace.

The music began, and she kept her eyes closed, ensuring her wayward thoughts stayed heavenward. She sang, the opening item flowing into the worship time that again provided those heart nudges she needed in order to align herself with God's plans and purposes.

Later, the sermon—which her heart attended to more fully this time—reminded her again of the need to submit and surrender to God's ways. Doing things in her own strength never got her far. And sometimes it seemed she was all too keen to plow on regardless of those whispers to stop, rest, and take time to allow God to refresh her heart and spirit. Surrendering to God didn't mean giving up. It just meant a more active trust that He would work things out for her good, regardless of what that looked like. She could trust Him. With her life. Work. And with whatever this thing was with Jai.

Pastor Josiah switched up the service a little, this time concluding with the item. Allie kept her heart and eyes focused away from the man in the back corner, relief cascading through her as her voice decided to cooperate this time. Maybe that's what she needed to do: have a run-through on life where she could mess up the trial run and smooth things out for the real go. Except life didn't work that way at all.

"Good job," Chrissy said as they exited the stage. "Hey, you free for lunch?"

"I, um, maybe?"

"You want to see what your hunky guy has to say, huh?"

She straightened. "He's not my hunky guy."

"Coulda fooled me, the two of you chatting with your parents earlier."

Yeah, hardly chatting.

"You let me know how that goes, okay?" Chrissy said with a wink.

"Um, sure."

Chrissy grinned, her wavy hair bouncing as she moved to join a bunch of friends. Leaving Allie standing alone, conscious of a pang of envy at the ease with which they talked, the friendly manner of their interactions, all smiles and laughter. If only Allie knew what that was like. She glanced around the room, loneliness crowding in. Maybe she should leave. Where was—

"Loved your singing this morning," a woman with a grey bob said, patting Allie on the arm.

"Th-thank you."

"Well done," another stranger said.

Gloria Abraham caught her gaze from across the room and gave a thumbs-up. Allie smiled. This was nice, but where—

"Finally."

She spun.

Jai smiled. "Hi again."

"I th-thought you were leaving."

"Yeah. I did. Then I came back."

"Why?"

You would think that after several years working at one of Chicago's premier arts establishments, she might have a better filtering system in place. But no. Her words—when they worked—seemed to tumble from her brain and ricochet out of her mouth with nary a thought to direct them.

"Well." He shoved a hand through his hair. "I could explain, but it might take a while, and after this morning, I'm afraid any conversation I have will get hijacked by someone else."

She nodded. Her lifetime of church attendance seemed to suggest that would indeed be the case. It was like people thought the only time they could catch up was after the service, like phones or paying visits weren't true options for congregation members. If this service was anything like her usual earlier one, there'd be plenty of people guaranteed to interrupt any chance of privacy. Not—she could feel her cheeks heating—that she had any right to expect Jai might wish to speak to her alone. Maybe she should just leave now and save herself the embarrassment of realizing he was just a nice guy with a slightly flirtatious manner. She shuffled a half step away.

"Are you going?"

"Um…" Oh, how eloquent *was* she?

"I was hoping I could talk to you," he said softly.

He was? She grasped the back of a nearby chair, needing to hold something to stay upright.

"But maybe we might need to talk somewhere else."

"M-maybe."

He angled slightly closer. "How *maybe* is that maybe? Like, do you really want to go somewhere with me and talk more, like over a meal or at least a cup of coffee—or anything else you like if you don't drink coffee or because it's pretty warm outside? Or *maybe* as in you don't really care and are just blowing me off because that's kinder than saying, 'Hey, Jai, go away and stop pestering me'?"

She laughed, her amusement rippling deeper.

"And now she's laughing at me," he complained. "I guess that's a no then."

"No!" she said with another spurt of amusement. "It was the first one."

"*Was* the first one, or still is the first one?" He hooked an eyebrow.

"St-still is," she murmured, her skin prickling in self-consciousness as Pastor Jo drew near.

"Great," Jai said. "What do you want to eat?" He stilled, stiffening as their pastor paused.

"Hey, don't let me stop you," the pastor said, his eyes twinkling. "Just pretend I'm not here."

As if. Allie fixed her smile back into neutral, her gaze sliding from Josiah to Jai, then back again.

Jai cleared his throat. "So, um, great sermon."

"Glad you thought so," Josiah said before turning to Allie. "I was coming over here to say well done to this young lady here. Really anointed. I appreciated you putting yourself out there, Allison."

"Th-thanks."

"I guessed that was what you were both doing, chatting about the anointing."

"Uh huh," Jai said, shoving his hands in his back pockets.

"Well, don't let me interrupt. Actually, may I give you a piece of advice?"

"Sure," Jai said easily as Allie nodded.

"Maybe you'd be better off discussing the anointing or whatever it is over lunch someplace nice." He slid a look at Allie, winked. "Maybe someplace with a nice view and nice tablecloths and nice menus and—"

"Thanks," Jai said, his lips twitching as if trying to keep a straight face. "I'll be sure to keep that in mind."

"I'm glad to hear it." Josiah glanced at Allie again. "Hey, are you a ribs or seafood kind of girl?"

"I'm the kind of girl who, if I see food, I'll eat it, ribs or not," she quipped, suddenly finding herself blessed with one of those indiscriminate moments of ease like with her own family.

Jai laughed, and she knew a heart ping of victory. Maybe

there could be something to this, seeing he seemed to like her sense of humor.

"You'd better watch this one." Josiah smiled at Jai before patting Allie's shoulder and moving to talk to some elderly congregation members.

"I already do," Jai murmured as if unaware she was standing right there, an impression he only reinforced when he turned and faced her, his eyes widening, cheeks growing red.

The joy of knowing he paid attention to her tumbled her heart but was chased by a desire to ease his embarrassment. What could she say to smooth things over?

"Do you mean to sound like a st-stalker?"

Yeah. That wasn't the way.

"What?" His eyes rounded. "I'm not a stalker. Seriously. I just wanted to talk to you, and all those people this morning made it so hard, and I really don't want you to feel uncomfortable. So if I am, then tell me and I won't bother you anymore—"

Somehow her hand reached out of its own volition and touched his arm. She felt his muscles ripple and contract under her touch. Felt her heart ripple and contract a millisecond later.

He exhaled, and she dropped her hand quick smart, her fingertips still tingling, every nerve-ending pulsing with energy. Whew. Had he felt that heated electricity too?

"Allie."

"Jai." Was this seriously happening? She'd just touched the fastest left wing in Chicago's history. And he was looking at her, talking with her, in a manner others might call flirting.

No. *Don't be silly.* She was misreading things. She stepped back. She should leave. She should leave *now*—

"Allie." He placed a hand on her arm, and again she felt that frisson of intense energy between them, which seemed to quiver all the way up into her chest and lungs. "What do you say?"

What should she say to what? Oh, right. She'd just accused

him of being a stalker. Yeah, that wasn't the way to make him hang around. "Um, it's okay."

"Really?" He drew nearer, his smile holding its own kind of heated energy, sparking life into her pores and draining volume from her voice.

She could only nod.

"So, if I was to ask if you'd like to go out for lunch, you might say yes?"

Her lips tweaked. "I might."

"I might need something a little more definitive than that."

She drew in a breath. Caught a tang of something woodsily enticing. "Yes."

"Yes, you'll have lunch with me?" he clarified, his eyes holding hers.

"Yes, I'll have lunch with you," she murmured.

His grin created its own forcefield, absorbing her attention. "Awesome. Want to go now? I know this great place…"

She nodded, only half listening to his words as her heart danced and thrilled and sang. Jai Mullins, heart-throb of her life, was actually about to take her on a date!

HE WAS SO rusty at this. Small talk. Compliments. Likes and dislikes. The usual stuff that constituted first dates. But somehow, Allie made it easy with her—surprising—tease and laughter. The shyness Jai had witnessed earlier seemed to have melted away. Her slight stammer he'd put down to nerves, which he fully understood, given his own nerves zapped his mouth into overdrive and a tendency to overshare. But now the strain had notched back to ease as they ate and talked and got to know each other. She was fascinating, this classy artistic lady who knew a few things about hockey.

He leaned back in his chair, watching as she daintily ate the last bites of her cheeseburger. Okay, so Mario's wasn't exactly fancy tablecloths and fine dining, but the food was tasty and delicious, and the atmosphere—with its painted walls of Italian scenes—made for some fun conversations.

"So you've been to Italy but not Germany," he said as she sipped her drink.

"And you've been to Switzerland but not Russia," she countered, placing her glass of iced tea on the table.

"I've played with a few Russians in my time, but I still can't get over the fact that you've been there."

"Plenty of great art in Russia," she said.

"Okay, so I want to know more. You said in your talk that Seurat is one of your favorite artists. Who else do you like?"

Her lips curved. "You remembered?"

"Well, of course I remembered," he said. *You fascinate me,* he could've added, but didn't.

Allie tilted her head, her gaze meeting his then dancing away, as if such an acknowledgment was too much to take in.

"So, favorite artists. Go."

She laughed. "Come on. That would be like me asking you for your favorite hockey players."

"Easy." He counted off his fingers. "Gretzky, Orr, Messier, Lemieux, and Howe."

"Okay then." She counted off her fingers. "Seurat, Pissarro, Monet, Manet, and Renoir."

"Impressive."

"Do you mean Impressionists?" Allie teased.

"I mean it's impressive that you didn't bat an eyelid when I mentioned those hockey greats."

"That's me. Impressive." She rolled her eyes. Before he could ask about the self-deprecation, she continued. "So, tell me why you picked those players."

"They're all super skilled, put up big minutes, huge goal

scorers, were legends in their seasons. They all have different qualities I'd like to emulate in my game."

She nodded.

"How about you? Why'd you pick those artists?"

"I like the Impressionist period. I always have. And these artists were highly skilled in their own ways."

"Why do you like Impressionism?"

That animation he'd seen before sparkled to life again. "I love how things can be suggested or implied—that it's not trying to be a photograph but allows the viewer to infer more than just what can be seen with the eyes. That's the impression the viewer gets, which allows them to make their own interpretation of what they're seeing. I like that. And…"

At her pause, he pressed. "And what?"

"And that's all."

"That's not all. Go on. Tell me."

Her gaze turned shy. "And it's the kind of art I enjoy creating, too."

"You're an artist as well? Wow."

She shrugged. "It's just something I do."

"Don't apologize. I want to know more. When, how, why? Tell me everything."

"You'll be here for hours."

"So we'll have dinner as well. I'm not doing anything else. Are you?"

Her cheeks turned pink. "No."

"So tell me. How did you get started in art?"

"My grandmother was an artist. I never realized how good her work was until I was in after school art class and discovered the skill involved in using oils. Then I wanted to try and do the same, and I realized how much I loved it. Art let me be creative, and I-let me express myself without worrying what others thought of me."

"You shouldn't have to worry."

She shot him a look of disbelief.

"What are you worried about? You're smart, you're pretty, you're talented."

"And I st-stutter."

"I hadn't really noticed."

"Come on."

"No, really. I hadn't. You sound so polished to me. When I heard you talk at the Institute, you sounded so smooth it was a bit intimidating, to be honest."

"Liar."

"Excuse me? I don't lie. I hate liars." Like his dad, like Kat's loser husband. "So when I say I really like your voice, I mean it. It's like you're a newsreader or something."

"Or l-like I'm on Valium."

He laughed, then was relieved when she cracked a smile. Allie sure had the funniest things to say sometimes. Funny as in ha-ha. He was glad to see she could laugh at herself too. His mom couldn't. Neither could Kat.

The uncertainty in Allie's face drew his hand to meet hers on top of the table. "Truth is, we all stumble over our words at times. You've heard me, trying to impress you and tripping over my words."

"You wanted to impress me?" she whispered.

See? Tendency to overshare. But, "Yeah. Look, I'd rather people be honest about who they are, and I think you hear more honesty in slight stumbles than in polished eloquence. In fact, I'll let you in on a little secret. I don't really trust people who don't stumble over their words. If someone is too smooth, too glib, I think they've just rehearsed what they're going to say, that it's a little fake."

"You don't have to say that to make me feel b-better."

"I'm not. It's like prayers. Call me judgey, but I think there can be a world of difference between someone who has all the right phrases and Christianese terminology and those whose hearts keep their prayers real and raw. I think that's what Jesus was about too."

She looked thoughtful at this.

"All of this to say, I don't mind if you occasionally trip over your words. I'd rather realness than polished perfection with someone fake."

Allie bit her lip, the uncertainty in her eyes rushing more words to his mouth. "I mean, I like that I can be myself with you, and I hope you feel the same way too."

She nodded again, but still her eyes held a hint of hesitation. Did she doubt him?

He did his best to dispel her worries, insisting she eat dessert. She refused but compromised on a coffee. While they were drinking, a couple of guys who looked to be in their late teens moved up to their table.

"Excuse me, are you Jai Mullins?"

"Hey." The price of his contract. He shot Allie an apologetic look.

"Sorry to interrupt, but we wondered if we could get our pictures taken with you."

"Uh, sure."

They insisted on a selfie but then turned to Allie and asked if she would mind taking a picture. She nodded—that seemed to be her go-to—and clicked the phone camera a few times, showing it to the guys, who pronounced themselves happy.

"Sorry about that," Jai said once the guys had left.

She shrugged. "I bet you get that all the time."

"Sometimes. I don't mind it when they want pictures or signed posters. But some fans are scary, acting like they know you, sending the team personal stuff that's a little *too* personal, if you know what I mean." *Jai, shut up.* "I've even heard of fans tattooing certain players' faces on themselves."

Her eyes rounded. "Really?"

"Crazy, huh?"

Another nod, paler cheeks. "Crazy." She glanced at her watch.

Oh. Did she want to leave? "You want to get out of here?"

"I p-probably should go."

His heart sank. So she hadn't enjoyed today as much as he had. Maybe it was the talk of the crazy fans. Jai paid, and they went outside to where he'd parked his car, right behind her yellow Subaru. Surely this wasn't the end of what had been his best date in years?

"Hey, it's Speed Machine JM seventeen!"

A group of girls—women in their early twenties—waved and blew kisses, casting Allie wide-eyed looks. One even snapped a photo. Jai glanced behind. Allie was fiddling with her car's door handle.

"Allie," he said. Her dark eyes met his. "Please don't let the crazy fans scare you away."

He noticed the ripple at her white throat as she swallowed. "Y-you think they're crazy?"

"Well, yeah. They don't really know me." *Not like I want you to know me*, he longed to say, although he sensed the moment was too soon.

"I need to go," she said, her gaze dropping.

Disappointment creased his chest. "Well, before you do, could I get your number?"

She stilled. "What for?"

He smiled. "So I can call you sometime. So we could maybe do this again. Except without the crazy fans."

It was only a fraction of movement, but she seemed to withdraw.

"What is it?"

She shook her head.

"Allie?" Another head shake. "Look, why don't I give you my number, and you can decide if you want to call me. Or send me a text. Or anything really." Man, how desperate did he sound now? He rattled off his number, but she made no effort to type it into her phone.

Whoa. Maybe this really wasn't gonna happen.

Frustration surged. "Hey, you got a pen?"

She blinked. "Um, yes. I think so." After a moment's scrabbling through her handbag—honestly, women were kind of awesome the way they managed to hold a world of useful stuff in bags—she handed him a pen.

He whipped out one of his old promo cards the organization gave the players, then scribbled his phone number on the back. "That's my number. If ever you want to call me or go out again, then please do. I've had a lot of fun, even if being interrupted by fans wasn't quite what I bargained for." He wouldn't push her for her number. After her stalker comment before, he didn't want to come across as that desperate or creepy.

She studied the card, lips pressing flat and tight.

"Or not, as the case may be," he felt compelled to add, half tempted to whip the card away again. Wow. Way to make a guy feel wanted.

"Th-thank you," she whispered, her gaze touching his again.

Oh. At the softness in her brown eyes, his heart settled back into a kind of normal. Maybe she had enjoyed herself after all. "I promise the next time won't be surrounded by the stalker fans."

Her gaze whipped away, and he was left wondering what he'd said now. And as she thanked him for lunch and hastily started her car—it sounded like it needed a service, judging from the dirty growl—he wondered what he could do to make her realize that he really meant what he'd said. That he wanted to pursue this, that he wanted to see if they could be friends, maybe turn these sparks between them—surely she'd felt that too in that moment when they'd touched—into something real. Something that would last, something that would be true. He didn't want polished perfection, even though Allie seemed plenty perfect to him. He just wanted to be able to be truly honest and have that person trust him enough to be completely honest and real too.

~

HAWKS & SQUAWKS ONLINE CHAT

TubularBells: Did you guys see this? JM17 on a date!
PucktheMagicDragon: OMG!
CoolplayismyJam: I didn't think he dated.
PucktheMagicDragon: The picture is blurry.
CoolplayismyJam: When did he last date?
Destinysoffspring: She's not that great looking.
TubularBells: Coolplay six months ago?
PipeDreams27: Coolplay a year ago?
Destinysoffspring: She looks pretty average, def. not hockey hubby worthy.
PucktheMagicDragon: Don't be mean! She looks sweet, but it's hard to see bc the picture is blurry. Hey, does anyone have a different picture?
TubularBells: Calm the farm, Destiny. No one is talking wedding bells.
CoolplayismyJam: When was this taken? And where?
TubularBells: Today. The other forum said it was Mario's.
PipeDreams27: Down near the Pier?
TubularBells: Think so.
Destinysoffspring: He's so hot.
CoolplayismyJam: I love his hair!
Destinysoffspring: I hope they break up.
PucktheMagicDragon: OMG Destiny. That's so mean!
PipeDreams27: Who *is* she?
ArtHeart101: OMG.

CHAPTER 6

She could never tell him the truth. Allie studied the posters staring down at her from the ceiling, at those black-lashed hazel eyes that had, mere hours ago, been smiling into hers. How could she tell him the truth?

Hi, Jai. I started an online forum for your fans where we post about how great you are. Sure, it isn't as smutty as some of the internet groups out there, but I just thought you'd like to know that those crazy stalker fans you're so worried about? Yeah, well, I'm the president of your own personal crazy fan club.

She exhaled heavily. Granted, she didn't have a tattoo of his face on her forearm, but pretty much everything else. Jai Mullins posters? Check. Mullins 17 jersey? Check. Jai Mullins bobble-head? Yep, she was that sad. How could she admit all that to him and spoil this most wondrous of beginnings, this dream-come-almost-true?

And now, to add to the collection of JM17 memorabilia, she had a card *with his phone number* burning in her pocket.

Maybe that was enough reason to tip this feeling of unreality into a more solid "Jai Mullins likes you." Which didn't make sense. Which freaked her out a little. Because while today had been so impossibly good, and Jai had been *so* nice, so interested in her, like he could see past the stutter and truly see her, it had also reinforced just how ordinary and non-special she was. She'd seen the way those girls had looked at Jai, then looked at her, then looked back at him, their eyebrows inching up.

Yep, she kinda felt the same way—total disbelief that someone like him would even deign to look at someone like her. Impossible, right?

Her fingers pressed into her forehead, willing the headache to stay away. Should she tell him about the online group? What should she say?

Thoughts whirled and spun, tossing and tipping her heart like a yacht lost at sea. This was too much. She needed to calm down. She needed—

Her gaze found her artwork, sitting forlorn on the easel in her bedroom's corner, the half-finished trees begging for her to come play again. She hadn't touched her painting since that first encounter with Jai. Thoughts of *him* always intruded, stealing her motivation as her imagination spun rainbow dreams of impossibilities and fairytales that always ended in happily-ever-afters that were simply too good to come true.

She wasn't that girl. She wasn't right for him. And that poor picture was going to have to go another day without any further paint, because she had no energy to do anything more on it today. Maybe food—although she was still full from that delicious meal at lunchtime—might help shake this funk.

She carefully tiptoed downstairs from her bedroom to avoid disturbing her parents watching TV in the living room—she'd yet to face them with the truth about how she knew Jai, and had no idea how to explain that either—and grabbed an apple from the fruit bowl in the kitchen, as silent as a thief in the night.

"Allie!"

She jumped. Turned. Sighed as her heart raced a million miles an hour. "Dad. I didn't see you there."

"Yeah, I kind of got that impression. We didn't realize you'd come home."

"I'm back." She bit into the apple. Maybe she could avoid answering the inevitable questions if she ate this now.

"How was lunch?"

"Good," she mumbled over a mouthful of apple.

"Where'd you go?"

She shrugged, pointing to her apple, hoping her expression offered innocent apology and not avoidance.

"Who'd you go out with?"

Heaven help her. How could she admit the truth about her lunch companion to one of the Hawks' biggest fans? Dad might have a heart attack, and after the angina scares of the past two years, she couldn't risk that. She swallowed. "What makes you think I didn't go out by myself?"

"Because I know you, sweet pea. Lunch by yourself isn't something you do."

Fair enough. Quick, change the subject. "How was lunch here?"

"The usual. Busy. Good. Fun."

"Allie!" Mom swooped in with a pat on the arm on her way to the fridge and iced tea. "How was lunch?"

See? This was why living at home was problematic. She loved her parents, and she knew they loved her, but this intrusion into her personal life was a little hard to manage sometimes. Sometimes she wondered what it would be like to live in a place far, far from home. Like London. Or at least L.A.

"It was good." She quickly bit her apple again.

"Who'd you go with?"

Unfortunately, she'd swallowed, so she couldn't avoid the question. "Just someone from church."

"Uh huh." Dad grinned. "Someone like Jai Mullins?"

Allie choked.

"Jai Mullins?" Mom said, her voice pitching up. "Why would

Allie go out with Jai Mullins? They don't even know each other. Now, Peter, don't tease our poor girl like that." She wrapped an arm around Allie's shoulders in one of her sympathy hugs that always felt a little condescending. As if her mother, who hadn't even remembered Allie telling her this morning that she'd be singing at both services today, could be counted on to know exactly what Allie did or thought. She who seemed content to package Allie up as the shy daughter who stuttered and must be destined for failure because she'd never learned to overcome her inability to talk smoothly.

Dad nodded. "I know it must have been hard to talk to a famous guy like that. I don't blame you for running away."

"I didn't run," she muttered.

"Oh, you ran," Dad contradicted, his smile holding its own version of patronizing pity. "Hey, you never mentioned how you know him."

"Know who?" Mom enquired.

"Know Jai Mullins," Dad said.

"I don't—"

"You *know* him?" Mom said over the top of Allie's protest.

"No." Except that wasn't really true anymore. Today at lunch she'd discovered that all she thought she knew about the man—that he was kind, that he was patient, that he had a nice sense of humor—all the stuff she'd speculated over on her fan forum was actually true, and then some. His own nerves and obvious awkwardness had somehow soothed hers, leading her to want him to feel at ease, until she'd felt something she'd never felt with a guy before and had certainly never expected to feel with him: relaxed. Like he was a family member who just knew her, with whom she could just be.

Mom stared at her hard, forcing Allie to take another bite of apple, then glanced at her husband. "Why did you say Allie and Jai know each other?"

His brow wore a faint crease. "I thought he said you did."

"Why would he say that?"

Sensing this could go on for some time, Allie swallowed and said, "He brought his nephew to the museum the other day. We met then."

"And now he's here at church? What are the chances?"

What *were* the chances? That was the million-dollar question. As for the chances of anything more, well, that was slim to zero, she was sure.

"Well, that must have been such a thrill. It's no wonder you couldn't find your words," Mom said with another of those pats on the upper arm that spoke of tolerant sympathy. "He seemed quite sweet. It was a shame he couldn't come for lunch. I wonder what he was doing at church?"

What would they say if she told them his phone number was burning in her pocket, had burnt itself into her brain? Not that she could ever call him. Not with all his talk about crazy fans. Not when she was the most hard-core crazy fan of them all.

The front door banged, which likely meant Carissa had finally come home. Sure enough, two seconds later, her younger sister had joined the kitchen pow-wow, flicking her long wheat-colored hair behind her ear as she glanced between them all. "What are you talking about?"

Please, God. Just for once, please don't let Mom and Dad say any—

"Oh, Allie here has met someone!"

Allie sighed, bracing herself. Here goes…

"Really? Who? Oh my gosh! I thought this day would never come. Oh, I'm so pleased." Carissa engulfed Allie in a hug that smelled of Ralph Lauren's Romance. "Who is it?"

"No one," she muttered.

"No one?" Mom exclaimed. "You call Jai Mullins no one?"

"Jai Mullins?" Carissa's eyes enlarged to the size of the delicate saucers Mom displayed in the china cabinet. "Oh my gosh! I saw some handsome new guy at church, but Jake was chatting and I didn't want to leave him, and oh my goodness, Allie! Is that who you were talking to? Jai Mullins? The Hawks' left winger? Number seventeen? Really?"

Allie nodded.

Carissa fanned herself. "I can't believe it!"

"Neither can we," Mom inserted.

Thanks, Mom.

"Where'd you meet him?" Carissa asked.

Dad rushed to fill his youngest daughter in with the little he knew, adding proudly, "I've always said Jai is the best of the Hawks."

Allie's lips twitched. He'd only started saying that when he first learned Jai was a Christian three years ago.

"Wow, Allie." Was that—heaven forbid—*respect* in Carissa's eyes? "Why didn't you ever say anything?"

Allie shrugged. "There wasn't anything to say. There still isn't," she added firmly, quashing the speculation she could see filling her parents' eyes.

"Wow. I can't believe this," Carissa continued. "You've only had a crush on him for ages. Is he nice? What did you say? More importantly, what did *he* say? Oh my gosh! It's like God is finally answering your prayers!"

Allie's amusement at how Carissa's enthusiastic rush of verbiage resembled Jai's own died at that last comment. Just because they'd met—which was, technically, an answer to many prayers over many years—didn't mean God would permit anything more. And just because she possessed Jai's phone number didn't mean she would do anything about it. How could she? Not when they were too different. Not when he hated crazy stalker fans. Not when she'd never—as her family so clearly believed—ever be the right match for him.

~

SUNDAY AFTERNOON STRETCHED into evening with no call.

Monday, too, possessed a weird kind of expectant heaviness as Jai's hopes for Allie to call or at least text him battled with the feeling that he'd come on too strong and said something—he couldn't figure out what—that had scared Allie off. Of course, the fact that he was so out of practice in talking to girls and figuring out expectations made him second-guess everything. He at least figured that she probably wouldn't want him to just show up at her work like he was the stalker she'd teased him about being. Or maybe he should. Should he?

By the time Monday evening rolled around, he was relieved to have the normality of visiting Pastor Josiah's house for the online Bible study with the hockey guys. He usually arrived an hour or so early so he could have dinner with Josiah and Gloria —Gloria's cooking beat Jai's bachelor efforts by a long shot. Tonight was her famous quesadillas, perfect for a hot day like today, and conversation centered around the weather and other innocuous subjects.

"I wonder if Brent will join us today," Josiah mused. "He seems so much more happy and relaxed now. I think he's enjoying married life."

"As he should," Gloria said with a smile. "It must've been hard when he and Holly lived so far apart for so long."

She shot Jai a look, which seemed a prompt for him to nod and murmur agreement. But yeah, Brent living in Detroit while Holly lived in Australia must've been a challenge. Sure was different to seeing each other in church. He blinked.

"You okay there, son?" Josiah asked.

"Yeah," Jai managed, although his words caught on a choke. What was he even thinking, daring to allow thoughts like that? He really needed to get his brain into gear.

"I think Holly is supposed to move back to Calgary soon," Jai offered. "Last I heard she had another short track event." Something in Utah or some hot place where it seemed strange to have ice skating competitions in summer.

"Hmm. Well, maybe we won't see Brent tonight then. He's had a busy year."

Jai nodded. Brent was one of the top forwards in the NHL, playing at a caliber Jai could only dream of. And to know Brent now had a wife, a gold medal, and a Cup? Envy reared. He pushed it down. Maybe it would be good if Brent didn't show tonight. Jai needed to get these stupid emotions checked.

The hour for the online Bible study arrived, and sure enough, Brent was a no-show, Mike Vaughan explaining that his wife, Bree, who also happened to be Brent's twin sister, had gone with Brent to cheer her best friend on at the Desert Classic in Salt Lake City.

"Brent sent his apologies when he called in the other day. I'm on dad duty." Mike grinned, then ducked out of screen and picked up a small chubby child.

"Aww, cute," Beau said, his Southern drawl thick as ever despite playing in Arizona these past two years. "I meant the daddy love, although little Caleb is cute too," he teased.

Dan Walton, who played for another of the Original Six teams in Toronto, offered a smile but said little, as was his way. Man of mystery, was Defenseman Dan.

"Um, I think Caleb needs his face wiped," Jai offered. "Just offering some uncle advice here."

"What?" Mike groaned. "You threw up again? Dude, you're killing me here. 'Kay, I'll be back in a moment."

"How's life in Chi-town?" Dan asked.

"Hot. How are things in Toronto?"

"Hot. But I'm still up here in Muskoka, so it's pretty good."

"How'd your camp go?" Beau asked.

"Yeah, it was good. Great to see some new faces, although it's getting so popular now I'm wondering whether I'll have to add another one. Or at least get some other leaders."

Dan ran a camp that gave city kids the chance to hear about Jesus while experiencing some real wilderness adventure two hours north of Toronto in a super scenic part of Canada called Muskoka.

"I'm happy to help out next year if you need me," Beau offered.

Jai felt obliged to offer too, though truth be told, he didn't like camping. Not that he'd ever admit that here. Kids needing to hear about God's love for them was way more important than the number of mosquito bites he'd score each day.

"Thanks, guys. Appreciate it."

"I saw the TV special on YouTube," Chris Thomas, a player from Vancouver who'd recently joined the group, offered. "Your place there looks awesome."

Dan shrugged, a smile playing around his mouth. "Yeah, it's pretty nice."

Pretty nice was an understatement. Jai had seen the TV special too, a glimpse into the vacation homes of some of the NHL players who seemed to be earning pay packets twice the size of his. But hey, he couldn't complain. Not with his apartment with its million-dollar view over Lake Michigan. And especially not when he considered the type of house in which he'd grown up. It had been a golden day when he could finally afford to move his mom to a brand new house in a nice suburb, to know she'd never need to worry about mortgage repayments or drug-based shootings again. He might get some things wrong, but that was something God had blessed him with the means to get right.

Mike returned, and the study continued. Tonight was like God had Jai's number—all about envy and comparison. Josiah read from the Bible about the need to take every thought captive, to focus on his own lane, to not worry about the way other people were running their races for God, or what prizes they might collect along the way.

"Envy is yet another of those things Satan likes to attack people with," Josiah shared. "Envy is born from comparison, which basically stems from the question: Does God love me as much as He loves the next guy? And if we're asking that question, then what does that really say about our understanding of God's love?"

Ouch.

"God loves you," Josiah continued. "Not based upon how good you are or how much money you make or the good works you do. He loves *you*. And when the enemy tries to tell us otherwise, we need to combat those lies with the truth of God's word and take every thought captive, wrestling it down, nailing it to the cross."

Jai joined the murmurs of agreement from the other guys. How he needed this reminder.

Chris nodded. "I'm so glad we're doing this tonight. I've gotta admit, as much as I love my kids and my wife, sometimes I look at you single guys and wonder what that would be like."

Jai internally winced, hoping Chris's wife hadn't heard that admission from her husband. But still, this online Bible study was a place for honesty and openness, a place where they could be real and talk about what really mattered. So if that was what Chris felt, then fair enough.

The conversation veered as Mike shared the latest news from his work with Mission Possible for Future Generations, the charity he was a spokesman for that worked to educate kids from the slums in the Philippines. Jai himself had two kids' faces on his fridge that he prayed for and supported. He suspected most of the guys here did.

"And we'll have another fundraising calendar this year," Mike said. "I'll put a post up soon so you can tell your friends. Oh, and speaking of, you might've heard about Tyler Woletsky getting traded to L.A.? I was talking with him the other day and sensed TJ could do with any spare prayers you've got."

Mike's grace toward someone who owned an enforcer tag that had seen Mike concussed with broken ribs a few years ago was nothing short of miraculous. Still, Jai joined the chorus of agreement. From Jai's own run-ins with the hotheaded Woletsky, he figured that TJ could use all the prayers going.

Other prayer points were shared, then prayers were prayed, then more tease and banter and their time was done.

Jai lifted a hand in farewell as Josiah flicked off the screen. "Thanks, Jo. That was a good one. I think I needed it."

"Sounds like you weren't the only one. Funny how God can set these things up for when we need it most."

Jai nodded.

"So, envy, huh?"

"Not anymore," Jai joked.

"If only it was that easy, right?"

Right.

"So, what's Jai got to be envious about? You want a little Caleb in your life?"

"Not any time soon," Jai said, thinking of his nephew.

"Well, yeah, you need the wife first." Josiah's gaze sharpened. "That it? You want to settle down?"

Settle down? Jai hardly lived the high life cruising the party scene.

"How did things go with Allie the other day?"

His heart kicked. His lips clamped together, clamping harder still as Gloria appeared in the doorway.

"Did I hear Allie's name mentioned?" she said, her dark gaze shifting between them.

"Gloria, it's not nice to listen in," her husband admonished.

"This has nothing to do with niceness and everything to do with caring about two of my favorite people in the world. And I can't help but be curious about how things went, especially when I couldn't help but see the two of you leaving church together the other day."

"What?" Josiah said, eyes wide as he turned to Jai. "The two of you—?"

"There is no two of us," Jai was forced to admit. "I did take her for lunch—"

"Ooh, where'd you go?" Gloria asked, coming to sit on the armrest of Josiah's sofa.

"Mario's," Jai admitted, to her nod of satisfaction.

"I told you to take her somewhere nice," Josiah complained.

Gloria nudged her husband. "I thought you were just saying that you didn't know they'd left church together."

"I didn't *know* they'd gone to lunch." Josiah pinned Jai with his gaze. "So, how was it?"

Great. How to explain… He shrugged. "I think the fans scared her away."

"What? What fans?"

Jai explained about the guys, the photos, the girls.

Josiah frowned. "I wouldn't have thought that would be enough to scare her off. Her family are the biggest Hawks fans I know and"—he tapped his chest—"that's saying something."

Maybe that was a red flag. He didn't want to get involved with people who might not be in it for the right reasons.

"She's a sweet girl," Gloria said, "but a little shy."

Jai nodded. Allie had owned as much the other day.

"Maybe she wouldn't cope too well with all the attention," Gloria added thoughtfully.

Jai swallowed. Was it unfair to place someone in the spotlight like that? Not that it was inevitable. Some people—like Brent—had managed to keep their relationship pretty much under wraps. None of the Bible study guys, apart from Mike, had even known Holly was on Brent's radar until November last year, when her injury at a World Cup event in Michigan had led a panicked Brent to request prayers on her behalf and they'd realized just how much he cared about her.

So, relationships could be conducted on the down low. But

was it fair? Holly was a champion skater who seemed plenty resilient. Bree, Mike's wife and Brent's twin sister, had grown up with hockey, so she knew the ins and outs of what the sport involved. But while artistic Allie might know something about his team, did she have any idea of the degree of speculation that the girlfriends of NHL players had to suffer?

"Allie is tougher than she looks," Josiah reassured.

Gloria nodded. "I guess you have to consider whether a relationship with her and all that could be is more important than wondering what others might think of you. And she needs to figure that out too."

A relationship? How crazy to be thinking this way at all, when for years he'd been happy flying solo. "We've only gone out once," Jai felt the need to protest.

"But was once enough?" Josiah prodded.

No. Not at all. For the first time, something other than hockey had grabbed his attention. But maybe Allie thought once was enough, given she hadn't called him yet. Was he being unfair, putting the pressure on her to make the next move? If she was shy and reluctant to put herself out there, then maybe he should just man up and go visit her again at work. For he couldn't shake this sense deep in his gut that pursuing her might be worth it after all.

CHAPTER 7

The question of whether to call Jai or not had to be put aside when Myra called Allie into her office on Monday morning to say she was going away on a work trip and that Allie was in charge for the week. Allie's surprise at the sudden work trip faded to the background as Myra added, "Oh, and Mr. Weinberger asked to see you."

Allie's chest grew tight. "What about?"

"How should I know?" Myra glanced at her watch. "But I shouldn't take too long if I were you. He's a busy man."

"He wants to see me now?"

"Didn't you read your email this morning?"

Well, no. She'd been busy trying to find a parking spot. "When do you leave?"

"As soon as I can get away. I've left instructions here on my desk. You might as well take them now." Myra thrust a bunch of papers at Allie, then straightened, her sharp-cut bob and asymmetrical black silk shirt swinging at the movement. Another glance at her watch, then back at Allie. "Well? What are you still doing standing here?"

"I hope you have a good time," Allie offered.

"I'm sure I will." Her lips curled in a smile she rarely wasted on Allie. "Now, go."

"Of c-course."

Allie hurried through the corridors until she found the executive offices and smiled at Meaghan Baldrick, the administration secretary who normally dealt with such appointments.

"I b-believe Mr. Weinberger wants to see me?" Allie said.

"What's your name again?" Meaghan asked.

"Allison D-davis." She clenched her fingers into clammy palms. What on earth did Mr. Weinberger want her for? Would she ever be able to talk like an adult and not a child?

"Ah. No, I'm afraid your appointment is for tomorrow. Wasn't that in your email?"

The email Allie still hadn't had a chance to check. "I'm s-sorry."

Heaven help her. At least when she slipped on her *s* sounds she merely sounded like a snake and not incompetent.

"See you tomorrow then."

Allie nodded, not wanting to waste any more words here.

Why had Myra told her the wrong day? Honestly, if Allie had half the suspicious mind Selina possessed, she'd be inclined to think Myra had wanted her away. But why?

She exhaled. No good ever came of diving into the political rabbit-holes of bureaucracy. That way anxiety lay. And she had enough on her plate with this unexpected promotion to the frontline of what Myra did, starting with informing the rest of the team—including Selina—just what delights Myra had saved for them while she was away.

"Mr. Weinberger will see you now," Meaghan said the next day.

Allie nodded, wiping her damp hands on her straight, knee-length black skirt, glad at least for the day's notice about this interview, or whatever it was, to ensure she looked as professional as possible. She'd barely been able to sleep last night, wondering what it was about. Which made two sleepless nights in a row, as she'd barely slept on Sunday night after torturing herself with the pros and cons of calling Jai. Or at least texting. Writing a message allowed plenty of time for do-overs. She just hoped she wouldn't need a do-over after the next few minutes.

She pushed open the door into a spacious office decorated in warm whites and camel tones. "Ah, Miss Davis. Please, come in." Mr. Weinberger gestured to the tub chair opposite his desk. "Take a seat."

Allie forced her lips to tilt upwards. Okay, if she was being invited to sit, it probably meant she wasn't going to get hauled across the coals. Not that she could think of any coal-hauling misdemeanor she'd done lately. Unless Myra had complained?

"You're probably wondering what this is about."

She nodded. Best to save her words for when they really mattered.

"Last week when the Donohues were visiting and caught the end of your presentation, they were most impressed."

Allie nodded, then thought she'd better show she wasn't a mute. "G-good."

He smiled. "There's no need to be nervous now. You might not know that they're on a dozen different boards, including the Vancouver Art Museum, and as we were talking, they made some suggestions about different ways cultural institutions such as ours can partner with other important businesses and groups within large cities. I was hoping you might be able to consider thinking of some ways our museum could partner with other institutions that might provide a win-win scenario."

For some reason, thoughts of Myra and her liaison with the Holborne Museum's programming director floated through her head. That wasn't a win for Neil Blanchard's wife.

She took a breath, forcing herself to speak slowly and

calmly. "F-forgive me, sir, but I would have thought this was something Myra—I mean Ms. Fordley—should be involved in."

"Yes, well." He glanced at the paper lining his desk. "Myra has other things on her plate, and as her second-in-command, well, it's only fair that you be given the opportunity to show what you can do."

"I'm sorry, sir, but I'm still at a loss as to what you want me to do."

"The bottom line is that we need more visitors in order to continue to attract the levels of funding and sponsorship necessary to offer what we do. Now, I know it's unorthodox, but I've been speaking to various employees in a variety of roles and responsibilities and seeking avenues to see how we can best move forward. Your name is consistently mentioned as one of the most engaging guides we have here, and so we want you to be more active in reaching a wider cross-section of our community. That is your role here, after all."

She nodded, surprise at his flattering comment clamping her throat. People thought she was engaging?

He explained some more about just what would be involved, then leaned back in his chair. "So, I hope that's clear?"

"Yes, sir." Sort of clear, anyway.

"You'll be reporting directly to me."

Another nod.

He smiled. "So, Miss Davis. Let's see what you can do."

It was one thing to want to see Allie and quite another to actually make it happen. Especially when clever him still didn't know her last name and the reception people out front weren't too keen on sharing personal information. Which was fair enough, Jai supposed. But when he was trying *really* hard to remember just what the proper name for the public relations thing she did was called—she'd mentioned it the other day—it didn't help that the museum people eyed him with raised eyebrows like they thought he was really dumb. But hey, those looks weren't anything new. Growing up in Chicago's 'burbs and wanting to play hockey, he'd grown used to certain types of people sharing that wrinkled-nose, bad-smell look as they questioned why a less-than-middle-class kid from a broken home might dare to play a sport some associated with thugs and fights instead of skill and speed.

Whatever. He straightened. "Allie's the one who gives awesome talks about Impressionists. And does great kids' talks too," he added in a rush.

"And you wish to speak to her, why?" A woman with hair a shade of red that certainly came out of a bottle eyed him over her narrow-rimmed glasses.

How to explain? "As she's part of the public relations team and I'm a member of the public, I wish to have relations with her."

Whoa. That so didn't sound right. And judging from the tilted head and sudden blinks, the woman definitely agreed.

"I mean—" *Shoot him now.* "Oh, forget it." Trying to explain himself to over-educated haughty women who wore disdain like others wore fur coats in winter was pointless.

"Sir," another voice intruded.

Jai swiveled to see a large woman with golden-brown skin and a wide smile. "If you wish to hear today's talk about Impressionism, it starts in two minutes."

Of course. What an idiot. "Thanks so much"—he peered at her nametag—"Celeste."

"Just go up those stairs there and hang a right."

"Yes, ma'am." He saluted and hurried away.

Okay, so just because Allie hadn't called or sent him a text didn't mean she didn't want to stay in touch. Maybe it was her shyness, or that natural ladylike elegance she conveyed. Maybe she'd read that book Kat had raved over years ago, something about rules on dating, when Kat had been all gung ho about her new independence after her loser of a husband finally kicked himself to the curb and right on out of their lives. Jai had snatched a look, wondering if the mysteriousness of a woman's mind might spill some secrets in the pages, but no. Either he was too dumb to live or just too dumb to love.

His steps slowed. Was that why Allie hadn't called? His mom might think him a catch, but did Allie just think him ignorant?

By now he'd reached the Impressionists room, and sure enough, there was a crowd, all patiently watching the museum employee give the spiel he was starting to recognize. But it wasn't Allie. It was a preppy-looking chick whose expression of boredom was a million miles away from the vivacity that had filled Allie's face the last time he'd stood here.

So where was she?

He turned, studying the huge painting that Allie had said was her favorite, wondering again at those little tricks the artist had used to draw the eye. Were all artists like that? Adding a little sneaky something that only some would notice and start to wonder over, and giving depth to something others might dismiss as mere paint dots?

He leaned closer, then drew back, conscious the burly guy in the corner was watching him askance. He sent the guy a wave and apologetic smile. Yeah, like anyone could snatch this picture and run off with it under their arm. It'd take a truck. Maybe a crane. The thing was huge.

But maybe...

The woman was now spouting her knowledge about Monet and his haystacks, so Jai took the moment to steal closer to the guard. "Hey there...Dave," he said, squinting at the guy's badge.

"Sir."

At least some people here showed him respect. He gestured

to the museum guide. "She's not the usual person who does these talks, is she?"

"No."

Fount of information. "I was hoping to hear Allie," he confessed. "Blonde, pretty, wears glasses."

"Allie Davis?"

Bingo. He hoped. He nodded anyway.

"Miss Davis is otherwise engaged," the guard said.

"Oh. Is she sick?"

"No."

What, did he have to play twenty questions? "Is she on kids' talk again?"

"No, sir."

"Man. I just wanted to talk to her."

The man pressed his lips together, a Sphinx-like expression crossing his face.

So this was yet another of his crazy-dumb ideas. Still, what had he expected? She was working, and any chance to talk would be eating into time she should probably be focused on what she got paid for. And any minute now she'd be going to get lunch...

An idea sparked. He retraced his steps to the giftshop near the entrance, and—phew. Bought the postcard, begged for a pen, and scrawled his note.

Let's see what the elusive Miss Allison Davis might say to that.

ALLIE PRESSED HER LIPS TOGETHER, her shoulders pounding with tension that had nowhere to go. Surely second-in-command didn't mean totaling two jobs in one? But the more time she spent in this role, the more she became convinced that was exactly what Myra had done—dumped all her work on Allie while expecting Allie to meet her usual role requirements as well. Coupled with the new expectations Mr. Weinberger had placed on her, was it any wonder she felt like she might collapse into a heap?

At least taking Myra's role meant she could pass off some of her responsibilities, such as some of the talks and tours—hard as it was to give up the Impressionists one. She had a funny feeling that Selina, whose interest lay in more modern and avant-garde pieces, would not bring the depth of feeling that Allie believed was essential to drawing the guests' interest. But juggling all this work was hard, and the policy Myra had left for her to report on was something she was sure had been pushed aside so Myra wouldn't have to deal with it herself.

Myra's absence had caused some comments the first day, her business trip not on any official correspondence so far as any of them could find out. Selina had been just as mystified, even wondering aloud if Myra was using *business trip* as code for something more illicit. Allie hadn't wanted to think along those lines, but now the seed had been planted, and she couldn't help but wonder if Neil Blanchard was taking an unexpected "business trip" too. In fact, she was more than halfway tempted to call the Holborne Museum just to speak to him and have her worst suspicions dismissed.

Stop it. She needed to get a grip. Or at least get some fresh air and get away from the mind-numbing statistics and reports drier than the Sahara. Anyway, it was way past her lunch break, so she was overdue for some carbs. Even if it came in the form of another salmon sandwich. Oh well. She wouldn't be seeing— let alone speaking to—Mr. Hot Hockey Player today anyway.

Ten minutes later she was walking under shady trees near to her favorite seat. She probably couldn't afford more than twenty minutes away from her desk. It was funny how Selina seemed to have lost all motivation for anything beyond the minimum, almost like she didn't want to work hard because Myra wasn't there to see.

Sorry, God. She drew in a cleansing breath, savoring the coolness on the air. Her feet slowed as she reached the wooden seat, where a postcard lay. A postcard of her favorite picture: *A Sunday Afternoon on the Island of La Grande Jatte.*

She glanced around. No one, except for the usual lunchtime joggers and picnicking couples and families with strollers. Who —? How—?

She picked it up, glanced at the back, then slumped into the seat.

Hey Allie.
I hope you find this and that you know you're still in my
thoughts, even if I'm not in yours. Maybe I am now!
Anyway, I ~~hope~~ *pray you're having a good day.*
J.

Her eyes pricked. Seriously? He was the only person who knew this was her favorite picture. It had to be him. Didn't it?

She glanced around, pinching the thin cardboard in a firm grip like it was a hundred-dollar bill. Was he nearby? Could he see her? The thought sent a delicious shiver up her spine. Okay, so maybe there was a slight sense of stalkerdom in that thought, but if she concentrated on the gesture, on his message, the fact that he seemed to want to be in her thoughts and that he *prayed* for her…

Oh. Breath hiccupped and she wiped away a tear. Was this what it felt like to be cared about?

Her sandwich lay forgotten next to the eco-bottle of water. Was he around here?

A shadow crossed her, and she glanced up. "Oh!"

"Hey, Allie."

"Hi, Celeste." Was it wrong to feel a sense of disappointment? "On your lunch break too?"

"Uh huh." Celeste glanced at the card that Allie hurriedly shoved in her lap as she hastened to move her water and food so the other woman could sit down. "What have you got there?"

A nervous laugh escaped. "N-nothing."

"Sure don't look like nothing to me. Hey." She clicked her fingers, and Allie reluctantly passed it over, hoping against hope the guard wouldn't turn it over. "That's your favorite picture, right?"

She nodded.

Celeste nodded, then handed it back without glancing at the other side.

"Must be your favorite if you have to take it outside with you."

"Mmm," Allie offered, the only answer she could give.

She took a bite of her sandwich, sure her break was now going to take a lot longer than she'd planned. But she couldn't leave right now, not when Celeste had just sat down.

"There was some man asking after you earlier."

A piece of salmon caught in Allie's throat, and she choked. "Who?"

"Didn't catch his name. But he was *fine*." She flapped a hand like she needed to cool down. "Of course..." She chuckled.

"Of course what?" Allie demanded.

"He seems to have the gift of the gab too, if you know what I mean." Allie didn't dare enquire. "You shoulda seen Francine's face when he said he wanted to have relations with you."

"What?"

Allie caught the echo of her shriek and slumped back in her seat, hoping against hope Jai wouldn't make a sudden appearance that would force her to face the man when she had nothing to say. "He said what?"

"Poor thing. He looked as embarrassed as you look now. No,

no. Don't get your panties in a twist. He just couldn't remember your job title and got a bit mixed up. Bless 'im."

Allie exhaled, mind ticking over all that had been said, emotions vacillating from shock to outrage to amusement at Celeste's "poor thing." How many times had the Hawks' fastest winger been called that?

"Anyway, just thought you'd like to know that."

"Thanks."

"Must be nice to have an admirer, huh?"

This sparkly feeling inside *was* nice. She'd never had an admirer before.

She soon had to make her excuses and return to work, which Celeste took as an invitation to accompany her until they parted in the main foyer. A twist of hallways later, and Allie was back at her desk, the afternoon's pile of files awaiting attention chasing her former lightness away.

"Whatcha got there?" Taylah asked, snapping her gum.

"Just a card."

"Oh, that's the painting you like, right?"

Allie nodded. She liked the painting even more now, thanks to the message on the back. She was in his thoughts? In his prayers? Oh my.

The next few hours ground by, and it was nearing five when the door opened and Billy walked in, holding a bunch of flowers not dissimilar to the one from last week.

Her heart skipped a beat. Then tripped over the next. Was that from—

"Flowers for you, Miss Davis."

Mouth drying, she accepted the perfectly sweet bouquet and inhaled the scent of gardenias and pink roses, her fingers trembling as she plucked the card from its envelope.

Hey Allie. I wasn't sure if you'd see my postcard on your seat in the park, but in case you didn't, I hope you'll call me soon. If you don't, then I know not to bother you again. But I hope you'll bother to bother me. Just in case you lost my number, here it is again. Hope these flowers make you smile. J.

His number—the one burned into her brain—lay at the bottom of the card.

"So you still don't have a boyfriend?" Selina asked, her expression hard to read.

What was Allie to say to that? *I don't. We're just friends. I think. But maybe he wants more. And I still don't know what to do about it, because I'm, like, his biggest fan, and he doesn't want to date fans.*

But while she didn't know what to call this most surprising development, she was sure of one thing: Jai deserved a thank you at the very least.

ai's phone buzzed, and he muted the TV and slowed his treadmill to a walk as he glanced at the screen. He pressed ACCEPT CALL. "Hey."

"Hey yourself." Beau's drawl, as Southern as fried chicken, met his ear.

Jai swigged water. "What's happening?"

"Training camp starts soon, so I'm doing what I can."

"Yeah. Same here."

There was a pause, then, "So, there's talk I'm moving to Montreal after all."

"What? Why didn't you mention this at Bible study?"

"I just got the call from my agent. There are rumors that they're looking to replace their goalie, and they don't like the backups, which is why they don't play them much even though Haslip hasn't been great these past few years. But seeing as his contract expires next season, well, who knows? It's only whispers, but it might finally be happening."

"You're excited, right?" Jai asked. "This is what you've wanted."

"Yeah, but it's funny how you can want something and it can

seem impossible, but then when you're on the verge of getting it, it feels a little overwhelming."

"Yeah." Jai remembered that feeling, back in his rookie year when the dollars being flung his way seemed impossibly high. He got paid to do this sport he loved? He got paid *this* much to do this job he loved? Unlike some guys who immediately bought expensive cars and status watches and clothes, Jai's life of frugality and care had meant he'd not squandered a penny, preferring to build his bank balance until he'd finally been able to buy his mom the type of house he wished they'd grown up in. The kind she actually deserved.

"There's nothing confirmed yet, but watch this space. These might be my last few months playing here in the desert."

"It's been better than you thought though, right?"

"Yeah. I miss my family, and I sure miss being able to swing by for Mama's cooking, but it's been nice to see a different part of the country."

Jai smiled as the Southerner's twang thickened. "And now you're looking at seeing a different country altogether."

"Canada's not like Cameroon, man. I think I'll be fine."

"You'll definitely be colder in Montreal."

"Yeah, but I heard they do this thing called heating there, so I think it'll be cool."

"Cool for sure."

Beau laughed.

"So why Montreal of all places?" Jai asked.

"I don't know. It's just always been my thing."

"What if you get there and you don't like it?"

"What's the point in having dreams if you can't be bothered chasing them?" Beau asked. "You only get one life. I want to make the most of mine."

"Well, I'll be praying. Let me know how you go, okay?"

"Will do. Nothing's guaranteed, but the way things are shaping up, I might need to invest in some warmer clothes next year. Hey, that reminds me. What's this I hear about you and alternate captaincy?"

Jai's heart kicked. "What have you heard? That's news to me."

"Oh. Forget I said anything."

"Dude, you can't say something like that and not expect me to bite. What have you heard? And where did you hear it?"

"Just some gossip around the traps. But Tesci's gone, and they'll be looking for another captain, won't they? And who better than you?"

"Yeah, they haven't thought like that before," Jai said dryly.

"You were younger then. And now you've got some more seasons under you, I think they'll be looking your direction."

"Dude."

Beau chuckled. "Now, don't go gettin' huffy like a granny without tea."

Now Jai laughed. "Where d'you find these expressions?"

"They just come naturally. It's a gift."

Jai released a snort of amusement. Yeah, like Jai had a gift for naturally embarrassing himself with bouts of verbal diarrhea. Would Allie ever contact him again, or was that bridge burnt and done?

"Look, you can call me prophetic and thank me for the heads-up later."

"Sure thing." Jai rolled his eyes. As if they'd ever tap him for captaincy.

"Okay, gotta go. Have a good one."

"You too."

The call ended, and Jai pumped the treadmill back to eight. The only way he'd maintain his fastest man on ice credibility was by ramping up the training. And while he knew he didn't have an awful lot going for him in some areas, he'd always taken a little bit of pride in this thing he could do—the thing that had first attracted interest from a friend's dad, who'd suggested Jai might want to try out for hockey. Jai's speed on ice at that kid's birthday party had won him even more respect when he admitted he'd rarely skated until that moment.

But maybe he could be more than just Speed Machine Mullins. Maybe one day others could see him as a leader and someone worthy of respect. And maybe a classy chick like Allie might feel the same.

His thoughts flicked to her, and he prayed for her again. Then prayed for Beau. Then Jai's sponsor children. Then his mom, Kat, and Kyle. Then Allie again.

Praying was better than stressing. He'd learned that long ago. And while he, like Beau, might want certain things, if he lived too much in dreamland about the future, Jai found it stole a lot of living from today. He'd rather shove it all at the feet of Someone who knew the future and could do something about it. That same Someone who offered peace. Who promised to work all things out for Jai's good.

He dialed the notch higher and ran harder until sweat slid down his back and his singlet clung to him. Good thing Allie wasn't around to see him now. He bet he stank too.

From the apartment window, he could see the evening shadows falling over the lake, the apartment tower's shadow darkening the park where he'd left the postcard on the bench seat. He sure hoped Allie had found it and not some stranger. He hoped she'd keep it and not toss it away. He hoped she liked the bouquet he'd organized Mom to arrange and deliver.

His phone buzzed with another message.

Unknown number.

THANK YOU FOR THE FLOWERS.

He grinned. Wait. Did that mean someone else got the—?

Another message notification.

AND THE POSTCARD.

All right. He fist-pumped himself, switched off the machine, and slid into his leather lounge, knowing any chance of multi-tasking was about to be severely hampered. GLAD YOU LIKE

THEM, he tapped back before quickly stowing the number in his contacts list under Allie Davis.

He waited, but when nothing more came, he tried again. HOPE YOUR DAY WENT WELL.

A half minute later: IT IMPROVED AS THE DAY WENT ON.

The smiley face she finished the message with matched the one on his dial. I'M GLAD.

He tapped out another one. ARE YOU FREE FOR DINNER SOMETIME?

Allie: SOMETIME IS PRETTY OPEN-ENDED.

Jai smiled. EXACTLY.

Allie: HA. ARE YOU SURE YOU'RE NOT A STALKER?

Jai: WOULD A STALKER ADMIT TO SUCH A THING?

Allie: A CHRISTIAN ONE MAY.

Jai laughed. YOU'RE FUNNY, he typed.

Allie: YOU'RE PERSISTENT.

Jai: YOU'RE SWEET.

Allie: YOU OBVIOUSLY DON'T KNOW ME WELL.

Jai: I OBVIOUSLY WANT TO CHANGE THAT.

Silence.

Jai tapped out another message. DINNER? TOMORROW? PLEASE?

He chewed his lip. Did that make him look desperate? He deleted the please and pressed send.

More silence, then...

OKAY.

IT WAS one thing to be scooped up in a wave of inevitability after church on Sunday and taken to lunch. It was quite another to receive a dinner invitation from Jai Mullins, left wing extraordinaire of Chicago's premier sports team and secret love of her life.

Allie exhaled, swiveling as she studied her reflection in the mirror, then wincing. So maybe eating all those muffins in her efforts to encourage Mom to keep on baking had been a bad idea. The muffin top today seemed very real. Unless she wriggled into the super uncomfy slimming shapewear that would guarantee she couldn't breathe. Or eat. Or enjoy herself much at all. She would at least look good. But was looking good more important than enjoying herself? Maybe she should just wear something other than this dress. Maybe Jai was more a jeans and plaid kind of guy, and when he'd said dinner, he was simply thinking of another Mario's-type experience, which she'd enjoyed, but which didn't exactly scream dinner date.

Not that she knew what to expect. She wasn't like Carissa—Little Miss Popularity, with a million boyfriends before she'd settled for bald Jake. Carissa, who'd only had to bat her eyelashes for a man to open a door or throw his coat over a muddy puddle so she could walk with unsoiled foot. Okay, so the latter wasn't exactly true, but still. Allie knew zip all about dating, while Carissa could write the encyclopedia.

Last night, when Jai's invitation had come, Allie's stunned expression had been enough for Carissa to demand to know what was going on. All Allie had said was that she'd been invited on a date, refusing to speak Jai's name, as she knew her sister would never be able to keep her mouth shut. And maybe because it still felt so unreal, like a shiny detergent bubble that was guaranteed to pop. Instead, she'd admitted that she'd met this guy at work—which was true—and, with an assertiveness that had stunned both of them, had declared that her private life was supposed to be private, thank you very much, which her sister, after threats of removing her from chief bridesmaid status, had eventually given in to with good-enough grace.

Carissa's advice: wear a nice dress. Nothing too fancy, but enough to show she'd made an effort. She'd then bulldozered her way into Allie's room and wardrobe, selecting a range of appropriate outfits (*range* meaning two, seeing as the rest of her wardrobe consisted of work attire or slack-off Saturday comfy clothes) and insisting on offering Allie some shoes, hair, and makeup advice.

"Not that you don't always look nice," she'd said, to Allie's internal eye roll, "but Mr. Whoever-he-is needs to know you're interested."

But now, Allie thought, eyeing her expertly applied makeup and professional-standard curls, she didn't actually look, let alone feel, like herself. What would Jai think? Should she care what Jai thought? She sighed.

"What is it?" Carissa asked, coming back into the room. "Don't you like it?"

"I do." Even Allie heard the doubt loading that last word.

"Too much?"

"I really appreciate the effort..."

"But you just don't feel like you?" Carissa guessed.

Allie nodded. And even though she really wanted to make a good impression, surely Jai should like her for who she was. Warts and all. Well, maybe not warts— thankfully, she was free of them—but stutter and all.

"Okay. So, do you like the hair?"

She nodded.

"Makeup?" Carissa studied her, brow pleated. "Maybe a different lipstick shade."

One that didn't make her feel like a wannabe 1950s movie starlet would be good. Something way more bland. Skin-toned. Neut—

"But definitely not neutral. We want him to know you're kissable."

Her heart tried to have a heart attack. Jai? Kissing her? She needed to lie down. Or at least sit down. She didn't know the first thing about how to kiss a guy.

"He *is* someone you'd want kissing you, right?"

Not on the first date. Just the thought was enough to make her hyperventilate. Imagining the act—even though she might have imagined it a million times in her dreams—was very different to the shiver-laden thought that it could one day be real.

Allie exhaled. How stupid to get so carried away. She needed to focus on what was real. "We're just going out for dinner," she mumbled.

"But dinner can lead to kissing and more," Carissa countered, waggling her diamond-clad ring finger in Allie's face.

"Not tonight."

"Hmm. Is he a Christian?"

Allie cut her a look.

"Okay! Wow. I've gotta say, I'm impressed you could find one of those working where you do."

Art museums were renowned for employing people who held more humanistic, hedonistic views on life.

"It's not Jai, is it?" Carissa asked slyly.

Allie jumped, smearing the lipstick Carissa had been applying.

"*Is* it?" Carissa demanded, her voice pitching high as her eyes widened.

"You c-can't honestly think he'd ask me for a d-date, can you?"

"You're stuttering again. It is!"

Allie shook her head.

"Come on, Allie," Carissa wheedled. "You can tell me. *Is* it Jai?"

God bless Allie's eyes' inability to hold a secret as they crept up to meet her sister's in the mirror.

"Oh my gosh! Oh my gosh! Oh my gosh!"

"Shh!" Allie placed a finger over her mouth. "Mom and Dad don't know."

"Why not?"

"Can you imagine?"

Carissa's head tilted, and she wrinkled her nose and nodded. "Point taken."

Allie grabbed her hands. "*Please* don't tell them. I don't want anyone to know."

"Why ever not? Man, I'd be telling everyone from here to Timbuktu if I was dating a guy like him."

"You think Jake would be happy with that?" Allie had always sensed he was kind of possessive.

"Hmm, maybe not. But seriously," Carissa continued, "what's the problem with people knowing? Apart from Mom and Dad, of course. They would get a little carried away."

"There's no way anyone could know without them finding out. And when they find out, they'll tell him about these stupid posters." She pointed to the ceiling—she *really* had to get them down. "He'll find out I'm one of the crazy fans he loathes, and then it will be done."

"Yeah, you probs should get rid of the cardboard Jai."

Allie winced. Okay, perhaps her most excruciating admission: she had life-size cardboard cutouts of Jai and the Hawks' captain. Not that she'd ever hugged the captain. Yep. True tragic here.

"And shut down the site," Carissa advised.

Allie sighed. Two years ago, Carissa had crept into Allie's bedroom and busted her as she wrote on her website. Allie had gained the impression that Carissa had been horrified but also slightly awed. But close the site down? "Maybe," she hedged.

"Definitely," her sister said firmly. "Come on. The people who go on sites like that are just sad, desperate losers without lives of their own."

Indignation rose.

"Present company excepted, of course," Carissa added hastily.

Except, the way she'd said that, there was no *of course* about it.

"You really think I'm sad and desperate?" Allie said, turning to eye her sister.

Carissa sighed, shifting to sit on the edge of Allie's white embroidered bedspread. "Allie, can I be honest with you?"

"You mean you usually aren't?"

Her sister rolled her eyes. "Look, we both know you've been inclined to hide behind your stammer and not go out or try new things because you worry about what people think of you. Don't you think this is a good chance to see if there's more to life than dreaming it away on TV, books, and fan forums?"

Allie flinched, wishing she could leave. Wishing her sister would leave, actually, as her words cut to the core. "I have a life," she began. "And—"

"But are you happy? What are you doing to step out of your comfort zone?"

"Why do I need to get uncomfortable?" she protested.

"Because there's a world of possibility out there, and you'll never know who or what you can be if you always play it safe."

But safe was good, safe was easy, safe was…safe.

Her sister smiled. "Allie-pops." The old childish name drifted over her offense like cool air on burned skin. "You know I love you," Carissa rushed on. "You know I think you're incredibly intelligent and talented and clever, and the way you've managed to do your job given…everything, well, I think that's great. And I know you might be happy living here with Mom and Dad, but one day you'll be all alone. You're almost thirty, and then what?"

"Life doesn't end at thirty if you're single," Allie protested.

"But each year that drifts by, it gets harder and harder to find guys one might consider Mr. Right. So maybe God has put Jai in your life right now for a reason."

"So he can be Mr. Right Now?" And not forever after?

"So you can have a great time and get to know him and see where this could go."

Carissa's smile, filled with tenderness and understanding of all Allie's insecurities and fears, tickled her ever ready well of emotion into tears.

"Stop crying!" Carissa implored. "You'll wreck my amazing makeup, and you truly look beautiful, even if I do say so myself."

Allie sniffed, then blinked hard several times, willing the emotion away. "But what will he say when he finds out about the fan forum?"

"You'll have closed it down, so it won't be a problem," Carissa said confidently.

Allie nodded. It certainly looked like that was what she'd need to do. "And you won't tell Mom or Dad? Or Jake?"

"Of course not," Carissa said. "What do you take me for?"

Allie bit her lip. Studied her reflection one more time. Thanked her sister, who gave her a hug. Then pushed her shoulders back. She was intelligent, and yes, she'd even be prepared to admit she now looked beautiful and not like a Marilyn Monroe impersonator.

Lord, help me, she prayed as she hurried out the door to her car. And help Jai to see she might be the perfect woman for him.

CHAPTER 9

The sweat trickling down after a workout was nothing compared to what Jai could feel right now. When was the last time he'd done something as fancy as this? Not that it was *too* fancy. Just fancy enough to make a statement without making a statement of intent. He hoped.

But now that he thought about it, agreeing to meet Allie outside the restaurant seemed a dumb idea. If he'd picked her up, as he first suggested, they would've had the whole car ride over here to lose the awkwardness so they could get into the meal and the real conversation. But he'd bowed to her wishes. Maybe it was some feminist empowerment thing, or maybe it was because she'd had bad experiences with guys and wanted to call the shots should she wish to leave early. Either way, here he was, pacing outside the Thai restaurant, hoping she'd turn up soon and he could get away with nobody else recognizing him.

Imagine if the Hawks won the Cup. He wondered what it was like for Brent to have won the Cup and a gold medal. Did people mob him on the streets? Of course, it probably helped that Brent lived a little way from the action of downtown Detroit and visited places like Toronto and Calgary fairly frequently. It'd be a different matter for a homegrown dude to lift the Cup. But even so, he could imagine how Chicagoans would go crazy.

A yellow Subaru drove past, and he lifted a hand, catching Allie hunch in the drivers' seat then brake as if she recognized him. Fortunately, there was a parking lot nearby that he could point her to, and he hurried to meet her as she parked and got out.

"Wow."

She smiled, and his heart did another flip.

"Allie, you look…" Words failed him.

Her brow creased. "Is it too much? My sister insisted on helping me, and I…I didn't have the heart to t-tell her to stop."

"Tell your sister I like her work. Not that I didn't like your work before, I mean…" Oh man. *Why, God, why?* "Allie, you look very nice, but then you always do," he said as sincerely and carefully as he could.

"Thank you." Her lips twitched, like she understood his gift for foot-in-mouth. "You l-look very nice t-too."

"I tried," he replied honestly.

He wanted her to be a little impressed so she wouldn't see him as just a dumb jock. He'd even given some thought to what sorts of topics of conversation might be helpful: art, travel, favorite museums. He could tell his world would get a lot bigger with Allie in it.

"So, you like Thai?" he said as he gently steered her to the restaurant's front door.

"I haven't had it much," she confided. "But it was very t-tasty, if a little hot."

"We won't get too hot and spicy tonight then," he said, wincing as he heard the echo of his words.

Fortunately, she laughed, and he knew another ping of relief. Maybe tonight could be as easy and comfortable as that first meal had been.

A waiter took them to their table and talked them through the specials, where they both agreed to keep the chili factor down to mild and easy. And it *was* easy: easy conversation, despite her apparent nerves, and easy laughter as they shared about their days. He liked the fact that with her he didn't have to try too hard. She understood his verbal fumblings and looked past them to accept him, just as he hoped she felt he did the same with her.

She fascinated him, this woman who wore a black fitted dress like she was a model, this woman who talked in those low musical tones about things he'd never realized he wanted to know about until now. She was elegant, humble, perhaps a little shy, but he didn't mind that, as it pushed him to be bolder, to want to draw her out and boost her confidence.

The first round of food was served: some tasty morsels of deep fried he-didn't-know-what. But it didn't matter, as Allie seemed to know, like she'd memorized the menu.

"I can't understand why it's taken so long for us to meet, especially given we go to the same church."

She opened her mouth as if to speak, then closed it again.

"What?" He touched her hand, noticed the little jump she gave.

She shook her head. "It's nothing."

"Quit doing that," he said gently. "You know I want to hear what you think."

She drew in a breath as if bolstering for courage. "I never really thought someone like me could be accepted by the cool c-crowd."

"What do you mean?"

Her gaze met his shyly, apologetically. "I mean, you hang out with some pretty popular people, and I'm just...me."

Wow. Sadness twisted his insides at what she wasn't saying. "You really think that?"

She lifted a shoulder in a half shrug.

"Allie, I've never been part of the cool crowd." He swallowed, wondering whether he should own his past then figuring being vulnerable might help her feel safe to be the same. "I grew up kind of poor in a broken home. My dad left when I was two. My mom had to scrimp and save and work three jobs just to get me and my sister Kathryn through school."

Her eyes grew soft, and she bit her lip, her sympathy compelling him to go on.

"The only reason I got to play hockey was because I went to a kid's birthday party when I was six, and they'd paid for everyone to ice-skate. I discovered I could do it, it was fun, and one of the dads ended up sponsoring me to have lessons and join a youth hockey club."

God bless Mr. Bicknell. His generosity had steered Jai into a very different world from his neighbors and peers.

"That became my life—working hard, getting sponsorships and financial aid where I could. I always got the uniform cast-offs and knew some of the rich kids sneered at me." He clenched his fingers, released them. "It made me work harder to prove that I deserved to be there. Then as I grew older, I worked out more and ran faster and did what I could to keep proving them wrong, that I belonged there more than them."

He stopped, surprised at his admission. Was this what being the fastest man on ice was about? Was this why he wanted the alternate captaincy role—so he could finally feel respected?

"Do you still feel that way?" Allie asked softly, like she could read the secret places of his heart.

"Sometimes," he confessed.

Her fingers, which had lain tantalizingly close on the table, now touched his. Heat sparked between them, causing him to blink.

Her mouth fell open—her very pretty mouth—then snapped closed.

The remains of the first course were removed, their drinks replenished, and the mains were served.

When the waiter had gone, he asked her what she'd been going to say.

Another half shrug. "I can't remember."

He hooked an eyebrow. Saw her blush. Smile. Laugh.

"Okay, okay. I was just going to say that I completely understand. People have always treated me differently just because I sometimes find it hard to speak."

"But you've done amazing things at the Art Institute." He paused. "Do…do you mind me asking, how did you get that role if you've found talking difficult?"

Her gaze met his, then slid away as she studied her main of chicken and cashews. "I've had to work hard, to practice and rehearse what I say. It helps when I don't feel nervous, which usually happens when I've built some confidence after doing something a few times."

"I think you're remarkable."

She rolled her eyes.

"No, really. It takes courage to do something like that. You haven't let anything hold you back."

"That's not what my sister thinks," she murmured, her mouth twisting to one side.

"Your sister?"

"Carissa. I don't think you've met her."

Yeah, because he hadn't met any of her family.

Her eyes rounded, like she'd said something amiss.

"What is it?"

She moved her head as if to deny it, then seemed to realize what he'd say, and smiled. "She's a fan of yours too."

"Too? Does that mean you're a fan?" he teased.

She blinked, the candlelight doing nice things to the contours of her face. "Y-yes," she whispered.

How much of a fan? he longed to ask, but he figured that'd sound arrogant, so he didn't, instead settling for, "I guess you wouldn't have finally said yes to going out with me if you didn't like me to some degree."

She bit her lip and glanced away, and he followed her gaze to a large picture of a tropical beach and turquoise sea he figured was someplace in Thailand. "Some degree, yes."

He chuckled, and her gaze switched back to him, the little smile playing around her mouth inviting him to wonder about the softness of her lips.

Whoa. Way too soon to be thinking like that. But maybe one day. One day soon. Like their next date. Like... "I think we should do this again."

"Eat Thai food?"

"Go out. I'm having fun."

"Me too," she murmured, her gaze holding his.

He exhaled and put his fork down on the gold-rimmed china plate. "Really?"

She nodded.

Yes! "So, um, when are you next free?" he asked as casually as he could.

"I'm pretty free all the time," she said, lips curving with wryness. "But don't you have training camp coming soon?"

Oh, yeah. "You know about that?"

She nodded, her gaze dropping. "I, um, might've had to look up a few things to make sure you wouldn't think I know nothing about what you do."

Huh. Just like he'd done. The thoughtfulness of that wove warmth around his chest.

"How do you feel about this coming season?" she asked.

His shoulders relaxed, and he didn't mind the question he'd been asked a dozen times already this week. "To be honest, I think with some of the new guys we have that it should be an exciting year. I actually dare to believe we're in with a chance at going deep into the playoffs, or at least as good a chance as ever."

"Confident."

He nodded. "You kind of have to be. If you don't believe in yourself, there are plenty of others who are only too willing to knock you down."

"True."

"Do you find that in your line of work?"

"Sometimes." She stirred the rice grains on her plate, put her chopsticks down. "I find it hard to not take on board what some of them say," she admitted, adjusting her glasses.

He loved that they were at this level of honesty already. "It's a good thing we don't need to take other people's opinions on board."

She nodded, lips twisting again in a sideways maneuver that made him wonder just what she was thinking.

"What are you not saying now?" he asked.

"It's good neither of us ever feels the need to prove ourselves to others," she said innocently.

"Ouch. But yeah." Surprise tickled his heart at her tease. Or was it challenge? When was the last time someone had gently challenged him like that? Pastor Josiah? Beau?

Wow.

He watched her as she smiled and bent her head to concentrate on delicately finishing her meal. Her skin was creamy, and her blond waves curled around her ears, begging him to find out if they were as silk-like as they appeared. Maybe it really was true, and in this artistic, graceful woman he'd found someone way more than just a pretty face for a dinner date. He'd found that, sure. But maybe in Allie Davis he'd also found an iron-sharpening-iron kind of friend.

~

ALLIE'S WEEK passed in a blur of responsibility and wonder. She —little old tongue-tied Allie—had been on a date with THE Jai Mullins. She could barely believe it.

She could barely believe so many things, like the fact that Carissa *still* had not told anyone about the identity of Allie's mystery date. God bless her sister. And the fact that the ease she somehow felt in Jai's company was still there. Even after that awkward moment when he'd asked if she was a fan and she'd wondered if she should just confess the whole truth in all its awful technicolor glory, seeing as they were exchanging confidences.

Whether by design or God's good management, the moment had passed, and their mutual exchanges had knit their bond even tighter. Or at least, that was how she felt. Like they were friends.

Was it such a bad thing that she'd known half his background story already? That the reason she admired him as a player—apart from the fact he was a Christian—was that he'd had a rough start in life? She'd always been one to support an underdog, having felt like one for most of her own life. But was it weird that she'd had to pretend she didn't know already when he told her these things?

She hadn't known everything, though, and the sympathy she'd felt for him had certainly been stirred in a deeper, more poignant way. Now he wasn't *the* Jai Mullins, Speed Machine. He was simply Jai. Sometimes awkward, like her. Funny, like she wished she could be. Compassionate and kind.

She'd noticed these last two traits even more as their date drew to a close. He'd insisted on paying, and while she might have enough feminist principle to insist on driving herself on a first (real) date, she certainly wasn't going to stand on ceremony and deny a guy who earned ten or twenty times her salary to pay for food he'd insisted on her having. She'd seen the way Jai had noticed the waiter, a guy whose complexion screamed

Mexican rather than Asian, and asked how he was doing, only to learn he was studying computer science. Jai's tip had been more than twice what would be expected, and this fact, coupled with the fact that he didn't flash his cash in fancy clothes or the latest car, drew a new appreciation for the man. He was humble, and she liked that. And she still didn't know how to tell him.

Was Carissa right in insisting that Allie spill the beans about the website? What if she just let it die? The thought reminded her to check the latest updates on the site, then prompted another thought that she should message the other adminis-trator and let her know Allie's thoughts.

But even that was problematic. How to explain that Allie no longer wanted to run the Jai Mullins's Girlfriend fan forum because she dared to think he might want to date her in truth?

Not that there was anything particularly daring about thinking that. He'd made that obvious, not just during the meal but later, in the car park, when he smiled at her and her heart missed several beats.

"So, about that next date," he'd said.

"What about it?" she'd said, smiling at how coy and self-possessed she thought she sounded.

"Would you like to go out again with me?"

The way he'd asked, all deep and raspy, and the way his gaze had trickled to her lips then back again, had caused yet another hitch in her heart. Maybe she'd need to see a cardiologist.

"That would be good," she'd finally managed, wondering whether he'd inch closer, and whether he was the kind of guy who kissed on first dates.

Just that thought had been enough to cause a delicious shiver, which Jai had noticed and misread, insisting it was getting cooler and she should probably get in the car. What to say: *No, I shivered because I was wondering if you'd kiss me, and it's been my dream for years now, and I'm so clueless because I've never dated, so I wouldn't even know what to do.*

Yeah. So not going to fly.

He'd shifted closer only to bend down and give her a light hug—something she could almost consider brotherly, except she'd never had a brother to compare it to.

But his closeness, his scent, the way every fiber of her being stood to attention in awe of his muscles, had caused this feeling of lightheadedness and wonder, like she really was living some kind of alternate reality as a movie heroine in a role that others dreamed about—except it was real.

And now it was Friday night, and they were going out again. She'd once again insisted on meeting him somewhere, not wanting her parents to intrude on their time—at least, not until she could figure out if this friendship was sturdy enough to handle other people's opinions and pronouncements.

It felt almost illicit, this secret bonding with the man of her dreams. No one apart from Carissa knew they'd gone on that first date. And to have her private life be actually private for once—at least from her parents—was such a novel feeling. And so empowering. When speaking to Carissa about that first date, Allie had tried to be non-committal—which her sister had seen through, of course—and hadn't told her anything about tonight. From what Jai had said, he hadn't told anyone either. And so the secret of their dates became another thing they bonded over, causing Allie's heart to twirl and her imagination to soar as she wondered, hoped, and prayed.

~

HAWKS & SQUAWKS ONLINE CHAT

TubularBells: Guess who I saw tonight?
PucktheMagicDragon: I'll bite. Who?
TubularBells: JM17. With his blonde lady friend.
PucktheMagicDragon: OMG!! Where?

TubularBells: Cantina Cantina on First.

PipeDreams27: Really? I thought he hated Mexican.

CoolplayismyJam: Maybe she's Latino.

TubularBells: She's a blonde.

PipeDreams27: Insert eye roll here.

PucktheMagicDragon: Pics or it didn't happen!

TubularBells: Give me a moment. Here.

PipeDreams27: Why? Why her? She wears glasses? Really? I don't understand.

PucktheMagicDragon: She looks classy.

TubularBells: She did seem nice.

PucktheMagicDragon: You SPOKE to her? Did you speak to him too? (OMG!)

TubularBells: They were sitting at a nearby table. Spoke to the waiter who served them. He kept going on and on about the large tip JM17 left him.

PipeDreams27: They get paid the big bucks so why not?

PucktheMagicDragon: She's so lucky…

PipeDreams27: He's probably getting some.

PucktheMagicDragon: You're just jealous.

PipeDreams27: Darn straight.

PucktheMagicDragon: Who *is* she?

TubularBells: Where'd they first meet?

PipeDreams27: I want to meet him there too.

PucktheMagicDragon: In your dreams.

PipeDreams27: In YOUR dreams.

TubularBells: That's our mission. Find out who she is. Spread the word.

PucktheMagicDragon: But don't you think we should let him be happy? He looks really happy in this pic.

PipeDreams27: That's what you get for being famous. Fair game. It's on.

TubularBells: Good night.

CHAPTER 10

"Okay, men. Drills!"

Coach Quartermaine was a gun of a coach. The sprints and drills he insisted on—or got his assistant coaches to insist on—were key in reshaping this young crew of athletes to something more. It felt funny to Jai to realize he was now one of the older guys, to know that his thirtieth birthday ticked ever closer, now just two months away. Before that, though, they had a trip to Switzerland, as Chicago had been scheduled to play a series of exhibition games against Detroit in early October. At least he'd be playing against Brent, which always made for some classic match-ups, given that Brent was widely considered to be one of the best power forwards in the NHL, with both the speed and size to grab and protect the puck. While Brent may have boasted of slicing seconds off his times due to his girlfriend-now-wife's short track secrets, Jai reckoned he still could take him.

He'd been relieved to see he'd likely still score the title of Speed Machine here. They'd be hosting a mini tourney at the end of the week, a chance for the Hawks' supporters to come and meet and greet the new team members and do signings with the others. He liked these times and always relished the opportunity to share with others whatever encouragement he could, conscious his was a privileged position and that some of the youngsters who came were likely hiding pain of their own.

But this year would be a little different. He'd asked Allie if she planned to come to a special event on Friday night, and while she'd hesitated, he hoped his powers of persuasion might finally convince her that it'd be fun.

He'd really like to see her again. They'd now had five dates, six if you included that first lunch after church, and his desire to make things more official was only growing. It would be a good chance for her to connect with some of the other players' wives and girlfriends. He blinked. Not that he was thinking quite so permanently just yet. But the more time he spent with her—they'd now tried Thai, then Mexican, Indian, Cajun, and Italian—the more he wanted to share with her. More time. More laughter. More talk. More...

He swallowed. He really shouldn't be thinking about kissing her. It was still way too soon. He hadn't even properly progressed to handholding yet. Mainly because every time he did, the electricity between them seemed too hot to handle—literally. And just that thought made his mind wander other places he begged God to help him control. Because he really didn't want to move too fast and take Allie places that neither of them were ready to go.

"Mullins!"

He winced, forced his head back into the now. Too much of this daydreaming would not go well.

More drills, more sprints—which Jai still managed to win, although young Farriss was inching nearer—then passing and shooting practice.

The practice time wound to a close with instructions about what the coming days would bring. Then the group rose from the circle of bent knees to move to the dressing room.

"Men!" Coach barked, bringing them all to a standstill. "Before you go, we've got one more thing to say." He gestured to Connor Lays, the baby-faced captain alternately known as Laser, due to his stellar shot, or Captain Grim, because he rarely cracked a smile.

"As you know, Tesci has left us, which leaves us with a position open for alternate captain."

Jai glanced at the tape wrapping his stick. "Count it all joy..." What an important reminder that had proven to be—countless times as he'd struggled to overcome feelings of inadequacy, disappointment, and rejection.

He looked up, wondering if it'd be Stamos or Thompson who'd make it.

"...Mullins."

Huh?

"Jai, come on out here."

Come here for what? He skated slowly to the front of the pack as two dozen pairs of eyes watched him. Maybe he should have listened harder instead of thinking about that verse.

But it became clearer when he was handed a brand new jersey, one with a 17 on the back and sleeves and a capital A stitched on the front. "Me?"

The corner of Connor's mouth twitched. "You."

Wow. How insane. If only Ray Bicknell could see him now. Heat pricked his eyes, and he had to choke down a really unnecessary spurt of emotion.

"Thanks," he said gruffly. Somehow he managed to stumble through the correct sorts of things he supposed someone should say, glad that for once his mouth's propensity for carelessness seemed to recognize the magnitude of this honor and behave. He ripped off his practice jersey and slipped on this new one, feeling his chest puff out a little.

Nods, applause, pats on the back, more throat tightening and feelings that probably belonged on some of those soaps Mom liked to watch, where characters gazed at each other for long seconds while a tear trickled down a cheek.

But wow. He couldn't wait to tell Mom. Josiah. The guys. And Allie.

"Really?"

"Really," Jai said, smiling as he heard Allie's gasp. "Hey. You don't need to sound so surprised. I am apparently considered to be very mature."

"By whom?" she teased.

Well, he guessed she was teasing. Hoped, anyway. "Look, my mouth doesn't always go and do its own thing. Sometimes it knows how to behave."

"Good to know," she said softly, before adding, "Jai, I'm really pleased for you. You thoroughly deserve it. They would've been stupid to give it to anyone else."

"Right? I said as much in my acceptance speech—"

"You didn't!"

"Okay, well, I might've thought about saying so in my acceptance speech, but mature me decided I really didn't need to point out everyone else's inadequacies."

"That *was* very mature of you."

"Thank you for noticing." He grinned, the light inside his apartment revealing his reflection in the window as the dark of a Chicago storm flashed by. "I hope you had a good day."

There came the faintest sigh, something which dimmed his grin a few degrees. "What is it? What happened?"

"Oh, nothing for you to worry about. It's just that now Myra is back, well, she hasn't been backward in coming forward to tell me all the things I did wrong last week when she was away."

"Really?" He frowned.

"You'd think a week away would make her happier, but it seems things didn't end well, and she's been snapping at everyone. Honestly, I was glad to escape right on the dot at five today."

"I wish you could've come to see me. Or me to see you."

"Then it would've taken me hours to get home. Maybe next time."

"Tomorrow?"

She chuckled. "I'm flattered, but I have music practice tomorrow."

"But you are able to come on Friday night, right?"

A pause. He gritted his teeth. He was fast coming to learn that when Allie hesitated, he probably wouldn't like hearing what came next. "Allie?"

She coughed, a sound that gave vibes of indecision, not illness. "Remind me what it is?"

"It's the special Hawks function of training camp week, a time to meet the others in the team and get to know some of the other partners."

He bit back a groan at those last two words, hoping she wouldn't misread too much commitment into one little phrase. But while they weren't at official status yet, he'd heard via the grapevine that was Lays and Brunton, the other alternate captain, that their respective girlfriends—they were too young for marriage, or so the gossip chamber echoed—wanted to know if Jai had a significant other in his life, and if so, they'd like to meet her. Given he'd never had a significant other significant enough to introduce to anyone before, he hoped Allie might consider it. Then wondered if this would all prove too much pressure.

She still hadn't said anything, so he asked again. "Please?"

There came a long sigh, and his heart sank. "I...I just don't know."

"What don't you know? I mean, I know it's kind of soon—"

"It's really soon."

"Okay, really soon."

"Like way, *way* too soon," she reproved. "We've only gone on a few dates."

"That could change. I could take you on ten dates between now and then, and—"

"Jai!" Her low chuckle lifted the corner of his lips.

"Allie."

"I'm sorry," she said softly.

Yeah, he was too. He stared at his reflection, seeing through it to where the storm clouds swirled into grays and dark blue. "It's okay," he finally conceded.

Another few beats of silence passed. Then, "I'm so honored that…that you would even ask me."

"I like you, Allie," he admitted, the baldness of his honesty drawing his attention to his feet as he hoped, desperately, to hear words that conveyed something of her feelings toward him.

He knew she liked him. It was there in the warmth of her smile, the way her gaze lingered, the way she would lean forward and touch him ever so briefly, like she, too, felt the scorch of skin. But there was something about hearing her say it, hearing her articulate the emotion his heart hungered for. Affection hadn't been huge in his house growing up—blame the father who walked out for that, leaving a mom too busy and too tired and stressed to ever show much love.

But Jai seemed to have been born with a faulty heart that demanded to know he was loved, which no doubt had contributed to certain levels of focus and determination to prove himself, to be the best, to have high expectations of himself, which then naturally flowed to others. He'd talked it over with Josiah before and knew this was an area he needed to take to God. But still, in moments like these, he craved to hear the acceptance and affirmation that he hoped she would give.

"Jai."

The way she spoke his name, with a kind of caress, drew an intensity to see her. "Allie."

"I…"

He waited, heart pounding, then wondered at himself for practically forcing her into such a proclamation. How mature. Not.

"It's okay." He rushed to fill the silence so he wouldn't have to hear her make polite excuses. "You're right. I guess my need for speed overtook my brain there for a moment. Forget I said anything, okay?"

Another pause, then a small, "Okay."

"Unless of course you want to," he hastened to add. "No pressure. Either way."

She gave a small chuckle. "Good to know."

"I mean it. Whenever you're ready to make things official, you just say the word and we'll attend something."

"Make what official?" she asked softly.

Okay. Yet another case of motormouth in action. "Um, this friendship thing?"

"So we're friends?"

"Well, yeah. Friends who like to eat together."

"Uh huh."

"Actually, I have other friends who I eat with, so maybe this isn't the same," he admitted.

"No?"

"No. See, I don't think about"—*kissing*—"uh, wanting to hold their hand all the time."

"Do you?"

"Do I what?"

"Want to hold my hand?" she murmured so low he had to press the phone hard against his ear.

"Very much so."

Another pause. "Oh."

Was that all she had to say? "So, uh, do you ever think about holding my hand?"

He heard her intake of breath.

"Allie?"

"Sometimes," she finally acknowledged.

"Maybe we could do some of that the next time I see you."

"That'd be good."

"Okay then." His heart lifted. And maybe after an appropriate length of time, hand-holding could progress to exploring just how soft her lips seemed.

"I...I'm sorry about Friday night," she said again. "I just don't want to be put in the limelight, not when I haven't said anything to my family yet."

"I said something to my mom." He'd had to. The number of bouquets he kept organizing for Allie had to be explained. Mom was pleased for him. Thought it was about time he found a girl. "So we talk to your family. Maybe after church."

Another pause, longer this time.

"What is it?"

"I...I don't know if I ever explained that my family are huge Blackhawks supporters."

"Really? I thought you said your mom was a teacher and your dad a dentist."

"You can be a dentist and still love your sports, Jai."

"You can? Who knew?"

She chuckled.

"Look, I like you," he said again. "I want to know where this can go, so I don't care about how much your family likes the Hawks." They couldn't be as bad as that over-friendly couple he'd met that first time at church. *Lord, spare me.* "I'd like to meet them."

Another sigh.

He laughed. "Come on, Allie. It can't be that bad."

"That's because you haven't met them yet."

"Please?"

A beat, two more, passed. "You…you might not like what they have to say."

"Are you worried they're going to spill the beans on you? Show me your baby pictures or something?"

"It's the *or something* I'm worried about," she muttered.

His chuckle escaped again. "Come on. I don't think there's anything they could say that would make me run away. They're fans, so they obviously have good taste."

"They're superfans," she corrected. "And didn't you say you disliked superfans?"

"I don't dislike them," he said, trying to think back to what he'd actually said. "Just maybe find them a little exhausting, if I'm completely honest."

Another beat. "Do…do you find me exhausting?" she asked.

"You?" Allie was one of the most restful people he knew. "Not at all. Why? Are you a superfan too?" he joked.

"M-maybe."

He grinned, affection for her swirling warmth around his chest. Man, he liked this girl. Liked this banter, liked that she could tease.

As for meeting her family of die-hard Hawks supporters, yeah, okay. He'd once thought he didn't want to get involved in something like that, but he'd put up with them. He'd put up with anything for Allie's sake.

How hard could it be?

ALLIE GLANCED AROUND HER ROOM, freshly shorn of all Hawks memorabilia, which she'd stowed in the closet, waiting for that rainy day. The dream-like bubble that had surrounded her since that first encounter with Jai at the Art Institute had burst with a mighty big pop when Jai had basically insisted on meeting her superfan family after church. Her imagined and her lived worlds were about to collide in a way she hoped would not prove catastrophic.

What would Jai say when he found out just how much of a superfan she'd been of *him*? At least she'd deactivated her blog. Her involvement in recent times had been non-committal at best, and the Jai Mullins's Girlfriend fan forum was no more. She hoped. Deleting it, deleting all the content that had spilled over so many years, had proved more traumatic than she'd thought it would. Not because of the loss of content. She'd grieved more for the loss of the life she now realized she hadn't been living. Her sister had been right. And while Allie and dozens of anonymous others had been so busy observing and admiring Jai and others of his ilk and making comments about their lives, she'd not been doing much living of her own. Deleting this sad part of her history was a way of declaring she was ready to live life now. Even if it felt surreal. Even if it felt doomed.

Jai might have said all the right things about meeting her parents, and she'd tried to hint and give him some fair warning, but she couldn't help but feel today was going to go down in the record books as the worst meet-the-parents scenario in history. She even suspected he didn't yet realize exactly who her parents were, and that far from meeting her parents for the first time, he was going to learn—in, oh, approximately two hours—that he'd met her superfan parents before.

Trying to figure out how to explain to her parents what was going on with one of their favorite Hawks forwards had proved so overwhelming that she'd been almost grateful for the fact that Myra's change of rosters had meant Allie had needed to work when the Hawks' training camp festival was on. Dad had complained, but she had been firm, conscious of the escape clause it was—at least until another day. That day being today, when she'd leave it to chance—or at least pray that God would somehow redeem today's encounter of the superfan kind. What would her parents say when they found out that Allie's dates with "someone she'd met at work" actually meant dates with Jai Mullins?

"Allie, how could you keep this a secret? Why didn't you want us to know?"

"Allie, we're so thrilled! You and THE Jai Mullins! Who would have ever thought this possible?"

"Allie, do you think this will mean we can meet all the other players?"

She cringed. She'd have to somehow speak to Jai, to explain, to confess her stupid, shallow, fan-girliest of weaknesses before her family confessed them for her.

Lord, help!

Even her prayers seemed to overwhelm her, the magnitude of this day pressing deep. To have seen her prayers miraculously answered, then to know this day would see them end—when she'd never even held his hand!—oh, she was so desperate, hopeless, faithless, sure this day would see the end of her finally-fulfilled dreams.

"Are you ready, Allie?" Dad called from downstairs.

She cast a last look around her room, knowing that tonight she'd be pulling all her posters back out.

Was she ready for what was guaranteed to be the worst day of her life? No.

"Yes," she called.

Here went nothing.

CHAPTER 11

Here goes nothing.

Jai straightened his shoulders and opened the glass doors, nodding to a few people he semi-recognized from his time at the early service before.

"Jai!"

He turned, met Gloria's welcoming smile. The nerves pattering through his veins slowed a mite. "Hey, Mrs. A."

"How are you?"

"Fine." Well, not really. Not since his stupid mouth had insisted on the rest of his body coming today to meet Allie's family. He wiped clammy hands down his jeans.

"You sure? You look, I don't know, a little nervous or something."

Awesome. Just the look he was going for. He smiled weakly as she grinned and moved away.

The doors opened behind him, admitting another chattering group of church-goers, propelling him into a desire to find his seat before much more time passed.

"Hey, it's Jai!"

The over-enthusiastic man from his last visit came up and pumped his hand. Oh no.

"It's Peter, remember?"

Jai nodded. How could he forget?

"And this is Merrilee, my wife." Peter wrapped an arm around a woman with dark-blonde hair. "Good to see you again!"

"Good to be here." It'd be better when he spotted Allie, but hey, he guessed he should be polite.

"We're having lunch at our place after the service, and you're more than welcome to join us if you like."

"Thanks, but I think I have plans already."

"Any time. And I mean, *any* time. Don't worry, we try to make sure things are pretty healthy, although I'm always telling the girls I don't mind if they want to add more sweet things, as it's good for the family business, you could say." He leaned in conspiratorially and winked. "I'm a dentist, you see."

Jai nodded as a vague memory of a conversation about dentistry flared then faded. It didn't matter.

"You gotta know how thrilled we all are about a Hawks player—the new alternate captain, no less!—being here, part of our church home, and maybe one day being in *our* home." Peter's bushy eyebrows waggled like he thought this was an invitation.

If Jai hadn't made a commitment to meet Allie here, he'd leave right now. This guy was all the reasons why he didn't date fans. Their families were often fully weird. Which only made Jai feel more weird. Like he wasn't weird enough already.

"Thanks, I'll keep it in mind."

"You do that. And hey, if your plans today change, know you're always welcome."

He nodded, hoping his face spoke of pleasantness and not *please leave* as the man and his wife smiled and moved on. Where *was* she?

He pushed to his toes, scanning the milling crowds as they moved through the glass doors into the auditorium, noticing the way some people nudged each other as they passed him and smiled. Another woman—he vaguely recognized her from last time—smiled and said hello, to which he responded automatically. But while he appreciated these people's friendliness, he just wanted to know where—

"Jai?"

A quick glance behind and his nerves melted away in a sugary sweet rush like chocolate ice cream dripping down a waffle cone. "Hey, you."

He leaned in to give her a hug, then figured her parents might be around, so turned his forward movement into a pat on the shoulder. Great. Maybe people should change his Speed Machine moniker to something more fitting like Awkward Man.

She glanced around, biting her lip like she, too, was worried about what others around them might be thinking.

"Want to sit together?" Honestly. It wasn't like they were in grade school. They were adults. Able to make their own choices, regardless of what anyone else here thought.

"Um, sure? But maybe over there." She pointed to the back corner of the auditorium, right where he usually sat when he came for the second service.

"Sure."

The chattering crowds were dispersing, and he got the impression that Allie was almost rushing as she threaded her way through the rows of seats until she claimed the spot next to the far wall.

"Hey," he said when they finally got their seats and she'd slumped down, like she didn't want to be seen. "Good morning."

Her gaze met his with a tentative smile that chased away more of the tension boiling away inside. "G-good morning."

He picked up her hand, heart zinging at the touch, at once

aware of how soft her skin was, the delicate weight of it in his much larger palm, and the statement this made to both her and anyone watching. "It's gonna be okay." He gently squeezed. "We're gonna be okay."

Her shoulders dropped, as if she was ready to buy that too.

"Are your parents here?"

She nodded, but before he could ask where they were seated, the music began, drowning out any further conversation. He settled for simply holding her hand, glad for this chance to be with her, glad for this chance to connect, glad for this chance to worship God together in this moment of time that blocked out the stress to come.

The music, the prayers, the sermon, all of it worked to settle his heart, to refocus him on what was important—that whatever happened today, God loved him and had good plans for his life. Just as God had good plans for Allie's life too.

He shot a look at her as she studied her Bible, following Josiah's message. How was it possible that he'd been so lucky—no, *blessed*—to find someone like her, who believed and felt the same way as he did on so many different things? What were the chances?

As if she felt his gaze, she glanced up and smiled, that sight releasing yet another of those tiny knots within that questioned what her parents would think of him. He hoped they weren't so fanatical as Peter seemed to be and that he'd impress them enough to show them he was normal. But he knew Allie's intelligence and gentle class meant she had to have pretty classy parents. Probably the quiet kind, like a poised silver-haired couple he could see down near the front. Whatever. He was just glad to be with her. Glad for this time. Glad today would mean they could finally act like a couple. Which also kind of freaked him out, because he'd never felt like this before, and he knew he'd dived deep and fast headlong into this relationship. But this was what he wanted to do, felt like something he was *meant* to do. And nothing would ever change his mind.

The service concluded, and he shifted. "That was a good one."

Allie nodded. "Josiah always preaches a message with something to say."

"Yeah. We always get a lot out of the Bible studies he leads online."

"How did that start?" she asked, straightening in her seat.

Jai thought back. "I knew a bunch of us were Christians from various tournaments and things over the years, and we'd catch up and try to encourage each other when we played against each other. Eventually the internet made it easier to connect, so that's what we try to do, meeting up every second Monday, which works if we don't have games."

"And how did Pastor Josiah get involved in it?"

Jai glanced up, saw the pastor approaching, and smiled. "You might need to ask him yourself."

"What are you two lovebirds talking about so intensely over here?" Josiah said, a twinkle in his eye.

Jai choked, not daring to catch Allie's eye. "Lovebirds?"

"No?" He cast a pointed look at their joined hands, which seemed to instantly remove Allie's fingers from his. "My mistake, and my apologies."

Jai chanced a look at Allie. She ducked her head, but he could see her face was bright pink. He had to divert attention.

"We were talking about you," Jai said.

"Me? I'm flattered."

"Allie was asking how you got involved in the online Bible study group," Jai explained.

"Aha." Josiah nodded and faced Allie. "You know that I am a big fan of Jesus and a big fan of hockey, and hey, when Jai told me about wanting to have a place where there was an opportunity to encourage him and some of his friends in matters of the Lord, well, I couldn't resist."

"So you started the group," Allie said, looking at Jai.

He shrugged. "It's been really good."

"That it has. And lately, seeing some of these fine young men"—Josiah clapped a hand on Jai's shoulder—"moving forward in their lives, getting married, having babies, well, I'm so grateful to think we've been able to encourage each other in this walk."

Okay, so Jai had always regarded Josiah as something of a father figure, but did he have to keep going on about the relationships thing? The man had the subtlety of a machine gun.

"Looks like I'm needed. Hey, Jai, before I go, loved your work at the festival this week." Josiah's gaze cut to Allie. "Did you see our man in action?"

"I had work."

"Fastest man, three years running. Or is that three years skating?" He clapped Jai on the back. "Proud of you, son. Oops, the way Chrissy is looking at me tells me I'm in trouble for something. I'd better go. You two have a good day, okay?"

"Thanks," Allie mumbled.

"Catch you later," Jai said.

Josiah gave him one of those upraised brow kind of looks that hinted the next time they talked there'd be some interesting questions. He left, and Jai exhaled.

"Sorry," Jai said. "I don't think he could've been any more obvious."

"D-don't apologize," she said.

"Really, I am sorry—"

"No, really," she said more firmly. "Don't apologize."

"But you were embarrassed by what he thought."

"Maybe. Or maybe I was just flattered that he seemed to think this could even be a thing."

"Really?"

"Really."

Wow. He studied her, and for once she didn't look away, holding his gaze with a little smile that begged him to know more about the softness of her lips. "You're really beautiful."

Her nose wrinkled, which caused her glasses to slip. She pushed them back. "And you're really blind. I thought those glasses you wore were for disguise, not because you actually need them."

"You're really beautiful," Jai whispered.

The moment stretched, the sense of the world around them dimming down to just two despite the knowledge that this bond that had awakened between them was something others seemed to recognize too.

Speaking of... "Are you going to introduce me to your parents?"

She closed her eyes, bit her lip, and nodded.

They rose, collected Bibles and belongings, and moved to the middle of the church, where various clumps of people were standing chatting. He noticed the man from earlier, Peter, turn and look at them and lift a hand. "Hey, Allie. Are you ready for lunch?"

Jai bit back a smile. *Watch Allie say no, buster. We've got bigger fish to fry.*

Before Allie could respond, Peter turned to him and grinned. "Jai! Hey, were you talking with Allie? Oh, that's right, I remember. You met at her work ages ago."

Last month, actually, but whatever.

"Hey, Jai, I know you can't come for lunch today, or at least said you couldn't"—he winked—"but I just wanted to tell you how great you were this week. I was there cheering you on—you might've heard me. Merrilee often says I get too loud." He grinned with no sign of apology. "But I can't help but be excited, especially now we've talked and I feel I know you."

Jai nodded, smiled, said something polite and non-committal. "Excuse me, sir, but I really need to go meet somebody." He turned to Allie. "You ready?"

His words faltered at the agonized look she gave him, her smile holding a side of cringe. "What is it?"

"You want to meet my family?" she asked.

"More than anything." Her parents might be superfans, but they couldn't be as bad as Peter here. More full-on than a dead skunk in the trunk, as Beau might say.

"You want to meet her family?" Peter asked.

Wow. Jai knew a new knot of frustration. Since when did strangers think it okay to admit to eavesdropping? He narrowed his gaze at Peter. "Excuse us."

"Us?" Peter glanced at Allie. "What's this all about?"

Allie sighed, and Jai's skin rippled with trepidation. No. Uh uh. Couldn't be.

"Jai," Allie practically whispered, "meet my dad, Peter Davis."

~

SHE WANTED to sink into a hole. She wanted to crawl away and hide. That look on Jai's face said it all, really. Her dad's confusion had lasted a few seconds before his eyes had rounded and he'd said, "Are you together?"

How to admit the man she'd been dating was Chicago's one and only Speed Machine? And that yes, while they had gone on several dates, and yes he'd finally held her hand, there still had not been any conversation about what this meant for them. Not that it mattered. Not when it was obvious that Jai was about to walk away.

"We're friends," she rushed to say.

"Whew!" Dad swiped a hand theatrically across his brow. "For a minute there I thought you were gonna tell me something else."

She sensed rather than saw Jai's confusion. She was going to have to explain this, and soon. "So, you've met my dad, and you've met my mom before. And my sister Marcie says she's met you."

Jai nodded as Marcie drew near holding a broad smile.

"Are you coming for lunch, Allie?"

Her smile grew taut, and she turned to Jai and raised her eyebrows.

He seemed to chew his lip, as if undecided, which instantly drew a mix of pity and offense. Yes, she knew he found superfans exhausting, and he probably wasn't very happy with her now saying she hadn't admitted to the truth. But Dad's enthusiasm for the Hawks shouldn't be so easily dismissed. He was a loyal supporter and had poured countless dollars and hours into cheering on Jai's team. Couldn't Jai see that was worth something?

Jai glanced at Allie. "You never said—"

"I'm sorry."

He sucked in a breath, the consternation in his face fading as he turned back to her dad. "Well, I guess there was some miscommunication. Looks like I'm coming to lunch after all, sir. If that's all right with you."

"All right?" Dad seemed suddenly possessed of an unearthly glow. Any second now beams of light would shine from his ears. "You coming for lunch would be the best day of my life!"

"Dad," Allie protested, her cheeks heating.

"What about the day I was born?" Marcie said with a teasing smile.

"What about the day when we were married?" Mom said, nudging him hard in the ribs.

"Those were good days too," Dad said, winking at Jai like he was the son he'd never had. "But to think I'll have a real live Hawk in my house! Wowzers!"

As her father turned to her mom and whispered frantically about doing a barbecue, Allie chanced a look at Jai.

He met her with an *I told you so* expression, then muttered, "How many real *dead* Hawks have visited?"

"They're not dead," she murmured back, appreciating his attempt at humor. "Just cardboard cutouts."

"You're serious?"

"Unfortunately, yes."

Okay, no way was she ever going to admit that she herself had been the person to collect the cardboard cutouts of Jai and the captain when they'd been advertised on a secret sports website. Far better to pin that all on Dad, who obviously knew no shame.

"So, I'm having lunch at your parents' place?"

She nodded. Best to just deliver all the news at once. "And mine."

"You live there too." His eyes widened. "Wow. I didn't know."

Deal-breaker, she could almost hear him say. But hadn't she already broken the deal by saying they were only friends? Yet another thing she was going to have to explain on the drive over. That is, if Jai was to ever come to her house. "I'm really sorry," she whispered.

He studied her a moment longer, then his mouth pulled up on one side. "It's okay."

The compressed feeling in her chest eased, and she wished she could grab his hand. But obviously, any admission of a status more than friends was going to have to wait until Dad came down from the rafters of sheer exhilaration. She could only imagine how excited he'd get at the knowledge his daughter was going out with Chicago's Speed Machine. That was, if Jai were to ever forgive her.

Lord, please help this day get better. And help Jai forgive me one day too.

CHAPTER 12

The clatter and chaos of what seemed to be a million people filled the yard with so much noise. Jai wondered how he'd ever been tricked into something like this. When Peter had discovered that Jai was in fact able to come for lunch, it had sprouted a bunch of new invitations to what seemed to be at least half the church and a fair sprinkling of near neighbors. And now, here he was at the center of it all, like the freak around which a macabre circus performed.

Jai glanced at Allie now, the keeper of secrets he really wished he'd known. It felt a little like he'd been led into a fully sprung mouse trap, and now he was caught and unable to move. Allie had apologized a dozen times on the way over, and amid her at times rambling explanations he kind of understood why she hadn't said anything before. So he didn't really blame her. But still, this situation made him uneasy, and at times felt a little like the nightmare he'd always tried to avoid. Nightmare on Elm Drive, to be precise.

Allie glanced up from where she'd been studying her plate while he was peppered with questions about his training, his thoughts on Chicago's season, their schedule, and a million other things.

"You okay?" he murmured.

She nodded, but she'd barely said a word. Not that people here let her get a word in. In fact, he'd become aware of just how little they seemed to notice her, despite these people being her family and friends. One bald guy seemed to roll his eyes whenever Allie spoke, his patent lack of tolerance for her firing Jai's protectiveness.

But even her sisters, Marcie and a perky blonde called Carissa—who seemed to eye him like a cat might cream, despite a sparkling rock on her finger that said she was engaged— seemed inclined to talk over the top of Allie, not waiting to let her finish her sentences. Her mother, Merrilee, did the same. And Allie's dad, the super excited Chicago fan who was a dentist —seriously, how could Jai not have put two and two together?— seemed to be living on a euphoric high that ignored the fact that his middle daughter was withdrawn. With such a family, was it any wonder that Allie sometimes might feel shy?

She excused herself, collecting plates, and Jai moved to help her.

"No, no!" Peter protested as Merrilee placed a hand on Jai's shoulder and gently pushed him down. "I want to know all about how you think you'll do in the preseason against Detroit. You're going to Switzerland, huh?"

"Yeah."

Allie paused, her gaze meeting his for a second before she moved to collect some more plates. Had he told her about going to Switzerland? Granted, they'd had a lot of conversations in recent times and his memory wasn't the best at keeping track of all he'd said. But surely he had. Hadn't he? Note to self: another thing he'd need to clear up as soon as they got a minute to finally talk.

Her father began a story about a conference he'd once

attended in Lausanne, something his wife seemed to have heard a dozen times, which she admitted as she leaned closer to Jai. "Now, don't mind him. And I hope you won't mind Allie's lack of conversation. Poor thing." She sighed.

"How so?" he asked.

"Oh, you probably haven't noticed, seeing you don't know her very well. But my poor girl has had quite a severe stammer all her life. I've taken her to countless doctors, therapists, and psychologists, and nobody knows the real cause. It just is."

He couldn't say anything, acutely aware of just how embarrassed Allie would be if she ever knew that her mother was speaking about her so.

"She doesn't tend to do it when she's relaxed with people," her mother continued.

Huh. So was that why she didn't stammer much with him? His heart grew soft.

"And she uses musical intonation to mask it a lot of the time."

"Uh huh." He remembered Allie had explained something like that before, only she'd said she always thought it made her sound like she was on Valium. He smiled.

"But you mustn't laugh at her. She'd be so mortified. I know it's a cross she must carry all her life."

Wait. Her family pitied her? Didn't they know the amazing job she did at the Institute? Weren't they proud of her and all she'd overcome? "You must be really glad to see how well she's doing in her career."

"Oh yes," her mother said in a tone that suggested she hadn't really heard him.

It only fired new indignation on her daughter's behalf. "I think Allie is remarkable."

Of course, that truth bomb had to land in the middle of one of those sudden silences that came from nowhere. All eyes turned to him, some speculative, some shocked, some frankly disbelieving.

Quick. He had to get out of this. On the ride over, Allie had explained that she'd said that thing about only being friends to avoid her father's overreaction. At the time, Jai had appreciated her foresight. But now, his mouth having gone where it probably shouldn't have, he realized he had to get out of this gracefully, to still be honest without causing Allie any more embarrassment.

"Yeah, I um, heard her speak at the Art Institute last month. She really knows her stuff." There was a visible easing of tension, the looks of speculation dropping away. "She ran this kids' class that my nephew attended. She's great with people."

Whoa. That might've pushed the rumor mill back to high, judging from those raised eyebrows. "Great with kids," he mumbled.

"How well do you know her?" Carissa, the younger sister who was getting married, asked with an evil-looking smile.

Uh oh. How much did she know? Had Allie said anything to her? He shrugged, hoping he looked way more calm than the tightness of his shirt's collar seemed to suggest.

"Did you know she's always—?"

"Enough talk about Allie," Peter interrupted. So maybe it was a general thing, and he didn't mind which daughter he spoke over the top of. "I want to hear more about the Hawks."

"Oh, give the man a break, honey," Merrilee said with a sympathetic smile for Jai. "I'm sure this has all proved overwhelming."

"It's been nice," he admitted. And surprisingly, that statement was mostly true. He'd enjoyed the relaxed nature of the meal, the easy tease and camaraderie—very different to how his own family behaved. Sure, the number of questions thrown at him had been a little overwhelming, but for the most part it had been nice to feel appreciated and honored, to be seated here among real fans who could reel off Hawks statistics better than he could. Fans who seemed to have some canny insights for those who were often dismissed as armchair experts.

It *had* been better than he'd expected—apart from a growing concern for Allie, who still hadn't returned from the house.

"I might have to go." He pushed to his feet, brushing off the requests to stay for cake and ice cream. "Thanks for a great meal, but I really need to run." Like, literally. He'd have to exercise to deal with the carbs he'd consumed today.

"Oh, but—"

"Let him go, Peter," Merrilee said. "I can walk you out, Jai."

And be forced to listen to more of her "poor Allie" Mom secrets he really didn't want to hear? "Thank you, ma'am, but I know the way." He nodded to the general population. "Good to meet you all."

Of course, his exit was delayed as some of the neighbors had hurried home only to return and ask him to sign pucks and cards, which he obliged. He now *really* wanted to find Allie and have that conversation the short car trip before hadn't really allowed. Where was she?

ALLIE'S HANDS plunged into scalding water, and she released a little hiss of pain. But the heat on her skin could never match the scorching mortification of hearing her mother—her *mother* —describe Allie's condition and voice the pity she'd always known.

To Jai.

It was this last that was the worst. She'd heard her mom say similar things to others in the past, and while she'd known a sense of shame, it had been a picnic compared to today's humiliation. It was no wonder Jai seemed keen to leave, mobbed as he was by rabid hockey fans. The star of the show, who seemed to resent the spotlight. She didn't blame him for wanting to rush away without saying goodbye.

Her eyes filled, and she angrily blinked them away. No. She couldn't blame him. She'd basically hijacked him into coming. He'd been quiet in the car on the way here, and she'd wondered if maybe he'd drop her off then burn rubber to get out of here, away from the lying lady with the crazy family of fans. The relief she'd felt when he nodded and said he'd still come—after she'd given him that option to escape—had turned her into a bone-puddling mess.

Jai had been mature, and so must she, and though she longed to hide in her room under the pretext of finishing her painting at long last—while sobbing out all her hurt and confusion—she would instead stay here and get this done. No one out there would miss her anyway. And if she disappeared, like she was sorely tempted to do, she knew there would be more questions about why she hadn't stayed, and the speculation that had shaded Marcie's and Carissa's eyes would leak out in questions for which she didn't have the answers.

Allie finished washing one glass. Another glass. Another. What *was* this thing with Jai? A friendship? Relationship? What? The fact she could barely define it in her mind meant she'd have no hope of articulating it to others, even if she had skills in that department. Not that it mattered. Not when today's little surprise had pretty much wrecked any chance of a future.

She moved on to washing the special plates that wouldn't fit in the dishwasher. How strange it was to see the imagined connect with the real. In all of her fantasies about meeting her Mr. Hockey Right, she'd never realized just how she would feel to be the person who would forever be in his shadow. Jai was famous. People liked him. People wanted to speak to him in a way they struggled to speak to her. She'd seen the way Jake had rolled his eyes when she tried to say something earlier. Honestly, if she didn't know better, and didn't love her sister as much as she did, she'd be half tempted to tell Carissa just what her fiancé was like. But that way lay discord and hardship, and given that Carissa had kept a fairly important secret, Allie had no desire to say or do anything that would cause her sister upset.

Another glance out the window saw her heart drooping a little more. Of course! Now Jai was signing pucks. At least it didn't seem that anyone had admitted Allie's involvement in the online fan forum. Not that anyone knew. Apart from Carissa.

She finished the washing and wiped down the counter, the dishwasher humming merrily away. Should she stay here? Go upstairs? There was no point in going back outside. No one would miss her anyway. Perhaps today she didn't need to be brave, and she could just run away.

A step, two, toward the stairs—

"Are you leaving?"

She gasped and turned to face Jai, who had come inside. The sight of him standing there, filling the doorframe, concern in his eyes, seemed to prick her composure, and she bit her lip to stop a sudden wobble.

"Hey."

The compassion in his voice coupled with all that had happened—the shame, the hurt, the confusion—whirled up, and she had to turn away to hide her emotion.

"Allie."

She placed a hand over her face, struggling to suck in enough breath to hide the desperate need to cry. "I'm so sorry."

"Sorry?" He touched her shoulder, his fingers splaying across her upper arm in a caress so gentle she wanted to cry again. "What have you got to be sorry about?"

Her breath was shaky as she turned, her eyes blurring so that she had to remove her fogged-up glasses.

"Allie."

Before she knew it, he'd wrapped her in a hug that saw her

drawn against his chest, where she could hear his heart thud against her ear. She took a breath, inhaled something enticingly musky and very male as a small part of her wondered how this could be true. Was Allie really standing here in his arms?

Noise outside—her dad's booming laugh drawing near—startled her from his embrace. Jai's eyes widened, his concerned look propelling her to the stairs. "You should go," she whispered.

"We should talk."

Yes, they should. But… She glanced at the back door, then back at Jai.

He seemed to understand, tilting his head to the front door. She nodded, and he grasped her hand, escaping into the hall and out the front door just as the back door slammed.

Jai hurried her to his car, and they jumped in and drove away, the ridiculousness of the situation causing spurts of hysteria-tinged laughter.

Jai's chuckles joined hers as his car veered around the corner. "Dramatic much?"

She nodded, then leaned forward, placing her head in her hands.

"Allie? You okay?"

She dragged in a deep breath, wiped her face, and put her glasses back on. "I'm sorry," she said again.

"Hey." He reached across to grasp her hand. "You really need to stop saying that. You don't need to apologize."

"Oh, b-but I do."

He shot her a quick glance, then released her hand and steered the vehicle onto the highway.

"Where are we going?"

"Somewhere we can talk," he promised.

She nodded, content to watch the houses and trees flash by as they headed north, the high-rises of the city growing smaller behind them. It was funny how, after the turbulence of earlier, she could find a quietness with him. His kindness, his compassion, were like a quilt upon her soul, providing a comfort she'd never expected to find.

She drew in several more steadying breaths, noticing they'd turned into a more wooded area. "Have you brought me here to dispose of my body?" she asked, shooting for tease.

"Huh?" He frowned.

"Today. Lunch. Your worst nightmare, right?"

He sighed, and she winced internally again.

"I hope I didn't give that impression."

"You didn't," she assured him. He'd been remarkably patient in his dealings with those who seemed to think it their right to poke their noses into his business, enquiring about everything from where he'd first learned to skate to when he'd become a Christian.

Of course, if she were still running the fan forum, she'd have a wealth of information to share now, having learned so much herself. But instead, his honesty was like a special treasure, something to ponder over, to keep to herself as she discovered hidden depths to this man some might dismiss as a mere jock.

That Jai had grown up with some challenges, he'd admitted to her before. But the way he'd described how those experiences had shaped him, how they'd dug deep into wells of compassion which motivated his support and sponsorship of other kids like him, had only enlarged her respect for this man. He'd even mentioned a missions project one of his hockey friends was a spokesperson for, something about helping underprivileged kids in the Philippines, which had seen more than one person whip out their phone and look it up online and tell Jai they'd just sponsored a child. Jai's gratitude had squeezed fresh appreciation for him within her chest, chased by the awful fear that he'd disappear from her life without a backward glance as soon as the meal was finished. And yet, here they were, his kindness in helping her escape daring her heart to believe there was a tiny possibility that there could be a future together after all.

He pulled into a fancy country club and parked in a spare spot by the grass, his black car fitting in with some of the expensive makes parked here already. Before she knew what he was doing, he'd grabbed her hand and they were moving toward a screen of evergreens, out of sight of the main building.

"Um, are we supposed to be here?" she asked, glancing over her shoulder to where the enormous peach-bricked building loomed, a circular structure like an out-of-proportion turret keeping guard on top.

"Relax."

"Are you a member?"

He shot her a look.

Oh. Okay.

"Come on, we're almost there," he said as the foliage grew thicker.

"Where? The burial chamber?" she joked.

His footsteps slowed as he frowned at her again. "Why would you say that?"

Because she was bad at jokes apparently.

"Allie, I'd never hurt you."

The sincerity in his eyes prodded her heart to believe a little more. She nodded, and he exhaled.

The green of pines had changed to the reds and golds of autumn foliage, and she looked up, marveling at the sight. "It's really beautiful."

"Yeah. Now just wait a moment longer and...voila." He waved his arm at the scene before them—a strip of sandy beach fronting Lake Michigan, which glinted in the late afternoon sun.

"Wow. This is lovely. How did you find out about this place?"

He drew her to a bench seat not dissimilar to the one at the park where he'd left the postcard. When they were seated, two handbreadths away from each other, he exhaled. "Have I told you about a guy called Ray Bicknell?"

She shook her head.

"He was the man who first noticed my capacity for skating and did what he could to help me succeed. It's safe to say I would not be where I am today without his support." He pointed to a house that was barely visible in what must be the adjoining property. "That was his house there."

"Was?"

A muscle ticked in his jaw. "He died two years ago. Left most of his fortune to a bunch of charities for underprivileged kids. I was one of the kids he'd helped for many years, so that's why I know about this place." His gaze moved to the lake. "He used to bring some of us here to the club on our significant birthdays, like on my eighteenth. He'd show us around the club, introduce us. He said it was important for us to learn to mix with people from all walks of life. I guess I've always seen myself as a bit of a jock—a bit of a dumb jock—so it was good to come here and be exposed to a different world. He also showed us how this little section of land could be accessed, and that though we might not have the money or the connections, we could still gain entry to what both those things could buy."

Her heart was reeling over what he'd said, his raw admission of his opinion of himself chasing her shame from earlier far away. "He sounds like he was a good man."

"A very good man."

"Like you are," she said softly.

He shot her a swift look. "I'm not very good," he said. "You know what I was thinking this morning in church?"

"Apart from how embarrassing it was to talk to my dad?"

His smile flickered. "I was thinking about the fact I wanted to kiss you."

Her breath hitched. *Oh my heavens. Oh my stars. Oh my goodness!* He had?

"You don't need to look so shocked. I'm pretty sure I'm not the first man who's wondered that."

"Wondered what?" she finally managed to say.

"What it would be like to kiss you."

Wryness escaped in a chuckle. Yeah. "Pretty sure you're the only one." Wait—did this mean they might still have a chance? Or did the fact he'd used past tense meant it *had* been something he'd thought, but now he didn't anymore? But the way he was looking at her now…

"Allie."

"J-jai."

His lips slanted up. "What was going on before?"

"When? T-today has been a crazy day, and I—" She cringed. "I'm so sorry about my dad, and my mom—"

"What about your mom?" he inserted quickly.

She shrugged and studied her suede boots, unable to meet his gaze any longer. "She overshares sometimes. I-I'm sorry you had to hear that."

"Allie." At the touch of his fingers on her hand, she looked up. "You don't need to apologize."

The sincerity in his eyes caused hers to well again. Great. Another reason for him to want nothing more to do with her. Who wanted to have to deal with such an emotional woman?

But the way he inched closer, breathed her name and wrapped an arm around her shoulders, suggested that Jai didn't really mind. And the way he drew her close to his side and pressed his lips to her hair, murmuring her name once again, said maybe he cared. He cared? How could he? She was such a mess, felt so hopeless it was all she could do to sit there stiffly, hoping he didn't notice just how awkward she felt in this moment when she could scarcely breathe.

Oh, she was so *hopeless* at this. She couldn't read a man if her life depended on it. And yet, for some inexplicable reason, Jai still hadn't left. He was still holding her near. She'd been so right about him all these years: he really was the loveliest human being.

"Allie. Your mom loves you. I think she'd be upset to know you're upset by what she said."

Yeah, he didn't know her mother that well. "I know she loves me. But I…sometimes I get the feeling that she would've been very happy with just two daughters."

"No."

"Y-yes." Her mind tracked back to all those times when her mother had taken her to medical and specialist appointments, even surgeries, with thinly veiled sighs and murmurs of the inconvenience this was. Her sisters, too, had not been backward in their complaints about how Allie got so much more attention at their expense. It was no surprise that they'd instead turned outwards and soon had scores of friends, while Allie had always struggled to connect. Except when it came to connecting online, where she could be as warm and witty as anyone else, it seemed, her brain and fingers tapping out her words the way she wished her tongue could. She winced.

"What is it?" He pulled back, eyes serious.

She swallowed. She was going to have to tell him about the fan forum, about starting *his* personal fan forum. She was going to—

"Allie, you can trust me. I know today wasn't easy, but you can trust me."

Could she, though? What if this admission proved the final straw?

"Allie, please. Tell me what was going on before."

Before? How much earlier did he mean? "You mean at home?"

He nodded.

Her mind spun back, and she shrugged, conscious his arm lay heavy across her shoulders. "I guess I f-felt like it was too much."

"There was a lot of food."

"No, I mean that I should have told you earlier about my superfan dad—"

"You did warn me." His lips pulled up on one side. "I thought it was the gray-haired couple down the front at church."

"The Hendersons?" Amusement spurted. "That would've been quieter for sure. He's deaf, so he doesn't say much."

"Ah."

"But it wasn't just that. It was the realization that I really don't fit in your world. I do art, not sports. You're famous, I'm not. I-I'm so very boring and ordinary and—"

"Clever and talented and beautiful and—" He stopped. "Whoa. Sorry."

The heart lifting stopped at that last word. "Sorry?" For calling her beautiful?

"For interrupting you there." He took her hand, gently kneading her knuckles with his thumb. "I couldn't help but notice today that some people talk over the top of you, seem to want to finish your sentences, and I don't want to do that."

Her throat cinched. He'd seen that? What else had he seen?

He glanced away. "Your mom had something else to say."

Great. Fount of information was her mom.

"She mentioned that you're fine talking with people you feel comfortable with." His grasp tightened. "Does that mean you feel comfortable with me?"

She nodded. "Yes."

"I'm glad," he said simply.

"Why?"

"Because I love hanging out with you. I love spending time with you."

"Even after today?"

"Yeah." His grin grew crooked. "Even after today."

She swallowed. "So...so you forgive me, for not telling you about it all?"

"Of course. But hey, there wasn't anything to forgive. I've gotta admit I was disappointed to not see any cardboard cutouts though."

Her smile froze. The ones she'd stashed in the closet in her room.

"Maybe I'll just have to visit again sometime."

"Really?"

"Well, yeah. If that's where you live, then that's where I want to be."

Her heart did a flappy-armed chicken dance. "Really?"

"Of course it is, Allie. What do I have to do to prove that I want to see where this relationship can go?"

He wanted a relationship? *Oh my goodness, oh good heavens, oh my word!*

His eyes darkened. "Actually, I know."

Any thought of further confessions was lost as he drew nearer still and gently clasped her face in his hands. He lowered his head, pausing for a tantalizing moment when his mouth was an inch from hers.

Her breath suspended. Was he going to kiss her? She'd never kissed anyone! What should she do? Close her eyes? Pucker her lips? Tilt her head? Thank God she'd not eaten salmon today! Oh my stars, he's getting nearer—

And as his lips touched hers, her eyes closed automatically and fire roared between them as her heart began to sing. This was heaven. Sweet perfection. Better than any dream.

Oh my stars!

Indeed.

CHAPTER 13

"Hey, Allie."

Her happy face shone at him from the computer screen. "Hi, Jai."

"I really wish I could've seen you in person today."

"I'm sorry. Work finished late, so I was speeding to get to church music practice on time."

"Do you think that's what they mean when they talk of Jesus taking the wheel?" he teased.

"Probably not," she said with a chuckle. "How was your day?"

He shared about training, about his mom's repeated plea that he bring his girl to meet her, about how some of his teammates' girlfriends were requesting the same—which was met with a blush and "maybe if they're there on Saturday"—then he returned the question.

His grin grew as he listened to her share about her work, including some special project for the deputy director, then her time at music practice. "We've got a new Sarah Maguire song and I love it. Her music always speaks to me."

Like Allie's joy always spoke to him.

Later, after she admitted her parents wanted to say hello,

which drew the conversation to a close far sooner than he wanted and without the lingering goodbyes they shared when it was just the two of them, Jai pushed back against the leather seat and contemplated this series of events.

So this was what it was like to have a girlfriend, to feel cared about and wanted. He understood why some guys on the team or in the Bible study group with wives or girlfriends seemed to offer less of themselves. They, like him, had given their focus, their heart, away to someone else. Not that he'd admit that to anyone yet, or that he'd said the *L* word. But as the weeks passed and the preseason came and went, with each day of connection he'd felt that word weaving more strongly through his chest.

He'd changed. Brent had noticed it back in Switzerland, when they caught up for a few meals. Jai had asked about Holly, and Brent had shared about her recent success in Venice, getting a bronze in the 500m final.

"I'm kinda relieved," Brent had admitted. "I wasn't sure if getting married and living between Detroit and Calgary would impact her training, but these results suggest it'll be okay."

"That must be hard, being apart like that."

Brent shrugged. "It's a heck of a lot easier than when she was living in Australia. I guess that perspective helps. One day I hope we can be in the same place full time, but you've gotta be thankful in whatever circumstance you face, right?"

"Right." A good reminder.

Brent eased back in his chair. "So, what about you? Is there someone back in Chicago?"

Jai swallowed. He hadn't admitted to anyone in the Bible study group—apart from Pastor Josiah, who had guessed—about the way things were with Allie.

"There is?" Brent's eyes widened. "Go on. Spill."

Jai shared a little about Allie, about her work, about how he felt outclassed by her in every way. Then he shared about her crazy family of fans.

Brent had laughed. "One thing I'm super thankful for is my in-laws. Nicest people you could hope to meet. I know Holly misses them, and we hope to visit next summer in our break. But hey, with them living in Australia, it means they'll never be in our face."

Now, Jai glanced out his apartment window and groaned. Not that he was thinking in-law status just yet, but a little less "in your face" would be nice. When he returned with Allie to her parents' after that infamous Sunday lunch—after that amazing, heart-hitching first kiss—they'd been greeted with concern and consternation.

"We didn't know where you were, Allie," her mom had complained. "We were about to send out a search party."

"I left my phone behind," Allie explained.

"That was my fault," Jai owned. "I insisted on taking her out."

"But why?" her mom asked as Allie's dad's eyes widened.

Jai exchanged looks with Allie. "Because I like her, and I like going out with her."

"What?" Allie's mom rounded on her. "You mean these dates…"

"Were with me," Jai said, hooking an eyebrow at Allie. "They were with me, right? Unless you've been seeing other guys."

"No other guys," she said softly, her face holding that same luminous glow it'd held since he first kissed her. What a kiss that had been…

"Allison Enid Davis—"

He caught the way she winced at her middle name.

"Do you mean to tell me you and Jai Mullins are dating?" her mother said.

He loved how Allie's parents always used both his names when referring to him, like there were a dozen other men named Jai floating around the place.

Allie shot him a look, her cheeks pinking as he nodded. "Y-yes."

He grasped her hand, threading his fingers with hers. "Most definitely," he asserted.

Her parents shared simultaneous blinks, looked at each other, then looked at them both, their expressions hovering in the regions of shock and confusion.

It'd only been when Jai lifted Allie's hand to kiss the back of it that her parents had seemed to snap out of their astonishment. They'd rushed at them and engulfed them in fierce hugs and loud cries of joy that'd made him wonder at their level of enthusiasm and whether this relationship was worth having to put up with this degree of affection all the time.

But Allie *was* worth it, he knew. And while things had been a little awkward with her family, over the past few dates things seemed to have settled into a version of normality he supposed he could live with. Peter was always wanting his insider tips on hockey, and Merrilee was always happy to share more Allie stories. While he tried to be polite for Allie's sake, he was glad that not many dates required parental involvement. Allie's work being near his apartment meant they could spend more time together here in the city rather than on Elm Drive.

Jai released a breath, his mind flicking to her comment during their earlier chat. This Saturday night would be the first time she attended one of his games as his official girlfriend. Her work commitments and his away games had postponed things until now, and he couldn't help the rush of anticipation now that she had finally agreed to meet some of his teammates and their girlfriends. Beau was also likely to be there, as Chicago was playing Arizona, and Jai knew this would prove a big deal. It was one thing to mention Allie to Brent, but to have her meeting Beau, with his charm and goalie swagger, made Jai's stomach clench a little. He knew she was nervous about meeting the other girlfriends, but meeting a guy who Jai considered almost like a brother was another thing. Still, if this relationship was to have any future, there could be no secrets. And Allie was fast making a grand statement in his life.

~

IF ONLY THE girls on the online fan forum could see her now.

Allie studied her reflection. Jeans, her suede boots, and her well-loved, well-worn Mullins jersey, the one without this year's A. She lifted her hair. To ponytail or not, that was the question.

"Put it up," Carissa commented from the door. "You'll look cute."

"Cute?" Allie made a face.

"You don't want cute? It's kind of hard to go for sophisticated wearing that." Carissa gestured to Allie's ensemble.

"You don't think this is okay?"

"It's perfectly fine," Carissa assured, but with a tweak to her lips that suggested she was being generous.

"Okay, fine. What would you do?"

Carissa grinned and moved forward to adjust a few things, pushing Allie's long sleeves up and fetching a belt that drew her jeans in a little tighter. "Now, earrings, makeup and hair."

"I don't want to be overdressed."

"Honey, have you seen how some of those girls dress?"

Allie nodded, trying to keep the misery from her face. The wives and girlfriends, or the WAGs as some called them, had a reputation for dressing in a style that was far removed from Allie's usual attire of business shirts and skirts. Whenever she'd attended games before, it had always been a simple matter of jeans and jersey and no fuss. But now, knowing she'd be expected to meet some of these people she'd seen talked about on online forums—not that she'd ever permitted her forum to get so nasty—she knew a certain standard in her appearance was expected, which put her in as much of a nervous state as did the expected conversation. What would people say about her?

A few minutes later, having succumbed to more of Carissa's ministrations and advice—*Just be yourself!* Yeah, right—Allie was at the top of the stairs, and Dad called that it was time to go.

He and Mom were taking her, while Carissa and Jake, and Marcie and Steve drove separately. Jai had promised to drive Allie home, so she didn't have to feel *too* little kid about it.

Except this time on the drive to the United Center, sitting in the back seat like she'd done a hundred times before, she was conscious of a new feeling of respect from her father. It was there in the way he kept eyeing her in the rear vision mirror when he asked her opinion on something about the Hawks, something he'd rarely done before. He usually spouted his opinions like they were foolproof claims of gold and expected others to agree. Which she had never really minded, knowing his was a personality inclined to get carried away and say things he might later regret.

Like when he'd asked her earlier this week if there was any way he could attend the post-game function she was attending with Jai tonight. She shivered. Thank goodness Jai hadn't been there to hear him. She'd been hard pressed to know how to fob Dad off, thankful for Mom's intervention when she said, "Oh, Peter, don't be so silly. This is Allie's chance to make a good impression. She won't want you getting in the way and stealing the limelight." Yeah, like Allie had ever craved the limelight for a second in her life.

But her mom's voice of reason seemed to have swayed her dad to sense, and he'd agreed not to do or say anything that would embarrass her. Not that he would ever do that deliberately, she knew. It was just that sometimes things had a way of happening.

They pulled into the parking lot and were soon in the crowds threading in long lines outside the arena. Red-white-

and black jerseys were worn by most, punctuated here and there by a sprinkling of brick-red and white, symbolizing allegiance to the Coyotes.

"Are you excited?" Dad asked her.

"Yes," she said as if he hadn't asked that ten times before.

"Don't worry, honey. You'll be great," Mom said, patting her arm. "Just remember that if you don't want to feel like all eyes and ears are on you, then turn your eyes and ears toward another."

Uh huh. Mom's advice for the ages. Sure had worked out well before.

But maybe there was truth to it. This morning as she'd been reading her Bible, she'd felt a conviction to not be so self-focused, to see if she could treat tonight as a chance to be a blessing to whomever God put her in contact with. And maybe that would mean staying in the background, being observant, being the eyes and ears that God might somehow use to bless another person. Maybe tonight didn't have to be all about her own personal comfort and enjoyment.

Exhalation. She could do this. "Let's go, Hawks."

THE UNITED CENTER was an awesome place to watch a game, with twenty thousand fans screaming their support punctuated by music and lights and everything that pumped the atmosphere into extreme. But this time felt very different, Allie's heart in her mouth as she watched Jai in the pre-game warm-up skate. He'd said he'd look for her in the stands—they were in Dad's usual rink-side seats—and she was waiting, waiting for him to notice her.

His helmeted head lifted, and as if an electric wire stretched between them, his gaze found hers, zapping her straight to the heart. He smiled, lifted a hand, and she felt another jolt of energy.

"Hi, Jai!" Dad bellowed.

"Dad!" Allie tugged his jersey to get him to sit down.

"What?" Dad said, still at mid-roar. "You can't expect me not to want to say hi to your boyfriend, can you?"

She heard mutters of "Boyfriend?" around them, leading her to slink down in her seat.

Thanks, Dad, for not wanting to embarrass her.

Jai nodded and skated off, his focus returning to the drills they were executing as the lights and sounds continued.

The Jumbotron displayed the Hawks' pre-game video, and she watched the snippets displaying this Original Six team's long and storied history. Several Championship Cups, the most recent many years ago—they were well overdue. Dozens of Hall-of-Famers. Snippets of players from previous games, smiling, joking, laughing. Video of action—some of the big hits, the great goals, those moments that caused the crowd's anticipation to build. One goal.

Then the countdown began, complete with player introductions for those who were on the first line and would begin the game today.

"And from Chicago, Illinois, please make some noise for our homegrown number seventeen, Jai Mullins," called the announcer.

Her pulse climbed, and the crowd cheered as the red spotlight briefly highlighted the man she'd kissed the other day. How bizarre to think this could be true, that he actually felt something for her.

The anthem was sung—as the crowd performed its usual cheering throughout—and she watched him finally move into position. *Lord, keep him safe.*

The horn sounded, the puck dropped, and the game began.

. . .

"Wow. Awesome game," Dad said as he finally resumed his seat after cheering for the win. Around them, the crowd had started to disperse, the win against the Coyotes pretty conclusive at four goals to one. The fact that Jai had scored two assists as he helped their captain score only cemented this feeling of excitement.

But watching the game was a completely different thing to what was coming next. The action-packed game had distracted Allie from the knowledge that she now had to socialize. She'd have to pretend she was peppy as fear stole inside.

She watched the players exit, eyes trained on the man wearing seventeen, wondering if he'd turn and acknowledge her.

"Hey, Allie." Dad stole her attention. "We might need to leave. The traffic will be a nightmare. Now, don't forget to take lots of pictures and tell me everything you see."

"Okay."

"Wow, he played so good!" Carissa said, giving her a hug before smoothing Allie's hair. "Don't forget, have fun tonight!"

"Yes, ma'am."

Jake nodded, and Allie managed a smile that broadened when Marcie drew close to give her a hug. "I still can't believe my sister is going out with a Hawk. You could've knocked me down with a feather when Mom and Dad told us. How amazing is our God?"

Steve gave her a thumbs-up, then it was her mother's turn to hug her. "Have fun tonight. Remember, don't be nervous. And you don't have to feel the need to talk. Just listen and have fun."

She nodded, turning back to the ice only to see the players had all disappeared.

Great. That decided it. Next time she was going to sit by herself.

She stayed seated, glancing at her phone, wondering what to do now. This part had been a little unclear. Jai had said he'd message her, but she didn't know exactly how that would work. Didn't they need to have cool-downs and showers and things? How long would she be sitting here as everyone else left and the cleaners moved in to attend to the stands?

"…girlfriend."

She froze at the hushed whispers behind her and turned to see someone lift up their phone. A bright flash dazzled her, and the girls giggled and hurried away before she could find wits enough to realize what had just happened. Had someone just taken her photo? Oh my goodness. What did she look like? What would people say? Would they wonder how she could dare to call herself Jai's girlfriend?

Her phone buzzed, and she snatched it up, her fingers trembling.

COME TO THE TUNNEL, Jai had texted. TELL FRANK WHO YOU ARE.

Frank? Who was Frank? And what tunnel?

She grasped her bag and rose, glancing behind her, but it seemed the girls had gone. An enquiry of the cleaner proved the riches of embarrassment as she struggled to make the man understand. "Where is the t-tunnel?"

"What tunnel?"

Should she show him the message on her phone? Of course not. *Don't be silly.* As if Jai would want her to show anyone.

"You exit that way," he said helpfully, pointing to a green-and-white sign.

She nodded, thanked him, and moved up the steps to the concourse. Another enquiry of an attendant and she was once again directed to the exit. "Move it along now."

No. She had to find Jai. She pulled out her phone and tapped a message. I DON'T KNOW WHERE TO GO.

"Miss? Come along now. Just follow those signs to exit there."

"B-but I have to meet J-Jai."

"Who?" The burly security guard looked her over. "Lady, what you have to do is leave. Now, don't turn a good night into a bad night by being difficult, okay?"

She nodded but felt the panic rise. If she exited like they wanted her to, down one of those long escalators, she knew she'd be dumped right outside with no way of getting back in. And now that her family had all left, she had no way of getting home. Not unless Jai was to come to her rescue again. I'M AT THE TOP OF THE CONCOURSE, she quickly tapped, AND THEY WON'T LET ME BACK DOWN.

"Miss! I'm going to ask you for the last time—"

Allie snatched up her phone and showed the man. "Th-this is from Jai."

"I don't care if it's a message from the president, you need to leave."

She jumped as a hand clamped on her shoulder.

"Is this person bothering you?"

Yes, she wanted to cry, until she realized this new security guard meant her. That Allie was supposedly the nuisance. She, who had been attending games here since she was a child, was being eyed askance by those nearby like she was a drunk troublemaker.

She shrugged away, panic rearing all the more. What should she do? What should she—?

Her phone buzzed, and she realized she had two missed calls from Jai. "Just l-let me check my messages," she pleaded.

"N-no," the evil guard mocked her.

Her heart seemed to shrink to the size of a pea while shame swathed her in a coat that felt sickening as it stole her words away. Tears blurring her vision, she pressed the phone to her ear and tried to listen above the noise and the guard's jeers.

"Allie?"

Her breath was shaky. Oh, what had Jai said? Why couldn't she hear?

"Allie!"

Another hand on her shoulder and she spun around in frustration only to see Jai's flushed and helmet-marked face, his hazel eyes filled with concern, and two guards' mouths hanging down as she flung herself into Jai's arms.

CHAPTER 14

"Hey." Jai drew Allie close to his chest as around them fans paused, mouths gaping as wide as the two men on security, who seemed a little too stern. "You're okay," he murmured closer to her ear.

A nod of her head, then she pulled back. But her big smile wasn't fooling him. "Hi. Great game t-tonight!"

"Yeah." Jai studied her, saw the red-rimmed eyes, then glanced at the burly men. "What happened?"

"Sorry, sir. We thought she was just another fan."

"Nope. She's with me. Allie"—he wrapped an arm around her shoulders—"meet Jeff and Graham."

She nodded, but he noticed she did not meet the men's eyes, nor did she smile. What had happened to make the ever-polite and gracious Allie so upset?

"Allie?"

She shook her head in that way she did when she didn't want to admit something unpleasant. But even if she did, this was hardly the time or place, especially given the number of spectators, some of whom had their phones out and seemed to be delighting in what was going on. He'd just need to find out from her later. "Come on," he said. "Let's get out of here."

Another nod and he drew her away, back to where the players entered. He was so glad that Allie had told him where she was so he had some idea of where to find her. But her agitation suggested that tonight might not be the best time for her to meet his teammates.

"Hey, Allie, do you want to meet the others? Or would you prefer me to take you home now?" He didn't really want to leave —he was excited about the thought of finally introducing his girlfriend to his team. But if she needed to leave, then he would do that too.

She shook her head. "We can stay. If you don't mind."

"You're sure?"

"Yes."

He exhaled. Okay, so maybe this evening could be redeemed. "Hey, I'm sorry. I probably wasn't too clear in my instructions before. Next time, you can use one of my allocated seats. That makes this whole thing so much easier. That way you can get to know some of the other family and friends of the team."

"To be honest, I'd be really happy to not sit with my dad again."

A chuckle escaped. "Yeah. He's kind of hard to miss, isn't he?"

Peter Davis, the motormouth dentist who was a legend in Chicago's arena, the season ticket holder with the at times pushy reputation. How had Jai managed to fall for such a man's daughter?

But he didn't need to wonder about that now, conscious that Allie needed his support and encouragement. Whatever had happened before had upset her, but at least she was putting it behind her now. He liked that about her, liked that she was willing to keep trying, even though he knew something like tonight would likely be quite intimidating.

"I'm really glad you're here. Thanks for staying," he said now.

She nodded, and he clasped her hand and kissed it, relieved to see the return of a smile he recognized as genuine.

He led the way down another corridor, where men pushing equipment and gear nodded and said hi, and he took the time to introduce her to them and to Frank and the other security guards. The more people who knew to keep an eye out for her the better.

Down another hallway, this one leading to the function room, where a trio of players gathered near the door before disappearing inside.

He steered Allie to one side and smiled, tucking a few strands of golden hair behind her ears. "Hey, have I told you how good you look in that jersey?"

"No," she said shyly.

"You look really good in that jersey," he murmured, wrapping one arm around her waist.

"I like the number," she said. "It's my favorite."

"Is it now?"

She nodded, and the sweet smile there was begging for a kiss.

After a satisfying moment, he drew back. "Wow." His gaze absorbed her glowing face, the tension from before lessened, before trickling down to her jersey, which he noticed was absent of an A. Huh. One of the older styles.

He plucked at her sleeve. "Have you had this a while?" he teased.

Her gaze dropped. "Maybe."

Or maybe she'd gone out and bought what she could afford, like lots of fans who couldn't keep up with the crazy prices for new jerseys every year. "I'll get you a new one," he promised.

"You don't have to," she demurred.

"I want to," he assured her. "Now, are you ready to meet the others?"

Her lips lifted, but he sensed from courage more so than joy. "Ready as I'll ever be."

"Just be yourself," he advised, "and they're gonna love you too."

~

THE CONFUSION and panic of earlier drained away at that one word. Had he just said what she thought he'd said? Oh, if she didn't ask now, she knew she'd die wondering.

She swallowed and dared to slant a glance at him. "Too?"

He exhaled. "Look, I really can't speak for them, so maybe we should just say they'll be sure to like you."

Like? Or love? It was way too soon for love. Even if his kisses seemed to suggest a leashed passion that her heart liked to explore play by play at night when she lay in bed. But like or love, the fact he seemed to be willing to put up with her, to come to her rescue again, made her appreciate him all the more. And even though this next thing scared her, she knew she could trust him to be as kind and thoughtful as he'd always proved to be.

"You ready?" he asked, crooking out his arm like an old-fashioned gentleman.

"Y-yes."

"Relax. You look beautiful. Come on, let's have fun."

He pushed open the door and murmured similar encouragement to her as he introduced her to various players, coaching staff, and the wives and girlfriends of his teammates.

"Hi! I'm Amber," said the captain's redheaded partner, holding out a manicured hand possessed of a half dozen rings. "It's so nice to finally meet you!"

Allie shook the model's hand, noticing her own lack of polished nails and bling. Something for Carissa to amend for next time. "Hi."

Maybe if she limited her social interactions to words of one syllable, she might be okay. Before she knew it, Amber had tugged her away from Jai and was moving her around the room, introducing her to others: Brittany, Natasha, Lauren, Nikki, Tanja. The names went on and on, and even though Allie had chatted about them on fan forums for years, it was so different meeting them in person, and she had a hard time trying to keep up with who was who. But it seemed that every one of them was super pretty and super bubbly and—her heart sank—super nothing like her at all.

She exhaled. Was she the only woman in this room who had some kind of vision impairment? Or was that because—she scanned the room again—she was the oldest woman here?

One of the wives, judging from the rings blazing on her fingers, offered a smile. "Good to see Jai finally brought someone."

Was her name Ella? One of the Scandinavian players' wives? "He hasn't brought dates before?"

"Never," she confirmed. "And I've been worried about him. He sometimes keeps to himself, so it's good he has a girlfriend."

Her friendliness put Allie more at ease. "Can you p-please remind me who matches up with whom?"

Her new friend laughed. "There is a lot to remember, yes? So many faces. But you'll get used to them in time."

Allie nodded. How many of these kinds of events would she need to attend? How much would she need to step out of her comfort zone to feel like she was fitting in? And did she want to fit in with this crowd? Long nails and tans and hair extensions had never been her thing, especially not working in the gallery and with small children as she did.

"And what do you do?" another pretty blonde—Brittany?— asked. "Abby, right?"

Her tongue seemed to suddenly be gnarled in knots, and she couldn't speak, much less answer. A smile and nod had to suffice as she drew in a deep breath. *Relax. Just be natural. Be yourself.*

Yeah, right. Because this was what happened when she tried to be herself.

The blonde's plucked eyebrows pushed up as she waited for Allie to reply. *Lord, help me!* Her tongue unclenched, and she drew in a breath and finally felt her words release. "Actually, my name is Allie." Her voice had that sing-song quality again. "I work at the Art Institute."

"And does a great job, too."

At Jai's voice, she felt herself relax a little more. He moved beside her, holding her hand and giving it a little squeeze.

"Hi, Jai!" the sunny blonde said.

"Hey, Brittany," he said, bending to kiss her cheek.

Allie knew an irrational spike of jealousy and tamped it down. How could she be jealous of a social kiss when she was the recipient of something so much better?

Jai squeezed her hand again. "That's how we met, actually. I took my nephew to one of the kids' art classes Allie ran and met her then."

That seemed so long ago now.

"Oh! I love art," Brittany said, turning to Allie with a smile. "You'll have to show me around sometime."

"That's what she does," Jai said. "You should go hear her talk about Impressionism. She really knows her stuff."

"Have you been to any art museums in Europe?" Ella asked.

Allie's shoulders relaxed a fraction more. "A few. I th-thought the Louvre was amazing."

"So amazing."

Somehow the conversation centered on art for the next few minutes, putting Allie at greater ease. Perhaps she could find common ground with these women. That thought seemed more confirmed a little later when she was invited by the captain's girlfriend to a special dinner to celebrate her upcoming birthday.

"Connor will be away," Amber confided, "and, so I've invited all the girls to come. But not everyone can. Some people work, some people have kids, but if you're free, it'd be good to have you come too." She told Allie the date. "What's your phone number? Let's swap numbers so we can stay in touch."

Her kindness touched that well of ever ready emotion, and Allie nodded, typing her number into Amber's sparkly high-end phone as Amber typed into Allie's.

How long had it been since she'd been invited to such a girlish thing? Had it been Marcie's girls night out before her wedding, when she'd attended along with lots of Marcie's friends and realized just how hard it was to socialize when she couldn't really speak? But maybe this time would be different. She'd been getting better these past eight years. Maybe by the time Carissa's girls' night out rolled around, she might be able to discharge her chief bridesmaid duties well.

"Hey, Allie," Jai said, intruding into her thoughts. "I want you to meet someone."

She turned and encountered the large presence of a smiling man she vaguely recognized as tonight's opposition goalie. He stuck out a hand, which she accepted.

"Allie, meet Beau. Beau, this is Allie Davis."

"Well." Beau's eyes crinkled. "Jai is certainly punching above his weight. Hey, Allie."

"Hello." She released his hand, glad to see his tease.

"Jai was saying you were a smart lady, and for a moment there I thought he meant smart because you'd chosen him, which really isn't a very humble thing to say, is it?"

She laughed.

"But now I see you *are* very smart, not just because you're with him but because you obviously have an excellent sense of humor."

"That she does," Jai confirmed, repossessing her hand only to wrap her arm behind his waist.

"I…I'm sorry about your loss," she said carefully to Beau.

"Sorry?" Jai said. "I thought you were a Hawks supporter from long ago. Why be sorry this guy lost when it means we won?"

Beau chuckled and halted a passing waiter. "Hey, this looks good. Allie, care to try some?"

"What is it?" she asked, eying the dark substance on what looked to be a rice cracker.

"Who knows?" Beau said, shoving one in his mouth. "Who cares? It sure tastes good."

"Dude," Jai said, shaking his head.

"Trying new things is the spice of life. Wouldn't you agree, Allie?"

She nodded, then smiled at herself. How ironic. She, the stuck-in-the-mud, no-friends stutterer pretending to be one of those adventurers who actually had experienced "the spice of life." But then, look at her here. Doing something new. Having fun. And even though the start of this part of the evening had been trying, it had worked out in the end.

Maybe it was time to live a little, to step out of the box of other people's expectations and see just what else this life might hold for Allie Davis.

~

"Did you have fun?" Jai asked as they sat in his car outside her parents' house. Well, not quite directly out the front. He hadn't wanted to run the risk of Peter feeling the need to come outside and check on his daughter. Or feeling the need to talk through the game with Jai in a blow-by-blow manner like he had with other games.

So here they were, late at night, in a dark car under a tree that shadowed some of the light being thrown by the street lamp nearby. He wondered how many of the neighbors remembered his car from that Sunday a few weeks ago. Then wondered how many of them were such active citizens that they participated in something like neighborhood watch.

"It was good," she said.

"It improved," he amended. "I know the start wasn't fun for you."

"What do you mean? The game was great. Apart from my dad, of course."

He smiled in the darkness, threading his fingers with hers. "What did he say?"

She shrugged, then sighed. "He made a loud comment about you being my boyfriend."

"What's wrong with that? It's true."

"Yes, but as soon as he said it, I had people around me whispering, and I think one of them tried to take my photo."

"You're a celebrity now," he teased.

"Yeah."

She sounded so glum that he tried to help her see the bright side. "It could be worse."

"How?"

"We could be in Canada. From what Mike and Dan have said, it seems some of those fans get a little possessive."

"They're not the only ones," she murmured.

"How do you mean?"

She stilled.

"You mean the people who were watching when I was trying to save you from those security guards?"

She groaned. "That was so embarrassing."

"Forget it. Although, now I think of it, what was the problem there?"

"No, you're right, we should just forget it."

He recognized a diversionary tactic when he met one. "What happened, Allie?"

"You're really stubborn, aren't you? Has anyone ever told you that?"

"A few people. What happened, Allie?"

"Nothing. I didn't know where to go or what the tunnel was, and neither did anyone I asked. Then I think they thought I was just some random person, and they wanted to send me home."

But surely that hadn't been enough to make her almost cry. "What else happened?"

"I...I don't think he meant it," she murmured.

Alarm rose. "Don't think who meant what?"

She sighed. "One of the guards at the end who you talked to. It...it s-sounded like one of them made fun of me."

"What? What did he do?" Indignation roared across his chest. He'd see the dude fired.

"I...I was trying to explain, and I kept stumbling over my words, and he...and he stuttered back at me."

Jai knew a cold kind of fury in his bones. "Which one?" he asked.

"I can't remember. It doesn't matter."

"It matters, Allie. Which one made fun of you?"

"I...I don't know. It was all so confusing, and there were more people taking photos and pointing, and I...I—" Her voice broke, and his heart broke for her too.

"Hey, shh, it's okay," he murmured, drawing her near. "You have nothing to be ashamed of."

She shook her head against his chest. "I...I don't want to be the cause of any trouble."

"Of course not. But neither should you be the victim of anyone, either. So if something like that happens again, I want you to tell me." He pulled back and eyed her seriously. "Coach talks about the need to lead in the moment, that it's often easier to deal with stuff straightaway, and if I'd known what they'd said, I would've dealt with it right then and there and you'd have an apology at least."

Allie took a shaky breath. "I'm s-sorry. I didn't know what to say."

"It's okay. It's not your fault, remember? If it's anyone's fault, it's mine." He sighed. "I should have realized my instructions weren't too clear and that it'd be really hard to figure out on your own. I haven't done this before either."

"Hey," she said, giving his hand a gentle squeeze. "It doesn't matter. It all turned out okay in the end."

"So, you did enjoy yourself? You liked Beau and the other girls?"

She chuckled. "I don't think Beau would like to be described as a girl, Jai."

He realized how his words had sounded and his lips curved at her return to tease.

"But yes, I did. I can see why he's your friend."

"He liked you. And he's right. I've definitely punched above my weight with you."

"Are you serious?"

"Deadly."

Her exhalation this time seemed tinged with heaviness. "You know, I was a little—okay, maybe a lot—surprised at the girls."

"What do you mean?"

"They seemed nice. Not at all how they get portrayed on some of those online forums."

Wait. She knew about online fan forums? He'd never figured classy Allie as the sort to know about those kinds of things. "You might want to steer clear of those places. I've heard stories that they're not the most edifying places to hang out."

"Not all places are bad," she protested.

"Have you visited them much?"

There was a long pause, then, "A bit."

"Allie, I don't want to come across all macho protective or

anything, but we've had to do some social media training, and all the statistics point out that people who hang around in those sorts of places tend to end up having all kinds of social and emotional challenges. I don't want you getting hurt by what some of the trolls out there might say."

She said nothing, and he squeezed her hand, deliberating over what to say. *Lord?* "I hate to say this, but some of those people who took your picture may post it in some of those places, so you need to be prepared to cope with such things."

"I never thought it would feel this way," she whispered. "I don't want to be the subject of other people's gossip."

"I wish I could say that you won't be, but it's probably best to be aware and prepared."

"Is that why so many of the wives and girlfriends always dress so nicely? In case someone takes a photo and they get mocked about their looks online?"

"You don't need to let it bother you. Not everyone dresses up. You might've seen pictures of Brent's wife, Holly, the Aussie skater? She doesn't bother with dressing up too much. She's pretty relaxed about that kind of thing."

Her smile flickered. "Isn't she a gold medalist? I'd think if you're like that you can afford to not care too much what others say."

"You don't need to care about what others think," he said softly. "I like what I see."

"You do?"

"I really like what I see," he said hoarsely. "I really like you."

Somehow her little sigh proved impetus for him to move closer, closer, until not even breath separated them. He took his time kissing her, caressing the soft skin of her cheeks, his fingers sliding to her neck and down her throat. She kissed him back with a fervency he hadn't quite expected but which fueled his own desire for more.

They kissed and they kissed, and the windows fogged up as

the air heated between them. Just when he reached that point of wanting to part her lips for more, he pulled back, blinking, chest heaving. "Wow."

"Wow." She touched her mouth. "I think my lips are swollen."

"Sorry."

"I'm not sorry," she murmured, her mischievous look eliciting his laugh.

"Okay. So we know there's nothing wrong with our chemistry."

"Nothing at all."

But chemistry without good management could lead to fiery consequences one didn't wish for. "I think we'd better take this slow."

"You might be right." She exhaled.

Silence filled the car as they sat there, once more holding hands.

"Are you on music at church tomorrow?" he asked.

"Yes." She sighed. "I suppose I should go inside soon. It must be late."

"I wish I could be there."

"Me too."

But he had a trip to New York tomorrow, which would see games down the east coast before he returned next weekend for his birthday. "Hey, you know my mom really wants to meet you."

"You've mentioned that."

"So you'll be free to meet her Saturday afternoon before the party?" The blessing of a road trip: a rare weekend off.

"Y-yes."

He pressed a kiss to the back of her hand, a far safer prospect than her lips. "There's no need to be nervous," he assured her. "I think she's been kind of worried about me, so you'll be like an answer to prayer—if she believed in such a thing."

"She's not a believer?"

"Once upon a time. Mind you, I think that's how she regards faith now—as a bit of a fairy tale."

She squeezed his hand. "I'll be praying for her."

His throat closed. How blessed was he to have found such a woman? "Thank you."

"Well, I'd better go, seeing as I have an early service and all."

"I'm sorry I won't be there."

"It's okay. I know your games during the season make that hard."

Yeah. With missing church, it showed just how important the online Bible study was proving to be. "I'll see you next weekend?"

She nodded, her pensive look enough to propel him from the car to walk her to the door and enfold her in a hug he hoped wouldn't be witnessed by her dad. "I hope you have sweet dreams," he murmured against her cheek.

"You too," she whispered back.

"Oh, they will be," he assured her.

"They will?"

He smiled, dusting the lightest of kisses across her mouth. "For I'll be dreaming about you."

~

HAWKS & SQUAWKS ONLINE CHAT

TubularBells: Can you believe it?
PucktheMagicDragon: I'll bite. What?
TubularBells: JM17's blonde lady friend.
PucktheMagicDragon: OMG!! Where?
TubularBells: In the stands tonight! She was with some big hairy dude who kept yelling about how she was Jai's girlfriend.
PipeDreams27: So not classy.

Destinysoffspring: Tacky trash.

TubularBells: Destiny!

PipeDreams27: Insert eye roll here.

PucktheMagicDragon: Pics or it didn't happen!

TubularBells: Give me a moment. Here.

PipeDreams27: Wow. Still don't get what he sees in her.

PucktheMagicDragon: Wait—I think I saw another pic of her somewhere else. Wait a moment while I find it.

Destinysoffspring: Did you see that pic of Amber? Is that a bun in the oven?

PucktheMagicDragon: OMG! No way! Imagine a little Grimmet!

Destinysoffspring: Gross. He should be with me.

TubularBells: Have you ever met him?

Destinysoffspring: No, but don't kill the dream.

PipeDreams27: That dream might be over if Amber is pregnant.

PucktheMagicDragon: She's so lucky…

PipeDreams27: Got that pic, Puck?

PucktheMagicDragon: Oh yeah! Here.

Destinysoffspring: Seriously? She looks like she's about to cry!

PipeDreams27: Ugly cry, too.

PucktheMagicDragon: Aww, don't be mean.

TubularBells: So who is she?

PucktheMagicDragon: I think someone on the other forum was there and they heard JM17 call her Abby.

PipeDreams27: Huh. Well she looks boring.

PucktheMagicDragon: I wonder why she was crying.

Destinysoffspring: Maybe JM17 broke up with her.

PipeDreams27: You wish, Destiny.

Destinysoffspring: That's an old jersey too. Three, four seasons ago?

TubularBells: Maybe she hasn't had a chance to buy a new one yet.

Destinysoffspring: As if any of those WAGs need to buy a thing. They just get their super-rich boyfs to pay for it all.

PucktheMagicDragon: You sound jealous.

Destinysoffspring: Just telling the truth.

PipeDreams27: You're full of it.

Destinysoffspring: The truth? Yeah, I like to think I am.

TubularBells: So she's Abby with a hairy friend. Her dad?

Destinysoffspring: He can't be a boyfriend if he's talking about our man Jai like that.

PipeDreams27: Brother?

TubularBells: Find out more. Good work, Puck, finding those pics.

PucktheMagicDragon: Thanks! I try.

ArtHeart101: Her name's not Abby.

PucktheMagicDragon: What? Why do you say that?

ArtHeart101: I know her.

PucktheMagicDragon: OMG!!!

"Allie, could you please come here and show me what to do?"

Allie withheld a sigh and moved to show Taylah how to access the computer file. Again. Was it unreasonable to expect Taylah to know what to do by now? Taylah, whose internship had somehow turned into a permanent, part-time position. How that had happened Allie did not know. Maybe an email or staff discussion had slipped by while she'd been so distracted by Jai.

Jai. Her chest knew a fluttery sensation. How wonderful was he? Another bouquet of flowers had arrived today with a simple note—not in his handwriting, she'd noticed—that said: *Miss you. J.*

When the flowers arrived this morning, she'd thanked God that Myra was in a meeting, as the other women's eyes had all rounded before they turned to her.

"Oh my gosh! How lovely!" Taylah had said like the college student she was.

"From your boyfriend?" Selina asked.

Allie had hesitated before finally admitting, "Yes."

"Oh my gosh!"

"Who is he?" Selina's eyes widened, then narrowed slightly.

"Just…someone."

"Is he famous?" Taylah asked.

Compared to a Kardashian or the Queen? "No."

Her fellow staff members both wore puzzled brows. "Then what's his name?" Selina asked at the same time Taylah said, "Where'd you meet?"

Avoiding the first question, and figuring the second was easier to hedge around, she said, "Ch-church." Well, that was where they'd properly gotten to know each other anyway.

As per any mention of church, this answer was met with dismay and disappointment, although Taylah asked if they could meet him. Allie had managed a creditable and incredulous-sounding "Whatever for?" for which Taylah had no answer, and soon the interest had died down, and they'd completed their shifts without further excitement. Until Taylah's computer had "malfunctioned" as she called it—*driver incompetence*, Allie privately thought—for the third time in as many days.

The phone rang, and Allie answered. "Hello, Public Relations and Learning, this is Allie."

"Ah, Ms. Davis. This is Meaghan Baldrick. Mr. Weinberger would like you to call in as soon as is convenient."

"Today?"

"Yes, today."

Allie glanced at the roster, knew if she left now she'd be free. "I can be there in five minutes."

"Perfect. I'll let him know."

Allie collected the folder that contained the material she'd been working on and rose.

"Where are you off to?" Selina asked.

"I have to speak to Meaghan about something." Admitting she was seeing Meaghan was easier than going through the potential ramifications of having to explain why she was going to see Mr. Weinberger.

"But what shall I tell Myra when she returns?" she asked.

Beau's comment from the other day flashed to mind. *Trying new things is the spice of life.* New things: like being assertive. "You can tell her what I t-told you."

Ten minutes later she was sitting in Mr. Weinberger's office, listening as he outlined his plan. He'd talked about building connections in the community and beyond, and she'd come prepared with a list of various businesses and organizations to hand to him. He seemed impressed, eyebrows raised, nodding as he read through the sheet.

"I'm pleased to see you've taken initiative with some of these," he said, tapping the paper. "Some of the others that I spoke to about this project didn't seem to treat the assignment as something of importance."

"If I'm asked to do something, I do my utmost to keep my word," she said. It was what the Bible said, after all.

"That quality seems to be getting rarer these days," he murmured.

His phone buzzed, and he glanced at the message before nodding. "Right. Well, I have another meeting I must attend, but I'm very glad to see this. Thank you."

She rose and made her way back to the staffroom, taking a slight detour to see some of her favorite pieces of art from the modern era. The painted tiles of woodlands reminded her of a trip her family had taken to Lake Superior many years ago, evoking a sense of peace and calm. She could almost feel some of the crazy clutter of her heart fade as she studied it. That was what was so special about art—the fact that it was created to be a reflection of one's imagination and heart, yet one's inspiration could be interpreted and lead to inspiration in others. Which reminded her. Her easel at home should be dusted off and revisited. Maybe this would be a good week to do so, given that Jai's road trip meant he wasn't around to distract her.

A glance at her watch and she hurried to the staffroom only to hear the conversation die as she entered. A glance between Selina and Taylah revealed nothing, but she couldn't help but wonder what they'd been discussing. It was stupid to be paranoid, but she had the strangest sense it had been about her.

"Myra still isn't back?" she asked, more to give a sense of normalcy to the room than because she cared.

"No," Selina said, adding, "Oh, is that the time? I have a talk."

"Me too," Taylah said, and she hurried to join Selina, looking suspiciously like she intended to pick up the conversation that had just died.

Oh well. Allie couldn't help what others might say.

Her shoulders relaxed, and she sat at her desk, relishing the quiet, which allowed her to concentrate on the work Mr. Weinberger had assigned her. Far from merely coming up with a list of businesses, she'd sought creative ways to connect beyond the usual realm of arts-minded donors and was investigating their mission statements and policies on public record to see how to marry the two.

Her cell phone buzzed, and thinking it might be Jai, she snatched it up.

Hɪ Aʟʟɪᴇ! Jᴜsᴛ ᴡᴏɴᴅᴇʀɪɴɢ ɪꜰ ᴜ ʀ ꜰʀᴇᴇ ᴛᴏɴɪᴛᴇ ꜰᴏʀ ᴅʀɪɴᴋs. Aᴍʙᴇʀ.

Really? Had Amber sent this to the wrong person? Allie rarely did drinks. She rarely did anything outside her usual safe box. She picked up the phone, preparing to tap out an apology.

But again, that suggestion to try something new hovered about—to see if that spice of life might exist or whether, if she stepped out of her comfort zone, God might use her to bless another. So instead of tapping out her regrets, she said: Tʜᴀɴᴋs ꜰᴏʀ ᴛʜɪɴᴋɪɴɢ ᴏꜰ ᴍᴇ. Wʜᴇʀᴇ ᴀɴᴅ ᴡʜᴇɴ?

. . .

"So you've worked there for how long?" Amber asked above the thumping bass.

"Nearly eight years," Allie said. Her dream job, straight from college to the work she'd always wanted.

"And you love it?" Amber leaned forward, her cocktail nearly spilling with the motion. "You wouldn't want to work anywhere else?"

Allie nodded. Then shook her head. Then realized how confusing that must look and said slowly, to ensure her words flowed as evenly as they could, "I love it there, but if something came up elsewhere, then I'd need to consider it at least."

"But what about Jai?"

Jai. This all felt too new to have to take into account his considerations. "We'd have to see."

Amber nodded, clutching at the silver beads that swung low across her chest. "You looking forward to his party this weekend?"

"Yes," Allie admitted, although that wasn't quite true. The thought of meeting so many of his friends and family members —including his mom—filled her with trepidation. Meeting new people, being judged by new people—it was so much fun when one couldn't talk without messing up one's words.

"He's lucky to have people who care," Amber said with a moroseness Allie didn't understand.

"H-how is work going for you?" Allie asked, hoping to change the subject and that the music would hide the stammer.

"I..." Amber shrugged. "It's okay, I guess."

"You'll p-probably think that I'm an idiot, b-but what exactly do you do?"

"I'm an influencer," Amber said. "I do hairstyling, modelling, and fashion tips, but I earn money by telling all my followers what they should buy and do."

"Like the Kardashians?" Allie joked.

"Please. I can only dream of being that popular."

Wait. This was a real thing? "So you tell people they should visit someplace and they will?"

"Usually." Amber tossed her red braid over her shoulder.

"How many followers do you have?"

"Maybe two hundred on Insta? I don't know exact numbers."

Wow. That was unexpected. She'd have thought the girlfriend of the Hawks' captain would have way more than that.

"Two hundred thousand, that is." Amber laughed. "I saw your face."

Oops. "I'm not good at not being honest," Allie admitted.

"That's why I like you," Amber said. She finished her drink and put it down on the table. "Did you know I asked a bunch of the girls to come tonight?"

Oh. Allie's chest tightened. So she'd been a last minute invitation.

"Every single one of them had an excuse, only some of which I believed. I mean, okay, the boys are away, so I get that the moms among them might need to look after their kids. But the others?" She shook her head. "Way to go to make the birthday girl feel special."

Compassion twisted anew, followed by a surge of gladness that she'd listened to her gut—or at least the Holy Spirit—and that nudge that insisted she go. "You don't have family nearby?"

"They live in a little town in Ohio and can't stand to see me flaunting all this." Amber gestured to her low-cut top, which left little to the imagination.

Shame writhed that Allie had once been so quick to judge women who dressed like this, when really they were simply beating hearts that God loved too.

"I'm so sorry," Allie said, remorse stinging in a hundred guilty pinpricks. Amber, she of the two hundred thousand followers, was lonely. *Lord? What do I do?*

She glanced around, saw that the bar had a restaurant

nearby. "Do you want to have dinner with me? I know you probably have plans alread—"

"I'd love to," Amber said quickly. "I was going to drink myself silly then pour myself into a cab, but I'd much rather have dinner with you."

"My treat," Allie said, feeling a rush as she lifted her glass. "Happy birthday, Amber."

"Whoo! It is now. Happy birthday to me!"

"SO, ARE YOU READY?" Jai picked up Allie's hand and kissed it. Their kiss back at her house had been far less tame, and he knew he'd have to keep a lid on the simmering passion. But she was too easy to enjoy, and her eager response made it hard to refrain. And being apart for a week had made their reunion more special.

"Yes."

He chuckled. "You don't look convinced."

"I don't tend to do well with new people."

"What do you mean? Connor told me he felt so bad about missing Amber's birthday, but then you were there and she called him to say she has a new best friend."

"Oh." Her lips curved. "It ended up being more fun than I thought."

"She obviously thought so too and couldn't stop singing your praises. So if Amber Monroe thinks that, then my mom and sister are going to love you."

He hoped so, anyway. Mom, he was pretty sure, would be a solid yes. Kat would be a tougher sell, suspicious as she always was of people from a different background or more formal education than her. But hey, Allie was way more educated than he was, and they got on just fine.

He pulled up outside his mom's place, the first destination

for this afternoon of celebrating his third decade on the planet. Age might be just a number, but it felt good to finally be making choices he hoped would track toward his future. He glanced across at Allie.

She smiled. "What?"

"Nothing. Except you look really pretty."

"Oh. Thanks. Blame Carissa."

"Are she and Jake coming?" He caught the way her face tensed at that name. "What is it?"

She shrugged. "I think so? I don't know for sure. Carissa is plenty bossy when it comes to me, even though she's younger by three years, but she never steps out of line when Jake tells her what he wants to do."

His heart tensed as a red flag waved, Kat's situation still too raw. "Does nobody ever point that out to her?" he asked as calmly as he could.

"I don't think Mom and Dad see it, but I…" She stopped.

"You what?"

Another shrug. "He's not the kind of man I think Carissa deserves."

"What do you mean?"

"Sometimes I get the feeling he thinks I'm an idiot. He looks at me like I'm a fool."

"If he thinks that, then he's the fool."

"Right?"

He chuckled. "I'll pray for them."

"Thank you." She squeezed his hand. "It's weird, because I'm her maid of honor, and yet I sometimes wonder if he's the right man for her."

"You should talk to her."

"I've tried, but she tends to ignore me."

The front door opened, and he knew he'd have to exit before Mom moved down the path. He got the bouquet from the backseat and hurried to open Allie's door. She eyed the flowers, then him, and he smiled apologetically. "They're for my mom. To say thank you for having me thirty years ago."

The soft expression she offered was probably better than if he'd given her the flowers himself. "You're so sweet."

"You know it."

"And so humble."

"Right?"

She laughed as they moved hand-in-hand up the path to where his mom and sister waited, Mom studying Allie as she might a discounted Sears coat.

He gave his mom the flowers and both her and Kat a hug, then drew Allie closer.

"Mom, Kat, I'd like you to meet Allie. Allie, this is Bev, and Kat, my sister."

"Allie, welcome," Mom said.

"Th-thank you," Allie murmured, her smile shy, as he'd known it would be. Look at him, reading her like a book.

"Come inside," his mom invited, and Allie did, handing Jai her coat.

The next half hour passed in an exchange of get-to-know-yous, with Kyle running in and out like he was on speed. Kyle had certainly made his presence felt when he was introduced to Allie. He'd tilted his head and announced, "Hey, I remember you. You're the lady who talks funny."

Allie had pressed her lips together while Kat yelled at Kyle for being rude.

"He is right, though," Allie admitted. "I...I d-don't always s-speak well, especially when I-I'm nervous, so I guess that must sound f-funny."

Jai squeezed Allie's hand as he watched some of his sister's defensiveness fade from her face.

"You don't need to be nervous, Allie," Kat had said. "If Jai loves you, that's good enough for me. He's a pretty good judge of character."

Jai's eyebrows, which had shot up in warning at the *loves* word, had lowered again as he recognized the reason for his sister's comment. Yeah, he'd been unsure of Kat's husband from the moment he first met him, but with Kat pregnant and determined to reach the altar no matter what, he'd bitten his lip and kept his mouth shut—only to regret that decision ever since.

"So, who else is coming tonight?" Mom said now.

Jai listed some of his teammates who had RSVPed, Pastor Josiah and Gloria, and some other friends. It didn't seem any of the Bible study guys could come, but he'd known the competing schedules would make that tough. "Oh, and some of Allie's family, who I've gotten to know at church."

His mom looked between them. "So it's getting serious between you?"

"Mom," he protested.

She chuckled as he felt the heat of embarrassment shimmer in waves off Allie. Yeah. Totally knew how that felt. He drew in a breath. Oh well. Tonight should be fun.

"Jai!"

"Speed Machine!"

"We're gonna have a match-up and see who's the fastest."

"He's thirty. Can't keep this up forever."

Jai laughed, enjoying the camaraderie and jokes as he was engulfed in bear hugs, back slaps, and affection.

Turning thirty was supposed to be one of those big numbers worth celebrating, and judging from the number of people in attendance here tonight, it seemed his friends agreed.

The surprise arrival of Brent, Beau, and Dan had touched him more than they'd suspected, each man taking a precious day off to spend the evening with Jai. And meet Allie too.

"So, this is the famous Allie Davis," Brent said. "Hi."

"Hello," she said, cheeks pinking.

"I hear you're keeping the Speed Machine out of trouble." Brent slid Jai a smirk.

"It's a tough job, b-but someone needs to," she said solemnly.

Beau laughed. "See? Told you. Smart as she is pretty. You know she works at the Art Institute?"

As Dan began discussing art with her, Jai marveled at how she seemed to fit in, chatting easily with these friends he regarded as brothers. She seemed to be more relaxed with some of the others, too, smiling and talking with Amber and Ella like she'd known them for years, not mere weeks.

Friends, family, music, food, speeches, bad karaoke—the night was all he'd hoped for and more. Of course, not all of the karaoke had been bad. Dared by Kat, he'd dragged Allie up on stage and made her sing "Islands in the Stream" with him, something that showcased both his utter terribleness but also her awesome voice, which had seen requests for more from her.

She'd laughed, politely declining, and he'd wondered at how someone so unassuming could find the confidence to do such a thing before remembering that she'd nearly always had assurance when she could sing. But when her mom murmured that he was so good for Allie, that he'd given her so much confidence, he wondered again how much Allie's mom knew her own daughter. For he suspected that Allie had always had the willingness, just not been given the opportunity. And it made him wonder just what else Miss Allison Davis had in store.

~

HAWKS & SQUAWKS ONLINE CHAT

TubularBells: Did you see the pics of JM17's party?
PucktheMagicDragon: NO! WHERE?
TubularBells: Whoa, Puck, stop shouting.
PucktheMagicDragon: SORRy—had caps on. (oops)

TubularBells: Here.

PucktheMagicDragon: OMG! Is that Brent Karlsson?

PipeDreams27: Is that Dan Walton? He's FINE! I'd have his babies.

Destinysoffspring: Not if I get there first.

CoolplayismyJam: Is that Amber? And Brittany? And the non-Abby?

Destinysoffspring: I still don't understand what JM17 sees in her.

TubularBells: You don't have to. He must see something though.

Destinysoffspring: Did you see the pics of her and Amber getting drunk?

Destinysoffspring: Here you go.

PucktheMagicDragon: How do you know that's alcohol?

Destinysoffspring: bc Amber is in AA.

PipeDreams27: Get real!

Destinysoffspring: She's like, so fake. And looks like this Abby chick is just the same.

PucktheMagicDragon: Why do guys like them always go for girls like that?

Destinysoffspring: Abby needs new glasses. Or JM17 does. She's too ugly for him.

PucktheMagicDragon: Destiny! Be nice.

PipeDreams27: Her clothes make her look fat.

PucktheMagicDragon: Pipe! Pipe down. You girls are just jealous. I bet she's nice in person.

TubularBells: Where's ArtHeart when we need her?

Destinysoffspring: I want to know where Abby works. She looks like an accountant.

PucktheMagicDragon: You sound like a stalker, Destiny.

Destinysoffspring: She stole my boyfriend.

PipeDreams27: You're crazy. I'm out.

PucktheMagicDragon: Yeah. Be nice. If JM17 is happy—and

those pics with her say he is—then we should be happy for
him too.

Destinysoffspring: I'm not.

TubularBells: Maybe we should find out where ArtHeart works.
Didn't ArtHeart say JM17 once visited there?

Destinysoffspring: You think ArtHeart works at an accountancy
firm?

TubularBells: Or an art supplies store.

PucktheMagicDragon: OMG! You're such a detective.

TubularBells: Sorry I mentioned anything. Goodnight!

CHAPTER 16

November rolled into December and all the fun and fuss of Christmas and New Year. It was so strange and lovely to share this holiday season with Jai, to feel the times of family connection were cementing this relationship into something more like what his mother seemed to believe. That perhaps Allie might find a future with this man who drew her from her safe world into something more daring—such as visiting the top of the John Hancock building for a special New Year's Eve celebration.

For someone who had never liked heights, peering out from the top of the building was as terrifying as it was beautiful. The sun descended to the horizon over roads that stretched in straight lines for miles, their lights twinkling in the twilight like gilded dewdrops along a giant glowing spider-web. Queues of red car lights contrasted with the muted pastel windows of city skyscrapers, and the sun's last golden rays blanketed everything in rose.

"This is gorgeous," she breathed.

"This is certainly that," Jai said, leaning close to press a kiss to her cheek.

Her skin seemed to vibrate at his touch. And yet sometimes she didn't know if they'd gone too fast too soon. For someone who'd never kissed a guy, she seemed to have figured out what to do pretty quickly, or so Jai had teased, responding to her embarrassed admission of weeks ago. But now she just wanted more of him, to feel more of him, and her Christian boundaries were being put to the test by the euphoric pleasure that kissing him brought. Because whatever lay in their future, this relationship could not be pushed into anything more physical unless two rings were on her finger.

"You know what?" Jai said after their delicious dinner was followed by more snuggling in front of the huge picture windows overlooking Chicago's night lights. "I have a feeling that this new year will be the best one yet."

"Is that because you're playing so well?"

His chuckle vibrated warmly in her ear. "Maybe. Or maybe it's because I'm with you."

His words exploded in her heart like the fireworks with their red, blue, and gold sparkles. "You might have to stay with me then," she said.

He tensed. "Allie, I…"

"Oh my goodness! I didn't mean *that*. I just meant that you'll need to stick with me. That you're stuck with me. That—oh, I can't believe you would think I'd ever suggest *that*."

His chuckle rippled through his chest. "I didn't think that. Not really."

"Good."

"Good."

And it was good. *Very* good, as his kiss goodnight proved. As were his words, murmured in the car amid very thorough kisses: "I love you, Allie Davis."

She drew back, the heat of his lips on hers burning sense from reality. Had Jai Mullins, the great Jai Mullins, just said what she thought he had? Was this one of her fantasies? Her dream come true? "You love me?"

"Yes." He smiled, whipping her heart into a giddy flame.

"But why?"

He chuckled. "How can I not? You're everything I think wonderful."

He even seemed serious. This dear, *dear* man. She pressed her lips to his. "The most wonderful person is you. I love you too."

"Really?" His eyes shone in the streetlight.

"Yes," she assured him. She couldn't even begin to articulate the qualities that endeared him to her, those things she pondered over late at night that made her heart sing and dream and dance.

And as he kissed her long and deep until her soul seemed to shiver, well, okay. Maybe this would be the best year ever.

"THAT'S LOOKING GOOD, DEAR," her mother said, eyeing Allie's creation with a nod.

"Thanks, Mom." Allie dipped the paintbrush into the water and wiped it on a rag.

"Is Jai coming for dinner?" she asked, hope shining in her eyes.

"Not tonight."

"Oh. Is everything still going well with you two?" Mom asked anxiously.

"Yes." But she sensed her word would never satisfy her mom's need for explanations.

January had begun with a rush of resolutions. Paint more: check! Try more new things, like eating Egyptian food: check! Own her life choices and not be swamped by the overwhelming emotions and experiences that came with simply being in Jai's presence. It might not yet be a total check, but she was working toward it. There was enough pressure boiling away in this house already with the lead-up to Carissa's mid-February wedding.

For someone who could easily make so many decisions about other people's lives, Allie's younger sister had a surprising lack of decisiveness about a day that most people would consider the most important of their lives. If it wasn't questions over her dress, then it was questions about the food at the reception venue. She dithered about everything, from the color of the bridesmaids' dresses to what flowers the men should wear in their buttonholes.

"Mom! I can't find it!"

Her mother sighed at Carissa's cry, and after patting Allie on the shoulder, moved downstairs to whatever new drama seemed to be flavoring Carissa's day.

"Lord, help her," Allie mumbled aloud, which spurted prayers for her sister's peace, for Mom's wisdom, for whatever was lost to be found, even for—her nose wrinkled—Jake.

Allie's concerns over Jake's behavior—he'd said some things to Marcie's little boys at Christmas that had raised eyebrows and Steve's voice—had been shoved under the rug called keeping the peace, nobody wanting to add to the pressure filling the house on Elm Drive. Except, sometimes Allie wondered if God wanted her to speak to Carissa, to remind her she had options, that she didn't have to settle for Jake. Those kinds of questions had Allie in such a dither of her own that it was almost a pleasure to go to work. But even there it was a little strange.

Allie tilted her head, studying the landscape before nodding and adding a touch more green as her thoughts whirled back to work. The start of the new year had seen a change in shifts, and Allie had been on fewer tours as Myra, for some reason beyond sense, seemed to think Allie's skills would best be used in the Pacific and Asian art rooms, far from Allie's beloved European paintings. She didn't mind too much—she'd had years of talking about her favorites, after all—but she couldn't help but wonder if she'd done something that had put her on the outer.

Selina and Taylah seemed thick as thieves, and Allie often felt like she was left out, as the conversations that would cease at her arrival seemed to prove. Myra, too, was often absent, which meant there was a degree of friction and tension that Allie didn't really understand. Sometimes Selina or Taylah would ask a question about Allie's boyfriend that made her wonder if they knew the truth about Jai. She didn't want to hide Jai, but neither did she want for him to feel used, so when he asked to pick her up from work, she often refused. In these ways, having her independence gave her a sense of breathing room, that this relationship need not hurtle too fast to some inevitable place she wasn't sure she was ready for yet.

When he asked to meet her after games, sometimes she would, other times she'd go home with her parents. She still stayed in contact with Amber and Ella and some of the other wives and girlfriends, but by no means did she consider herself an integral part of their social scene. Which was good. It helped her feel more like herself—that she wasn't being consumed by Jai's world.

She placed the paintbrush back in the water container and studied the canvas before her. The trees—which had been in full leaf when she started but now wore clumps of white and ice— glowed in a vibrant landscape of color. Another way to feel more like herself—she was keeping a promise she'd made herself at New Year's: finish a painting by the end of January. She'd forgotten the joy of creating and had relished the chance to do something so different to Mr. Weinberger's reports and the talks she gave at work. There was life and energy and passion and joy in creating art. It was addictive, probably like Jai felt about hockey.

Chicago was tracking to make the playoffs, even though it

was only mid season, and she was happy to cheer him on both from the stands and watching on TV. For some away games, she'd go and visit Amber at the apartment where Amber lived with Connor. Often these times proved more than mere opportunities to watch their guys, as Allie felt little promptings of what to share with Amber.

Lord, help me to be a friend. Another dab of paint, another smear of viridian green. A touch of umber, a little ochre to add depth. If she finished it by the end of January, she could get it framed for Carissa's wedding on February the fifteenth.

"Allie?" Her sister's screech punched through her thoughts and pushed her to her feet.

She placed the brush in the water pot and turned the painting away from where Carissa might see. "What is it?"

"Have you seen it anywhere?"

"Seen what?"

"My wedding sample album."

"No."

Carissa sighed, and in leading lady fashion, flung herself on Allie's single bed. "Everything is so hard."

Allie swallowed, her thoughts from earlier spinning faster as a nudge to speak to her sister pressed harder. "M-maybe you could delay it," she suggested.

"Delay it? Delay the wedding? Are you crazy?"

Apparently, judging from that look on Carissa's face. "If it's making you stressed—"

"I'm not stressed. I just want—need—things done in a certain way," Carissa insisted.

Or was that Jake's certain way?

"Why are you looking at me like that?" Carissa frowned. "Don't you want me to be married?"

Allie bit her lip, the truth stubbornly locked inside.

Carissa gasped. "You don't, do you?" Her eyes welled with tears. "How could you be so cruel?"

"Is it cruel to want my sister to be happy?" Allie asked.

"I *will* be happy. As soon as I'm married on February fifteen."

"You don't need to be married to be happy," Allie said softly.

"Really? What would you know? I bet you're just jealous because I'm getting married before you."

Allie's heart hurt, and not just with the tiniest pang that said her sister's words had once been true. "I'm not jealous," she assured her.

But it seemed her sister hadn't finished. "I bet you're just jealous that Jai hasn't even said he loves you yet."

If only she knew. Allie held her tongue. For four seconds. "In case you hadn't noticed, I'm not like you. I've never been the sort to go announcing it to the world every time a guy talks to me."

"Is that because no guy has talked to you apart from Jai?"

Hurt flared across Allie's chest, and she turned, busying herself with her pots and paints, blinking back emotion. It didn't matter. Her sister was stressed. Allie would forgive her. Soon.

"Allie, I'm sorry," Carissa whispered. "I didn't mean it."

Yeah, except… "It kind of felt like you did," Allie said, her voice a little wobbly.

"I *am* sorry."

Any doubt about the sincerity of her sister's apology was lost as Carissa flung herself at Allie, wrapping her in a huge hug. "Forgive me. I've just been so stressed, and I know I'm taking it out on others, and I don't want to, but it's kind of hard not to."

"We can all do that," Allie murmured, stroking her sister's beautiful smooth hair, her heart easing at the moment of restoration with her sister. Her ever-emotional sister, so quick to fly off the handle, so quick to express contrition. Now wasn't the time to say anything about Allie's doubts about her sister's husband-to-be.

"I don't mean to," Carissa said again. "It's just that everything feels so overwhelming."

Allie wrapped her arm around her sister and sat beside her on the bed. "What feels so hard? What can I do to help?"

Carissa sniffed, and Allie found a tissue box and handed it to her. Her sister wiped her mascara-bled eyes. "You've been great. Organizing the bridesmaids' dresses, helping pick the colors for the venue, arranging the flowers and the bachelorette party." She blew her nose. "I don't know. I guess sometimes I just wonder…"

"Wonder what, Carissa?" Allie's pulse increased.

Her sister shrugged. "I wonder if…" She glanced down, studied her engagement ring, the one Jake had said cost him a month's wages.

"Wonder whether you should be getting married so soon?"

"It's not too soon," Carissa protested. "Not when we've been going out for two years."

"Then what?" Allie asked, before finally daring, "Wonder whether Jake is the right man for you?"

"How can you say that?" Carissa said, reverting to her defensive self. "How can you pretend to be supportive if you think that?"

An excellent question.

Carissa's face crumpled. "I thought you were happy for me."

"I am—"

"I thought you liked him."

A beat. "I do."

Carissa drew back. "Do you? Really? When you say it like that, it's not exactly convincing."

"I think he's nice," she said carefully. He was nice sometimes, at least.

"What don't you like about him?"

Put like this, her objections seemed to flee. *Lord?* "D-do you remember that time at Christmas when he growled at Marcie's boys?"

"Oh, come on. Ethan and Jon were being brats. You know it."

"He looked like he was going to hit them," Allie said.

"What? No."

"I think Steve thought so, which is why he got upset and told Jake to stop."

"That was Steve telling Ethan to stop," Carissa insisted.

Allie studied her and bit her lip.

"I can't believe you would think such a thing. You're wrong." Carissa blinked, shaking her head. "Jake would never hurt the boys."

"Has…has he ever made you feel unsafe?" she asked.

"Are you serious? What planet are you from? He's never even raised his voice to me. *Never.*"

Allie examined her sister's eyes, recognizing truth but also something else. "Then what is it? What's worrying you?"

Carissa shook her head. "Nothing. Nothing at all. Except I wish I knew where my wedding sample book was." She pushed to her feet. "And I wish I knew that Jake and I had your full support."

Allie rose too. "I love you, Carissa. I don't want you to make a mistake. And if you're feeling like something is wrong, then maybe that's God nudging you to think again."

"Or maybe it's that I'm upset because my sister, who is supposed to be my chief bridesmaid, can't even be bothered to back us."

"Carissa, please—"

"You know what?" Her blue eyes sparked. "I think maybe I'll ask Amelia to be my chief bridesmaid instead."

"What?" Hurt cramped within.

"I'd rather have someone I know has my best interests at heart standing next to me than someone who doesn't even like the man I love."

DOWNTOWN BARS WEREN'T EXACTLY his scene, but with Allie having blown him off again, here Jai was, hanging with some teammates, shooting pool. He kind of wished tonight was an online Bible study night with the guys, with those men who understood the challenges of balancing their career with life. But with the mid-season break approaching, the guys were all busy with games or were travelling, and even Josiah had another meeting tonight. Leaving Jai here, wondering why Allie didn't want him there, and wondering how he was going to not self-combust from all the frustration roiling away inside.

His cue hit the ball with a thwack, and it spun away from where he'd aimed, scoring chirps from Jeremy Stamos and David Eccles, their new goalie who'd been a recent trade from Colorado. Jai shrugged, moved to prop himself against the wall as music pumped around him.

It was funny how, now that he'd admitted his feelings to Allie—feelings he'd never admitted to another woman—she seemed to want to put distance between them. Sure, she might have said she loved him back, and her kisses certainly weren't lacking intensity, but he still felt this strain between them, like she didn't quite know what to do with him anymore.

He'd asked her about it a few days ago, but she'd simply denied there was anything wrong. Then sighed.

"I had a big argument with my sister."

"Carissa?"

She nodded. "How'd you know?"

Because Carissa seemed the opposite of her quiet, elegant sister. And Marcie seemed too preoccupied with her own family to bother arguing with Allie.

Allie went on to explain, finishing with, "And now she doesn't want me to be her bridesmaid anymore."

"You did the right thing," he'd assured her. Then he'd

explained about his sister, how Kat had married a guy who'd proved to have a quick fist behind his silver tongue. "I've always regretted not saying something."

"Mom told me I shouldn't have said anything, that she thinks Carissa is an adult. Which might be legally true…"

His lips curved now at the memory of Allie's wry humor. Yet another quality he liked about her.

"Mullins, you gotta stop thinking about your woman," Stamos called.

"What?" Did he have a sign over his head or something?

Connor pointed to the table. "Your turn."

Oh. "Right."

He pushed away from the wall and sighted his ball. Playing pool wasn't his kind of thing, but he was trying to make more of an effort to connect with the guys, especially as Allie had forged such a great relationship with Amber and some of the others' girlfriends and wives. His lips quirked. Look at him, not thinking about Allie again.

A crack of his cue, and this time the ball dropped into the socket, allowing him to line up for another shot. It was funny how he could be so fast on the ice but kind of slow in so many other ways. But he couldn't move slow with Allie. He felt a kind of urgency to claim her as his own. Maybe it was this intensity that had scared her, that made her want to back off. Maybe he should—

Whoa. Missed.

"Dude. You really need to get your head in the game," Stamos said.

Yeah, he really should.

"Anyone need a drink?" Jai took beverage orders and moved to the bar, waiting as the girls finished serving the group of men at the end.

A squeal snapped his gaze up from the beer-stained menu. Wait, was that—?

He drew out his phone, texted Allie. What's your sister's fiancé called again?

Ten seconds later the phone dinged. Jake.

Is he with her at the moment, do you know?

She's home with me, discussing flowers. Why?

He hesitated. How to explain that Jake, or at least his doppelganger, had just pinched a woman's butt and even now was laughing with her in a way Jai never would if he was an engaged man?

Just thought I saw him somewhere, he typed back. Hope you're having fun.

Thanks! Hope you are.

Not as much fun as if I was with you.

She sent back a smiley face emoji followed by a love heart and one of a blown kiss. If he couldn't have the real thing, he supposed that was better than nothing. At least she cared about him.

He sent back a heart of his own before the bartender drew close to take his order. As he waited for it to be filled, his gaze shifted to where the Jake lookalike flirted with the woman. Jai's lip curled. He hadn't had much to do with Jake, not since that incident at the Sunday lunch when he'd caught the man's eye rolls when Allie struggled to answer. But something about the man was off. Now he thought about it, he'd noticed it at his party, where Jake had stayed on the sidelines, watching Carissa laughing and chatting, his eyes on her unless a pretty woman passed by and drew his gaze. And given the number of Jai's teammates with model girlfriends, Jake had proved as much of a bobble-head as the plastic figurines he'd seen in cars.

Another squeal, another laugh. The itching feeling inside wouldn't let him prop up the bar another moment. He straightened, moved toward the man. He had to be sure.

"Jake?"

The man's head snapped up. "Yeah?"

"We met at your fiancée's parents' place for lunch. Remember?"

He noticed how the woman beside Jake inched away. "Your fiancée?" she said.

"After church."

A beat. "Yeah."

"Who is this guy?" the woman asked.

Jai ignored her, kept his focus on Carissa's husband-to-be. "So I'm just wondering what you're doing flirting and touching another woman when you're supposed to be getting married soon."

Jake straightened. "I'm not flirting."

"I saw you. I heard her." Jai gestured to the woman.

"I don't know what you think you saw, but it wasn't that."

Jai hooked an eyebrow.

"It means nothing, man."

"I think it'd mean something to Carissa if she knew."

"Mullins? What's going on?" Stamos asked, drawing near.

"I'm talking to my girlfriend's sister's fiancé about how he shouldn't be touching another woman just a few weeks before getting married."

Stamos nodded, his gaze veering away, and Jai remembered the man had experienced his own marriage troubles after a picture of Stamos kissing his wife's best friend had surfaced online. No wonder he'd gone quiet. Sure, Stamos should never have messed up, but how anyone thought posting a picture on an online forum was necessary was beyond him. He hated those things, hated how private matters became public fare, hated how such things could mess with people's lives.

"Jai? All okay here?" Connor asked. "You know this dude?"

Jai nodded. "Just talking."

Jake said nothing, just eyed him with a loathing Jai could feel.

Connor tugged at Jai's jacket. "Come on. We have a game to finish."

"And drinks," Stamos said.

Jai could feel the tension abate, and he pointed to the tray waiting on the bar.

"You gonna tell her?" Jake finally said.

"What should I tell her?" Jai said, watching the man's gaze flicker. "I'm not going to stand by and watch an innocent woman get hurt. Don't you think she should know the kind of man she's marrying?"

Jake swore and took a step forward.

Jai braced but didn't shy away. Connor moved beside him. "You need to tell her, or I will."

Jake's hand clenched. "Why do you go out with a freak like Allie anyway?"

Heat roared through Jai's chest, and before he knew it, he'd delivered a few thumps to Jake's chest as he wrestled him to the floor, scattering tables and chairs as people backed away with shouts and screams.

"Dude!" Connor yanked at him, dragging Jai away. "He's not worth it. Come on."

"So not worth it," Jai muttered, wiping at the blood smeared next to his eye.

No way could Carissa marry this creep. But how would he ever tell her what her fiancé had done—or tell her what Jake had said about Allie?

~

HAWKS & SQUAWKS ONLINE CHAT

CoolplayismyJam: Did you see this?

PucktheMagicDragon: OMG!!

TubularBells: A fight? Wow. I didn't think JM17 had it in him.

PipeDreams27: Don't you remember the brawl in Dallas two years ago?

CoolplayismyJam: A fight from the new alternate captain? Coach won't be happy.

PucktheMagicDragon: I wonder what it was about?

TubularBells: His girlfriend?

CoolplayismyJam: Was she there?

Destinysoffspring: She's so ugly. I hope they break up.

TubularBells: Hey ArtHeart, do you know?

CoolplayismyJam: Why would ArtHeart know?

ArtHeart101: I've asked. She always denies it.

CoolplayismyJam: How do you know her?

ArtHeart101: She works at the Art Institute with me.

PucktheMagicDragon: OMG!!

CoolplayismyJam: No way!

ArtHeart101: Way.

PucktheMagicDragon: Pretty and smart.

PipeDreams27: ArtHeart?

PucktheMagicDragon: Well, I'm sure that's so. But I meant Abby.

Destinysoffspring: That's it. I'm going to see her.

TubularBells: You talk a big game, Destiny.

PucktheMagicDragon: Aw, don't pick on Abby. She looks really sweet.

ArtHeart101: Her name is Allie. She's a tour guide like me.

CHAPTER 17

$\mathcal{A}$llie studied the beautiful stained-glass artwork salvaged from an old church, which showed the Good Shepherd with his sheep. Poetry in glass, she thought as she gently squeezed Jai's hand and felt the return of pressure. After his travel and the turbulence of recent weeks, it was wonderful to have some time to reconnect, such times as this only fueling crazy-but-maybe-not-insane hopes for a romantic Valentine's Day with Jai. She'd known he'd have some time off during the mid-season break and so had scheduled a few days off of her own, which had allowed for daytime dates like this. Work and the pressure of Carissa had been a lot.

The Institute had noticed a recent upswing in visitors, something for which the public relations team really couldn't take credit, as they'd had had no special exhibitions or done anything differently. Mr. Weinberger was pleased, but it seemed the visitors weren't the usual, or so Celeste said, with the odd enquiry about someone called Allie who might work there. Of course, there were other Allies who worked there, and the privacy of employees was protected, but still, it was weird, and if she thought about it too much, kind of unsettling.

But now, here with Jai, feeling that sense of connection as they wandered around the stained glass art museum on Navy Pier, admiring the works of artists from long ago, she foolishly did wonder if his mom had been right when they last visited, when she'd whispered to Allie that maybe she might expect a proposal on Valentine's Day. Of course, her stupid heart had immediately latched onto this, had immediately leaped a thousand steps ahead and imagined a dress and her reception and all the decisions that she'd advised Carissa on—how she would change those for herself, for what she'd want for this mythical marriage to Jai.

It was stupid, she knew, but sometimes the way he looked at her, the way he kissed her, made her wonder just where he wanted this to go. Those days when she said no to dates with him helped give her a sense of breathing room, a sense of her own identity separate to him, and she wondered if this might prove the difference between her relationship with Jai and Carissa's with Jake.

Carissa's world was so thoroughly entwined with Jake's that she seemed unwilling to listen to anyone else, and while marriage would obviously mean that would be the case to an extent, if she was marrying the wrong guy...

"What are you thinking about?" Jai asked, nuzzling her neck.

"Just about marriage."

Her neck cooled as he moved away.

"Um, Allie—"

"Oh, I didn't mean with you. I mean, not me and you. Oh, I'm saying this all wrong. That's a lovely picture, isn't it?"

But he didn't turn to look at the specimen of Tiffany glass. Instead, his eyes remained fixed on her. "Allie," he said, seriously, "I thought you wanted space from me. I didn't realize you were thinking..." His voice trailed away.

Embarrassment flushed her cheeks. *Way to go, Allie.* Make the guy you'd like to propose one day feel both a sense of expectation from you *and* a sense of retreat. How to fix this awkward strain, a pensiveness she'd felt a few times in recent days? Maybe with the truth.

"Do you want to see any more pictures?"

"Only if you do."

"I've been here before. I only suggested it because you hadn't been. I wanted to do something touristy that a local rarely does, and I thought this would fit the bill."

"It's been cool," he said, "but I'm happy to leave if you want to."

She took his hand, and they wandered back outside onto the pier but away from where the music and amusement rides blared. Honesty required quiet. This relationship required candor. And a comfortable seat in a warm café overlooking the ice-strewn lake.

When they'd settled on a coffee shop and found a quiet corner and ordered, Allie finally found her courage to speak. "The reason that I've sometimes said no to spending time with you is because I find that...that when I'm with you I..." She ducked her head. "I want to do things that I really shouldn't, and that's embarrassing to admit, but true."

He blew out a silent breath, grasped her gloved hand a little tighter in his. "I know what you mean."

He did? Some of the tension lining her chest disappeared, and she glanced up. "I...I don't really know what's normal or expected in a relationship," she admitted shyly, "not having had a relationship before. B-but sometimes when I'm with you I feel that I'm o-o-overwhelmed and I forget about me. It's like I just want to drink you in and I c-can't stop."

Her cheeks were so hot. But sometimes the feel of his hands on her back made her wish he'd touch her elsewhere, shameful as such a thought might be.

"I know what you mean," he said. "You're my sweet addiction."

As lovely as that phrase might be, she didn't exactly mean that, and she stumbled mentally to find the way to best express things. "I don't know what you think about the future, but I don't want to g-give you everything if there's no future in it."

Like poor Brittany. Amber had mentioned that Brittany and her boyfriend had broken up and she was now moving out of his home, out of his life, like an unwanted coffee cup. Amber had whispered it might get super complicated, as Brittany was worried she was pregnant, something that had twisted Allie's heart.

The waiter delivered their steaming drinks—his black coffee, her hot chocolate dotted with pink and white marshmallows. They sipped and watched the white ice on black Lake Michigan shift and slide.

"Allie." Jai shifted to face her in the padded booth and tucked a strand of hair behind her ears. "You know I love you."

"Yes." Her heart danced crazily. She might know it, but believing it still seemed surreal. She kept waiting for the other shoe to drop.

"You know I want our relationship to continue."

"Yes." She placed a hand on his chest, was sure that despite the many layers, she could feel his muscles underneath. Or maybe she just wished she could. *Dear Lord, help me.* "And I have no wish to rush you or make you say anything you don't want to say. If I've made you feel unwanted, I'm sorry. I just see what's going on with Carissa and Jake, and my heart feels sad. I don't want to be like them."

There it was again. That slight tensing in his face. "What is it?" she asked.

"What's happening with Carissa and Jake these days?"

She sighed. "It looks like the wedding is still going ahead."

He nodded, glanced away.

"Jai?"

He pressed his lips to her gloved hand. "I'm sorry you'll be going to it alone," he said.

One of Dad's more crushing blows in life: the discovery that Chicago was going to be away playing a game on his youngest daughter's wedding day. He'd been making noises about changing the date, but neither Carissa nor Mom would hear of it. Allie herself had been disappointed—it would've been nice to have gone to a wedding with a date for a change—but she'd known that even if Jai did attend, everything else would fade in his shadow. So it probably was a good thing he couldn't go.

"But I'm also kind of not sorry."

"Pardon?"

He sighed, rubbed his forehead. "I didn't know how to tell you this. I didn't know what to say or whether he would say anything—"

"Whether who would say anything?"

"Jake." His tone was flat. "I saw him in a bar that night I messaged you about him."

What? "I thought Carissa said he was at work."

"Yeah, unless he's got a job downtown at a bar picking up women, then I don't think that's the case."

"Picking up women?" She pulled back. "What do you mean?"

He explained what had happened, how he'd accused Jake of getting overly familiar with a woman and that Jake, who'd at first denied it, had gotten very defensive.

"I can't believe it!" she gasped.

"You can believe it," he admitted grimly. "There are photos online."

"Online? What do you mean?" She hadn't looked up the fan forums in months. "Photos of what?"

He shrugged. "A fight."

"You got into a fight with Jake? Oh my goodness!" Shock warred with admiration. He'd done that to protect her sister?

She touched the scab marking his face. "Is that how you got this cut?"

"It was just a nick, but it bled a bit."

"Oh my goodness, Jai. And how about Jake? I haven't seen him."

Another shrug. "I don't know what I ended up doing to him, but I know that he would've felt it the next day."

"Wow." She studied him, this man who'd protected her sister's honor. "You're like a superhero."

"Yeah, such a superhero, who's really glad that he doesn't have to put on a smile and pretend he's happy about this wedding."

"But they can't get married now. You have to tell her."

"I would have, but I'd hoped he would."

"I don't think Jake knows the first thing about being honest," she scoffed. "Not like you," she said.

"Not like you," he repeated, tugging her closer to give her a kiss.

But even as his lips enticed and teased with the taste of coffee, part of her mind wondered. In all her honesty and sharing of vulnerable things, she'd never actually owned up to the truth of once running an online group devoted to him. She didn't have to, did she? Not when she'd deleted it and it was obvious that she wasn't part of it now and hadn't been for months. But still, a little thought whispered that if he were to discover what she'd done, he might be upset, as his expression seemed to suggest earlier when mentioning the photos.

But Jai wouldn't blame her. He'd understand, wouldn't he? *Lord, let him understand.*

"So I hope you can understand why going to the wedding would be difficult," he finally said.

"But there won't be a wedding," she said. "We're going to have to tell her. Actually, *you're* going to have to tell her. She doesn't want to listen to me. And we can show her the pictures as proof if you like."

He grimaced. But finally agreed.

IT WAS funny how his claims of honesty seemed to occur right at the time when his conscience pricked with a little reminder that he hadn't been completely forthcoming. But how could he admit the true reason for his fight? No way was he going to tell Allie exactly what Jake had said. His chest grew tight, and he forced his fingers to unclench. *God, give me grace.*

He pushed open his car door and hurried up the path to Allie's house—the site of tonight's talk with Carissa, which Allie had pleaded with him to do as soon as possible.

Allie. That girl made him do all kinds of things. Like go online to find that stupid picture someone in the bar had snapped, which had somehow been uploaded to half a dozen different sites. He hadn't even known half of these websites existed. Hockey fights of shame? Hockey girlfriends and wives? Chicago's Hawks and Squawks? Who looked at these things? The bigger question was who thought they were a good idea to begin with. Whoever they were, they should be embarrassed, because the types of comments he'd barely skimmed showed that these people knew nothing about his life or those he knew at all. His mind flicked back to something he'd come across, something that had dug a little fear. Was Allie now a target because of him?

Blood heating, he drew in a cold, sharp breath, working to calm his heart as he knocked on the door. It wouldn't help matters if he let his anger consume him before they'd even had a chance to begin.

Allie opened the door and drew him inside. "Hey, you!"

In her arms and lips, he felt some of the tension melt away, knew a surge of protection for what she didn't know was being said about her. His Allie. His lovely, beautiful girl. How dare people make comments when they didn't know them at all?

"And if it isn't Chicago's fastest man on ice!" a voice boomed.

He drew reluctantly away from Allie's mouth and turned to meet the man he'd maybe one day call father-in-law. "Hey, Mr. Davis."

"It's Peter, Jai."

Sorely tempted to say *it's Mr. Mullins, Peter*, Jai refrained and instead clasped Allie's hand, threading her fingers with his. "How was work?" he asked her.

"Good," she murmured. "How was—?"

"So what brings you here tonight?" Peter interrupted.

Ticked by the man's blatant overriding of his daughter's question, Jai kept his eyes on her. "What were you saying, Allie?"

"I...I just wanted to know how your day was," she murmured.

"It was kind of boring," he admitted. He'd been really tempted to visit the Art Institute and drop in on her, but he knew from previous comments that such an action might prove awkward for her.

"Thanks for coming tonight."

"No problem. It's the highlight of my day." Well, he figured the upcoming discussion with Carissa wouldn't be, but at least he'd be guaranteed another kiss with Allie before the night was over. And he might even see if they could have another kind-of conversation about the future...

"Can I get you a coffee, Jai?" Peter said. "Water? Anything?"

"Thanks, but I'm good." Although, if Allie's dad were to take a request, it would mean he'd leave. "Actually, maybe a water would be good. Thank you."

Her father nodded. "Allie? Anything? Or are you two going out? I swear it's hard to keep up with what's going on with my daughters these days."

Allie squeezed Jai's hand. "We just wanted to have a chat with Carissa."

Her father blew out a breath. "I don't mind admitting I'll be glad when that girl is married. It's like I can't see my baby girl any more. There's a word for it, isn't there? Bridezilla or something?"

Awkward family moment Jai didn't want to comment on. "I remember my sister was a little stressed before she got married." And that was the reason why he was here today. If he'd realized just why she was stressed, that she was wondering about the wisdom of marrying a man she barely knew, and he'd said something, helped Kat see she had options, that there was a way out, then maybe her life would have turned out very differently.

Women didn't need to be put on a fast track to a crash course in regret. If only they could realize that their self-worth was not to be found in a man. So, if tonight a life could be saved from the tears and pain Kat had endured, then he'd be happy. In some ways, Allie's confession yesterday made so much more sense, and he knew a reluctant admiration for her stance in not needing to be with him all the time. Some of the guys in his team complained about how needy their girlfriends were and how they had to be their girlfriend's all in all for self-esteem. Maybe it was Allie's faith that had propelled her to find her identity in God, or the fact that she'd experienced a few more years than some of the others, who seemed very insecure. Allie might have her issues, but at her core she knew who she was—Whose she was—and that God's love for her persisted no matter her circumstances. He prayed that would continue and be true for Carissa tonight too.

Allie guided him to the family room and said she'd be back with Carissa in a moment.

Jai nodded, leaning back in the floral-fabric sofa, working to get comfortable. Tension knotted his shoulders, and he rolled them to release. Great. Looked like he was going to get some of that confrontation he hated. He knew he'd have to somehow scoot Allie from the room, but then what? How should he begin?

Hey, Carissa, good to see you. I don't know if your fiancé told you, but I saw him pinching another girl's butt last week.

Hey, Carissa, your fiancé is a loser, just like the scumbag who married my sister then left her two years and one baby later.

Hey, Carissa, did you know your fiancé called your sister a freak?

Allie's father returned, deposited a tall glass of water on the wood-and-smoked-glass coffee table, and sat on the opposite sofa. "So, what do you think the chances are of Chicago making the playoffs this year?"

Jai's thoughts scrambled at the shift in direction. "Um, yeah, good, I think. We're playing strong, people are healthy. If we can keep clicking, then we've got as good a shot as any."

"You know, I really feel this is our year."

Jai smiled. He always liked it when fans took such ownership that they identified with the team in that way. "I'll likely have a few spare tickets, if you know anyone who might want to use them," he said in a burst of stupid generosity.

As soon as the words escaped and the man's face lit, Jai knew regret. He could see it now: Peter hassling him about tickets until he sorted it out. But Mom and Kat weren't so keen on hockey, although they appreciated the bills hockey paid. He'd promised Josiah and Gloria could have some tickets if the Hawks made it that far this year. But what he wanted most was to see Allie there when he scored a goal, to look up in the stands and see her joy, her pride in him. That, more than anything, would be the icing on the cake.

Fortunately, any further talk of hockey tickets had to be put on hold at the arrival of Allie and Carissa. Allie offered a tight smile and shrug, while Carissa's face revealed a mutinous expression. Oh boy. This was gonna go well. *Hey, God? Help, please.*

"Hey, Carissa, good to see you." He rose and gave her a hug.

She seemed surprised, murmuring the same to him, and he waited for her to sit.

Carissa looked between the two of them. "Allie mentioned you wanted to talk to me about something."

He nodded, then slid a look at Allie which, just like their pre-arranged roleplay, prompted her to request her father's opinion on something about a frame upstairs.

"Is this for your new painting?" Jai asked.

She nodded.

"I can't wait to see it."

Her smile wavered. "One day. Maybe."

When they'd gone, he turned to Carissa and drew in a deep breath. "Hey, I know this is kind of weird, but I thought it important—like, really important, especially before you get married."

Her eyes narrowed slightly, losing the uncertain ease she'd worn before. "Is this something you and Allie have cooked up? You know she doesn't want me to marry Jake. She thinks he's only going to hurt me."

He swallowed. "And there might be a good reason for that."

"What?"

He explained about his sister, about how she'd married a guy whose true colors had only been revealed after the wedding. "I just would hate to go through this again, to know I could have stopped an unhappy marriage instead of dealing with the mess after they'd said *I do*."

"Jake isn't like your sister's ex."

"Carissa, I hate to be the one to tell you this, but I saw him fooling around with another woman last week."

She shifted back as if slapped, her eyes rounding. "No. That couldn't have been him."

"I spoke to him, Carissa," he said gently. "He denied it, but the woman is here with him in these photos." He tugged out his phone and handed it to her, displaying a screenshot from the online fan forum site.

Her mouth fell open. Then closed. Her lips pinched very tight.

"I'm really sorry."

She shook her head. "No, I can't believe it. What did you see him do?"

He shared about what he'd witnessed, hating that every word was hurting her but knowing he needed to own the truth. "I'm really sorry, but I couldn't stand by to see another woman I care about make a mistake with a guy, not after what happened with my sister."

Her chin wobbled, and she studied the image again. "You got in a fight?"

He wasn't proud of it, but, "Yeah."

"Wow." Her tone was colorless. "Allie is one lucky girl, isn't she?"

What did Allie have to do with this moment?

"And she knows? You've showed her this?" She handed him back his phone.

"Well, yeah. She is my girlfriend. To be honest, I wasn't sure what to say to you."

Her face tightened. "You know she's always spoiled things."

Huh?

"Marcie never noticed, because she was older, but I was always stuck trying to grab whatever crumbs of attention Mom and Dad had to spare."

"Carissa, I don't think that's true."

"What would you know? All my life my parents' attention has always been fixed on Allie, running her around to appointments instead of taking me to ballet or music lessons. And if there wasn't enough time for me then there certainly was never enough money. Do you know what it's like to feel second best all the time?"

"Actually, I do." Story of his childhood.

"Really? Big hockey star like you? You don't have a clue about it, or about us or about anything."

"I know what I shared isn't what you want to hear, but I don't think it's fair to take it out on your family," he said as kindly as he could.

"Right. Because you know them all so well. You think because you've been hanging around our family for the last six months that you know us? You don't even know your own girlfriend."

"What?"

"Allie. You think she's so sweet and innocent, don't you? I bet she's used the line *I've never had a boyfriend* on you, hasn't she?"

"What's that got to do with anything?"

She studied him narrowly for a moment. "Did she ever tell you about an internet fan forum site called 'Jai Mullins's Girlfriend'?"

"What? No." His stomach tensed. "Is she on it?" he asked, dreading to know the answer. "I saw pictures elsewhere, and—"

"She's not on it, because she *is* it. Your precious Allie started the whole thing."

What? He laughed. No. "Not Allie. That's ridiculous. She'd never do something like that."

"She did! She started this online group devoted to you years ago, because she's always dreamed about you and had this ridiculous wish that you'd be her boyfriend. Maybe not so ridiculous, seeing as she still has you while apparently my man is a cheat. But hey, that's beside the point."

His amusement faded at the intensity in her eyes. "I don't believe you."

Her eyebrows rose. "She *admitted* it me, Jai. You should ask her."

Nausea rippled his insides. "I can't believe it."

"Yeah? Well, I can't believe my own sister, pretending to be so weak and meek when really she was luring you in. Clever Allie wins again! I bet you've just loved being adored like that, haven't you?"

Dread lined his stomach. Surely this had to be the ravings of a disappointed woman. "No. She wouldn't have done that. She's too classy."

"Classy? Check this out."

Before he realized what was happening, she'd disappeared and run upstairs, judging from the *pound, pound, pound* of feet.

Jai stayed in his chair, dreading whatever Carissa returned with.

He heard a car door slam, and seconds later, Allie's mother entered the room. He pushed to his feet. "Hello, Mrs. Davis."

"Jai! How lovely to see you. What brings you here tonight? Well, that's a silly question, isn't it? Allie, of course. I'm so sorry I wasn't here earlier. We had a parent-teacher meeting tonight, and oh my goodness those things go on a long time." She peered around. "But where's Allie?"

"Upstairs."

"Oh." A wrinkle creased her brow as she unwrapped her scarf. "And no one else is here with you?"

"Um, I was talking with Carissa until a few moments ago," he admitted. Breaking her heart. Before she took a few potshots at his own.

"Poor Carissa. She's been so stressed about this wedding. And it feels like we're always shelling out more money. Honestly, having three daughters and paying for their weddings is such a trial! It's a good thing Peter earns a good living at his dental practice." She eyed him. "How large a wedding do you think you'll have?"

He coughed, heat spilling up his neck. "I, uh…"

"I know." She leaned forward and patted his hand. "You

probably haven't thought about it at all. So like a man. But I know Allie has been dreaming about getting married for quite some time, which is why it was so good when she met you."

His chest grew tight, and he withdrew his hand from the overly touchy-feely woman. Where *was* Allie? Now her sister and mom had both sown seeds of doubt, and he needed to see her before his impression was blurred any more. She couldn't have started that online group. She couldn't have—

"...no, no!" More high-pitched words came from upstairs.

"I wonder what that could be," Allie's mom said, peering up the stairs then gasping. "Girls! Whatever are you doing?"

Jai slowly pivoted to see Carissa trudging down the stairs, holding a cardboard figure, and Allie clutching the other end as if tugging it away.

What the—?

With a grunt of victory, Carissa jerked it free, and Allie gave a whimper of pain.

He took a step toward her, then saw her pale face, the moisture tracking down her cheeks. "What is it?"

But she shook her head, refusing to face him as Carissa pulled the cardboard cutout and turned it to face him. A cardboard cutout of a hockey player. A cardboard cutout of him.

No.

She propped it upright, the cardboard head flapping brokenly down. He studied it with a degree of dumbstruck fascination. The same kind of fascination he suspected he felt for Allie. Allie, who was even now half sobbing.

"Please, I can explain."

He turned to her, disbelieving. "This is your dad's, right?"

"Dad's?" Carissa laughed, a sound that seemed to hold a note of hysteria. "It's hers," she said, pointing to her sister.

"Allie?" he asked, even though the misery on her face proclaimed it as true.

"Carissa, that's enough," her mother said.

"Oh no. Jai needs to know the truth. He likes to speak the truth, so he might as well hear the rest of it."

There was more?

"Go on, Allie. Why don't you tell him about your online Jai Mullins's Girlfriend group?"

"What group?" her mother said.

Allie refused to meet his gaze.

"Allie?" he asked, waiting until she finally lifted her red-rimmed eyes. "Is this true?"

She paused a long moment, her eyes filled with mute appeal, then finally nodded.

His heart caught as a riptide of emotion threatened to drag him away. "What?" What did she know about him? He shuddered. What had she posted about him? How much of this relationship had been real? Was he some kind of notch on her belt of sick fantasies? "Are you…are you some kind of stalker?"

She shook her head.

"Is it true? Did you really start an online discussion group about…me?" It sounded so far-fetched still, although Carissa seemed plenty confident. And the person who just might have been responsible stood before him, head bowed, glasses off as she wiped her eyes again.

"I'm s-s-sorry."

All he'd thought he'd known about her shattered into shards of hurt, stabbing his chest with physical pain. He swallowed. Glanced at the broken-headed figure of himself. Noted the gleeful expression of Carissa, the shocked face of her mother, the mortification of Allie. The woman he'd loved. The woman who had basically lied to him, saying she knew "a bit" about hockey, that she "might've heard of him a time or two." She had his cardboard figure in her bedroom?

Who *was* this woman? Certainly not the person he'd thought he'd known. Talk about a body check to the heart. What a fool he'd been. A sucker for a pretty face and a musical voice. She'd played him well and good.

"Wow." He had nothing else. No clue. No discernment. And especially no girlfriend. Not now. Had any of this been real?

"Jai, I *promise* you I deleted it months ago." Allie grabbed his arm. "Please believe—"

He shook off her hand, stepped away, nodded to Mrs. Davis, flicked a look at Carissa. "Hope you're satisfied."

He glanced at Allie. How could meek *Allie* have played him? He swallowed. Clenched his fingers. Jerked his chin. "We're done. Goodbye."

CHAPTER 18

Was it possible to die of dehydration thanks to all the tears she'd spilled?

Allie shifted her water bottle and straightened the files on her desk, wishing she could order her life the same way she could order the mess here. But it seemed no matter how hard she tried, everything showed her just how much of a bad human being she was.

She hated feeling like the loser she knew she was, the loser Jai undoubtedly felt he was as, game after game, Chicago continued a losing streak that only compounded her guilt.

Because Jai was playing really badly. And she could only blame herself.

As, apparently, did everyone else.

Mom. Dad. Even Carissa, who hadn't talked to her since that night three weeks ago.

She hadn't dared attend a game, hadn't replied to any of the girls' texts, although Amber's persistence had seen Allie finally answer, as Amber insisted on talking to her soon.

I can't believe you two have broken up!

Oh, Allie could. This hurt felt like a car had run over her chest.

Everyone was saying you two were perfect together.

Were being the operative word.

I know you might not want to see any of us, but I miss you. Let me know when we can catch up for a coffee.

The kindness in Amber's comment had touched her enough that she'd replied okay.

Yay! Thinking of you. Don't worry what anyone else might say.

Amber's message had sparked softness chased by fear. What were others saying about her? She knew she shouldn't look, but she couldn't help it. Allie had started trawling through all of the Hawks' online groups that she knew of.

She's so ugly.

She's so fat.

Good riddance.

Tacky trash.

JM17 needs MY babies.

What did he ever see in her?

Each phrase punched her heart, plunging her spirits lower and lower. What *had* he ever seen in her? She was a liar—he'd definitely not seen that. A scammer—yep, pretty accurate. And all these comments about how she definitely didn't belong with a player like JM17? Definitely true.

Hopelessness seemed to have shrouded her days in a freezing kind of fog. Outside, inside, deep in her heart, it was all much the same. Gray. Cold. Miserable.

Valentine's Day came and went. The only one she'd ever hoped might be the one she'd finally learn what all the fuss was about. Nope. She'd lost her chance at any proposal now. Her face and name was splashed all across the internet so everyone would know to avoid one Allison Davis, the Blackhawk Black Heart, as some wannabe wit had named her.

No one would have anything to do with her. Even Pastor Josiah had only managed a nod rather than the usual smile. And who could she dare to try to explain to? Nobody wanted her explanations. Nobody wanted to know her. And she didn't blame them. At all.

Her phone buzzed. Marcie. She let it go to voicemail rather than answer. Then, when Marcie left a message, listened.

"Hey, Allie. I just wanted you to know that Steve and I are praying for you. I know things are hard with Carissa right now, but remember she always blows up and then it blows over. Don't give up. Love you. Oh, and let's do something together soon, okay?"

"Okay," she murmured as the message died. If *soon* meant in several months.

These days she had just enough energy to manage attending work. Of course, work was its own special level of hell, with Selina and Taylah asking questions about what had happened to Allie's mystery boyfriend.

"You know, some people have wondered if maybe you sent flowers to yourself because you wanted others to think you had a man."

Shocked outrage had filled her chest, stealing any words she might have shared if she'd had the ability to articulate them.

She could've shown them the highlight reel on her phone. The pictures she and Jai had snapped in so many different places—restaurants, parks, the selfies they'd taken together. If only she could show them now.

Taylah had looked at her—not unkindly, she'd dared hope—and finally said, "You know, some people think that you and Jai Mullins were a thing. *Was* he your boyfriend?"

Oh, how she hated the past tense of that. Oh, how she wished—

Oh, why not tell the truth? It didn't matter anymore anyway.

"Y-yes."

Taylah's eyes had rounded and she'd slumped back in her chair. "Wow."

Yeah, she wanted to say. *Bet you didn't think little old stutterer me could get a guy like him, did you? Or that someone like him had kissed me and said he loved me, did you?*

As if they'd believe her.

Work provided some solace though. At least, when the other girls weren't there and Myra wasn't looking at her askance.

Allie's phone buzzed. Amber. HEY, YOU FREE TONIGHT?

She was now free every night. She had no commitments, not even music practice, as she'd told Chrissy she wanted February and March off.

SURE, she tapped back to Amber. WHERE AND WHEN? Maybe a night out, just the two of them, where she could find out if maybe Jai had said anything to Connor or the other guys on the team. Maybe she could learn if he'd ever find it in his heart to forgive her. And maybe, just maybe, she could stop this pity party and see if God still wanted to use her and all her brokenness to help another.

"ALLIE! YOU MADE IT!" Amber wrapped her in a hug as Allie stood at Amber's apartment's front door. Sounds from within suggested the TV was on and that they could have a nice night of mindless drama instead of that which had enveloped her life. "Oh, girl. We've gotta do something with that hair."

"Might as well," Allie said, shoving a hand in the long bushy tresses. "I feel so gross and plain."

"You can't complain about feeling plain if you never make to effort to make a change," Amber said. "That's what I tell my clients, anyway. You want me to do a little restyle?"

Judging from the gleam in Amber's eye, Allie figured *little* meant *whopping huge*. But she didn't mind. "Sure. While you're at it, maybe you can organize a restyle of my life too."

Amber laughed. "See? It can't be all bad if you still have that sense of humor."

She was pretty sure Amber had never heard of black humor, but okay.

"Come on in. The others are here somewhere."

"Others?"

Amber flashed an apologetic grin, as shiny as her new engagement ring. "Did I forget to tell you? My bad. I meant to, but stuff happened and, yeah, sorry. Just a few girls. I think you know them all."

Allie followed her hostess blindly, letting out a silent scream. *No, no, no, no.* As they rounded the corner into the living space with its 180-degree view of the lake, she pasted a smile to her dial and lifted a hand. Yep. Brittany, Natasha, Lauren, Nikki, Ella, Tanja. "Hi."

On a purely academic level, it was interesting to see the various expressions cross their features. Pity. Dismay. Anger. Sadness. Gladness. Alarm.

"Okay, so we're gonna watch the game, and there are snacks"—Amber pointed to a long oblong tray of antipasto —"and drinks, so help yourself."

Mmm. Allie didn't think she'd be driving with any of the beverages on offer. Looked like plain water for her.

She managed a weak smile for Lauren, who turned and moved to speak to Natasha. Brittany, too, seemed to avoid Allie's eyes, grabbing her drink and brushing past her without responding to Allie's quiet hello.

She blinked away tears—she couldn't blame them—then startled at the touch on her sleeve.

Ella. "I'm so sorry about you and Jai."

Allie blinked hard, but a tear escaped, and she had to take her glasses off to wipe it away.

And before she knew it, she was weeping again, the center of a dozen awkward pats and murmured condolences as Ella and Amber wrapped her in a hug—a big hug of awkwardness, as Ella's pregnant belly poked into Allie and Allie was pretty sure she'd snotted into Amber's hair.

"Oh, girl. It's not easy, is it?"

"I c-can't even blame anyone, because it was all my fault."

Amber steered her to a chair and pushed her down. "Sit. Spill. We're your friends, aren't we girls?" She seemed to say this to someone over Allie's shoulder, which suggested that sentiment was more hope than truth. But she appreciated the murmurs of affirmation all the same.

"I still don't understand why Jai would dump you like that," Tanja said.

"It's obviously affected his game," someone—Lauren, maybe? —said.

"Poor guy. He hasn't scored in weeks."

"And we're not just talking about Allie now," Amber said.

What? Oh! Her cheeks heated. "Um, we never—we're Christians. I don't—" *Oh, Lord, what do I say?*

"Are you serious?" Natasha asked, looking at Allie like she was crazy. "You were with him all that time and didn't put out?"

"I...no." She shrugged. What else could she say?

"Wow." Amber eyed her, like she didn't know what to say either. "No wonder he's frustrated."

Well, this certainly wasn't a conversation she'd planned on having tonight. Her cheeks must be bright red. She glanced longingly at the door.

"Don't mind them," Ella said. "They're just young."

"Thanks, Grandma," Lauren said with a hair flick. "Like you're so much older than us anyway."

"How old are you, Ella?" Amber asked.

"Twenty-eight."

"Girl, you don't look it," Amber said admiringly.

"Two kids at twenty-eight?" Natasha said.

"Jonas and I knew each other in high school and got married young—saw no reason to wait."

"I met Connor in high school," Amber said.

"I've been with Alex since college," Lauren said, hair flicking away again.

Brittany said nothing, just looked down, and Allie knew a surge of compassion for her that prompted her to say, "Well, I thought I knew Jai for years, but I only met him in August. I'm pretty sure he thinks he didn't know me at all."

There was silence for a moment, then a snicker, then some giggles, then a round of laughter.

"See? This is why I like you," Amber said, lifting her glass to tap Allie's lightly. "You're one funny chick."

Allie hoped she meant funny ha-ha rather than funny peculiar. She'd choose to go with that one, anyway.

"Did you ever write about any of us?" Brittany asked when the cackles had died down.

Allie shook her head. "No. Call me desperate, but my site was just about Jai. I'd delete anything that wasn't focused on him and always tried to keep the conversation positive."

"What was it called?" Ella asked, retrieving her phone from her bag.

"Jai Mullins's Girlfriend," she said, shame layering each word. "But I deleted the site back in November."

"Oh, I remember that site! One of my posts got deleted. So that was you," Tanja said, oblivious to the ramifications of what she'd just said.

"What did you post about, Tanja?" Amber asked.

"Yeah, if Allie had to delete it, it must've been pretty bad," Lauren said.

Tanja reddened. "Nothing that concerns anyone here."

"But something that must've hurt somebody else, huh?" Brittany asked quietly.

Allie knew a new sense of shame. See? This was why she should never have started that online group. Sites like that were toxic. Toxic for self-esteem, toxic for relationships, toxic for life. She might've deleted the site, but who knew whether what had been posted had been screenshotted and shared to goodness knew where? A person's digital footprint could never be fully erased. It would forever be somewhere for employers to see, for future partners to see, for children to see.

"I'm really sorry," Allie said. "I might have started that website innocently, but I never realized just how harmful it could be. So I hope you know just how much I regret it, and I hope you'll forgive me."

"Forgive you?" Amber laughed. "Honey, I think half of us are in awe of you."

"I beg your pardon?"

Amber stuffed a green olive in her mouth and drained her wineglass. "I think it's safe to say that we've all seen our share of the sites, and yeah, some of them are like cesspools. So if there's some way we can control the lens of how people see us, to know we're not all bimbo puck bunnies, even though some like Tanja are"—Amber paused, meeting Tanja's thrown olive with a smile —"then I think, good on you!"

Good on you? There was a first time for everything. "Um, thanks?"

"No, seriously, girl. I'm impressed."

She was?

"More power to you!" Amber clinked Allie's glass again.

"Well, if you really want to 'more power' me, then send some visitors my way."

"Huh?"

"You know I work in the PR department of the Art Institute."

"Yeah."

"I've had a special project where I'm supposed to boost visitors, and while I've had some leads, it'd be great to find some more."

"Do you just mean regular people, visiting the museum?" Ella asked.

"Do you know who you're talking to?" Amber said. "Influencer, blogger, hairstylist, makeup queen, DJ, influencer." She looked around the room as she pointed to each of the girls in turn. "What do you want? People to go to the Art Institute and ask for Allie?"

She laughed. "Don't be silly."

"Nothing silly here, girl. You want me to post about it? Come visit you? Hashtag *I Heart this Art?*"

Allie blinked. "You'd do that?"

"Girl, I'm not just a pretty face. You know I don't mind me some pretty pictures."

One of the others laughed and displayed Amber's Instagram feed. Picture after picture of beautifully curated artistic displays.

"That's lovely," Allie admired.

"Right? Now, back to the good stuff," Amber said. "Where do I find this thing?"

"What thing?" Allie said.

"Your online fangirl thing for Jai."

"I deleted it," she reminded them.

"No, you didn't," Ella said. "Look, it's still here."

"What?" Allie grabbed the phone and saw that the posts had continued in the past months, that pictures of them on some of their dates had been uploaded for the world to see. "I don't understand." Nausea traveled through her stomach. "I don't know what to say."

"Hey, it's okay."

"No. No, it isn't. I told Jai I deleted it. Oh, he'll never believe a word I say again!"

∽

MONDAY NIGHT—BIBLE study night. Jai was in Florida, the Hawks' road trip meaning he had a rare Monday night off. He'd had his fill of dinner conversation, had his fill of Connor sharing all the details of his Valentine's Day proposal—the day Jai had hoped to pop his own question. Why the man felt like he needed to share, Jai didn't know. He'd put it down to an excited phone call from Amber, which had led to other guys talking about their girlfriends and wives in ways he'd needed to escape, sure the words and images they conveyed would singe his heart and ears.

Not that his heart hadn't already been branded by Allie anyway. She seemed to have somehow burned logic from his brain and any skills from his body. He'd played so poorly since their breakup he was fighting hard to keep his spot on the top line. Escape from the wreck of his life via the online Bible study might be the respite his mind and soul needed.

"And he's back!" Beau said as Jai's image flickered on the screen.

"Hey, guys," Jai said, lifting a hand, forcing a smile.

Dan, Mike, Brent, Chris, and two new guys—Tim Carruthers from New York and Edmonton's Ryan Guillemette —appeared in little squares, offering their own versions of waves, salutes, and greetings.

"How's Florida?" Dan asked.

"Warmer than home, that's for sure."

"You hoping the warmth will help your game?" Beau chirped.

Jai shook his head. "Yeah, I'm gonna plead the fifth."

"I've decided I hate the cold," Brent announced. "I want to move to Australia. You know it's summer there?"

"I'll come with you," Chris said. "Vancouver is always raining."

"I enjoyed it this time last year," Brent said with a smirk.

Yeah. Brent had the gold medal to prove it.

"How's Holly?" Mike asked. "Bree says hi, by the way."

"She's good. In Moscow now."

"Wow." Ryan looked impressed.

"We had preseason games in Finland a couple of years ago," Tim said. "Closest to Moscow I've ever been."

The mention of Moscow drew Jai's thoughts back to another girl who'd visited that city, but for the art, not for skating. His spirits dipped.

"How's Allie?" Beau asked.

The question hit Jai in his solar plexus. He managed a shrug, begged his lips to smile. He couldn't do this, not with Mike and Brent going on about their great relationships, not when he was one of the oldest guys here and he'd just had the rug pulled out from under him. Explain to all these guys just what an idiot he'd been? Nope. Couldn't do it.

"You okay, man?" This question came from Dan, the quietest member of the crew and the one who seemed the most discerning. Maybe it was a defenseman thing. Mike was often observant too.

"Did she turn you down?" Beau asked.

"What?"

"Valentine's Day. I was sure you'd be hitching a ride on the proposal train the way you were talking about her."

"I thought the train too crowded," he managed, adding a raspy-sounding fake laugh.

"Just gonna keep her hanging?" Beau said, a crease folding his brow.

This wasn't right. Jai couldn't pretend they were still together. Not when he was—as Carissa had all too aptly pointed out—all about honesty and owning the truth. And not with this band of Christian men he considered brothers.

"We broke up," he admitted flatly.

"What?"

"Huh?"

"Man, I'm sorry."

He willed himself to keep it together, managed a shrug. "Stuff happens."

"Really? I can't believe it," Beau said. "She seemed so nice and down to earth."

"Yeah, she certainly seemed that." Jai winced. Had he said that aloud?

Judging from the faces staring at him, it appeared he had. "So, um, is Josiah talking tonight? Are we gonna do a Bible study or not?"

"He can't make it," Mike said. "Anyway, even if he could, I think we need to be talking with you."

"I don't want to talk about it."

"Dude," Brent said. Was he giving Jai a pitying look?

"I don't need your pity, and I sure as heck don't need your platitudes."

"I think everybody here has had some relationship issues one way or another," Dan said quietly. "There's no shame in admitting things are tough."

"Especially if you thought you might marry the girl," Beau added.

Jai hissed out a breath, shoved both hands on his head. "Will you quit saying stuff like that? It's not gonna happen. Allie lied to me, man. She pretended to not know me, when all this time she was running an online fan group about me!"

Beau's mouth dropped open. "No way!"

Brent laughed. "Seriously?"

"That's awesome," Chris said. "I should get my wife to start one about me."

That scored a chuckle from both Ryan and Dan.

"I think you're missing the point here," Jai said.

"Yeah, I don't know that I'd be so ticked if that happened to me," Chris said. "It's a bit of an honor if you think about it."

"I'm kind of impressed," Beau admitted.

"What? Are you serious?"

"Hey, just saying." Beau shrugged. "She didn't seem the sort to do that."

"Right? It's weird. Like, really weird. Like, a little psychotic."

"And also maybe a little sweet," Ryan offered.

"No, it's wrong. And I feel violated. Like everything I knew about her is a lie." Jai exhaled. "And don't you think it's a bit stalker-like?"

"I can see you might think it's a little creepy," Mike said. "Of course, I wouldn't have minded if Bree had thought to do something like that." This last was said in a louder voice.

"Something like what?" a fainter female voice said.

"Something like Jai's girlfriend and started an online fan group for me."

"Jai's girlfriend started an online fan group for you?" Bree said, clearly confused.

Dan laughed, which seemed to trigger the others' amusement and even managed to hitch Jai's mouth up a quarter inch. "Fine," Jai said. "Make fun of me all you like. I still think it's weird."

"What's the name of it?" Beau asked.

He sighed. "There's no point looking it up. She said she deleted it."

Tim made a noise that stole his attention. "Yeah, sorry to be the bearer of bad news, but you might want to check that again."

"What do you mean?"

"I mean, the Jai Mullins's Girlfriend fan website is up and running. And there's a picture of you with her at some fancy restaurant."

"What? She told me, she *promised* me she'd deleted this." She was such a liar. Jai scrambled to click buttons and press search engines until he found what Tim was staring at.

A picture of her in Jai's arms, smiling up at him with all the adoration Carissa had accused her sister of.

A picture taken at the top of the John Hancock building, on that day when he'd thought this year would see the fulfilment of all his dreams. On that day when he'd first confessed he loved her, back on New Year's Eve.

CHAPTER 19

*A*llie gripped her disposable coffee cup firmly and escaped Chicago's early March cold as she moved inside the Art Institute. She walked across the mosaic tiled foyer, nodding hello to those on the front desk.

"Hey, it's our celebrity," called Celeste, which earned a roll of Allie's eyes.

"You're really funny."

"I wonder how many people will be asking for Allie today?"

"You'd think people would get a life." Except that had been her for how many years? "I hope it's not proving too distracting."

"Oh, I don't think the other guards mind. It doesn't hurt to have a bit of fun, especially this time of year when it's still so cold outside."

"Thrilled to be bringing the fun factor," Allie said wryly.

Celeste laughed. "I don't know what we'd do without you. Everyone else"—she glanced around and lowered her voice —"they can be so serious, like all they do is think about Rembrandt and Monet all the time."

"You mean you don't?"

Celeste's grin flashed. "There it is again."

Allie smiled and lifted her cup. "Have a good day."

"You too. Love the hair, by the way."

"Thanks."

Allie's smile faded as she moved through the staff areas along carpeted halls. Well, she would try to have a good day. Admittedly, knowing she had some friends—namely the team's wives and girlfriends and a few people like Chrissy from church—the days had been getting slightly better, even with the stir caused by people asking for Allie at the front desk. She guessed many of them were trolls or people wanting to see the infamous woman who had broken their poor Speed Machine's heart and thrown the Hawks into something less than certain playoffs contention.

She drank the rest of her coffee and moved inside the staff bathroom to toss the cup away. Amber had reminded her, as they'd watched the Hawks lose again, that Jai was just one member of the team, and if people thought Allie was responsible for whether Chicago won or lost, then they were simply proving just how stupid they were.

Allie appreciated Amber's support and encouragement, both with her recent visit to the Art Institute, which had resulted in hashtags and Insta photos that saw an increased visitor count the next day, and also her unique dress sense and take-no-prisoner attitude. Amber's confidence seemed to be contagious, and Allie had even allowed the hairstylist to "fix her hair" as Amber called it. The result: a bob that made her look and feel far more chic and confident than before. Mom called it sassy. Amber called it hot. Allie had started to ditch the glasses occasionally too, wearing contacts when they were out.

Amber insisted that Allie go out. "You can't hide at home forever. And if people want to talk about you, they'll do it whether you're crying at home or out at a party having fun. So you might as well make the most of life and have some fun."

It was good to get out of the house. Carissa still hadn't forgiven her, though their parents and Marcie and Steve all understood. It seemed Jake had moved on, not even deigning to meet Carissa to discuss what he'd been accused of, something which had deeply hurt Carissa. Of course, such an action only proved the measure of the man. In this case, a very, very small man, one without an ounce of honor.

The same could not necessarily be said about Jai, she knew. He, at least, had honor enough for the two of them, even if he lacked forgiveness. She'd sent messages and emails and flowers to his apartment. No response. She sometimes took her lunch outside, braving the cold as she wondered if she'd recognize him among the joggers. No luck.

She'd now reached a point where all she could do was pray and ask God to help her, to help Jai finally show some grace. While she might not have always had the most pure motives, her conscience was clear in that while they were together, she'd never posted a picture or a word about him. Something she'd explained to him in every apologetic message and note.

Allie drew in a breath. God would be enough for her. God would *have* to be enough for her. A few nights ago, she'd been listening to another Sarah Maguire song that talked about finding one's identity in Christ rather than circumstances. She'd known that, but somehow the truth of it had never passed down from her head to her heart. It had spurred her to more Bible study where, amid more tears and repentance, she'd confessed that for way too long she'd been putting Jai's and other people's feelings toward her ahead of remembering what God said about her.

It was funny how one could go to church all one's life and still get led astray by the heart's fickle fancies. And while Jai was a good guy, she knew giving herself space from him was wise as she prayed and sought God's direction for her life. And while she loved her new hair and style, she knew the enjoyment of such things would pass soon, and that only one Person could really satisfy. So it was to God she'd need to keep turning. It was God whose ways would protect and bumper-lane her through life. God first. No matter what happened with Jai or anyone else.

As far as it depends on you, live at peace with everyone. She'd read that just this morning in the Bible, and she knew she had to apply it within her heart. She wasn't responsible for how others thought about her. She needed only to keep a clear conscience before God.

She entered the public relations staffroom, hung her coat on the hook near the door, and switched on the coffee maker and her computer. This time of day, before the others came in, was always a good chance to breathe.

A search through her emails revealed one from Mr. Weinberger. Her heart skipped a beat or four. Last week when they spoke, he'd mentioned something about a job opening at a museum of European art in San Francisco, and she'd known the strangest hankering to go visit.

"It could be a great opportunity for you," he'd said. "You could be the head of your own department, which is not a bad prospect for someone of your tender years."

Tender years? She'd take it. The tender years part, not necessarily the job. Although… "When would you need to know by?"

"You would like to apply?"

"To be completely frank, I suspect Myra will be happy to see the end of me. At least, the end of my working here. I don't think I can go any further in my career while she's here."

He'd nodded and discussed more details, and this was his follow up email.

Her chest grew tight. Imagine leaving Chicago. Leaving all she'd known, flying to the other side of the country, and having a chance to restart her life. The thought equally thrilled and scared her. How would she cope? How would she make friends?

How would she learn to conquer her fear of talking? A situation like that, with all its new responsibilities, would mean she'd be having to face those fears on a daily basis. But didn't she have God with her? She could do this with His strength. And with no relationship, and a chance to finally flee the family nest, the thought of moving to a city known for its arts scene was enticing.

The door opened, and Taylah and Selina walked in.

"Allie, you're here bright and early," Selina said.

"You know it." Funny how her stutter didn't bother her so much these days. Maybe it was just that she didn't care. If people wanted to judge her for how she talked, well, that said a lot more about them than it did about her. And if she was able to score a job in one of San Francisco's top art museums, then what these people here thought didn't need to matter. If she scored such a job, maybe she'd finally be considered worthy of respect from the likes of Myra and Selina. But did she really care what such people thought? *No.*

Surprise at her inner revelation moved Allie's feet to the coffee pot. "Taylah? Have you been caffeinated yet?"

"Um, no. That'd be good."

Allie poured a coffee for Taylah and Selina—practicing what Josiah had preached on Sunday, doing good to one's enemies, or at least to one's non-friends—and had just returned to make her own when Myra's phone rang. As the second-in-command thus anointed by the Institute's deputy director, Allie rushed in and answered breathlessly, "Hello, Public Relations and Learning, this is—"

"Myra? Is that you? Honey, I'm so sorry, I should never have said what I did."

Recognition of the man's voice clamped Allie's throat.

"Look, I'm sorry for wrecking what should have been a wonderful break, but if you'd heard her go on and on about wanting me to stay home, well, you would know—Myra?

Honey? I know we haven't talked for weeks, or maybe it's now months, but I thought you'd speak to me at least." Neil Blanchard gave a raspy chuckle. "I was sure you'd have plenty to say. And you still could if we could meet. What do you say?"

What *could* Allie say? Should she just hang up? Let him know he'd spilled the beans to someone other than Myra? Myra, who would eat Allie alive if she ever knew Allie had taken this call.

"Myra? Look, let's just say the offer is always there. Nobody will ever know, nobody needs to get hurt."

But Allie's conscience protested that wasn't true. Hadn't he just said that his wife hadn't wanted him to go? Surely his wife had to know. And if she didn't, Allie had to speak up for what was right. Especially after everything that had happened with poor Carissa. As much as she hated confrontation, she wouldn't let another man get away with destroying other people's lives. "N-no."

"N-no?" He laughed again. "Come on baby, you don't mean that. And you definitely don't need to start talking like that idiot you work with."

"What idiot?" Surely Myra didn't speak that way about Taylah.

"The one you're always covering for. The stutterer. What's her name?"

Breath escaped in a whoosh, followed by a cramping kind of hurt across her torso. Myra spoke like that about *Allie*?

"Myra? Are you there? Look, come on. We can work things out—"

"No," she said, words pushing from her mouth. "Allie Davis."

"Allie—that's the one."

All the little drops of hurt from this conversation clotted into anger. "No. *My* name is Allie Davis. How dare you say such things?"

There was a second's pause, then he hung up, the dial tone beeping in her ear. Breath shaking, hand trembling, she replaced the phone, struggling to believe. Far from having the respect of her peers, they instead laughed about her? Made fun of her?

She rose unsteadily, clutching the side of the desk.

Taylah moved to the door. "Allie? Are you okay? You look really pale."

She shook her head. "I...I need to..." She didn't know what. Return home? Resign? Pursue the job Mr. Weinberger had spoken of?

A flash of the door revealed Myra had returned. "Allie? What are you doing in here?"

It was like the lens had shifted, like she could finally see this woman, her boss, for who she really was. Not someone she'd tried to win as a friend but as a selfish, self-centered, malicious woman who would always seek personal gain no matter the cost to others. Allie paced back, put a hand against the wall.

"Are you unwell?" Myra placed her bag on the desk. "I hope you haven't contaminated anything in here."

"No." Because the contaminant had just returned.

"Well?"

As Allie scrambled for something to say, Myra's phone rang again. "Hello, Public Relations and Learning—oh yes, John." She eyed Allie, the line in her forehead becoming more pronounced. "Are you sure I can't help you?" A beat. "Well, of course, I'll send her right away."

She replaced the phone, eyed Allie with an expression that promised to dip into a scowl. "Mr. Weinberger wants to see you."

Allie nodded. Whew. She inched to Myra's office door. She was saved.

She hurried to collect the folder from the locked drawer and had nearly fled the room when her name was called.

"Allie, before you go, why were you in my room?"

She glanced at Myra, then at Selina and Taylah, and swallowed. "Y-you had a phone call. I answered it."

"Anyone important?"

Out of nowhere, Beau's comment flipped through her mind: *Trying new things is the spice of life.* Why not try to be brave right now?

"Neil Blanchard w-wants you to call him. Apparently he wants to make up for the trip you took away together, the one his wife didn't want him to go on."

Myra's jaw sagged. "Allie—"

"He thought I was you, so he also called you honey. Then he made fun of my stutter, because apparently you've done that too."

Gasps from Selina and Taylah. Myra's face paled.

"Excuse me," Allie managed, hitching the folder to her chest. "I have a meeting with Mr. Weinberger."

IT WAS FUNNY how some conversations seemed to linger in one's soul and, like a whirlpool, suck the negativity away. It had felt that way since the conversation with the Bible study guys. It was like they'd seen the flipside, and Jai could appreciate that perhaps he'd overreacted just a little. Not that he was willing to make amends with Allie just yet. Even with all the notes and messages of apology she'd sent. He might forgive—one day—but that day was not this day. Even if his Bible reading that morning suggested he should have forgiven her long ago.

"Dude, you're coming to the party, aren't you?"

Connor's engagement party. Something where all their teammates were guaranteed to show. They and their wives or girlfriends, and he'd be going stag. Again. "Sure."

"It won't bother you that Allie will be there?"

"Nope." He knew that Amber and Allie were good friends. And he could show up and show everyone that they were still friends. Even if the thought of seeing Allie made his palms sweat and his lungs struggle to breathe. He could do this. He *would* do this. Prove this to everyone. And himself.

The party was on Saturday night, one of those rare times on the schedule when they were home without a game. He knew it would likely get wild and hoped Allie knew that too. Even as he dreaded seeing her again.

The venue was an upmarket Gold Coast hotel, something worthy of the Hawks' captain and his influencer bride-to-be. Jai went inside, saw one of the Hawks' girlfriends at the turntables, vibing away as the crowd danced and partied. So not his usual scene. But then, Jesus didn't hang out just at church, either.

Connor and Amber met him, and after backslapping his captain, Jai kissed Amber's cheek. "This is great."

"Right?" Amber said. "Hey, have you seen Allie?"

No. They were getting to this already?

"She's over there," Amber said, pointing to a group of women that included a blonde with a sexy haircut and a purple sparkly dress that left the haircut for dead.

That woman was Allie?

"She looks different," he finally managed.

"Doesn't she look hot? It's amazing what a new dress and haircut will do to a woman. And isn't that what they say? A woman gets a new haircut when she gets over a man?" She winked, her smile shifting to Connor as she kissed him. "Not that I'll ever be changing my hairstyle, baby."

Jai got the message and left the lovebirds alone, moving through the throngs of people to the food. He didn't love danc-ing, but he couldn't help seeing Allie's dress glimmer as it caught the strobe lights. She was spectacular, like a disco ball he just wanted to be near.

But he couldn't. Everyone would be watching them, if Amber's wink was any guide.

He took some time to talk to teammates, checked out the food, talked more, ate more, as every minute his eyes strayed to

Allie. No. He could do this. He could be strong and avoid her. Even if he hadn't been able to forget her soul-searing kisses that had marked his heart like a brand.

But somehow, whether it was natural shifting of crowds or his feet just didn't get the memo, he found himself in her vicinity when the music dropped. And like magic, each woman she'd been dancing with glanced at him, glanced at her, then melted away, leaving her to turn and face him. Alone.

Her eyes rounded, and her jaw fell. "J-Jai!"

So, she was nervous of him. He wasn't sure if that was a good thing or not. "Allie."

Her gaze connected with his for a long moment as her lips parted, and he knew a sudden savage longing to kiss her again.

Then she blinked, paced back, and turned, moving away toward some friends, exiting their little faceoff like she wanted out of his life for good.

"Allie, wait." He glanced at the other women. "Excuse us."

"Us?" Allie's chin rose. "There is no us. You made that clear weeks ago."

He couldn't have this conversation here, not in front of a million ears and waiting phones. "Can we talk? Please?"

Her mouth set in a mutinous line, and he thought she'd refuse. But then, after a swift glance around the room, she sighed and moved to a door that led outside. "What do you want, Jai?"

He was half enthralled, half in fear of her new confidence. "I want to talk."

"What do you want to say? Or is it more what you want me to say? Because if it's an apology you want, well, I've apologized a million times. Now it's up to you. You can forgive me or not. But I'm not going to waste my life wishing you'd come back."

"Allie, I…" *still love you.* Surprise at the truth lodged the words in his throat.

"Look, I know I made a mistake. I should've told you, I

could've done things better, but I didn't." She paced back, her silver strappy shoes gleaming in the light. "I'm human. I'm sorry if your impression of me took a dive—more sorry than you'll ever know. But it's done. I can't change the past, no matter how much I might want to."

Hurt wove between them—his confusion, her regret, simmering in a bubbling mess of raw emotions.

"Well? What did you want to say? Or have you dragged me out here for nothing?"

Where was his soft-hearted girl? He barely recognized her now. His chest hurt.

"Allie, I…" He swallowed. "You said you'd deleted that online group."

"I did shut it down." Her chin tilted. "I *did*. I can tell you think I lied."

"No, I—"

"I don't know why, but I think the other administrator restarted the group, and kept it open. Maybe because you and I were a thing and she thought the site could get more traffic or sponsorship or whatever. But it wasn't *me*." Her voice broke. "Do you really think I want that horrible reminder of this stupid crush and stupid phase of my life?"

His stomach clenched. He was a stupid phase?

"Have you even read what they're saying there? There are pictures your fans must've taken, and so much is obviously fake, talking about dates we were never on. Why would I post about that?"

A sick feeling gnawed within. Had he misjudged her? "Allie." He moved toward her.

She backed away. "I understand you despise me," she said, her voice lower, softer. "I don't blame you. But me being the sorriest creature in the world won't help anything until you can forgive me. And I can't help with that. That's all on you."

Her words slammed into him with the force of a Zamboni.

He *needed* to forgive. For himself as much as anyone else, in order to release the poison whirling through his heart and brain. *God, help me…*

"Nice to see you, Jai. Excuse me."

Frustration wrestled with guilt and admiration as he watched her walk away. Sassy. That's what Kat would say. That's what Kat *had* said when he finally admitted the whole situation to his mom and sister.

"But she seemed so shy," Mom had said. "Such a meek little thing."

"Appearances can be deceptive."

"Huh. Well, I still like her," Kat had said, eyeing him with a smirk. "If she can turn your head once, then she can do it again."

Please.

"I like her," Kat had said again. "She's a sassy little thing."

That was for sure. Honest. Upfront. Direct. And more. Was that a swing to her hips? Who'd taught her that? Amber? And that glittery dress she was wearing sure wasn't one he'd seen before. Which was probably just as well, because if she'd worn that when they were going out, well, Peter might've had to bring out the shotgun.

"Allie, please don't go."

He raced to catch up to her, touched her arm, noticed her flinch.

Her flinch made his own heart quail. This was Allie, his Allie, who had once nestled into his hugs like she wanted to beat inside his heart. Did she now dislike him so much that his touch made her recoil? If only he could say the same. But touching her had ignited a fierce need, the desire for more, to hold her, kiss her, taste her, love her.

"Allie."

"Jai."

Her eyebrows rose in challenge as his fingers itched to touch that wild curl near her ear.

She turned to leave, and he grasped her arm again, felt her stiffen.

"Allie?"

"What do you want from me?"

The emotion fringing her words dug deep into his conscience. She might've called herself the sorriest creature, but he was more sorry if he held this remorseful woman's sins against her. "I…I want *your* forgiveness."

"What?"

"Allie"—*I still love you*—"could you ever find it in your heart to forgive me?"

She blinked. "Forgive you for what?"

"For flying off the handle. For not giving you a chance. For not reading all your notes. For not realizing I should've believed you. I'm really sorry. I was wrong."

She took a step toward him, then hesitated. "Yes."

"Yes what? You forgive me? Yes, I was wrong?" *Yes, you're prepared to overlook my stupidity and want to be with me again?*

Her lips twitched up, but wariness remained in her eyes. "Yes to both."

His chest released. *Thank You, God.* "Allie."

"Jai."

He swallowed. "Would you ever consider going back to how things were?"

"You mean…?"

"You. Me. Us. Together again."

She bit her lip, studying him for a long time, her eyes seeming to delve between his hopes and his heart. What did she see there? Why was she shaking her head?

His insides knotted. "Allie? What is it?"

"I can't go back to how I was. I'm done with stupid crushes, with watching others live their life while I sit around and check the boxes of other people's expectations. I'm making changes in my life. I want whatever God has for me, and I'm not that same sad, pathetic person anymore. I'm moving on with my life."

"Moving on?"

Her head jerked. "I'm going to San Francisco."

~

Hawks & Squawks online chat

CoolplayismyJam: Did you hear about Connor and Amber's engagement do?

PucktheMagicDragon: Pics please!

CoolplayismyJam: Here you go. Don't they look so happy?

PucktheMagicDragon: OMG!!

TubularBells: Is that Allie in that picture? Wow!

PucktheMagicDragon: OMG! She looks amazing!

PipeDreams27: She looks hot.

CoolplayismyJam: Revenge haircut? I wonder what JM17 thought.

PipeDreams27: Was he there?

CoolplayismyJam: He'd have to be there. He's part of the leadership group.

Destinysoffspring: Huh. She actually looks good.

TubularBells: Found a pic of him. He looks so good in a suit.

CoolplayismyJam: So hot I'm melting. Those shoulders...

PucktheMagicDragon: I hope they get back together. They were so cute!

CoolplayismyJam: As if she would say no.

PipeDreams27: When is Amber's baby due?

TubularBells: She's pregnant?

CoolplayismyJam: Why else would they be getting married?

PucktheMagicDragon: I hope they have a little girl.

TubularBells: Nobody knows if she's even pregnant. You're all such gossips.

CoolplayismyJam: Says you.

PucktheMagicDragon: I do hope they have a little girl—one day. And that JM17 and Allie get back together.

Destinysoffspring: They're probably together right now, if you know what I mean.

PucktheMagicDragon: Destiny!

CHAPTER 20

*A*llie squared her shoulders, working on remembering her pitch, which she'd memorized as best she could. She could do this. God was with her, and regardless of how today's interview went, she could trust Him with her future.

The door opened, and a man with familiar broad shoulders and brown, wavy hair was silhouetted in the doorway. Her heart stabbed. Jai!

But no. Foolish her. It was a man who'd looked a bit like him, except now he'd turned, and she could see his man-bun. So, not Jai at all.

She exhaled. What was she thinking, imagining him here? He was in round one of the playoffs, courtesy of the Hawks' strong beginning to the season. He was focused on games against Nashville, not on her. He'd made that clear. She might say she was over him, and her jagged feelings since seeing Jai at Amber's engagement party had been buffed smoother by the past few weeks of prayers, but sometimes her emotions still held a weight, like the pain would never go away. Praying for God to take these feelings away had helped, and reminding herself of what God said about her had brought a sense of calm and helped her balance out those shards of shame with faith for something new. Until moments like this, when regret snuck up to shock like a defibrillator and she was forced to refocus on the future, not the past.

The future. Like this job she was seeking in San Francisco.

She lifted her chin, straightened her shoulders, breathed in calm. Ran through the answers she'd rehearsed since she'd been told about the interview. Whatever happened, God was with her. She could trust Him to straighten her paths.

"Miss Davis?" A woman spoke from an opened door. "They're ready for you now."

She nodded, collected her bag, and followed.

Inside, there was the usual cast for these kinds of interviews: senior executives and board members, and a representative from the team she'd be leading here, should she get the job. Usually these panels incorporated someone from outside the museum too, so no calls of nepotism could be made. She offered a smile to those on the other side of the desk, then her mouth dried. No.

"Good afternoon, Miss Davis." Mr. Holt, an elderly man with a surprisingly youthful face—surgery, perhaps?—gestured for her to take a seat.

When she was seated, he began the introductions, and she murmured hellos to people whose names she'd heard, read about, watched on interviews. And someone she'd spoken to not so very long ago.

"And lastly, our representative from another institution is a colleague who is also from your neck of the woods and a dear friend. Neil Blanchard."

Why was he here? She kept her expression neutral, wondering how Neil was going to play this. Pretend he didn't know her? Give her a bad mark? Or perhaps he'd be keen to see her leave Chicago for the other side of the country?

"Now, Mr. Blanchard assures me you have not met or had

any professional working relationship before, so his role here can be considered unbiased."

Allie's gaze flicked to Neil's hooded eyes. Except that wasn't exactly true. *Lord? What do I say?* She cleared her throat. "It is true that we've not had any professional working relationship," she said carefully.

Mr. Holt's eyebrows lowered as he glanced between Allie and his friend. "Neil?"

"I've never met the woman before," Neil said.

Technically true. But when she'd encountered Neil and Myra engaged in actions that even now made her blush, that had hardly been the time to introduce herself. Did the phone call from several weeks ago count?

"Miss Davis. Are you ready to start?"

No. Everything she'd rehearsed seemed to have flown out the huge tinted window. She nodded anyway.

"Let's get on with things, shall we?"

"Y-yes."

What followed proved a tightrope of questions and answers where she hovered between honesty and careful explanations. Neil Blanchard obviously knew who she was, knew her role as subordinate to Myra. Were they still together? Was he Myra's spy to get Allie out of her hair? Or were such thoughts just paranoia?

"Miss Davis," Mr. Holt continued. "I am going to pass you over to the other panel members for them to ask you questions."

She nodded, her chest pulling tight. So far the questions she had met with were much as she'd expected, and she'd been able to offer her rehearsed answers and just tweak on the spot a little. Such a thing had allowed her to speak well, with fluency. She suspected that would now change. *Lord, thanks for being with me.*

Just the reminder of His presence helped to calm her, and through taking her time, adopting that musical quality Jai had once said he loved about her voice, she was able to fend fairly well, she thought. Until it was Neil Blanchard's turn.

He eyed her, his expression holding something that resembled a sneer. Her heart sank. "Miss Davis, would you be able to tell us why you wish to leave such a renowned art institution in Chicago to move halfway across the country over here?"

She swallowed, took a deep breath, then slowly exhaled. "I have enjoyed my time working at the Art Institute, but there comes a time when everyone wants to push their personal boundaries and discover what else might lie in their future. My passion is for European Art, and particularly Impressionism, and while the Art Institute in Chicago has one of the best collections of Impressionist art in the country, I feel I know and understand those pieces so well that it's time to explore something else."

"So you don't wish to leave your work there for any other reasons?"

Like what? She studied him, working to discern the reason for his question. "If, by that question, you are hinting that I have personal reasons for wanting a career change, then you are mistaken. I've really enjoyed my time there and really enjoyed my colleagues."

"All of your colleagues?" he pressed.

What was he playing at? "I will admit that, as in any work environment, there are some personalities that get on better with others, but I think that all of my colleagues would recognize me as a hard worker and someone who is very committed to her job."

"Your immediate supervisor in your current role did not write a reference. Would you care to speculate why?"

Because Myra had resented Allie asking for one, saying that she could not in all good conscience promote someone beyond her capabilities.

"You cannot articulate as clearly as one in a senior role

ought," Myra had said. "I know it must be distressing, but surely you can see that it would not be in your best interests."

Not in Myra's best interests, perhaps. Not when Allie had carried the bulk of their work over the past years.

"Miss Davis?"

"I...I cannot say why," she finally managed.

"Is it true that you have something of a speech impediment?" he asked.

Her jaw sagged as murmurs around the table took on a protesting tone.

"Now really, Neil," Mr. Holt said, cutting Allie an apologetic look. "You don't need to answer the question," he added quietly.

"But I w-would like to answer it," she asserted.

"Very well then."

She drew in a deep breath and shifted so she faced Neil Blanchard, and the words that for so long had felt trapped suddenly began to flow. "I don't know if that's a question you've asked all of the candidates or simply one you have reserved for me, Mr. Blanchard, but I would have thought, from our last conversation when you mocked my stutter, that you were only too aware I have had such challenges in the past."

"Miss Davis?" Mr. Holt glanced between them. "I'm afraid this seems a little unnecessary."

"I agree," she said. "I have worked v-very hard to get to where I am, and Mr. Weinberger, whose reference I am sure you *have* read, will attest that many of our museum's guests would agree. If you will allow me to return to your previous question concerning the lack of reference from my immediate supervisor, then Mr. Blanchard, I would ask you to recall our last conversation, when you said my immediate supervisor, Myra Fordley, your mistress"—gasps filled the room—"mocked me, and you called me an idiot."

His jaw clenched.

"Neil?" Mr. Holt wore a heavy scowl. "Is this true?"

"Of course not. She's lying."

Allie laughed. What was the point in trying to hold onto whatever shreds of dignity she might still have when it was obvious the job would not be hers? Far better to speak honestly and let Mr. Holt know the truth about his colleague and dear friend.

"How could it possibly benefit me at all to admit such things about myself?" she asked incredulously. "I cannot see it. Just as I fail to see the relevance of your questions about my speaking ability."

"You certainly don't seem to have a problem speaking now," one of the other board members murmured.

"Ex-exactly," she said, lips twitching at the irony. Of course her mouth would choose such a moment to let her down.

Allie glanced between them all, offering a small wry smile as she rose from her seat. "I thank you for this opportunity. I feel like I could have been a great fit for this role and would've loved the opportunity to prove you were right to interview me today. I'm sorry if you feel you've wasted your time. I wish you all a good day."

She stretched out a hand to Mr. Holt, who shook it, seemingly surprised at the rapid escalation of events. She didn't blame him. She was surprised herself. A nod and smile for the other members, apart from Neil Blanchard, and she took herself out of the room, head held high, even as she wanted to shake and a weak part of her wanted to cry.

So, it didn't look like she was going to be moving to San Francisco. A pity, for she liked the hills and street cars and harbor and quirky buildings, so different to the flatness of Illinois.

She pushed her shoulders back. As disappointing as this had proved, she was going to have to trust God to show her what was next.

~

THE LOCKER ROOM held a kind of intensity unique to playoffs season. Focus, less laughter—this was the business end of the season, when everyone from sponsors to players to fans would kick up an extra gear and do all they could to ensure sweet victory.

Around Jai, other players were taping their sticks, each with their unique methods. White tape, black tape, wrapping to protect the stick's shaft and blade. Jai grabbed a marker and reminded himself of what was more important tonight.

Count it all joy, Jai wrote, the black marker bold against the white tape. The verse from James was one of his favorites, a reminder that trials produced patience and perseverance. It was so true in hockey, so true in life. Trials, drills, practice, pain, long suffering—all of it was used to develop a man and train him to be better.

And these days he needed that reminder all the more. Needed it as he tried to do life without Allie in it. But the longer she was away, the more he realized he wanted her in it. She was like the puzzle piece his life had only now realized was missing.

No. He couldn't afford to think on her. He had to focus on tonight's match against Nashville. Two games at home, then two games in Tennessee, then a game apiece until one team had won four. Then whoever won would progress to the second round, then the Conference finals, then play for Lord Stanley's Cup. Despite Chicago having home ice advantage, most of the punters were backing Nashville, due to Chicago's less-than-stellar efforts in the second half of the season. But with games tied at three apiece, a win tonight would see Chicago move on to the second round, something they hadn't done in years, and would fuel the city's pride.

They had a job to do. Sink more pucks in the net than Nashville did. Simple.

It wasn't long before they were skating out onto the ice for the warm-up exercises. The United Center was loud, the music thumping, the fans as frenetic as Jai's own pulse. He knew he had to put in a good showing tonight. *Had* to. He couldn't let his teammates down.

As he skated, his gaze flicked to the stands, to where Allie's family stood cheering. His mouth ticked up. Not that they would see that, but it made him wish—hard—that he'd worked a little more to convince Allie to stay. She was in San Francisco?

He felt the urge to pray for her, that God would bless her and open the right doors at the right time. *God, bless her*, he gritted out, in his millionth unselfish prayer.

The puck slid his way, and he slapped it toward the goal. He really needed to get out of this funk and focus on the job.

Two hours later, the clock was counting down the last minutes in the third period. Chicago was tied with Nashville, two goals apiece. The puck ricocheted off the boards in front of Jai, and he hammered toward it, outskating Nashville's bruising Russian defenseman, scooping it up as he headed to the opposition's net and the wide yellow jersey of the opposing goalie doing his best to block the space.

A slide, a hit, a thwack, a ping. The puck slid around the back of the net, so Jai raced another Nashville player to retrieve it. Skirmish on the boards, a shove, a curse, a check, a hit. Then he flicked the puck free, sending it to Connor, who flicked it deep to David as Jai moved into position and yelled for the puck to be sent his way.

David slammed it to Jai, and he slid it toward goal—straight between the legs of the Finnish goalkeeper. The horn blared, the lights strobed, and Chicago had its goal.

Jai was surrounded in a mass of helmet thumps and back pats as his teammates celebrated. With only forty seconds left on the clock, they had a shift or so left where all they'd need to do was protect their lead.

He skated to the bench, downing a drink as Nashville removed their goalie. The strategy of having an extra attacker could pay off, as they could get that necessary goal, but sometimes it backfired spectacularly, such as that time when a goalie had cleared the puck only to see it rebound off the boards before sliding straight and true into the opponent's empty net. One of hockey's more insane moments, for sure.

The cry of "Let's go, Hawks!" filled his ears as the whistle blew for the next start of play. The countdown on the clock revealed thirty seconds, twenty seconds, ten…

The siren blared, revealing the end of the period and the end of Nashville's hopes to further the season. Job done.

As was traditional at the end of a post-season bout, each team faced off and went down the line with handshakes, back slaps, and muttered congratulations or commiserations. He was glad to be on the side being congratulated tonight.

Then it was back on the ice to join the others as they raised their sticks to thank the crowd—screaming fans wearing Blackhawks wigs and masks, waving banners, shaking flags. There was Mr. Davis, cupping his mouth as he yelled out his support. Jai's gaze shifted to where his mom sat with Kat and Josiah in the seats reserved for them, and he shot them a smile and a salute. His smile faded. They were right next to the seat he would've had reserved for Allie if he'd been able to get ahold of her. Had she blocked his calls? Blocked him from her life?

He didn't know what to think. Except it seemed awfully weird to be standing on center ice in the middle of celebrations, having scored the game winner that was sending them to the next round of the playoffs, feeling a sense of loss because the woman he still stubbornly loved wasn't here tonight.

HAWKS & SQUAWKS ONLINE CHAT

CoolplayismyJam: They won!!!

TubularBells: Through to take on Calgary or L.A.!

CoolplayismyJam: Hope it's Calgary. Mike Vaughan is hot!!

PucktheMagicDragon: But married. With a little baby that is so cute!

CoolplayismyJam: Don't kill the fantasy, Puck. JM17 looks hot with that beard though. I think my ovaries might've melted.

PipeDreams27: That's kinda gross, Coolplay.

TubularBells: JM17's last goal was awesome. Best I've seen him play in weeks.

PipeDreams27: Probs bc he and Allie are back together.

TubularBells: Are they though? I didn't see her at any of the games.

PucktheMagicDragon: Where is she? I hope she's okay.

CoolplayismyJam: Maybe they have broken up. If so, hello JM17!

PipeDreams27: Get in line, Coolplay.

TubularBells: As long as he keeps playing well I don't care if they're together or not.

PucktheMagicDragon: Aww, but don't you want JM17 to be happy?

CoolplayismyJam: I could make JM17 happy.

PipeDreams27: In your dreams.

CoolplayismyJam: Exactly!

CHAPTER 21

"Okay, and then we'll begin that medley, right? And Allie, you'll be okay to introduce that series of songs, won't you?"

"Of course." Allie pasted a smile on her face, but the debacle of her San Francisco interview had led to a plummet into self-doubt, as if the flare of confidence had been a momentary aberration. Sure, she might still have the hair and clothes that said she was spunkier than she felt, but inside, the old habits, the old shy Allie, was clawing to get out.

It was this battle that had propelled her to rejoin the music team at church, sure that this would be the place where she could recalibrate her soul and, with renewed focus on God, get the niggles and wrinkles of doubt dealt with as she surrounded herself with God.

God. Her savior. Lover of her soul.

The church auditorium was gradually filling with people. She looked out and spied her parents and Marcie and Steve and the boys. Huh. Carissa was here as well? She hadn't been to church much in the past months, preferring to watch online worship services at home, or so she said. Whenever Mom and Dad asked Carissa what she'd watched, she never could remember what the sermon had been about, which only made Allie wonder just what Carissa was doing instead.

Their relationship still had not resolved, and no matter the prayers or the pleadings, Carissa still spoke very little to her these days. At least they'd progressed to occasional comments. They might be comments like "Did you use my hairdryer?" which really had more of an accusatory feel than otherwise, but they counted nonetheless. Perhaps it was a good thing work kept them both so busy that they barely saw each other—except for weekends, when Carissa would often hide in her room and binge-watch TV, while Allie worked on her art and her heart as she struggled to deal with the joy and pain of watching Jai in the playoffs, wishing she could be like Amber and Ella and the others and be there cheering the boys on.

She lifted her chin. Enough. Now wasn't about that. Noticing Josiah and Gloria had moved to their seats, Allie found a smile and lifted a hand. They both smiled at her, any tension Allie had once felt with her pastor long gone, as he'd made clear in enquiries about her welfare. Last week's lunch at their place had led to honesty about the breakup and her shame, and they'd assured her that they valued her happiness as much as Jai's. She'd left feeling very relieved that at least one of the strained relationships in her life had tipped back into normal—and that Jai hadn't made an appearance, something she had to admit she'd wondered about. She loved her pastors but wouldn't put it past them to hatch a plan like that…

Enough! She refocused. Josiah nodded to indicate she could begin.

"Good morning, church," she said into the microphone. "Welcome. It's so good to see you here today. Let's pray and then we'll begin."

She breathed and prayed and the music began. The first song was another by Sarah Maguire, and yet another with words Allie loved. It was more upbeat than a lot of other songs from Heartsong Collective, but in selecting the song for today, Allie had sensed it would be appropriate.

"Our God, our God, He can do anything, our God, our God, He can do anything," she sang.

What a great reminder. God *could* do anything. He'd healed Mrs. Henderson, sitting there in the second row, of cancer. He'd saved Mr. Baznik from a terrible fire. She closed her eyes, letting herself sink into the truth of the words of this song. God could do anything. God could heal, God could restore, God could save.

And whatever happened with her job, whatever happened with Carissa, whatever happened with Jai, the words this Sarah woman had penned for this song sang directly to Allie's soul.

"And we can trust Him," she sang. "We can trust Him with it all. We can trust Him"—higher harmony there—"we can trust him with it all. Yeah!"

She grinned at her uncharacteristic *yeah*, opening her eyes as she glanced at the musicians—those who, like her, were sensing the energy in the room picking up as the congregation joined in remembering who God was and what He'd done. Faith was rising, a sense of expectation.

God *could* do anything. God did heal. God did restore. Her gaze drifted across the congregation, her heart pinching at the stony-faced glare of her arms-crossed sister. For a moment her heart wavered, then steadied as that long-ago comment of turning her perspective from herself to others sparked again. Instead of self-focus, she should start expecting God to do wonderful things. God loved her. She could trust Him with her sister. With her job. With—

Her mouth dried. Jai.

The music shifted to the bridge, but she fell several beats behind, the shock of seeing him here, at the early service, chasing the words she was supposed to sing far from her mind. She glanced at the lyrics, but they didn't make sense, and she lost her place, shrugging sheepishly as Chrissy took over. What was he doing here? He'd had a game last night. He never attended the early service after a game. And wouldn't they all have been celebrating until the early hours? Amber had invited her to a party, but knowing that she'd be leading worship this morning—and that Jai would be at the party—Allie had declined.

The music shifted again, reminding her she had a job to do. That she was out the front and people could see her. Through a haze of clamoring thoughts, she finally returned to the song, hoping the fact she'd come in where she had would look planned and not the result of being dumbstruck by her ex-boyfriend's appearance here today.

The song finished with a flourish of drums, then she exhaled. Caught her breath. Steadied her heart. Opened her mouth to speak.

No words.

Nothing. Like that car was parked right on top of her chest again, refusing utterance. *Lord?*

She closed her eyes as mortification, her old friend, swathed her in familiar heated shame. Skin prickling, she stood still, wanting to cry, wanting to flee, but just as her tongue seemed clenched within her mouth, so her feet appeared rooted to the stage.

"And now, let's press in a little more."

Allie's chest released a fraction at the sound of Chrissy's voice. God bless the woman. Did she know why Allie had failed again? Surely it must be obvious to everyone here why she'd failed.

Failure.

The word taunted, a whisper she'd heard many times before.

But then the absurdity of listening to that voice when she'd just been singing about trusting God struck her. She might be a failure, but this song, another by Heartsong Collective, spoke of God using broken things. Broken people—like her.

She drew in a breath. Another. One more. Then sang.

"All of my pieces, broken and scattered, You've seen it all."

God *had* seen it all. Even if others here might've had to check their first impressions of her, she'd never taken Him by surprise.

"And yet You still love me, And yet *You* still love me"— emphasis on the God-focus there—"I know I can trust You with it all."

The tempo picked up. Maybe if she didn't look at Jai, she'd be okay. She opened her eyes, saw the congregation was singing along, some with raised hands. Gloria smiled encouragingly, Josiah gave her a thumbs-up. She relaxed.

As the music grew, so did the swirl of assurance. Yet another song about trusting God—how typical that God had known what she'd need to proclaim today, even if she'd picked the songs—and she sang of God's goodness, sang of His love today.

God's love. It would be enough.

Her eyes opened and zeroed in on Jai's playoffs-bearded handsome face. He smiled at her, and her heart skipped. *No, no, no.* She dragged her gaze away. God would be enough for her. *God* would. Not Jai.

The battle for her focus continued through the rest of the songs, then finally they were released, and she took her seat next to Chrissy, just off the stage. "Sorry about before."

"He's a bit distracting, huh?"

Allie winced. Great. So much for hoping nobody had noticed.

Communion was followed by Josiah's sermon, a message about—what else?—trusting God, almost like God Himself had orchestrated the entire service today, seeing as Allie and Josiah hadn't discussed the focus of today's songs and sermon. God was obviously into promoting His message with all the different pieces linking together.

Announcements, then one more song as the offering bags were taken around. A repeat of the first song. God could do anything. God could heal, God could restore, God could save.

She closed her eyes. *God, I know You can do anything. Thank You for healing this relationship with Carissa. Thank You for working out my career. Thank You for restoring my heart to wholeness.* Faith statements, all. But wasn't that just what Josiah had instructed them to do?

The music concluded, and with a final, "God bless you, have a great week," Allie finished and replaced the microphone, feeling way more drained than usual. The service—or more correctly, God—had hit her hard today, and now all she wanted was to escape, get home, have a sleep, recalibrate her soul.

"Great job today," Josiah said. Gloria gave a smile before her attention was stolen by someone requesting prayer.

"You're kind."

"You pushed through. That takes grit."

"I didn't feel very gritty today," she admitted.

"It's a good thing we don't have to let our feelings decide our actions."

Was that some oblique reference to Jai? She could see him, hovering on the outskirts of her line of sight like he was waiting to talk to her. Or was that just wishful thinking?

"Trusting God. That's what it's about. With everything and everyone." Josiah winked.

Okay, so she might feel clueless about lots of things, but there was no mistaking what that wink was about. "Thanks."

But she wasn't quite ready to talk to Jai just yet. She didn't have the sassy front to put on today. It felt like that girl had gone away. Maybe she'd fled with a final *yeah* in that first song.

"Hey, Mom."

Her mother wrapped her in a hug. "Good job, honey."

Warmth enveloped her at her mother's praise. "Thanks." She peeked open her eyes. Jai had been trapped by Dad. Of course he had. "Where's Carissa?"

Her mother sighed. "She left. She's probably sitting in the car outside. I didn't want to argue—she's a grown woman after all. It felt miracle enough to have her join us here today. I didn't have the heart to insist she stay."

Concern for her sister chased away earlier questions. "I'll go check on her."

"Would you?"

Allie nodded and made her way through the milling congregation, glad she could escape without Jai seeing her. "Lord, I know You can do anything," she murmured as she hurried across the tiled foyer, her heels clicking. *Restore this relationship. With Carissa*, she added.

She made it outside to the parking lot, and sure enough, her sister's red-shirted figure was hurrying to the car. "Carissa!" Allie called, noting her sister's steps pause.

"What?" Carissa said, hands on hips. "What do you want?"

"Don't leave."

"Why not?"

"I...I want to talk to you."

"Yeah? Well, I don't want to talk to you."

"P-please, Carissa." Allie swallowed. "I want us to be friends. I want you to forgive me." Her eyes welled. "I don't want you to hate me anymore."

Carissa glanced away, shook her head.

Allie's heart plummeted. Her sister didn't want to stop hating her?

"Well, look who's here," Carissa muttered.

Allie turned to look. Jai stood there, several cars away, hands in pockets, looking awkward. Her chest grew tight.

What did he want? But no. Now wasn't about him. Now was about trying to fix this strained relationship with her sister.

"Is this another of your two-for-one specials?" Carissa asked, returning Allie's gaze to her.

"What do you mean?"

"You. Him." Carissa jerked a thumb to where Jai stood. Allie refused to glance his direction. "You've both come to tell me I'm wrong again, right?"

"What? No. I came out here to tell you I hate this feeling of tension between us and I want to do whatever I need to to make things right."

"What would make things right would be for me to be married right now," Carissa said, her words terse and pitching higher. "But instead, I'm stuck. Stuck in this hellhole of a life because of you!" She stabbed a finger at Allie. "And you!" Carissa turned to point at Jai.

"Carissa, no. You can't blame us for what Jake did. You know that we only said something to you because we love you, because I love you. Would you really have wanted to marry a man who wasn't faithful?"

"I want to be *married*," Carissa said with a desperate-sounding hiccup. "I want to feel chosen. I *felt* like I was chosen, that Jake loved me—and I was wrong."

Allie stepped closer. "You *are* chosen," she murmured. "You *are* loved. You know that we love you, you know that God loves you."

"But I'm not loved by Jake." Carissa's eyes spilled, and she wiped them away with an impatient gesture. "I just want a man to love me enough."

Allie bit her lip, conscious that Jai was within hearing distance but sensing that this would need to be said anyway. "Honey, you need to know that you are enough, that you don't need a man to tell you you're okay. Because you *are* okay. The fact that God loves you proves that you're okay. You just need to believe it."

Oh, and what a hard battle that was.

Allie clasped her sister's upper arms and drilled her with her eyes. "You *are* enough, Carissa. You *are* okay. But if you need a man to always tell you that, then the danger is you're always going to put him ahead of God in your life. Ask me how I know this," she added in a whisper.

Carissa took a shaky breath, her gaze swinging from Allie to Jai and back again. "You're still not together."

"No," Allie continued in a softer voice. "And I don't want to be in a relationship with a man unless I know I'm okay by myself. And you know, *you* know of anyone, just how not okay I've been. But I'm trying, with God's help, to get better."

Her sister's chin wobbled, then she gave a little sob and burrowed into Allie's neck, which soon grew damp with her tears. Allie wrapped her close and prayed, and gently shook her head at Jai, who still hovered. He nodded and stepped away.

"How will you ever know?" Carissa whispered in her ear.

"I'm not sure," Allie murmured back, holding her a little tighter as her heart refused to settle into calm. How that man disconcerted her. "I think it's when you feel like you don't need them anymore. That you can be emotionally healthy without them." She paused. Like she was now.

As unsettling as it was to see him, she no longer had that train wreck of desperate longing to be in his life. She no longer felt like he was her all in all. Because she knew that God was.

"Are you over Jai?" Carissa asked, her words muffled against Allie's neck.

What could she say? Admit he still gave her heart palpitations every time she saw him? But she knew that would fade in time. It had to.

"Do you still love him?"

Allie sighed. She knew what Carissa was really asking:

would she, too, be able to get over her heartbreak? Allie wanted to say *yes, you'll be fine, just like me*, but what could she answer but the truth? "I still love him," she admitted. "But I'm okay with the fact that it's not meant to be, and so I pray that God will take these feelings away. It's been good to focus on other things, to think about my job and future, without needing to make all my decisions revolve around him."

"You should get back together," Carissa murmured. "I shouldn't have blamed you both for what Jake did. I…I'm sorry for telling him about the website."

Allie sighed. Clutched her sister a little more firmly. "I should've told him ages ago."

"I was angry, and malicious, and—" Carissa shuddered out more tears.

"Shh, it's okay," Allie soothed. "I forgive you."

"I'm so sorry. But you can get back with him now, can't you?"

"I can't believe Jai really wants to give me a second chance."

"Are you serious?" Carissa eased away, wiping her face. "Isn't he hanging around just to talk to you?"

Allie's disobedient gaze tracked to where he now stood, surrounded by a group of people, which naturally included her father. She swallowed a groan.

"Dad is so embarrassing, isn't he?" Carissa said with a sigh.

"Yeah."

Carissa giggled. "You know what you were singing about in there?" She gestured to the church. "Don't you think that if you're going to trust God, then He might be able to work things out for good?"

"Well, yes. Of course."

"What if Jai is part of that something good?"

Allie's eyes returned to him, and as if some magic force bonded them, his gaze lifted to connect with hers. Another heart slam. Another hitch of breath.

"Go talk to him, Allie," Carissa said with a gentle push. "I'm okay. I will be okay."

"And we're okay?" Allie checked.

"Yeah." Carissa's small smile was now reflected in her eyes. "We're good. Now go. Go see if you can find something good over there too."

Allie swallowed and turned to face Jai. *God? Thanks for healing things with Carissa. Help me to trust You with Jai too.*

CHAPTER 22

*J*ai pivoted as Allie slowly walked toward him, the excited conversation around him fading into insignificance. He'd held back, sensing he couldn't get involved in what looked like a sister squabble, but not before hearing some of what Allie had said. His hearing was unfortunately too good.

"Jai? Want to come to lunch today?" Peter Davis asked.

"Not today," he said, eyes still on Allie.

"Right. Uh, okay." Peter shifted. "Allie! Want to convince Jai to join us for lunch?"

She shook her head, her gaze shifting to her father. Jai instantly felt the loss. "No."

Jai's lips twitched at the bewilderment filling Peter's face.

"But I thought—" Peter began.

"Excuse us," Jai said. He tilted his head at Allie, and she nodded, allowing him to lead her to his car, situated half a row away. "You okay?"

She nodded.

"Carissa?"

"She's going to be okay." Allie smiled, the sight sucker punching him again.

Words rose, fell, as he struggled with what to say. There was so much to say. He settled for, "I hope you don't mind me kidnapping you."

"You haven't exactly kidnapped me," she said.

"It's just we need to talk, and your dad—"

"I know."

The wry look she shot him brought greater ease. "You want to go somewhere? We can come back for your car later."

"Um, okay."

He unlocked her door, holding it open while she slid inside as she'd done a dozen times before. His chest tightened at the memories of the kisses they'd shared inside, and as he shut the door and moved to the driver's side, he batted them away. No. Today was about reconciliation, nothing more, even if such kisses persisted in his dreams. *Reconciliation,* he told himself sternly. Not like that farce from Connor's engagement party, when she'd flung words at him and then walked away. No, today had to be about something more real.

When he woke early this morning, he'd had a sense that he needed to be in church. He'd blown off an invitation from Josiah and Gloria to lunch last Sunday. He'd quit going to the early service after the breakup, using the season's games as his excuse. But he knew now that he needed to make things right with this woman who'd stolen his heart.

He drove them to a little Greek place that he'd driven past before and thought looked nice. "This okay?"

"Uh, sure."

A few minutes later they were being seated, the front manager's, "I'm sorry, sir, we're fully booked," soon superseded when someone called, "It's Jai Mullins from the Hawks!" and a table miraculously appeared. Fortunately, it wasn't in the middle of the restaurant but by a window, where he hoped they could eat without too much fuss.

But judging from the whispered conversations around him and the shy approaches from kids wanting autographs, his choice to eat here hadn't been his cleverest idea.

"And what can I get you?" Their server boasted a smile and hair flicks to rival Brittany, the way she looked Jai over, barely sparing Allie a glance, sending chills down his spine.

"Allie? What do you want?" he asked.

Allie looked up from the menu and glanced at the waitress. Whose eyes rounded.

"Allie? Allison Davis? Is that you?"

Jai could see the near-palpable tension emanating from Allie. "Yes."

The waitress placed a hand on her red-aproned chest. "Erica, from high school. Remember?"

"Yes." Allie's smile was tight.

"Oh my gosh! How long has it been? Ten years? No, it can't have been. We didn't see you at the reunion last year."

Allie said nothing, her lips tightening in a manner Jai recognized meant distress.

"I'll have the steak, thanks. Allie? Do you know want you want? Or do you not want to stay?" He hoped his interruption would give her the out she needed—if she wanted it, of course.

"I'll have the salad, thank you," Allie said, her gaze flicking from him back to her high-school friend. Or non-friend, if the lack of warmth was any indication. "With the chicken and avocado, and tzatziki on the side. Thanks."

Erica nodded, her forehead wearing a small crease. "Okay. Oh, and drinks? What can I get for you?"

Two iced tea orders later, Erica left, and Allie's posture rounded slightly.

"Are you okay? You know her?" Jai reached across to hold her hand, but she shifted away.

"She used to bully me in high school."

"What? Why?"

She sent him one of those looks he'd seen his sister wear, a look of the *are you stupid?* variety. Oh. Her stutter. "We can leave if you like."

"And let her win again? No way." Her chin tilted, and he knew a surge of admiration for this woman.

"The reunion?"

She shrugged. "I didn't get an invitation."

He frowned. "Did you move? Sometimes those things can get missed."

"We've lived in the same house all my life. Our phone number, email, hasn't changed."

"Wow."

"Right?"

He leaned forward and trapped her hand beneath his, feeling the spark of energy and her attempt to pull away. He waited until she met his eyes. "I'm sorry."

"It's okay," she said.

"No, it's not. Bullying is never okay."

She shrugged, and his grip firmed, then she nodded.

"Everything okay here?" Erica said, placing their drinks on the table.

Jai leaned back in his seat. "Yeah. We were just talking," he said. "I didn't know you two knew each other."

"Allie and I? Oh, we go way back. Don't we?" She flashed a smile at Allie, who didn't smile back.

"So, were you friends?" he pushed. He probably shouldn't stick his nose into this, but he couldn't let Allie think he wasn't about to stand up for her.

"Uh, sure. We all were." Erica glanced away.

Allie shifted on her seat. "It's funny how two people can look back on life and see things very differently." She pressed her lips together, as if wondering whether to speak, then shook her head and sighed. "We weren't friends. You and Gina and Tori used to mock me. I didn't go to the prom because of you."

"I don't know what you mean."

"Did you bully my girlfriend?" Jai now said, conscious of Allie's small gasp and a heat of indignation on her behalf that probably wasn't helpful right now.

"O-of course not."

His gaze narrowed. Was Erica mocking her again?

"Of course not, sir. I...I might've said some things, but what kid doesn't?"

He bet Allie never had.

Erica's gaze shifted back to Allie's. "I'm real sorry if I said stuff that upset you."

Allie eyed her for a moment, then gave a small nod. "I forgive you." Her sudden small smile held a sweetness that said it was true.

"I'll, um, just see about your meals. They're on the house," she said, sliding Allie a look before shifting back to Jai. "Is it true what they're saying? Do you play for the Hawks?"

He nodded.

"Wow. And Allie is really your girlfriend?"

"Yes." Well, she would be, as soon as they had the conversation he now *really* needed to have with her.

"I...wow." She hurried away.

"What's the bet she gets someone else to serve us?" Jai muttered.

"I don't care." And he could tell she really didn't.

"You're happy to stay?"

"Yes." A shy smile. "Thank you. I'd heard she worked here, but didn't want to let that stop me. I...I'm trying to be more brave."

He studied her, grasped her hand again, noting this time she didn't pull away. "I think you're amazing," he said honestly. Her courage, her strength, her willingness to be vulnerable. "Truly."

She shook her head.

"Allie." He squeezed gently. "You're the most amazing woman I've met."

"Oops! Am I interrupting?" Another waitress, older, wider, placed their meals on the table. "I'm Andrea. Erica said these are for you, on the house." She grinned at Jai, but this smile held no speculation. "Hey, it's the Speed Machine! Wow, thanks for coming here today."

"My pleasure." He hoped. The food looked good, and the company was perfect, even if the earlier encounter had been less than ideal.

"Can the boys and I get a picture? We're so excited about going to the second round. And that was all thanks to you!"

"It's a team effort," he said, knowing it was true.

"Only one man scored that final goal. And that was you! Go Hawks go!"

Her raised voice drew other cheers, and just like that, the atmosphere changed from something fraught and tense to something more upbeat. Just like this morning at church, when the music had shifted to a place of possibility. When he'd felt courage rise to dream again.

"Okay, you'd better eat while it's hot. We'll get a photo later, okay?"

"Sure thing."

"Woohoo! And can I say, you make a very cute couple."

Jai's lips twitched. She could say that all she liked. "Thanks."

Now, if only he could make that really true.

~

HOW TO KILL THE MOOD.

Actually, we're not a couple.

Actually, while he might hold my hand, I'm not even sure we're friends.

Actually, we just need to have a conversation about returning to friends status without constant commentary and interruptions.

Yep. Eating here had proved a great idea.

"Is that nice?" Jai asked, looking up from his steak.

"It's delicious," she admitted.

"So the food is good, at least. And the company is great."

Allie sipped her drink, feeling her cheeks heat. "You shouldn't have let them think we're back together."

"Why not?" he said softly. "Especially when it's what I want."

Her heart skidded. Okay, so this wasn't a conversation she could have here. Not when Erica might return at any minute and hear the truth. Change the subject. "So, your goal last night was really good."

"You were there? I looked for you but didn't see you."

"I saw it on TV," she admitted.

He exhaled. "You know you can come and watch in person. I'll have tickets for you. For here, there, wherever, whenever."

"Thanks. I still have work, so…" She gave a slight shrug.

"When we play here, though, you could come. Couldn't you?"

"Maybe." Her lips tweaked. "But you know that would mean my dad would insist on coming."

He sighed. "I guess I could cope with that if it meant you were there."

The way he looked at her, with that intensity in his hazel eyes that twisted her heart in knots, did she have a chance of saying no? "I'll see."

"I'll take it." He grinned and sliced another piece of steak. "So, last we talked, you were talking about San Francisco."

She swallowed a piece of feta cheese. "The interview didn't work out."

"What? Why?"

She explained a little about Neil Blanchard, about the secret relationship he'd had with her boss.

"I can't believe it," Jai said, eyes wide. "That's so wrong on so many levels."

"Yeah." She shrugged. "I didn't know what to say except the truth."

"You did the right thing," he affirmed.

Another knot in her chest released. It was so hard to know if she'd done the right thing, especially when she lived in second-guess land.

"You spoke the truth. Your conscience is clear."

That was true.

"If they can't see what an asset you are, especially in a situation like that, they must have rocks in their head."

Did he want her to leave? Oh, this was so confusing. Between the hand-holding and the girlfriend comment from before, she barely knew what to think. "You sound like you want me to get the job." *And leave*, she almost added.

He put his knife and fork on his plate. "I want you to succeed and be given all the opportunities in the world that you deserve."

Her heart cramped. See? This was why Jai Mullins was so impossible to forget. How could her heart ever truly let him go when he said such sweet things?

"Allie?" He reached across, touched her hand. "What's wrong?"

"Nothing," she managed in a voice that didn't sound completely wobbly.

"You've gotta know that the last thing I want is for you to move away, but if you did because it was best for your career, then I'd support you with that." His smile grew wry. "I'd even pray I'd mean it."

"You pray for me?"

"All the time. I was praying for you with your job interview before, that things would go well. Guess I didn't pray hard enough."

"I don't think it's how hard we pray that determines God's answers." She sipped her peach iced tea. "It wouldn't have worked out anyway."

"Why not? From what your dad said earlier, you loved your time there."

Wait, Dad and Jai hadn't been talking about hockey? "You were talking about me?"

"Of course." His grin flashed. "And hockey. I think that's inevitable with him."

She chuckled, and he looked surprised. "What?"

"I've missed hearing you laugh," he said.

That same push and pull was there again, the mix of feelings that made it way too hard to stay neutral. "Why did you want to talk to me today?"

"Because you were right." He exhaled heavily. "I checked out the fan forum and the stuff posted there was crazy. I knew it wasn't real, that you never would speak like that or say those kinds of things. There are some really delusional people out there."

Like she had been. She ducked her head. "I asked the other administrator of the site to stop, but short of a court order, I don't know that she will. And I didn't think you'd want to give this more oxygen, especially if you knew it was like someone's version of fan fiction, and not worth the drama and publicity a court case would mean."

"You're right. We'll never be able to control what others say, and trying to live according to others' opinions is a surefire way to insecurity."

She nodded. Oh, she knew that well.

"But we can learn to trust each other, and trust that God will help us through it all," he continued. "So I don't want to think about the forum, or other people's opinions, or let those things steal from us anymore."

Her gaze crept up to meet his again. Around them, the clatter and conversations seemed to fade.

"I miss you, Allie," he said hoarsely. "I want us again."

The way he said that, his voice throbbing with the intensity of a thousand kisses, made her shiver. But this time, she could feel her brain levelling out her emotions, unlike the last time, which had been a one-way ticket to lovelorn land, ultimate destination: Doomsville.

"You still want us, even knowing all I did?"

"Yes."

"Even knowing I want to one day leave?"

"Yep."

"Why?" The question came out as breath.

"Why?" He leaned closer, shoved aside his plate, shoved aside hers, and grasped her hands. "Because I love you."

A feeling like a hundred sparklers emitting golden light danced and fizzed within. "You love me?"

"Yes," he said, his smile holding tenderness now, like she would be silly not to believe him.

And in the echo of his word, there came the oddest sensation within her soul of a heavenly *yes*, as if God Himself might be pleased with this.

"I don't know what to say," she whispered.

"I hope you'll go with my new favorite word and say yes."

"I thought your new favorite word was *us*," she dared.

"You're right. I love that word too."

Was this what God had meant when He'd asked her to trust Him? That putting her focus on Him, on renewing her relationship with Him, had allowed her heart to shift into something more? How good was God? How good was Jai? "I can't believe you still love me."

"I can't believe you can't believe it."

"Well!" A new voice intruded. "I hope you enjoyed that."

Allie blinked, the perfect bubble of contentment popped by the return of the waitress.

"Yeah, it was great," Jai said, releasing Allie's hands.

"Mm-hmm." Andrea glanced between them. "Anything else you'd like? They do a mean baklava here."

Jai glanced at Allie, who shook her head. "I think we're good," he said.

"Okay. So, do you mind if we get that picture now?"

"No problem."

The next five minutes turned into a frenzy of photographs, as Andrea, then the cooks, then the whole staff—including Erica, who shot Allie a worried glance that Allie met with a relaxed smile—insisted on photos too. This spurred several other customers to approach for selfies with their phones, and Jai was kept busy signing autographs for a few moments.

He tried to give Andrea a tip, but she refused. "Least we can do. Just win the next series, okay?"

"Yes, ma'am. We'll do our best."

"Don't you *ma'am* me." Her eyes twinkled. "Just tell everyone how good the food is. Okay?"

"Yes, ma'am."

"Go on with you." She laughed, catching Allie's eye. "You've got a good one there."

Allie nodded. Actually, she had the best.

~

HAWKS AND SQUAWKS ONLINE CHAT

CoolplayismyJam: Did you see this?

PucktheMagicDragon: OMG!! They're back together!

TubularBells: Aw. That's sweet.

PipeDreams27: Where was this taken?

CoolplayismyJam: Some place in the burbs. My sister knows a waitress there.

PucktheMagicDragon: I'm so happy for them!

TubularBells: I hope this helps him stay focused. We need to beat Calgary!

Destinysoffspring: I still kinda hope they break up. But at least her haircut is cool.

CoolplayismyJam: No words, Destiny.

PucktheMagicDragon: I hope they live happily ever after.

TubularBells: That's real sweet, Puck. Just let them win!

"So, Jai, how are you feeling?"

"Good." A grin erupted across Jai's lips. "Okay, maybe more like freaking excited. But trying not to get too excited, if you know what I mean."

Brent laughed, Beau and Dan smiled, and Josiah fist-pumped from his screen. Tonight's Bible study had a more relaxed vibe, with several of the guys off travelling now their seasons were done, including Mike, who was in the Philippines again for his charity.

"I bet this was how you felt a few years ago," Jai said to Brent.

"You thought the past month was crazy? Well, strap yourself in," the former Cup winner replied.

Jai exhaled. May had passed in a blur of playoffs travel. Their second round match against Calgary had seen the Hawks sweep the Flames in four games and progress to the Western Conference finals against San José. San José had home ice advantage, so it had been a repeat performance: two games away in California followed by two games at home, then a game apiece until finally the Hawks had won their fourth game and the United Center had erupted in cheers when

Chicago finally closed the series. But now, with the unthink-able-but-forever-hoped-for first game of the Cup final looming ahead of them, it was all he could do to think of anything else.

"Just enjoy the journey," Brent advised.

"I've gotta admit, it's been kinda crazy."

Everything, from the Art Institute's famous stone lions wearing hockey helmets to the inundation of interviews and intensified media scrutiny, screamed playoffs craziness. As for the fans... He might've once dismissed people of Peter Davis's ilk as the type to avoid, but Peter had proved almost a haven of sanity among the wild people out there. Some fans acted like they owned you. Every place he went there was at least one person wanting an autograph and "just a quick photo," and some of the requests were so, so wrong. And after every article or interview, it seemed to get worse. What would it be like if they actually won the Cup?

"I'm so thankful that something's worked out."

"What's that?" Dan asked.

"Allie's forgiven me and we're back together."

"You are?" Beau said. "That's awesome!"

Jai grinned as the others congratulated him, and Josiah gave a nod of satisfaction. But Jai knew he needed Allie. He needed some normalcy, someone down to earth who he could just be real with. She was his breath of fresh air, the smile in his heart, the one whose kisses after their reunion had threatened to fold him inside out. But such sweetness had helped temper the past few weeks of intensity and travel, even if the travel, training, and crazy fans had curbed his ability to date her as he'd like.

They'd talked every night, and he saw her when he could. But the searing nature of their kisses meant it was probably good to have space from her, as such times only fueled a hunger for more.

Voices stole his attention back to the screen, and with a pang of guilt at his distraction, he realized the Bible study conversation had moved on.

"Hey, Brent, it's daylight where you are. Where are you again?" Beau asked Brent.

"Australia." Brent grinned. "Here with Holly, visiting the in-laws. Check out this view." Brent's screen wobbled, the living room décor veering to reveal a deck complete with a shot of the sea. "Pacific Ocean, baby. Although I'm told this part between here and New Zealand is called the Tasman Sea."

"Nice," Dan said.

"It's a tough life, for sure."

Jai's time in San José hadn't exactly allowed for beach visits to the opposite side of the Pacific, but he could appreciate the climate, could see why Allie might've liked to move out there. And from the professionalism of the San José organization, he would've followed in a heartbeat. Once his contract at Chicago was done, of course. Not that it mattered now, as she wasn't leaving. His heart crimped with gladness.

"Hey, Holly," Brent called offscreen. "Come say hi."

A moment later, a petite brunette sat on Brent's knee, curled an arm around his neck, and flashed them a smile. "G'day, guys."

There was a chorus of greetings and congratulations on last month's World Championships, where she'd placed second overall in her pet event.

"Thanks," she said. "I'm so glad to have done well, especially as I don't think I'll be racing next year."

"You injured again?" Beau asked.

"Not exactly." She murmured something to Brent, and they exchanged private words and nods. She faced the screen again. "I'll have other commitments," she confessed with a sweet grin.

"Like a baby," Brent said, kissing her cheek.

"A baby?" Beau asked. "Congrats, guys. That's awesome!"

Jai and Dan echoed the congratulations, which saw Holly blush and Brent's cocky grin widen.

"You know, sometimes I still wonder how this happened," Holly said, which brought Brent's protest and several snorts of amusement from the guys.

"I don't mean that, of course," she said, laughing. "But once upon a time I really thought that after getting married I'd want to have at least five years to focus on short track. But when this happened, well, all of that suddenly seemed less important than building a future with my husband in one place."

The look Brent shot her was filled with tenderness as he bent to kiss her cheek again.

"What will this mean for your career, Holly?" Dan asked her.

"I think by the time this little one comes," Holly placed a hand on her stomach, which Brent covered with his own, "I'll be well and truly ready for this new season in my life."

New seasons, new focus, new life. Jai's chest constricted. Others might be moving deeper into their happily-ever-after, but so could he. He'd sensed in their recent conversations that Allie's disappointment in not getting the San Francisco job had not assuaged her desire to find work that would require moving elsewhere. But even if she did, there was no reason why he couldn't follow. He didn't need to stay in an Original Six team. A shiver raced up his spine.

"How are things going for your camp?" Beau asked Dan.

Dan shared a little, and Jai remembered he'd offered to help at the camp in Muskoka too. But when he apologized for being unavailable, Dan just laughed. "Yeah, I think you have other priorities right now, and that's okay."

Jai nodded. Other priorities like winning a Cup, confirming a girl's heart was his, and seeing what might lie next in their future.

THE LIGHTS DIMMED, the anthems started. The United Center was awash with red and noise. Chicago had only played Philadelphia once in the regular season, so they'd need to figure out the opposition pretty quickly. Jai stood on the ice, his heart hammering. He glanced at his stick, taped, with *Count it all joy* scrawled on top. That's right. Breathe. Relax. Thank God that He helped deal with this kind of pressure. Jai glanced over to Jeremy Stamos, who looked nervous but had denied it when Jai had tried to reassure him earlier.

"Hey, man, it's all good."

"Dude, I'm fine." Jeremy had given his cocky smirk as Jai bit back a grin. He'd seen Stamos throwing up in the washroom earlier. Fine? Not.

The puck dropped. Initial face-off went to Chicago, Connor passing it to Jai, who quickly slid it back to Alex on defense. Jai watched for the puck, checking the Flyers as they tried to skate into the Hawks' zone. The puck slid his way, he skated hard, then bam! The hit came from nowhere. He shook his head and completed his shift, then skated off to the bench.

He grabbed his water bottle, watching the play of the next line. Philly players were skating closer, closer to the Hawks' net—

Goal. The stadium filled with boos as the guys came off, their faces filled with disgust. Jai patted them on their helmets and downed his water.

Second shift. Jai skated on with Connor flanking him. A Flyer saucer-passed the puck, but Jai stepped in to intercept. The puck hit his chest, then dropped to the ice, where he scooped it up. He back-checked a defenseman and skated hard into the Flyers' territory. He sent the puck toward Jeremy, who slapped it into the net. Goal!

The United Center erupted in cheers and the Hawks' goal song. Jeremy skated over with a huge grin on his face and a bigger hug. Jai slapped him on the back, then headed to the bench. A round of high fives, then it was time to catch his breath.

"Good effort." Coach Quartermaine tapped Jai's helmet.

The next few minutes saw more unforced errors, fueled by excessive energy, before a shorthanded breakaway led to the Hawks' second goal. The horn blared, the crowd screamed, and the guys came off, sweaty but excited. Jai completed his shifts, blocking shots, taking shots, giving hits, being checked, yelling for the puck. The score seesawed: Philadelphia scored on the powerplay, then again three minutes later to take the lead.

Back in the dressing room during the first intermission, Jai swigged more water. The adrenaline coursing through his body slowed, and he took a deep breath, paying careful attention to the coach's instructions. "Stop being so jittery and settle. We'll find our groove. Now get back in there and win." The line of trainers and assistant coaches slapped encouragement as they walked back to the ice.

Second period passed in a blur. Hawks goal, crowd cheers, Flyers powerplay, Flyers goal, crowd groans, Connor's snapshot, Hawks goal, yelling from the bench, another Hawks goal, screaming crowds, Flyers goal, swearing from the guys, siren for the end of another wild period.

"Nice plays, Mullins."

Jai nodded to Jock, the trainer, as he resumed his seat in the locker room. Five all. Someone in this room was going to score. Jai wanted it to be him. He had several points this playoffs season, but knew he could contribute more.

The third period began, and Jai waited for his turn to get back on the ice. The coach tapped him on the shoulder, and he clambered over the boards into the fray. He tangled with a Flyer, shoulder barging him out of the way and grabbing the puck. He skated, deked one of their forwards, and sent the puck to Jeremy on the wing. Jeremy skated closer to the Flyers' goal but was quickly menaced by a huge Flyers defenseman.

"Here!" Jai had to yell hard to be heard above the fans. Jeremy looked up and slapped the puck back to Jai. He took it and, with a hard strike, smacked it into the net. Goal! "Yeah!" Jai did a fist pump as he skated around the net. *Thanks, God.*

"Dude! That was sick!" Jeremy skated over and thumped him on the back, and they skated back to the bench for the next line change. Jai fist-bumped down the bench, then took a seat.

The tension magnified. Philadelphia was desperate to score again, but the Chicago defensemen were doing a great job keeping them from the net. The minutes ticked away, the crowd waiting in anticipation for the final siren. When it finally rang out, the United Centre filled again with Chicago's elation. Yes. One up in the best-of-seven championship finals.

"Excuse me!" An interviewer, TV cameraman by his side, motioned to Jai, forcing him to skate to the side. "Jai Mullins, congratulations on a great game."

"Thanks. It was a lot of fun." Jai grinned. "Sure was a wild one."

"So, as the number one star of the evening with two assists and that game winner, tell us about that goal."

"We wanted to win tonight. Home ice is huge, and the fans here are amazing." He laughed as the crowd's cheers grew louder. "We just needed to stay patient. Jeremy gained some ground, then sent that great pass." He shrugged. "It's always a team effort."

"Well, congratulations. Great game tonight."

"Thanks." With a quick smile and wave at the crowd, Jai skated off, receiving slaps on the back and high fives as he entered the locker room.

"Great goal, Speed Machine."

Jai stripped off his jersey as Coach Quartermaine gave a quick review. Next time, once their nerves had settled, they'd be better. Jai glanced at the board near the door. Media room: #2, #17, #25. He finished getting changed, then slapped on a baseball hat to hide his helmet hair.

"Jai, they want you for media."

Jai nodded and followed the media relations guy out to the room filled with journalists. He joined his teammates and coach at the table and chugged a bottle of water in between answering questions about his game. The adrenaline had eased off, leaving him tired. He glanced at his watch and winced. It was already late, but he couldn't wait to see Allie tonight.

A day away felt way too long. He yearned for her smile, her hug, a kiss. He studied the black cloth on the interview table. Allie in a black dress had looked so—

"Jai?" He looked up to see one of the NHL staff writers looking at him. "Would you care to comment?"

He blinked. "Sorry, what was the question?"

The man gave a tight smile. "As the only hometown player in the team, could you describe the level of expectation you feel?"

Jai nodded and leaned forward in his seat toward the microphone. "Chicago is a great city that loves its sports. It's fun to see just how much the city is getting behind us. I love it here. So sure, there's pressure, but we deal with it."

"And how do you personally deal with it, Jai?"

Jai eyed the brunette reporter. "It's great to have supportive family and friends around, and my girlfriend too. That keeps me grounded, for sure." He smiled. But what really kept him grounded? *God, help me express this right.* He took a deep breath. "I also try to get some quiet time each day, to be still"—*and know that You are God*—"pray, and get some perspective."

There. Do what you like with that, mockers. He caught a few cynical smirks. *God, touch their hearts somehow...*

"Thanks, guys. See you again soon." Coach Quartermaine closed the media session with a grizzled smile, and they were released.

Jai's phone buzzed as he made his way back to the dressing room.

"Just caught the live feed," Josiah said. "Nice one."

"It probably won't make the cut, but anyways..."

"Every little signpost helps, man. Don't forget it."

Jai went to his locker and was grabbing his gear when a punch in the arm made him turn. "Jeremy!"

"So, what are you doing tonight to celebrate?"

Jai had arranged for his mom to stay with him over the next few days, to avoid the to and fro of traffic. Allie was also going to meet them at his place for a quick catch up. "I'll catch up with my mom and Allie. Then sleep."

Jeremy nodded, smirking. "Yeah, I bet you're gonna ce-le-brate with Allie, huh?" He made a crude gesture, then laughed.

Jai tried to maintain an impassive face. He sometimes over-heard guys carrying on about their post-game exploits with such candor he felt sick. "Man, it's not like that."

Jeremy sneered. "Sure it's not."

Jai closed his locker door and turned to face him. "Are you calling me a liar?"

Jeremy's eyebrows rose, then he took a step back, his hands up. "Dude, I—"

Jai shook his head. "You heard Coach before. We need to sleep. Which means rest, not anything else." He started walking to the door to the car park. "See you tomorrow."

The drive home still wasn't long enough to contain his emotions. Elation at winning had been soured by Jeremy's dumb comments and mixed with the usual post-game let down, making his brain twitchy. It would be so much easier to keep his faith locked up and go along with the flow. He pulled up outside his apartment block with a sigh. *God, help me live for You.*

He wanted to give Allie a big hug and just wind down with her and Mom. He stowed his gear by the door and walked through to where he heard voices. Mom was talking on the phone to Kat, judging from the conversation, the TV muted but showing NHL highlights.

"He's here now," his mom said as the phone chirped in her ear. "Kat says great goal."

"Thanks." He moved to the sink, splashed water on his face in a vain attempt to look good for Allie, wherever she was.

"Okay, talk again soon. G'night." His mom ended the call and found him. "Great game, son."

"Thanks, Mom. It got a little crazy tonight. And loud." His voice was still raspy from having to shout louder on the ice to be heard above the fans. They chatted for a while about the game, then he looked around. "Where's Allie?"

His mom gave a small sigh. "She wanted to go home and let you have some time to relax without having to go out again."

Disappointment surged through his chest like a tidal wave. He moved to the window, staring out at the darkness. Jeremy's wild assumptions were so far off the mark it was ridiculous.

"Jai?" His mom's voice came from behind. "She said she'd see you tomorrow."

He had to fight the urge to drive to her house at once and check if everything was fine. "I'm gonna call her." He kissed his mom on the cheek. "G'night."

He hurried to his room, shut the door, then lay on the bed and dialed. And waited…

"Hi!" Allie yawned. "Congratulations. You were great tonight!" She chattered for a couple minutes about the game and the crazy atmosphere. "It was so exciting!"

"Did I wake you?"

"No, no. Dad insisted on reliving every highlight all through the drive home, and there were so many it took forever. You should've seen him and Josiah after the game. I think Josiah is planning on coming over to talk some more." She yawned again. "I wouldn't be surprised if they talk all night. They're like little kids in a candy store."

Jai smiled. He'd always suspected that about his pastor.

Allie gave a sleepy-sounding chuckle. "It's a good thing it wasn't you dropping me home—you'd still be stuck here."

His heart tipped. "So is everything okay? I was looking

forward to seeing you, but you weren't here when I got back..."
He glanced at her photo on the bedside table. Poor substitute
for what he really wanted.

"Yeah, I'm fine. I just wanted you to get some rest. I
imagine it's a hassle for you to have a big day with a huge
game, then come home only to have to drive me back here
again. I wanted to save you some time so you could get to bed
sooner. You must be pretty tired. I know I'm tired, and I
haven't done anything like what you've done today." She
yawned again.

"Okay, okay, I believe you. But for the record, I'd rather see
you than sleep anytime." A picture of Allie in bed filled his mind.
His heart started racing again. He slowly breathed out.
Oh, God...

"Hey, we saw you on the post-game interviews. I loved what
you said about prayer and perspective." He could hear the smile
in her voice. "It's tough to not sound like you're Bible bashing,
but we thought you got the balance just right."

Jai closed his eyes. "Thanks, Allie. I needed to hear that."

"So, will I see you tomorrow?" Another yawn.

Her yawns were catching. "We have training in the morning,
but I could meet you for lunch."

"That'll be great. Sleep well." He heard Allie try to stifle
another yawn. "I love you."

"You too. Goodnight, Allie." He ended the call with a smile
and his heart more at peace.

"I REALLY DON'T SEE why you should, Taylah. It's not like this
hasn't been explained enough times already."

Allie hesitated at the threshold, out of sight of Myra, whose
berating of the intern paused. Taylah murmured something
Allie couldn't quite hear.

"Well, if you think that, then you're sadly mistaken. Honestly, it's like I'm surrounded by imbeciles all the time."

Allie straightened and strode in, blood pulsing with indignation as she faced Myra. "How dare you speak to Taylah that way?"

Myra's face tightened, and it looked like she was debating whether to respond or not. Given she'd had very little to say to Allie since the debacle that was San Francisco, Allie wasn't sorry.

Allie glanced at a red-eyed Taylah, saw the relief wash over the youngster's face as she mouthed a *thank you*. Allie nodded and returned her attention to Myra. How ironic that the leader of the Public Relations and Learning team was so mean to her employees in private. Allie lifted her chin. She had nothing to lose by speaking the truth. "I think it's way past time your actions and manner toward us be reported to HR. You are a bully, Myra, and the way you speak to us is unacceptable."

Myra's jaw dropped. "I most certainly am *not* a bully."

Allie moved to stand behind her chair, clutching the top of it so the others wouldn't see her trembling fingers. "You've mocked me, you've made fun of Taylah, we both just heard you call us imbeciles. Your behavior is unprofessional and intimidates—"

"I have never intimidated anyone in my life!" Myra's voice rose in volume and pitch.

"Would you agree with that, Taylah?"

Taylah glanced at Myra, then back at Allie as Allie willed her to finally stand up for herself. "No," she murmured.

Satisfaction steamed across Allie's chest, and she moved to Taylah's side. "We're going to speak to HR right now."

"But what about the talks?"

"You can sort out the talks," Allie said. "Or better yet, do it yourself. Or get Selina, whenever she decides to show up, to do them."

"But, but…"

Ignoring Myra's pleas, Allie steered Taylah out of the room and into the hall, where they saw Selina approaching holding a disposable coffee cup and a bright red smile.

"Oh, hi there. Off to do your talks already?" She giggled. "I didn't realize I was that late. Oops!" She glanced between them. "What did I miss?"

Allie shook her head and drew Taylah on, ignoring Selina's call of "Allie?" as they moved down the corridor to where Human Resources was located. They had nothing to lose. Allie might not have gained the San Francisco job, but a person with her skills could easily find work elsewhere. As for Taylah, well, the girl was young and still studying. She could chalk this up to experience and learning to stand up for herself. Allie's lips twisted. *Something I should have learned to do years ago.*

They reached the door, and Allie paused. "You ready?"

Taylah gave a single nod but grabbed Allie's hand before she opened the door. "I'm scared."

"Honey, you've got this. We're going to tell the truth, something that's needed to be told for ages."

Taylah nodded, eyeing Allie with a look she couldn't quite decipher.

"What is it?" Allie asked.

"You've changed. Is it from going out with Jai?"

"Jai?" Maybe. Or maybe it was God. Allie smiled. "I think I'm getting bolder in my old age."

"Old?"

"I'm nearly thirty, Taylah. I remember thinking just how old that seemed when I was a teenager."

"Yeah."

Taylah's meek concurrence spurted amusement, which chased some of the agitation from Allie's heart. Things she wished she'd known when she was younger: thirty was not old;

you have a voice so use it; stand up for yourself; and start the way you mean to carry on.

Well, the last she had managed to some degree. She had always endeavored to be polite, to treat others the way she would like to be treated, just like Jesus said. And if it had taken her a while to find her voice, well, she figured that was okay too. She'd never have a silver tongue, and the tongue she had might be prone to misbehave, but she'd use her voice to help others as best she could regardless. How could she not, when her Bible reading this morning encouraged her to break the chains of injustice, to get rid of exploitation in the workplace, to free the oppressed—things which would require acting in ways that pushed her beyond her comfort zone, but which would make a difference in her world.

Anyway, she *could* do this. God was with her. He would give her strength.

"Let's do this." Allie pushed back her shoulders, opened the door, and walked inside.

CHAPTER 24

Jai pushed his glasses back on his face and hurried up the steps into the Art Institute's main entrance, then through the big doors into the main foyer, where Allie had said she'd meet him. So far, he'd been able to walk the distance here without being recognized. He put that down to the plain black cap and gingery whiskers that people really didn't seem to expect from his dark-colored hair.

He spotted Allie talking with an older man dressed in a suit, someone who was nodding to whatever Allie was saying as she stood, poised and elegant as ever. But something about her stance seemed off, a little tense—something he saw in her face as she shifted slightly and caught his gaze, which led to a slight relaxing. What was wrong?

The older man turned and spotted Jai, his brow wrinkling a little before he spoke to Allie again. "…and we'll set up a meeting in a few days."

"Thank you." Allie's smile held more than a touch of relief as she beckoned Jai forward. "Mr. Weinberger, before you go, please allow me to introduce my very good friend Jai Mullins. Jai, this is Mr. John Weinberger, the deputy director of the Institute and the one who encouraged me to consider the job in San Francisco."

Jai shook his hand. "You're the culprit then." Man. What a time for random mouth to appear.

"Culprit?" The man looked between Jai and Allie. "I'm afraid I don't understand."

"Ignore him," Allie said, gently shoving Jai to one side.

But it seemed Mr. Weinberger was having none of it. "Allie, if you don't wish to pursue the job offer, then please don't let me persuade you otherwise." He glanced at Jai again. "Especially not if you have commitments elsewhere."

"Sir, you must excuse me," Jai said. "I'm prone to bouts of foot-in-mouth."

"Aren't we all?" The older man's smile faded. "Actually, don't I know you from somewhere?"

"If you follow hockey, then perhaps you do," Allie said. "If you'll excuse us—"

"The game-winner from last night." The older man's face lit. "That was you."

"Well, yeah, it was." Huh. Who would have thought a stuffed shirt like this guy would know who Jai was, let alone now be insisting on a photo?

"You don't mind taking a photo of us, do you, Allie?" Mr. Weinberger asked. "You can add it to the Instagram account you've started."

"Uh, sure." She snapped the photo and quickly tapped on her phone while Mr. Weinberger asked Jai about his Cup hopes. "There."

The look she sent Jai had him winding up the conversation quick smart—even faster as he noticed a small crowd starting to gather. "Excuse me, sir. I best go before things get a little crazy."

"Oh, I see what you mean. Well, very nice to meet you. Good luck tomorrow. And Allie, I'll be in touch soon."

"Thank you, sir. I'm heading off for my lunch break now."

"Take all the time you need, especially given your morning."

She thanked him, watching until Mr. Weinberger had exited before grabbing Jai's arm and steering him to the door. "So sorry."

"I'm not. I love how people from all walks of life seem to be getting into our run for the Cup. I never would've picked him for that."

"Another case of checked impressions, huh?" They were outside now, and she steered him south along Michigan Avenue, then across Jackson Boulevard toward the parkland.

"What's the rush?"

She exhaled, her steps slowing, and shoved on sunglasses, pushing them higher up her nose. Her lips were tight, the tension still palpable.

"Allie, what is it?"

She shook her head. "What did you want to do for lunch?"

They were passing a hot dog stand. "I'd planned to take you somewhere nice, but—"

"Would you mind if we grabbed something here, then sat in the park? I'm starving, and I'm afraid I don't really want to be around people right now."

"Allie, what's wrong?" From the mutinous look on her face, he guessed an answer wasn't going to be forthcoming any time soon.

"What'll it be?" the guy serving asked.

When two plain dogs and a lemon shake-up and water were ordered and delivered, they moved through the park, across the railway line, then over Columbus Drive to Grant Park, where they found a shaded spot that gave a great view of Buckingham Fountain. The blue of the sky, the trickle and splash of the fountain, the pretty flowers, and the lake's warm, gentle breeze would normally make for an ideal afternoon, except he could see Allie's tension, even as she ate her food and drank her lemonade before putting the trash to one side.

Allie sighed and leaned forward on the bench seat. "I'm really sorry."

Jai had polished off his hot dog, even though it wasn't exactly packed with the nutrients he'd need for his game tomorrow. Still, he could remedy that later, and time with Allie was more important than fending off fans as they tried to have the serious conversation he feared this would be. He reached across and held her hand. "Allie, what is it? Is everything okay with work? Mr. Weinberger seems nice enough."

"He is." She chewed her lips again, and as he rubbed her back, he could feel knots in her shoulders. "I had words with Myra today and finally took matters to HR. We're going to have to see what happens next."

"That's not fun."

"No. But it was the right thing to do."

"I'm proud of you, Allie," he said. "I know it couldn't have been easy."

She turned to face him, removing her sunglasses and placing them in her bag. "It was actually kind of humiliating. Myra had called ahead of our arrival—"

"Our?"

"Taylah and me, the intern you met on your first visit. Myra was berating her when I arrived this morning, called her—and the rest of us—imbeciles."

"Wow." His fingers clenched.

"I couldn't let that happen. Not when Taylah was so upset. But by the time we arrived, Myra was spinning it all she could and reporting us for misdemeanors we've certainly never done. And then I couldn't get my words out, and it turned into such a mess, and..." She sniffed. "And..."

"Come here." He drew her close, wrapped her silk-shirted self into a hug as he silently prayed for her. "It's okay. You're gonna be okay."

"I know. But I really can't see how I can stay here working

with that woman anymore. And now there'll be an investigation and more reports, and it's such a big mess, and I didn't want to tell you any of this, because you have your game to focus on and…" She hiccupped. "And…"

"And you are really important to me, and I'm so glad you told me. I would've been hurt if you hadn't," he murmured.

"See?" Her voice pitched up. "This is why I can't help but love you, because you're so nice to me. I wish I could be half the blessing you are to me, but to you. Oh, I can't even make sense anymore."

"I know what you meant," he said, smiling against her hair before pulling away. "Allie, do you want to work there?"

"Yes. Well, sort of. Well, not with Myra, but I do love the place, except…"

"Except what?"

She glanced down. "Except sometimes I still wonder what it would be like to work elsewhere. It doesn't have to be on the other side of the country, but somewhere else would still be nice."

"Then why not apply for other jobs?"

"And let Myra win?"

"What's more important? Feeling like you're trapped because you don't want her to win, or taking steps toward your future?"

"But what about you?" she whispered.

Now it was his turn to exhale. "I have another year on my contract, but after that, I can talk to my agent and we could see." His lips twisted into a half smile. "I made some enquiries about San José when you were looking at the job in San Francisco."

Her eyes widened. "You did?"

"I love you, Allie. I want to be with you, wherever you are."

Her face softened for a moment, then she launched herself at him, pressing her lips against his in a kiss that melted all tension and soothed his questions away.

"I can't believe you did that," she murmured a few moments later.

Neither could he, now he thought about it. Leave Chicago and all he knew to follow a woman? Something Beau had said a while back about trying new things floated through his memory. "Trying new things is the spice of life, or so someone we both know likes to say."

She smiled. "I can't wait to see Beau find a woman to keep him on his toes."

"Maybe he'll find her in Montreal," he said.

"He's been traded? How did I not know?"

"I think nothing official is being said for a few more weeks."

"Wow."

He kissed her again. "Wow."

Her lips lifted in a tender smile. "Thank you," she said, caressing his cheek. "Gosh, I can't wait until this cheek stubble is gone. It's a little abrasive."

"Amber said you need to think of it as an exfungalitate."

She laughed. "An exfoliant?"

"That too," he said, loving that smile she gave him now.

"You're adorable."

He rolled his eyes. "You're a little tired, huh? Maybe we both need to sleep together." Her eyes widened, and he realized how that had sounded. *Oh man.* "I mean, you have a sleep at your house while I have my rest at my place, so we can both be okay by the next game. That's all." Until these games were done and he could finally focus on what needed to be said—and maybe in the not-too-distant future make those promises before God and Josiah. A long-distance relationship could work, couldn't it? Brent had made it work with Holly. Jai could do the same.

"I'd better return soon," Allie said, gathering her things.

"You've still got time. Time for a bit more of a walk with me. Come on, let's go see Cloud Gate."

"Haven't you seen this a million times already?" she asked

fifteen minutes later, as they checked out the massive stainless steel sculpture that looked like a giant shiny silver bean.

"Not with you," he said, tugging her near. "Come on. Surely you should be encouraging a man to explore his artistic side."

"That would be fun," she said. "I'd like to see you try your hand at watercolors."

"I'd like to see you teach me."

"Maybe that can be arranged," she countered.

"Maybe after a few more games."

She chuckled, he grinned, a camera nearby flashed, and he drew her aside under the shaded cover of more trees. "Will you be okay this afternoon?"

She nodded. "I'd already booked to leave early, so it's only for a few hours."

"I'll be praying for you, Allie."

"And I'll be praying for you," she said. "Get some rest, okay?"

He nodded, kissed her again, and they parted—her to work, him to sleep and pray and thank God for the wonderful distraction that was Allie, who had kept him from noticing just how slowly the clock had been ticking today.

ALLIE ENTERED the car and laughed. "Seriously, Dad? A painted face and a wig?"

"Honey, it's like your wonderful mother says: There's no point having stuff if it never gets used. I've had this wig for twenty years, and now I finally get the chance to wear it. Come on. It's not as if I'll be embarrassing you or Jai."

"He's got the whole corner on that himself," Carissa said with a laugh.

"Are you picking on your poor old dad?" their father complained.

"Never," Carissa said, winking at Allie.

Allie exhaled, sitting back in the seat, glad to see the return of her sister's sass. With everything that had been going on lately, it'd been hard to check in with Carissa as much as she would've liked, but their relationship seemed to have healed well. It had experienced a mild speed bump when Carissa had demanded to know about Allie's "work trip" out west. Allie hadn't shared the finer details with her parents, figuring to leave it until she knew whether a job would eventuate or not. But Carissa hadn't been content with polite deflections.

"You want to leave us?" Carissa had asked.

"No, but I wanted to see what I could do," Allie had said, before adding, "Weren't you the one to tell me not to play it safe not so long ago?"

Her sister pouted. "But what about Jai?"

"What about him?"

"You can't leave him in the lurch."

"Who says he'll be left? He could come too."

"Allie!" her sister had gasped. "You'd be like Yoko Ono, hated by everyone for breaking up the band."

"Maybe. *If* he came. But that's a big if. Anyway, I didn't get it, so there's no point wondering," she'd said.

Except, from what Jai had said yesterday, maybe he would've followed her anyway.

She shivered. He cared that much?

"You okay?" Carissa asked as the car pulled into the United Center's parking lot. "Don't worry. Jai will be fine. He *is* plenty fine, if you don't mind me saying so."

"Why would I mind my sister ogling my boyfriend?" Allie asked. "Not weird at all."

"Right?"

Allie joined her sister's laugh.

They made their way to the seats allocated to them, the atmosphere ten times the usual that filled the Madhouse on Madison. Josiah and Gloria waved from the places next to where Jai's mom sat. It looked like Gloria and Bev had been having a good conversation.

"Hello, Mrs. Mullins," Allie said, giving her a kiss on the cheek.

"It's Bev, Allie. Now, come sit here next to me." She patted the seat beside her, and Allie waved to her family in the next section, once more down near the glass. No, Dad's costume wasn't weird at all, especially given the number of other fans dressed similarly.

"I can't get over how excited everyone is."

Josiah grabbed his wife's arm. "Is that Michael Jordan?"

"Where?"

"Over there!"

Allie smiled. She'd seen Michael Jordan already—well, the statue out the front of the United Center, anyway—all decked out in a Hawks jersey and skate attachments.

The thumping music quietened a little as a spectacular light show began, with the repeated cry of *one goal*. The announcer introduced each Chicago player to thunderous cheers. "Number seventeen, Jai Mullins!"

"Woo hoo! Go Hawks!" Allie waved her rally towel as Jai skated around completing some warm-ups, then blew him a kiss when he looked up. He grinned and placed a fisted hand over his heart.

The roar in the arena escalated during the national anthem, then it was time to begin. But it was obvious from the get-go that tonight would be very different. The crazy goal-scoring frenzy of two nights ago had been replaced with serious atti-tude. The hits looked harder, the plays more controlled. Allie winced, watching some of the penalties as they were replayed on the huge Jumbotron overhead. Josiah was leaning so far forward he was almost in the next row.

"Cross-checking is dangerous," he muttered. "Philly should know better."

Allie swallowed. *Lord, keep Jai safe.*

Two minutes later, Bev was shuddering. "I think elbowing should be more than a two-minute minor. It can lead to concussion!"

Allie tried to reassure her, then turned back to watch the game, her heart filled with prayers. *God, keep him safe. Help Jai stay focused and play well.*

The siren blew for the first intermission, and they all sat back in relief.

"He's playing well," Allie said.

"Amen, sister." Josiah patted his large stomach. "I think I need another hot dog."

Allie bit back a grin. Josiah looked like he wouldn't *need* to eat for a week.

Josiah turned to her, a twinkle in his eye. "Now, don't you be looking at me like that, young lady. All this excitement is making me hungry." He hefted his large frame out of his seat and waddled off to the food stands.

Gloria shook her head. "I'm sure half the reason the man loves sports so much is so he can eat the foods they sell here."

"Allie!"

She turned at Amber's voice. "Hey, you." A hug revealed a little bump on Amber's otherwise svelte frame. "Amber!"

Her friend smiled. "I've got a little present coming in time for Christmas."

"How special! A true gift from God," Allie said, giving her friend another hug.

"I don't know how much God had to do with it," Amber said with a wink.

"You are blessed with a gift some women dream of having."

"Huh. Well, yeah, I suppose."

It might not be the salvation talk with Amber that Allie longed for, but every chance to drop a God-seed, she'd take.

"Are you feeling well?" Allie asked softly. "Is there anything I can do?"

"You're just the sweetest, aren't you?"

"You know it," Allie said dryly.

Amber laughed. "Come watch the next games at my house? I'd travel to Philly, but flying makes me feel sick."

"I'll be there," Allie promised.

"Allie, come sit down," Josiah called. "The next period is starting."

Allie peered past all the towels and scarves being waved around as the teams came back on the ice. It didn't take too long before the rough play resumed with hard hits into the boards. "There he is!" Jai's mom pointed as his line skated into the play again.

Allie held her breath, watching as Jai maneuvered around the Flyers' huge defenseman as he flicked the puck on the net.

"Glove save." Josiah shook his head as the crowd vented their disappointment. "Their goalie's good. But not as good as ours." Josiah stood up. "C'mon, Jai!"

"Ouch!" Bev winced as the crowd booed. "Poor Jai! That's going to hurt."

"What happened?" Allie stood to her feet, trying to see the ice, but there were too many bodies in the way.

"Jai got tripped. Look!"

Allie watched the replay on the Jumbotron—a deliberate trip, according to the commentators. Her stomach grew queasy as she saw the blood dribbling down his chin. "This is so rough!" She watched as he made his way back to the bench.

Bev sent her a sympathetic smile as Allie resumed her seat. *Lord, let him be okay.*

The next ten minutes saw more hard, gritty action. Each time Jai completed a shift, Allie's heart rate returned to something approaching normal. How Dad wasn't having a heart attack watching this was beyond her.

"Come on, Hawks!"

It was almost like a miracle. As soon as Jo's booming voice uttered those words: goal!

The crowd was on its feet. "Yes!" There were high-fives and hugs all around as strangers congratulated each other. Then half a minute later, goal!

The goal song boomed through the arena. Chicago was in the lead, 2-0.

The cheers had barely died down by the time Jai skated on for his next shift. Allie bit her lip, watching as he delivered a massive hit to one of Philly's players, into the boards. "Oh!"

Josiah grinned. "That's my man. Legal check. He wasn't targeting the head."

The crowd's cheering appreciation for the hit was drowned out as the horn blared for the next intermission. Allie sat back in her seat as conversation flowed around her. This felt surreal. Was the man out there delivering bone-jarring hits the same one who held her so tenderly? Her heart swelled in renewed respect for this man. She loved his intensity, his passion and zest for life—passion he'd kept restrained when kissing her these past few days.

The final period started, and another Chicago penalty soon led to a powerplay goal for Philadelphia. The United Centre held its breath, willing its boys to hold off the opposition. Chicago kept the Flyers contained, and despite a flurry of shots at the end, the horn sounded with the Hawks winning, 2-1.

Allie watched as a brawl began between several players. Was it any wonder that the physicality of the sport spilled over into high-flying emotions? Two games up, only four games to win. Could Chicago finally lift the cup of Lord Stanley once again?

CHAPTER 25

Jai pushed away his tray of food and glanced outside at the glowing lights on the plane's wings. His stomach clenched, protesting the meal. Or was it tonight's loss?

"Hey, Mullins, wanna play poker?"

Jai forced a smile. Why did Jeremy insist on asking him this every single flight? Was he just trying to make Jai look uncool to the others? Jai held up a bunch of cards. "No, thanks. I've got mail."

Jeremy shook his head and turned back to the other guys. Jai opened the first letter.

Hi Jai,
Can you please send my brother a card? It's his fifth birthday
soon and you're his favorite player.
Thanks, Caleb.
PS His name is Rohan.

Cute. Jai smiled, grabbed a player card and wrote a short

birthday message, then sealed the envelope and put it to one side.

The next twenty minutes provided more opportunity to reply to mail. Most of it was pretty innocuous. Some he put to one side for the front office to deal with. Others he put in a separate pile for follow-up, like little Ethan, a nine-year-old kid with leukemia who wanted Jai to visit. His heart wrenched. *God, heal Ethan.* He'd definitely prioritize that once at home.

He cleared the mess of letters and envelopes away, then leaned back in his seat and closed his eyes.

"Hey."

Jai opened his eyes as Connor slipped into the vacant seat beside him. "Hey."

Connor nodded, his blond hair flopping over his forehead. "It'll be good to be home."

"Yeah." Jai smiled. "Nice breakaway tonight." Connor's breakaway goal had robbed the Wachovia Center of its voice for a few seconds.

Connor shook his head. "I didn't think we'd lose both games."

"Philly is good." Jai shrugged. "They've come from behind several times in the Eastern Conference finals series." He smiled. "But so have we."

Connor finally cracked a smile—the first one all night for Captain Grim. "How do you always stay so positive?"

Jai's eyebrows rose all by themselves. People paid attention? *God, help me not to mess up my words.* "You know I'm a Christian, right?"

"Yeah." Connor's eyes slid away.

"Well, I think that takes away a lot of the fear and pain that often shapes our world. It helps to keep things in perspective." He motioned to the mail still sticking out of the plane seat's pocket. "Hockey's important, but it's not the be all and end all. Not when there are people out there having to deal with life-

and-death stuff." Jai tapped an envelope. "Nine-year-old with leukemia."

Connor grimaced. "I just don't get why stuff like that happens."

"I don't get it either. But at least this boy has hope."

"What? A transplant?"

Jai shrugged. "Not yet. No, he wrote that he believes God is helping him to stay positive for his parents and little sister, and he's trying to encourage them that even if he doesn't get better, that he'll see them in heaven one day. He believes in Jesus."

"Wow," Connor muttered. "Life and death sure give some perspective."

"It's God perspective." Jai swallowed. *God, help me say this right.* "This life is temporary, filled with trials. But we don't have to do it alone. There's Someone who cares about us, who wants to be our friend, who's helping us persevere and have hope, in this life and for the next. Christians know this, which is why we can count it all joy when we face trials of many kinds, because it's building character, building patience, so we can be mature and complete, lacking nothing. I write that on my stick to remind myself," he added.

Connor blinked and looked away.

Jai's heart raced like it did during the most pressure-filled moments of a game. *Lord, somehow touch his heart, despite my poor words.*

Connor cleared his throat. "Amber is pregnant."

"Really? Congrats. That's awesome. Isn't it?"

Connor nodded. "It's why I had to make things official. I want to marry her before the baby is born."

Jai nodded. A baby before marriage wasn't the way he'd do things, but Connor and Amber were on their journeys to God, and if this past year had taught Jai anything, he couldn't judge. "If there's anything we can do, just holler, okay?"

Another nod from Connor. "I'll do that. I...I know Amber

and Allie have really clicked, and Amber sees her like the sister she never had, so, well, maybe we'll have to get you guys to be godparents or something."

Jai's throat tightened. "We'd be honored. And anytime you want to talk, I'm here."

Connor stood. "Thanks."

The rest of the plane trip was a blur as Jai's prayers mingled with hope and excitement. *Lord, heal Ethan. Help his family continue to trust You, no matter what the outcome. God, thanks for Connor. Open his and Amber's eyes to see Your love for them. And help Jeremy and the others know You are real. And thanks that we're going home—home!—and that Allie will be there. Lead us into Your goodness.* He smiled.

Mr. Weinberger leaned back in his leather chair and studied Allie, prickling her skin. This meeting they'd set up a few days ago had certainly not gone the way she'd thought it would.

"I want you to consider it," he said. "You know your colleagues here at the Institute don't want to lose you—"

Except for Myra, she thought.

"—but Mr. Holt says it's a solid offer."

She licked dry lips. "I thought they didn't want me."

"You would be only too aware that the process before was clouded by, ahem, the misjudgment of a certain panelist. I think it'd be fair to say that if you were interested, then they would be more than willing to set up another interview as soon as possible."

Her heart hammered. Was this it? Could her dream be coming true after all? "When?"

"Well, the sooner the better, really."

When would Jai's games be? His next was tomorrow night, and they'd need at least one more, which would likely be two nights after that. She *really* wanted to talk to him, but how could she ask him for his thoughts about her potentially moving away when that was a guaranteed distraction? "Would a week's time be okay?"

"I really think it would be better to show you're genuinely interested by opting for something sooner," he advised kindly.

She nodded, fingertips tingling as he excused her and the wondrous dread of possibilities followed her back to her desk. She couldn't concentrate. She hardly dared believe. They wanted her? After all this? Even with the recent drama of Myra?

Breath escaped. Thank God Myra had taken personal leave these past days, that Allie didn't need to face her as she juggled the thrill of this job offer with the weight of what she'd be leaving behind. And the weight of what this would mean for her relationship with Jai.

SLEEP WOULDN'T COME. Jai tried to snooze, do the usual rest-time things before a game, but for some reason his brain was too wired for anything remotely restful. Even finding the world's slowest documentary on TV couldn't dampen the nerves tapping through his veins. Pictures of goals, of winning, all the visualization techniques the coaches asked them to do, refused to go away. Coach was switching the lines up tonight, hoping the combinations would throw off Philadelphia. Jai hoped—he prayed—it would work. The city that five years ago barely knew Chicago had a hockey team now seemed more invested than Kyle eating candy at Halloween.

He lay back on the bed and closed his eyes. It wasn't just tonight's game that had his heart and mind buzzing. He'd wanted to see Allie today, but she'd pleaded work, promising she'd catch him after the game tonight. He couldn't help but wonder if her boss had been making life difficult for her again, but when he asked, she'd denied it, which took the edge off his concern.

But still, his heart wrestled with what was concerning her, which soon rabbit-trailed into what their future might look like. Them here would be best. "Don't You think, God?" he said aloud.

There was no answer he could hear, nor settling in his heart, which forced him to confront the other option. Had he really meant it when he told her last week he'd follow her anywhere? Could he abandon his mom and Kat and Kyle and leave possible godparent duties behind? Obviously, anything like that might be a few years down the track, by which stage they should be settled into something more permanent relationship-wise.

He couldn't talk to Josiah about it. That man might know how to keep a secret, but he was the Davis family's pastor too, and it didn't seem fair to tell him this stuff when Allie might well be staying. Jai's mind whirled, the stress and strain of past months tugging at the peace he'd so blithely claimed in his recent conversation with Connor.

He needed to pray, or at least have someone else pray, so he reached for his phone in the dark.

Hey, anyone up and able to talk?

A minute later, his phone buzzed. Get some rest, dude. Beau.

The group chat continued.

Obvs he can't, otherwise he wouldn't want to talk to us. Eyeroll emoji from Brent.

What's up? This from Dan.

Ten seconds later, he had them on Messenger group chat, the screen displaying the faces of his three friends.

"Dude, what's going on?" Beau asked.

"Can't sleep," Jai admitted.

"Yeah, it's tough trying to rest, huh?" Brent said. "Busy imagining plays, what you could've done better last game, what to improve upon next game—"

"Yeah, and then some."

"Then some?" Dan asked, shrewd as ever.

"I'm trying not to think about the future."

"Then don't," Brent said bluntly.

Beau laughed. "Like telling someone that ever works."

"Weird. Holly says the same."

"How's she doing?" Jai asked. *Distraction, distraction.*

"She's good. None of this morning sickness stuff. Still insists on whupping me on the bike, so she can't be too bad."

"How's Allie?" Beau asked.

Jai paused. How to explain this so he didn't raise concern?

"Dude?" Brent frowned. "Is that site still going?"

"Allie's good," he hastened to reassure. "And the site has gotten so crazy that I think everyone knows just how fake it is. Apparently I took her on a helicopter ride over Manhattan two nights ago, or so Connor's fiancée told me."

"While you were at the game?" Dan asked.

"See? Completely unbelievable. It's almost funny seeing what crazy stuff they come up with."

"Glad to hear it's not that, then," Brent said.

"No. But I had this conversation with Allie the other day that got me thinking."

"Is this the thinking you can't shut off now?" Dan asked.

Jai nodded, then went on to explain a little about what was happening. "Be great if you could pray for her, and for me, to feel some peace."

"And to win tonight too, eh?" Beau said, emphasizing the *eh*, which scored eyerolls from Canadians Dan and Brent.

"You got it," Dan said.

"Already been praying," Beau reassured him.

"Thanks, guys," Jai said, feeling a little better.

"Now, go get some sleep," Brent said before grinning. "And then go win!"

~

HAWKS & SQUAWKS ONLINE CHAT

TubularBells: How about that game?
PucktheMagicDragon: OMG!! It was the best!
PipeDreams27: Apart from when poor JM17 got hit.
CoolplayismyJam: Draco has a mean streak.
PucktheMagicDragon: He can't stand to see someone outperform him. And JM17 was so awesome tonight!
TubularBells: That first goal was gold.
Destinysoffspring: Jai *is* gold.
TubularBells: Best goal of the tourney.
CoolplayismyJam: And why he got the second star tonight!
PucktheMagicDragon: I hope he's not hurt.
PipeDreams27: Heard it was a flesh wound. Two stitches. He'll be okay.
PucktheMagicDragon: So glad it didn't get closer to his eye!
TubularBells: That's why they wear visors.
CoolplayismyJam: So now we're back to Philly. I kinda hope they don't close it out there, because I'd like to see them win. Can you imagine how insane Chi-town will be if that occurs?
PucktheMagicDragon: IF???
TubularBells: Shame on you, Coolplay. WHEN they win!
Destinysoffspring: Was Allie there?
PipeDreams27: Yeah. She sat with the other WAGs and I think his mom.
PucktheMagicDragon: Aww, so sweet.
PipeDreams27: And some big dude who kept going crazy with the cheering.
PucktheMagicDragon: That might be his pastor.

TubularBells: He goes to church?

PucktheMagicDragon: How do you not know this? He's always going on about it in interviews and stuff.

Destinysoffspring: But he's so hot.

PucktheMagicDragon: You can be hot and a Christian, Destiny. Anyway, he's in some Bible study group the big guy leads, which other NHL players attend too.

Destinysoffspring: Like who?

PucktheMagicDragon: Beau Nash, Brent Karlsson, Mike Vaughan, Dan Walton, some others.

CoolplayismyJam: Like, all the hottest players ever!

Destinysoffspring: I still hope he breaks up with Allie.

ArtHeart101: Don't say that.

Destinysoffspring: I'll say what I like, thank you, Arty.

ArtHeart101: She's nice.

PucktheMagicDragon: That's right, Arty! You work with her.

ArtHeart101: I did.

PucktheMagicDragon: What? Did you lose your job?

ArtHeart101: I quit, and I've heard rumors she's losing hers.

PucktheMagicDragon: Oh no! Poor Allie.

PipeDreams27: Please. Poor? Not when she's got a rich boyf looking out for her.

Destinysoffspring: Hope she moves far away.

CoolplayismyJam: So you can get your shot?

PipeDreams27: As if, Destiny. He's too good for the likes of you.

ArtHeart101: And Allie is perfect for him. They make a good couple.

PucktheMagicDragon: Aww! I hope things work out for them.

TubularBells: I hope they win this next game! Three wins down, one to go. Go, Hawks, go!

CHAPTER 26

Allie stared around at the Wachovia Center, crowded with orange-and-white-clad supporters. Judging from the number of Hawks supporters, more than a few thought tonight would be the night, including Amber. Of course, it helped when the organization chartered a plane to take the team's family members to Philadelphia to watch the game. She was still blown away by their generosity—a delicious steak dinner, hotel accommodation, great seats for the game for Jai's mom, Kat, Josiah, and herself.

She knew Dad was a little sore that Josiah got the pass when he didn't. She'd even heard him mutter something about the nerve of a future son-in-law, which had scorched her cheeks and made her hush him, hoping Jai hadn't heard. She couldn't afford to think like that, even if Jai had murmured sweet nothings to her as she tried to soothe the aches and pains of the big hits from the last game two nights ago. For she knew the online interview with Mr. Holt in two days' time would impact their relationship regardless of what happened here tonight.

Uneasiness twisted her insides as the lights dimmed and the players were introduced, the Hawks to a chorus of boos from the biased arena. Allie watched as the team stood on the ice as a special duet of "God Bless America" was performed.

"It's kind of good they're here." Josiah leaned forward. "Away games can be easier; you don't have to face home-crowd pressure."

The Hawks won the opening face-off and it was on. The shouts and clash of sticks could barely be heard over the stadium noise. The two teams traded shots and hits, trying to create the momentum that would help the game go their way. Eight minutes in and the first penalty against Philly was called, sending their chief defenseman to the penalty box for mauling a Hawk.

Amber cheered from beside Allie. "If that guy is losing his cool already, that's means he'll have lost it completely by the end of the night. He'll be sent to the penalty box plenty more times before the night is over."

Allie bit her lip as the Flyers continued to try and muscle their way into the game. *Lord, keep Jai safe.* Another hit, a hope-filled roar from the crowd as a Hawk went to the box before an effective penalty kill. More big hits, then a high stick to the face saw the same Flyers defenseman back in the box again.

"Go Hawks!" Josiah and Amber were on their feet. And seconds later, the whole row was on its feet as the Hawks inched closer to the—

"Goal!"

There was no siren or fancy dance music here to indicate Chicago's goal, just a flashing light and loud booing from the Philly supporters.

"That's good." Josiah nodded once they'd all sat down. "Statistics say whoever scores the first goal usually ends up winning. But you can never count the Flyers out."

And sure enough, three minutes later the stadium erupted as Philadelphia scored on the powerplay.

The period ended and everyone sat back and breathed.

"The Hawks are outshooting them, but their goalie's a wall." Kat sounded hoarse already.

"This is so exciting!" Amber looked like she wanted to jump out of her skin.

Allie wanted to smile, but her nerves meant she only felt sick.

~

"WE'VE STARTED STRONG. We've made seventeen shots to their seven. You've won more face-offs. Now stay out of the box and we'll see more goals." Coach Quartermaine finished his locker-room lecture and conferred briefly with some of the other coaches.

Jai gulped down the Gatorade and threw the empty bottle toward the trashcan. Score. Now for that to translate on the ice. He stood, collected his stick, and followed his teammates back to the ice.

Second period. Jai leaned over the boards in front of the Hawks' bench and watched the reshuffled lines continue to stymie the Flyers, skating, passing, shooting, to no avail.

"Come on, boys!" His voice sounded rough. He grabbed more water. "Go Hawks!"

The pace was fast, but tonight's stakes meant the level of aggression had ratcheted up. He had to keep his wits about him. Just breathe. Play. Don't think about the Cup. Focus on what you need to do right now.

"Yo!" Jai clambered across the boards for the shift change. The puck was up near the Hawks' goal, so he skated quickly into position at point. He watched the puck skip toward him when it was intercepted by a Flyer. He raced toward it and—

Bang!

He threw a hand to his face as pain radiated around his chin. He took his hand away. Blood. Awesome.

"Mullins, keep your head up!" Connor turned to protest the play with the refs. "See? Blood."

Jai wiped it off. Sometimes penalties were about who could make the biggest fuss. Getting upset wouldn't help. It would only steal his concentration and rob him of his game intuition. But while he was opposed to diving or milking a penalty, he wouldn't mind seeing justice for this.

"But I was just finishing my pass!" The Flyer skated backwards, arguing with the ref.

Apparently the refs weren't buying. Jai gave a tight smile of satisfaction as a two-minute penalty was called. He nodded to Connor, who skated past looking as serious as ever.

Jai's shift soon ended, and he skated back to the bench to be greeted by the wolf whistles of his teammates. Jeremy laughed. "Mullins, you're so pretty."

Jai squirted him with his water bottle, then sat down, took off his helmet, and raked his hair out of the way. "I'll never be as pretty as you, man."

"Let's have a look." Jock squatted before him. "Looks like it's just a small cut. It'll heal." He wiped on antiseptic, then disappeared, and Jai leaned forward to watch the play.

Philadelphia had the puck. They were moving well, up the ice into the Hawks' zone. "Come on, Hawks!" His teammates were blocking shots—sometimes even leaping in front of the puck—but the wily forwards kept peppering the Hawks' goalie until they scored.

The horn blared, the fans screamed approval, and his teammates swore. 2-1, Philly.

"Come on." Connor had his serious face on. "They're desperate, but we're gonna win."

Play resumed, instantly followed by another couple of penalties. Jonas took the puck and skated hard to the net. Around the back. Wrap around goal! They were now tied, two all.

Jai went out for his next shift. Connor had the puck. He looked over. "Mullins!"

Jai collected the puck and slowly skated down the ice into the Flyers' zone. "Jeremy!" He sent a quick pass out to the wing while keeping an eye out for the tank-like defensemen who would try and block the shots. The puck skipped back his way. He shot, but it bounced off the side of the post with a ping. Jeremy stretched his stick out and pushed it in. Score! Back in the lead, 3-2. He skated over and hugged Jeremy. "Awesome!"

Jeremy's mouthguard hung loose. "It was, eh?"

Jai laughed and skated back to the bench for the celebratory high-fives and backslaps.

Another couple shifts and the period ended, then it was back to the locker rooms.

More stripping off of equipment to dry, re-taping of sticks, energy bars, energy drinks. With one more period to go, this could be it.

Jai exhaled, scribbling his favorite verse on the stick as Coach Quartermaine continued his instructions. *Count it all joy.* Jai smiled to himself, although his cheekbone protested. "Just persist."

Connor looked up from his stall nearby. "Did you say persist?" At Jai's nod, Connor stood. "Come on. One of us will score and be the hero. I know it." The mood subtly shifted as Connor stood in the middle of the locker room. "Just persist!"

It was the rally cry they needed as they headed out again—hopefully for the last time this season.

Five minutes later, Jai sat on the bench with ragged breath, watching the play. They were so close. They were still outshooting the Flyers, but the score wasn't changing. The third period had been filled with disciplined yet desperate hockey. Now, if they could just hold on for four more minutes.

He glanced up at the packed arena. The orange-clad fans

were screaming at their team to score, their despair fueling the threats and cajolery he could hear from nearby. "Go Flyers!"

His heart hammered as the clock ticked down. Three minutes to go.

The Flyers had the puck, their top forward was shooting... Jai held his breath.

Horn. Goal. Three all.

Curses flew from the Hawks' bench as the Flyers players fell on the goal scorer in relief. Jai sighed. Winning never seemed to come easy for Chicago.

More play. Another shift. Pass, hit, shoot. Save.

"Count it pure joy..."

THE NOISE LEVEL during the last two minutes of period three almost warranted covering one's ears. "This is crazy!" Allie yelled close to Amber's ear. Everyone was standing now, screaming, waving.

"No, this is the Cup!" Amber shouted back. "Look! Connor and Jai are on again."

Allie watched as Jai's shift stood ready for the puck drop. Her heart was beating louder than the drums at church.

Bang. The Hawks won the face-off, and Jai was quickly fed the puck. He weaved past the opposition, passed to Connor who shot. Foiled. Shift change.

Now it was Philadelphia's turn as they tried to swing momentum their way. Allie held her breath as the Flyers took aim, but Chicago's goalkeeper stood firm, preventing their goal. One minute to go.

"The Hawks' goalie is doing an awesome job," Josiah yelled as Jai's line came on. They passed, veered, passed again and moved closer to the Flyer net. Thirty seconds. Twenty. Jai pushed the puck toward Connor, who collected it, veering to the side before ducking in, shooting toward the goal. Suddenly he started shouting.

"Where's the puck?" Allie checked the Jumbotron, but it wasn't showing a replay.

"I think it's in the net!" Josiah yelled.

"But why hasn't the buzzer gone off?"

"I don't know. But I think we've won! Look at them!"

"It's in! It's in, boys! It's in!" Connor threw his gloves on the ice, his face splitting into the biggest smile Jai had ever seen as he skated down the other end to the Hawks' goalie.

Jai squinted at the net. Where was the puck? Why hadn't the horn sounded? But then…the dejected stance of the Philadelphia goalie and a defenseman gave credence to the goal. The goal! One goal and they'd won. Hadn't they?

His teammates continued celebrating as the officials rushed a review. It was nice to believe this was true, but until they had official confirmation…

The refs nodded and he knew: the Hawks had won! The crowd erupted in a chorus of boos and cheers. Soon everyone—coaching staff, trainers, and team management—was on the ice.

"Yeah, baby!" Jeremy had the biggest grin on his face as he gathered Jai in a bear hug. "I love you, man!"

Jai laughed. "Love you too, Stamos." He hugged, thumped people on the back, grinned, laughed some more, fist-bumped, and hollered. He gave Connor a huge hug. "Awesome goal!"

Connor smiled again. "Thanks, man."

Jai glanced over, his joy abating slightly at the disappointment crushing the Flyers. Dejected, looking down, some had crumpled to the ice. One looked like he was going to cry. Jai bit his lip. *God, thanks for the win, but please help these guys cope…*

The final handshake line was a chance to encourage his

opponents with a "good game" and to pat people he'd played with over the years on the back. The Hawks regrouped as the officials rolled out the red carpet and wheeled the trophies in.

The NHL Commissioner strode out, firstly awarding the trophy for best playoffs performer to the Hawks' captain. Connor had a quick photo before handing off the trophy for safekeeping and coming back to the team.

The Commissioner continued. "Ladies and Gentlemen, the Cup!"

Even the Philly fans quietened their boos at the sight of the huge silver trophy. Eighty-two games in regular season, twenty-plus playoffs games—no wonder this was the most coveted trophy in sports.

Photos, smiles, cheering, congratulations, flashes, noise—it was all a blur as the Cup was passed from the Commissioner to the captain to other teammates, then finally, to Jai.

He'd never seen it up close, let alone touched it, but despite its weight and size, he lifted it easily. The silver reflected the lights and camera flashes. Unbelievable. His childhood dream was being enacted for real. "Yeah! This is awesome! Thank You, God!" He passed the cup to Jeremy, then looked out into the crowd. Where were Allie and his mom? This moment was for them as much as for himself. If only Ray Bicknell could see him now...

"Photo!"

He joined his teammates and the staff and crowded in for the commemorative photo, grinning as he held up his pointer finger: their one goal had been achieved. After the official team photo, the ice was thrown open to media, Chicago staffers, and family members.

"Jai?" He turned around to see a Chicago television crew. "Congratulations! Can you tell us how you feel?"

"Yeah, it's amazing. Every kid playing hockey dreams of this moment, and here we are!"

He glanced across the throng of people and smiled. "Allie!" He wrapped her in a hug.

"Congratulations, superstar." She smiled her gorgeous smile and gave him a long kiss.

"Did you enjoy that?"

"It was pretty good." Her eyes were alight with laughter.

"Only pretty good?"

"You guys could've scored earlier."

"Uh, excuse me?"

Jai turned. Oh. The interview. Allie gave a soft gasp, and he had to choke back the laughter at her round eyes and hand on mouth.

The interviewer watched the exchange with a big grin. "Would you like to introduce us?"

Jai grinned. "This is my girlfriend, Allie." Then he noticed his family. "Mom!" He gave his mother a big bear hug, then squeezed Kat too.

"I'm so proud of you, son."

"You did good, bro," Kat said with the widest grin he'd seen in years.

"You did it, man!" Josiah thumped him on the back.

"I'm so glad you all came!" Jai's heart was filled to over-flowing.

The interviewer was enjoying the family reunion. "And this is your mom and sister?"

"And my pastor, Josiah Abrahams," Jai continued the intro-ductions, his arm firmly wrapped around Allie's waist the whole time. A few more questions, then the interview concluded, and finally he could celebrate with the most important people in his world.

"Dude! It's so awesome!" Jeremy appeared, trailed by his dad and brother. Jeremy grinned at everyone before honing in on Allie. "Allie!" He gave her a squeeze, winked at Jai, then moved on.

"What was that?" Allie raised her eyebrows, a smile on her face.

He could only do a palms-up. "That's Jeremy Stamos. He defies explanation."

Her snickers quickly ceased as, staring past him, her eyes grew round again. Jai turned, and there it was again. Large. Silver. Stanley.

"Oh-h-h." The collective sighing signified how important this moment was. There was a frenzy of photos before he reluctantly passed it to his next teammate and their supporters.

The next half hour was continued celebration before they eventually made their way to the locker room, which soon crowded with rowdy revelers. Champagne sprayed as the Cup was lifted high and his teammates hugged and cheered each other. But it was getting late, and they had to head back, so Jai found a quieter corner to make his farewells. "I'm so glad you were here."

"We wouldn't have missed it for the world," his mom said as she and his sister gave him immense hugs, then stepped back. "We'll be heading back tomorrow, so we'll see you back in Chicago."

"It's been awesome!" Josiah looked happier than Kyle at Christmas.

Finally, Jai turned to Allie. He cradled her face in his hands to block out the noise. "I love you."

"I love you, too. I'm so proud of you." She leaned in, and her lips met his in a long, deep kiss that said his bristles didn't matter.

He pulled back, blinking. "Wow."

"Wow yourself."

He exhaled. "I heard something about a parade on Friday." He shook his head. "How crazy is that?"

Her face stiffened. "On Friday?"

"You can come, can't you? I'm sure Mr. Weinberger won't mind."

She drew a hand down his scruffy cheek. "I'd love to, but I, um, have some work things."

He exhaled. Work? Who could think about work at a time like this?

"Allie!" Amber screeched. "Isn't this awesome?"

Allie nodded. "Super awesome."

"Come on, you two." Amber grabbed Allie's arm. "I think Connor said we'll be partying for days."

At Allie's look of panic, Jai slipped an arm around her, but a hand grabbed his shoulder. "Dude!"

He turned, met Beau's and Dan's grinning faces. "Hey! I didn't know you were here."

"We weren't sure whether we'd get tickets," Dan said, "but so glad we did."

"Congrats, man!" Beau drew him into a hug and thumped his back. "So proud of you!"

As his friends continued with their excitement, he noticed Amber and Allie in low conversation. Allie finally nodded, and he shifted closer. "Hey, look who I found."

Her face lit as she exchanged hugs. "Hi, guys."

Jai introduced them to Amber, then drew Allie aside again. "You okay? If you've gotta go work, that's okay—"

"It just depends on what time it is. But don't you worry about it, I—oh!" She gasped as they were sprayed with more champagne. Jeremy, of course. "It's getting crazy in here!"

It sure was. But he didn't mind. And the celebrations continued into the wee small hours, until he finally, reluctantly, had to say goodnight and goodbye to Allie, with the promise she'd see him later that same day in Chicago.

CHAPTER 27

"Miss Davis, I would like to formally offer you the position of Head of Public Relations and Engagement at the San Francisco Museum of European Art."

Allie gripped her folder, doing her best to appear calm even though John Weinberger had told her this was the crux of this morning's video call. She hadn't dared believe it. Not really. Which might be why she still hadn't found the courage to tell Jai why she couldn't meet him this morning before the parade started. In thirty minutes.

She'd greeted him last night when the plane of weary Hawks had finally arrived—some, she suspected, more wearied by their celebrations than by playing over one hundred games. Jai had been so hyped, even more so as he pointed out the city buildings lit up in red and Hawks images and slogans. But between not wanting to distract his focus during the finals and not wanting to kill the mood last night, she'd somehow ended up here, staring at a computer screen while the job of her dreams was handed to her on a silver platter and she wondered what to do.

She didn't want to be the girl who worked her life around her partner's, especially when nothing officially permanent about their relationship had been said. Was it selfish to seek her career above his own? But Jai had said he'd be supportive. And he *had* said he liked San José…

"Miss Davis?"

She refocused. *Lord, what do I say?* She cleared her throat and spoke into the microphone. "Thank you, Mr. Holt, for the honor of being offered this position." *Lord? Yes? No? Yes?* Her heart settled. She exhaled and told him what she thought.

FIFTEEN MINUTES LATER, she was hurrying through downtown, past the streams of fans dressed in red cramming every doorway. Somewhere out there were her family and Josiah. Somewhere out there were Jai and his teammates and the trolley cars and double decker buses the mayor had organized for this parade.

She reached the place where Jai had said to meet, but he wasn't there. Where? What should she do? She checked her phone. Nothing. Tried to call Amber. Nothing. Was it any surprise when everything was so noisy and chaotic?

There! She finally recognized the place, saw the buses waiting on the other side of the tall chain fence with fans ten deep cheering in front of her.

"Lord, help me."

She tried Jai's phone again. No answer. Tried Amber. Still nothing. She'd have to weave her way through the crowds to get to the fence and see if a friendly security guard might let her through.

"Excuse me," she murmured.

"Hey, watch it!" a red-clad supporter with a Hawks tattoo yelled.

The heat was intense, the mugginess of summer combining with the smell of sweat.

"Pardon me," she said, ducking past a trio of girls. They

narrowed their gazes, and the tallest one muttered something about pushy people.

Her cheeks flamed, and she knew sweat was trickling down her back. She wasn't surprised people looked at her askance—she was still dressed in her interview clothes, not having had a chance to change. She at least had a red-and-black team cap and hoped this made her look fan enough as she wove her way and finally reached the chain-mesh fence. Here she could see various workers moving around as players ascended the trolley buses along with their significant others.

Her heart thumped. This was where Jai had asked her to be. To make a public statement that she was his significant other. And she was here, trapped on this side of the fence, unable to be heard, unable to be seen.

"Hello!" she called. "Jai!"

"They can't hear you honey," a woman with black hair said with a glance at Allie's silk shirt. "Are you sure you're meant to be here?"

"Jai said he'd meet me," she said. "Jai!" she screamed.

"JM17, huh? He's a hottie, isn't he?"

Ignoring the woman, Allie moved closer to where a security guard stood, hands clasped behind his back as he surveyed the scene. "Excuse me!" she yelled. "Excuse me!"

He finally turned, not seeing her at first, the wave of cheering seeming to turn him into the celebrity he wasn't as he waved to the crowd.

"Excuse me!" she yelled again, waving her arms for extra effect and accidentally knocking a kid's hat from his head. "Sorry," she muttered, picking it up from the ground, hoping the crowd wouldn't suddenly surge and trample her to death. "Sir! Excuse me!" she called again.

Finally, the security guard noticed her and hefted up his considerable bulk as he ambled to the fence. "What is it, lady?"

"I'm supposed to be there," she said, pointing to the buses.

"You and everyone else here, lady."

"No, you don't understand. I'm Jai Mullins's girlfriend."

He looked her up and down as she clung to the fence. "Sure you are."

"My name is Allie Davis. Go ask him and he'll tell you I'm supposed to be there. Please, he's waiting for me."

"Then why are you here and not there?"

"I had an interview and I was late, and—"

But he'd turned as if she was no more interesting than a fly crawling up a wall.

Allie's breath hitched, and she swallowed a sob. Glanced at her phone. Tried to call. But his phone went straight to voicemail. "Jai? It's Allie. I can't get through. The interview went longer than I thought, and now they won't let me through." She swallowed another sob. How could she be expected to start a new job and life if she was crying all the time?

"Allie?"

Allie turned. The black-haired woman was frowning at her. "Please, can you help me? I'm Jai Mullins's girlfriend, and I'm afraid that if I miss this today, he'll always think I couldn't be bothered, and I love him too much to wreck things again."

"You work at the Art Institute?"

Who was this woman? "How do you know that?" she whispered.

The woman shook her head. Grasped the fence and whistled. "Yo, you there!"

The guard turned.

"She's Jai Mullins's girlfriend."

"How would you know?" the guard asked. Yeah, Allie echoed. How *did* she?

"See?" The woman held out her phone, complete with a photo of Jai and Allie from New Year's Eve.

Allie's breath hitched. The photos. That forum where she'd seen the horrible words that women had called her.

"She looks a bit like you," the guard said doubtfully.

"Because she *is* me," Allie insisted.

The woman eyed her—probably thinking she was the world's biggest flake and Jai would be better off without her—then sighed. "Let her through."

"Huh?" The crowd around her called.

"Let her through!" the woman called, which seemed to be incentive for the crowd to call, "Let her through! Let her through!"

Allie's eyes filled. She mouthed a *thank you*.

"Please. I have a pass and everything."

"Why didn't you say so?"

He moved to open the gate, but before she went, she grabbed the woman's hands. "Thank you so much. Please, what is your name?"

The woman shrugged and looked away. "Destiny."

"Destiny." The name on the forum. The one who'd called her tacky trash. "Is that Destiny's Offspring?"

The woman's lips tightened, and she jerked a nod.

Allie didn't hesitate. She wrapped her in a hug. "Thank you so much. I appreciate you." She looked into the woman's eyes, saw surprise and indecision, then Destiny gave another nod.

"Lady? Are you going through or not?"

"Coming!" With a quick smile and a "God bless you" for Destiny, she hurried to where the buses were parked and waiting.

She scanned them: In the first double-decker bus, the coach, Connor and Amber, and some people she recognized from the engagement party who must be Connor's parents.

"Hurry up, Allie!" Amber called.

The second trolley held Ella and Jonas, Alex and Lauren, and a sea of others, including some former players she knew Dad would be thrilled to meet one day. Which was great, but where was Jai? Around them, people on walkie-talkies muttered and directed, and the rumble and fumes of the buses choked her hearing.

"Allie?" a voice called. She glanced up. Tanja waved at her, then pointed behind. "He's there."

Allie clasped her hands in thanks and ran to the next bus. And there was Jai, his expression lighting as he saw her, and she shoved her pass in the high-visibility-clad worker's face and finally clambered up the stairs. She was puffing when she reached the top, glancing around until she found him, and was moving to him when the bus started with a jerk. She stumbled into Jai's waiting arms as the couple in front of them asked if she was okay.

She nodded, clutching Jai's arm as she finally gained her seat.

"You really are okay?" Jai asked, concerned.

"Yes."

"I didn't think you'd make it," he murmured as he tucked her close to his side.

Confess she'd just had her interview? Admit her life was about to change? With cheering crowds stretching twenty deep and Jai deserving to soak up the adulation? "I had some work stuff that took longer than I thought."

"Hey, it's okay." He kissed her cheek. "You're here now."

The words sank into her heart. This was one of life's rare moments. It wouldn't come again, so she had to make the most of it and ensure Jai had his special time too. She relaxed, smiled, and drew a hand down his shorn cheek. "I'm not sorry this is gone."

"Me neither. It was itchy."

The next hour passed in the chaos of cheering and crowds and confetti. People hung off street signs and balanced on precarious-looking office balconies in a sea of red jerseys that said how much this city loved this team. Police on horses kept the crowds back as paper fell from the skyscrapers, and around them the crowd called, "Let's go, Hawks!"

"There must be a million people here," Allie marveled as the buses drew to the end of the route.

"It's been a while since a sports team won something in Chi-town," Jai said.

The bus slowed and drew to a halt, and Jai was summoned to join his teammates and some team officials for a rally on the corner of Madison and Wabash. Someone sang, the mayor spoke, and they watched a highlights reel of the playoffs.

"Look! There's Jai!" Amber said, pointing as the video showed Jai's goal from the last game against Nashville.

Allie knew a surge of pride as the video showed him lifting his stick in victory, something she felt again a few minutes later when the players were introduced and gave short speeches. "And our homegrown hero, number seventeen, Jai Mullins!"

"Hey, everyone!" Jai said, waving. "How good is Chicago? I love you guys!"

Allie swallowed, the backs of her eyes heating with emotion. How could she ask him to leave? He loved this city, and it was obvious everyone loved him too.

"Allie? You okay?" Amber wrapped an arm around her. "I know, it's pretty overwhelming, isn't it?"

Allie nodded. Sure was. How could she share her news with him and possibly break his heart?

HIS APARTMENT that night held a special kind of tiredness—a joyous tiredness, filled with every kind of contentment. Today had been special. The past few weeks had been special. Jai tugged Allie nearer on the sofa. This woman made it special. "I love you," he said, moving to kiss her cheek, then settling for nuzzling her ear.

"I love you, too," she murmured, lifting the back of his hand to kiss it.

But something was wrong. He could see it in the way she hadn't fully relaxed, the way her gaze never held his long enough. "What is it, Allie?"

She shook her head. "I should've known I could never hide anything from you."

Alarm pushed his spine straight. "What are you trying to hide? Is it something to do with work?"

Allie nodded. "But I don't want to spoil today."

"How can anything you say spoil today?" He drew her closer. "I love you."

"I love you too."

But… He heard the *but.* "But what, Allie? What's happened at work? Was Myra mean to you again?"

"I had another interview with the San Francisco art museum."

He blinked. "You did? I thought that was over and done with."

"So did I," she confessed. "But Mr. Weinberger was contacted by Mr. Holt a week or so ago, and they wanted me for the job after all."

"You knew this and didn't tell me?"

"I couldn't distract you from the finals or your celebrations."

He exhaled a long breath even as his heartbeat picked up pace. "So you said yes?"

"Yes," she whispered.

He nodded, trying to wrap his head around what this would mean. "San Francisco?"

"Yes."

"When would you start?"

"They want me by July first."

"Wow." His thoughts whirled. He shoved a hand through his hair. "That's not much time."

"I know. It's why I couldn't say anything until now."

"But it's a good opportunity," he said, as much to convince himself as her.

"Apparently trying new things is the spice of life," she murmured.

Despite the tumult in his chest, he couldn't help but appreciate this boldness of hers to step into the new. Boldness he could maybe learn from too. He moved to face her, kneeling on the seat in front of her, and grasped her hands. "I'm so proud of you, Allie."

"You are?"

"Of course I am. You're so courageous, willing to chase your dreams, and I love that about you."

"But…you don't mind what this will mean for us?"

"That you'll be there and I'll be here?" He grazed her knuckles with his lips. "I don't have to stay here forever."

"But this is your hometown. Your family, your church, your friends. Your history."

"And I dare to think, to hope—" He swallowed. Oh, what the heck? Trying new things was the spice of life, after all. "I hope you'll be my future."

Her eyes grew shiny. "I want that too."

"Allie, I'm not the man I want to be when I'm not with you," he admitted hoarsely. "I like myself better when I'm with you. When you go, can I come too?"

"What? Jai, no, I could never ask you to give up this here."

"You're not asking. I'm telling you what I want."

"But what about your contract?"

He shrugged. "This year or next year, we'll get it sorted. I love you, Allie. I want to marry you and have my future with you."

"Do you mean it?" she breathed.

"I do," he assured her, pressing his lips to her knuckles again. "So, is that a yes? Do I get to move to San José? Please say yes."

"Get to move?" She chuckled incredulously, lining his heart with hope-warmed joy.

"Please?" He waited, watching her with hawk-eyed intensity. *Please say—*

"Oh, yes, Jai," Allie murmured before flinging herself into his waiting arms and lips and heart. "Oh, yes."

~

HAWKS AND SQUAWKS ONLINE CHAT

TubularBells: We won!!!
CoolplayismyJam: Got da Cup, baby!
PipeDreams27: LaserTaser is da bomb!
TubularBells: Been a long time, but we're ba-a-a-ck!
PipeDreams27: Did anyone make it to the parade?
PucktheMagicDragon: Me!! Well, kind of. I was hanging from my office building's window. OMG! There were so many people there! It must've been SO awesome to be down in the crowd.
CoolplayismyJam: Two million they say.
PipeDreams27: Did you get any pictures?
Destinysoffspring: I did. I was down where the players got on the trolleys.
PucktheMagicDragon: Wow! Did you see anyone?
Destinysoffspring: Yeah.
PucktheMagicDragon: Who? OMG! Did you talk to anyone? How exciting! Do you have pictures?
Destinysoffspring: Yeah. Here.
PipeDreams27: Is that JM17's Allie? She looks kind of weird.
Destinysoffspring: She almost missed the bus.
PucktheMagicDragon: Poor thing. Did she get on in time?
CoolplayismyJam: Can't you see the pic, Puck?
PucktheMagicDragon: Oops. But I'm glad she got there. He played so well! So happy for them!

TubularBells: Did you speak to her?

Destinysoffspring: Yeah.

CoolplayismyJam: And?

PucktheMagicDragon: Details! Give me juicy details!

Destinysoffspring: She seems nice. Normal.

PipeDreams27: Huh.

CoolplayismyJam: And?

Destinysoffspring: And what? She's just like one of us.

PucktheMagicDragon: Aww. I hope they live happily ever after, here in Chi-town forever.

TubularBells: As if he'd ever leave.

PipeDreams27: Can you imagine the ruckus if he did?

PucktheMagicDragon: Don't even put that out there, Pipe! Jai = Chi-town forever!

CoolplayismyJam: I wonder when JM17 will pop the question?

PipeDreams27: Did you guys hear about TJ Woletsky?

CoolplayismyJam: Gross. Don't pollute this page with him. Let's talk about hot guys instead. Did you see that interview with Dan Walton at his house in Muskoka? Hello!

PucktheMagicDragon: He's so dreamy. I saw this pic of him and his friend Beau Nash at a camp in Canada. OMG! Beau is so tall but so *fine*. I'd happily move for either of them.

Destinysoffspring: Isn't this page supposed to be about our Hawks?

PucktheMagicDragon: Woohoo, Hawks won!

PipeDreams27: We won the Cup!

TubularBells: I'm just thankful that we finally won. Go, Hawks, go!

THE END

Check out Hearts and Goals, the next book in the Original Six contemporary romance series

A NOTE FROM THE AUTHOR

Thank you for reading *Checked Impressions,* the third book in my new contemporary romance series, which combines my love of ice hockey with appreciation for the cities that comprised the NHL's original six teams. This story is partly based on my visit to amazing Chicago, and my love of the Art Institute there. While some of the references to places like the Stained Glass Museum at Navy Pier may no longer there, they certainly were when I visited, so I hoped you've enjoyed getting a taste for this amazing city!

Please make sure you check out the other books in the Original Six hockey romance series, a sweet & swoony, slightly sporty Christian contemporary romance series.

The Breakup Project
Love on Ice
Checked Impressions
Hearts and Goals
Big Apple Atonement
Muskoka Blue

Reviews help other readers find new-to-them authors, so if you can spare a moment to write a quick review at Goodreads / your place of purchase, I'd be very grateful.

I'd love for you to check out my other books and to sign up for my newsletter at www.carolynmillerauthor.com where you can be the first to learn all my book and contest news, and discover more behind-the-book details and photos.

A huge thank you to the following people for their encouragement and eagle eyes: Iola Goulton (who advised that half of my original *Love on Ice* could be fashioned into another story), Nancy, Brittany, Tamera, Lisa, Kaye, Bea & Becky - I appreciate you all so much! Big thanks to the ladies in my Facebook group, Carolyn's Books & Friends, for all your support in helping promote my books.

Please turn the page for a peek at *Hearts and Goals*, the next in the Original Six hockey romance series.

Chapter 1

Montreal, Canada
August

Oh, what were men to rocks and mountains—or at least to beautiful gardens? Magdalena Joly's heart was full as she surveyed the gardens of le Jardin botanique de Montréal, stretched beneath her. Was it possible to love a garden too much? To be too thankful for a job that permitted moments such as this? Surely no man could fill her heart with a fraction of the contentment she found here—except for the one she'd left at home.

She moved carefully on her perch high in the old oak tree, leaning back against the strong trunk, carefully lifting the camera to capture the scene below. Summer sunshine lit the Japanese Garden's manicured topiary and trees, creating few shadows and making it the perfect time to capture such beauty. She snapped one picture, then another, before taking a moment to check the shots. Serenity stared back at her, the flashes of gold and orange from the koi in the pond providing contrast to the pinks of the shrub peonies. Everything else, from the pines and maples to the foliage of rhododendron, offered dozens of shades of green.

Damp hair clung to her neck, and she blew out a breath in a vain attempt for coolness. She had been fortunate this morning to avoid too many visitors straying into view. Perhaps today's heat had kept them away. After a careful readjustment from her precarious position, she lifted the camera and focused in on the stone lantern arching across the water. There. A smile filled her heart. Was it truly possible to have a better job? What else managed to incorporate a love of photography as well as a love of horticulture? Maman often said she was blessed indeed.

A crunch of gravel drew her gaze to the path. Two men, one shorter with dark hair, the other very tall with a tawny man bun, walked along the winding path that led to the teahouse. She hoped they didn't think to look up and spot her here. It was enough that some of her colleagues thought her commitment to the job bordered on extreme, but she had no way of communicating exactly why she did this. How exactly did one explain the rebellious wish to step out of the ordinary and safe that confined every other part of her world? Neither had she any wish to concern the public or worry those who might think occupational health and safety should take precedence over capturing the perfect pictures to entice the public to visit. Like this morning's shots taken from her post high up here.

The men paused, the taller one gesturing to a little vantage point where a stone seat was positioned to best capture the view. She'd caught many couples taking advantage of this most romantic scene—even a proposal or two, which elicited feelings both of tenderness and regret.

"It sure is beautiful," the tall man drawled, his voice holding a Southerner's twang.

The other man murmured something she didn't hear, but

she saw his nod and wondered where they were from. Locals? The accent suggested *non*. Perhaps tourists, friends or work colleagues, then.

The men took several photos, then the shorter one pointed to the cultural pavilion, a building with the Peace Bell prominently displayed out front. It was funny how so many tourists just clicked a picture but didn't linger as these gardens had been designed for people to do. Oh well. If they moved on, then there was less chance of her being seen.

The big guy shrugged, then sat down, his legs stretching out as he clasped the back edge of the stone seat. From this position she could see how the T-shirt he wore strained across the breadth of his shoulders, the muscles in his arms and legs not unlike Alain's. She swallowed, pushing emotion down, and dragged her gaze away. She had a job to do.

"Come on," the shorter man called, stealing her focus again, his impatience evident in his shuffling feet and frequent glances at his watch.

The taller man murmured something she couldn't hear, but he obeyed, albeit reluctantly it seemed, as he rose and snapped another photo with his phone. She did not blame him. The Jardin japonais was widely considered to be one of the finest in the world. Her lips lifted as she recognized a fellow appreciator of beauty, and she waited, curving her body along the stretch of solid branch to maintain her discreet location as the men walked away.

It was funny how so few people looked up to see what might exist above them. But then, she had always been the type of person distracted by the shapes of trees, who loved the winter sculptural forms that held poetic beauty in their branches. Trees had another advantage, too. When they died, they often became a thing of beauty rather than leaving a hole in one's heart that could never be filled.

Maggie swallowed, blew out a steadying breath, and grasped

the nearest branch. Now was not the time to think on such things. Now was the time to take the shot and descend before the next visitors came and spoiled the view. She inched higher, stabilizing against the smooth bark of another strong branch, and lifted the camera, this time zooming in on the waterfall that provided soothing background music to this part of the garden. Like the garden below, the water cascading over rocks had been designed to evoke feelings of tranquility and to inspire meditation and, like the nearby stand of pines, helped to shut out the noise and bustle of Canada's second largest city. Another reason she loved to work in this oasis of calm.

It was not surprising that so many people enjoyed coming here, even if it was simply locals wishing to sit under the trees. How many others had found this place had brought healing to their soul? To know she had the privilege of working here, that she was part of the huge team that could use nature to minister to weary hearts, was something she did not take for granted.

The men had disappeared—probably wondering about the meaning behind the placement of rocks in the Stone Garden or marveling at the bonsai trees—and she carefully took the last series of photos before turning off the camera and slipping it into the pocket of her khaki work shorts, then buttoning the pocket carefully. She'd learned the hard way the consequences of not doing so.

A careful grasp of the slender branches, then she slid one booted foot to the deep fork where the branches veered away. High above, a chattering sound drew her attention to a squirrel, who seemed most indignant that she'd dared trespass upon his territory. "I promise I'm leaving," she assured the little creature. The squirrel scampered away, as if it didn't believe her. Ah well.

Another cautious movement and she was ready to descend. A quick glance side to side showed no visitors or—worse— fellow employees within sight, so she grasped the branch and swung her feet down.

But now the ground seemed too far away, the descent much farther than it had seemed when she'd climbed it in a burst of defiant tomboy exuberance not so long ago. A dilemma. What to do? Her arms were getting sore. She could jump, but such an action held an element of risk she was reluctant to invite these days. Oh, she should have thought this through. The garden's "no climbing trees" safety measures had probably been written with this in mind. Too late now.

Gritting her teeth, she calculated the distance. A couple of meters could scarcely cause injury, could it? Nevertheless, what choice did she have? How else was she going to get out of the tree?

"Miss?"

She squeaked and let go, the ground rushing to meet her as she yelped.

Bang.

"Ah!" Shock rippled through her body, followed by a wave of pain. Vaguely aware of the sound of pounding feet, she bit back words her mother would frown upon as she clutched her knee, startling again as someone grasped her upper arms. The hands instantly released.

"Miss? You okay?"

Did she look like she was okay? She winced, ignoring the voice as she checked her pocket with its expensive secret. Trembling fingers undid the button, and she drew out the camera, relief pulsing through her as it appeared unharmed. Until she turned it over and saw the viewing screen had smashed. Non. Oh non.

"Are you hurt?" the voice said again.

She finally glanced up, meeting startling green eyes and concern in the strong-featured face. Monsieur Man Bun from before. Her breath hitched. If his hair were out, with that scruff on his face she'd bet he would look like a modern-day Viking.

"Here, let me help."

He bent, arms reaching down, but Maggie shrugged away and pushed to wobbly feet. Then managed an equally wobbly smile. "*Merci*, monsieur. Now if you will please excuse me."

"Is your camera okay?" he asked softly.

The care in his voice buckled her composure, and she sucked in her bottom lip. Non. Today was a cry-free day. She raised her chin, lifting her gaze to almost touch his. At five-foot-ten, she was tall by most women's standards, but this man must be a good eight inches taller. "It will be fine. I will be fine. Merci."

His face lit with a smile. "I love how everyone speaks French here."

She only just managed to refrain from rolling her eyes, her earlier good opinion of his intelligence at appreciating the gardens dropping several points.

"Can you walk okay?"

Okay, so maybe she'd revise her opinion again. It *was* nice to have such a big man fussing over her. It had been so long—

"You really shouldn't be climbing trees."

Maggie looked away to meet the owner of the new and nasal voice—a wide man with graying hair and a disapproving turn to his lip. Looked about the perfect age and temperament for her mother. She shook away the disloyal thought and winced at the gathering crowd. "You're right," she murmured, easing away. "Excuse me."

"Wait—were you spying on us?"

"Pardon?"

"You were hiding, taking pictures," the fussy man said, gesturing to the camera. "Mildred," he called, beckoning an equally large and joyless woman forward. "This woman was taking pictures of us."

"No, no. I was not taking pictures of you, sir. Now if you'll excuse me—"

"Do you work here?" the woman said, eying the logo on her shirt.

Uh oh.

She moved to leave, but her knee buckled, and she would've collapsed on the ground had Monsieur Man Bun not swooped in, wrapping a strong arm around her shoulders. "Gotcha." He grinned.

Her lips lifted in automatic response, and she grew uncomfortably aware of a fluttering in her stomach. Non. *Non.* She was not going to find the man attractive. Even if the tingles evoked by his scent of moss and musk suggested otherwise.

"Beau, have you always gotta be charming the ladies?"

She peered back to see the shorter man from before studying them with his lips pulled to one side.

"I can't help it if women find me charming, Dodge," Beau said.

Dodge? What kind of name was that?

"I expect it has more to do with the accent than anything else. Although my folks did teach me the importance of being a gentleman."

The other man—Dodge—snorted, albeit with a reluctant grin.

"Tell me, do you think I'm charming, ma'am?"

It took her a moment to realize he addressed her. "Ma'am?" she asked.

His lips hitched higher as his friend laughed. "I guess that's a no, then."

"You can let me go," she murmured.

"I don't think I can," Beau Man Bun said, even as his actions proved the contrary. But as she staggered, he clutched her arm again, balancing her upright. "See?"

Hmm. It would seem there was no easy way out of this.

"I'm real sorry I startled you before," he continued.

Maggie blinked. He was apologizing for her stupidity in exiting the tree? "That was my fault."

"What were you doing up the tree anyhow?" he asked.

How to explain, how to explain…

"Miss!"

She exhaled as the voice from before drew her to peer over her shoulder. The gray-haired man now wore a scowl. "What's your name? I'll be reporting you to the authorities."

Maggie knew an insanely hysterical desire to laugh. As far as many employees here were concerned, she *was* the authorities.

"Now, sir, I really don't think things need come to that," Beau said, friendliness in his voice and face. "Not when the little lady is injured and all."

Little lady?

"Come on," Beau continued. "You wouldn't want to be making her day any worse now, would you?"

Challenged like that, the older man hmphed. "But she was spying on people," he complained.

"*Were* you spying on people?" Beau asked her, humor glinting in his eyes.

"But of course," she shocked herself by saying. What was it about today that dared her to act like the teenager she hadn't been for ten years? Climbing trees, engaging in tease… Was it simply a result of the heat of the day, or was it something about the appeal of the man that had melted sense from her brain?

His green eyes rounded. "You were?"

She nodded. "It's our new way to evaluate visitor engagement with the gardens. Some might use surveillance cameras, but we prefer old-school methods."

"Like climbing trees to watch people," he said, chuckling.

The sound tugged at her, reminding her how long it had been since she'd made an attractive man laugh, which further reminded her of the need to put up her walls. Non. She could not fall again.

"What is your name, Miss?" Mr. Grumpy called.

Oh dear. She'd forgotten he was still there.

"Sir, I really think it's inappropriate for you to be asking about an attractive young lady. And to do so in front of your wife just ain't right." Beau tsked tsked.

Maggie stifled another wild impulse to laugh as the man huffed away, trailed by his wife, who wanted to know what had been said.

"I'm guessing he won't be telling her the truth anytime soon," Beau said with a grin.

Non.

"Dude, we gotta go," Beau's friend said.

"But not before we see this lady safely to first aid." Beau turned to her. "Do you want me to carry you?"

She choked. "Er, I should be okay."

"You sure?" He grinned. "I don't mind showing Dodge a thing or two about how a gentleman ought to treat a lady."

She eyed his muscles. He looked strong enough to carry her. But fortunately, before her stupid emotions weakened her resolve, she spied one of the park's small golf carts being driven in the direction of the Chinese Garden. She pointed to it. "If you could please get Frederic's attention, that would serve well."

Beau glanced across, nodded, and told his friend to wave the employee down. The other man sighed, then jogged over, waving attention, then pointing to where Maggie stood, Beau's arm still wrapped around her. She winced. Eased away.

Beau glanced down at her, and again she was struck by the eloquence of his eyes. Right now she thought she read surprise and confusion, then fresh amusement, something that wrinkled her soul with the strangest sense of disappointment. "Well, it looks like your chariot'll soon be here," he drawled. "I hope you feel better soon," he added kindly.

"Merci," she managed, drawing further away.

"It was nice to almost meet you," he said, eyes twinkling again. "I'm Beau."

"I know."

"You do, huh?" he said, as if forgetting his friend had called him that already. "And you are?"

He might've proved sympathetic, but she didn't need her name getting her into any more trouble. And she definitely didn't need to be feeling any of these feelings being near him had stirred within. How desperate *was* she to be attracted to a stranger? She shook her head.

"You'd prefer to remain a woman of mystery."

"Oui," she said firmly.

Relief filled her as Frederic slowed and stopped. Maybe she could get away with nobody being the wiser—

"Maggie? Are you injured?" Frederic asked.

"Maggie, huh?" Beau said, smirking.

Ignoring him, she hobbled to the golf cart, murmuring thanks to the man called Dodge, who nodded before reassuring Frederic she was fine and only needed to rest.

"Yeah, and maybe get some ice for her knee," Beau called.

She glanced at him once more. "Merci."

"Stay safe, Maggie." His lips curled as his grin pushed to one side.

"You know him?" Frederic asked her in French as he drove her to the employees' section of the main building.

"Non," she said, refusing to give in to the temptation to turn around. Non. *Non.* She needed to tether these recalcitrant feelings, tamp down these emotions and focus on what was real. Like the threat of the chubby gray-haired man. Like the crack in her camera. Like the fact her injured knee meant she'd likely need some time off work.

"He seemed to know you."

She shrugged, bracing herself on the metal frame as the cart bumped over rocky ground. What would she do if she couldn't work? What would that mean for poor Noah?

"He looks familiar." Frederic's brow creased. "What is his name?"

"Beau," she admitted.

"Beau?"

At his gasp, she turned her head. "What?"

He swore in French. "I cannot believe it."

"Believe what?"

He grinned. "I think you just met Montreal's new goalie."

INTRIGUING THOUGHTS of dark eyes and hair and sweet sass were interrupted by Beau's new teammate's snort. "What?"

"Honestly." Jake Dodgewell—one of the NHL's most aptly named players—rolled his eyes as they continued the slow trek back to the main gate. "Could you have been any more obvious?"

"What do you mean?"

"Look, I know we're both new, but is that how you play all the time?"

"Huh?"

"You. You're a flirt, man."

"Moi?" Beau asked. "I think you're mistaking me for someone else."

"I think you're gonna have to work on your French, dude."

"Not the only one," Beau said with a grin. "Good thing they're setting us up with language classes, huh?"

Jake snorted again.

Beau would take that as a no, then.

He, for one, was glad for the chance to learn the main language spoken in Quebec. It was part of the fun of moving to a new team, part of the appeal of transferring from the desert to one of the NHL's Original Six teams. *The* Original Six team. The one with the most championships. The place where it felt like a dream to walk its hallowed halls. *Les Habitants.* This cosmopolitan city tucked beside the St. Lawrence River, a bastion of European tradition, had long held his heart for many reasons. Diving into the culture was just part of that. But Dodge's comment about flirting…

"I was being friendly, not flirting," Beau said firmly, as much to himself as to Dodge. So Maggie was pretty, with those sparkling brown eyes and dark hair. And okay, he'd liked her scent in that all-too-brief encounter when he'd helped her stand. But how could he even think of more when he didn't know where she stood with God?

"Is that what you call it?"

"Listen, I can't help it if you Wisconsin boys don't know the difference."

"Michigan."

"Same difference."

That earned him another snort. "I don't even know why Southerners play hockey."

"Ouch! Tell that to Tampa Bay."

Jake laughed, and conversation turned to teammates they knew who played in some of the warmer climates of the league and the challenges players faced when moving across the continent. But joining Montreal's team, Beau's third club in four years, was living his dream, and his introduction to the organization and city had proved relatively smooth. Of course, it helped to be negotiating this on his own, to not be assisting a wife and family with the ins and outs of language and cultural expectations. Not that learning French was a prerequisite—their head coach spoke English—but Beau wanted to immerse himself in the culture as much as he could, and not simply by eating poutine, smoke meats, and baguettes.

Later that night, he reiterated this on the call to the Bible study guys. The online group started by Jai Mullins and Josiah Abrahams had grown in recent years, with players from the Original Six teams—Mike Vaughan, Brent Karlsson, Jai, Beau, Tim Carruthers, and Dan Walton—now joined by others, like

Chris Thomas from Vancouver, Ryan Guillemette from Edmonton, and Luc Marchand who played for Winnipeg. Given the number of players based several time zones away, maybe one day they'd need a northwestern division of this Bible study group.

"So, are you settling in?" Jai asked. Jai had surprised them all a couple of months ago by announcing his engagement, then shocked them further by saying his upcoming season with newly crowned champions Chicago would be his last before he followed Allie to San Jose. The latest of the guys to find a girl and settle down. "Meeting some new people?"

A face flashed through Beau's mind. He suppressed it. "My new teammates seem cool. The ones I've met, anyway." He'd meet the rest in a few weeks when training camp began. "The apartment is nice."

"I bet," Ryan laughed. "What is it, the penthouse?"

"The sub-penthouse," he clarified.

"Oh, right. My mistake. The *sub*-penthouse. I bet that's really different."

"Yeah. A little smaller, one less bedroom."

"What? Only five?" Tim asked, mouth curled up one side in tease.

"Four," he corrected meekly. Could he help it if goalies were amongst the highest paid in the league?

"You're so humble with the flex," Jai teased, which earned Beau's good-natured shrug.

"Living in Montreal would be like living here in Toronto," Dan said. "You need privacy and good security, even if it looks ostentatious."

"You calling me conceited?" Beau bantered.

"I'm saying you're wise to be careful. Let's just say you don't want your address getting out to the crazy fans."

Beau nodded. He'd appreciated going under the radar—well, as much as his height allowed. But so far it seemed few people had recognized him, even though he knew his face had been splashed across the media since being traded back in July. He'd wondered if Maggie had recognized him today at the Botanical Gardens, but the fact she'd said nothing, and then after that little moment of intriguing sassy tease had basically withdrawn, said she didn't care to know him more and had put his vanity firmly in the trash. Dodge was so wrong.

After more catching up, including Mike sharing about his latest trip to the charity he fronted in the Philippines, Josiah joined them and the study began.

Tonight's message was from Proverbs chapter eleven, with a focus on the verses about generosity. "I think the Message version puts it best," Josiah said. "'The world of the generous gets larger and larger; the world of the stingy gets smaller and smaller.' And the next verse continues this theme. 'The one who blesses others is abundantly blessed; those who help others are helped. Curses on those who drive a hard bargain! Blessings on those who play fair and square!'" Josiah smiled. "Now, I know I'm preaching to the choir here, but I wonder how many of us can still take something away from these verses?"

"It's talking about giving," Luc said. "Not being a tightwad."

"And if you give, you get back, a bit like investing," Ryan said.

"But it doesn't have to just mean money though, does it?" Dan mused. "Things like generosity of spirit, forgiveness, or kindness are all things we can work on."

"Or trusting God," Brent added.

"Absolutely," Josiah said. "And as we give in these ways, our hearts expand, and when our hearts are bigger, we have more room to care and in turn be cared for."

Beau thought about his life and what areas God might be wanting him to trust Him in. *God?*

"I think it's fair to say we've all seen instances like this, where people try to protect themselves from further hurt. But so often it leads to isolating, to cutting off those very connections that can help promote healing."

"Like what bullies do, putting the walls up and attacking first," Tim said thoughtfully.

"Exactly." Josiah sighed. "I've seen this so many times in ministry, and I'm sure you've seen this with people you know too."

Beau nodded. "My mom has always been outgoing, but it took her some time after my dad died to bounce back. She was in shock for a while."

"Did she bounce back?" Jai asked. "Or was it a longer term thing? I don't know if my mom has ever really recovered from my dad leaving. But then, she's still on the God journey."

"That she is." Josiah nodded. "And getting closer to salvation every day."

"Amen," Jai said.

"I was only young when it happened," Beau said, "but I remember a few bleak years."

"Which is only natural," Dan said quietly.

"She did have Jesus, but it still knocked her around." Beau thought back. "I think it helped to have family and a great church community supporting her. And to know she had my sister and me to focus on."

Olivia. His thoughts shifted to his sister, who had struggled with her own loss. Sorrow panged. His father's death he'd come to terms with, but the loss of little Joey was something he'd really like God to explain. One day. He could only marvel at his sister's composure in the face of great grief. But perhaps that was part of what Josiah was talking about and the legacy of his mother's experience and faith. Liv had always been outward focused, others focused, and that longstanding habit meant that grief had not curled in upon itself, her faith such that she knew with certainty she'd see little Joey in heaven one day. He swallowed, emotion throbbing in his chest, and refocused on the conversation.

Ryan was sharing a prayer request for a teammate who'd injured himself in a painting accident by falling off a ladder, which brought memories of the woman in the tree today. Or more specifically, the woman out of the tree. Beau's lips flicked up.

"It's not funny," Ryan complained, obviously misinterpreting Beau's smile.

"I wasn't smiling at that," Beau protested. "Just, what you said reminded me of something that happened today."

"Spill," Chris said, which drew another smile.

"Okay, fine." He briefly explained about the woman and the tree-falling incident, which drew a round of stares and smirks instead of smiles. "What?"

"What's her name?" Brent asked.

"Maggie."

"Maggie," Chris said. "Uh huh."

"What? Why do you say it like that?"

"We've just never heard you even mention a girl's name," Brent said, arms folded, grinning in a way Beau didn't trust. "And here you are smiling over a girl."

"I'm not smiling," he scoffed, doing his best to tweak his lips down.

"Is she French?" Ryan asked.

"I think she speaks it," Beau said, shrugging.

"Well, yeah, Einstein. If she lives in Quebec she probably does," said Luc Marchand, a Quebecois-born newer member of the group who was still working on his off-the-charts sarcasm levels. He'd proved helpful with some of the expectations and adjustments Beau had needed to make in moving from Arizona to the city of Luc's birth, even if his tone sometimes had Beau digging deep for patience.

"Ooh la la." Chris waggled his heavy eyebrows.

"Dude, you know we French speakers don't actually say it like that, right?" Luc continued.

"Didn't know, don't care," Chris said. "If it impresses the wife, then I'll say it however I like."

"Christopher," Josiah cautioned. This wasn't the first time exchanges between Chris and Luc had become a little heated.

"Fine, fine." Chris held up his hands, and the time continued with other prayer requests that saw them praying for the health of family and friends, wisdom for the growth of the Philippines charity, and Jai praying over his fiancée's job before adding, "And bless Beau with the woman of his dreams."

"Amen," Brent said with a grin.

"Amen," Mike agreed.

"Amen," Ryan said, not bothering to hide his chuckles.

Beau wasn't sure whether to laugh or agree but figured it was only fair their attention had turned to him. He'd not exactly been shy about encouraging—okay, pushing—some of the guys, like Jai, to try new things. Like a relationship.

"Hey, I'm not opposed to the idea," Beau said. "But I don't think you should count on this Maggie woman being the one."

"Nobody said anything about Maggie, man," Dan said with a slight smile.

Oh. "I, um, ignore me."

"Never," Josiah said with a smile of his own.

"Yeah, ignore Beau Nash after all he's done for me?" Jai said. "Couldn't do that to you, man. Wouldn't do that to you."

Awesome. Looked like tonight's Bible study meeting had descended into studying Beau squirm. "Hey, look at the time," Beau said. "I'd better bounce—"

"You did *not* just say that," Luc scoffed. "You're living in the classiest city in North America, Nash. Live up to it, dude."

Said the man calling him *dude*.

"I'm looking forward to seeing what happens with you," Jai said.

"I just bet you are," Beau drawled.

"Trying new things is the spice of life," Jai said. "Or so I've heard."

Beau winced as his words from months ago came back to bite.

"Remember, friend," Josiah said. "The world of the generous gets larger and larger, so just imagine what trusting God might lead you to."

"The man's right," Jai said, his grin as wide as the St. Lawrence river. "Let's see what God has in store for you."

Purchase Hearts and Goals today

ABOUT THE AUTHOR

Carolyn Miller lives in the beautiful Southern Highlands of New South Wales, Australia, with her husband and four children. A long-time lover of romance, especially that of Jane Austen, Georgette Heyer and LM Montgomery, Carolyn loves to write contemporary and historical romance that draws readers into fictional worlds that show the truth of God's grace in our lives.

To find out more about Carolyn's books, and to subscribe to her newsletter, please visit www.carolynmillerauthor.com

You can also connect with her at

ALSO BY CAROLYN MILLER

<u>The Original Six hockey series</u>

The Breakup Project

Love on Ice

Checked Impressions

Hearts and Goals

Big Apple Atonement

Muskoka Blue

<u>The Independence Islands series</u>

Restoring Fairhaven

Regaining Mercy

Reclaiming Hope

Rebuilding Hearts

Refining Josie

Historical:

<u>Regency Wallflowers</u>

Dusk's Darkest Shores

Midnight's Budding Morrow

Dawn's Untrodden Green

<u>Regency Brides: Legacy of Grace</u>

The Elusive Miss Ellison

The Captivating Lady Charlotte

The Dishonorable Miss DeLancey

<u>Regency Brides: Promise of Hope</u>

Winning Miss Winthrop

Miss Serena's Secret

The Making of Mrs Hale

<u>Regency Brides: Daughters of Aynsley</u>

A Hero for Miss Hatherleigh

Underestimating Miss Cecilia

Misleading Miss Verity

'Heaven and Nature Sing' from the Joy to the World Christmas
novella collection